Advance Praise for *Pepperland*

"The early 1970s: sure, that was the era of drugs, sex, and rock & roll. But those weren't really the headlines. It was a time of energy crises, political upheaval, the war in Southeast Asia, the radical underground, and the dawn of the computer age. Into this shifting landscape blunders our lovable hero, Pepper Porter, a would-be rock star who chases the woman of his dreams through one illegal fiasco after another, all while being pursued by a mysterious ghost from his past. This book is a comic joyride that captures the frontier feel, the full-throttle attitude, and the breakthrough music of a remarkable period of American history. Pepper's journey is our journey, or would be if we had his rare combination of innocence, lunacy, and courage. *Pepperland* is an optimistic look into a funhouse mirror, and it offers us proof that dreaming big isn't really crazy after all."
—Clint McCown, author of *Haints*

"*Pepperland* is a rollercoaster ride that baby boomers will find vividly familiar and hilariously commemorative. Infused with muscled prose and pulsating desire, it careens along at a breathless pace, connecting the decades of the sixties and seventies with the present in a magical mystery romp so unexpected and touching that you will not be able to stop reading until the ride comes to its joyous conclusion. At once an ode to redemption, paean to rock and roll, and sweet chronicle of a time lost, *Pepperland* is original to its core. You've never read anything like this. I know I hadn't. This is one fun novel."
—Robin Oliveira, author of *My Name is Mary Sutter*

"*Pepperland* barrels ahead like a Keith Moon drum solo, striking every tom tom and crashing every cymbal until, in the end, the kit has been kicked across the stage and all that remains is a grinning imp with a pair of sticks in his hands and smoke coming from his ears. Which is to say, I enjoyed the hell out of this book. Both hilarious and insightful, *Pepperland* is a mightily satisfying amalgam that ties together every single socially, politically, and musically significant event from the early seventies into one frantic, nutty, and miraculously coherent plot. Read it and rock."
—Gregory Hill, author of *East of Denver*

Pepperland

BARRY WIGHTMAN

Running Meter Press

DENVER

Published by
Running Meter Press
2509 Xanthia St.
Denver, CO 80238
Publisher@RunningMeterPress.com
720 328 5488

Cover art and design by Nick Zelinger, NZ Graphics
Text design by D. Kari Luraas
Author photo by Chris Kirzeder

ISBN: 978-0-9847860-3-9

Library of Congress Control Number: 2013930624

First Edition 2013

Printed in the United States of America

For Jill
Claire, Ian, Graham
and Kevin

The system of society as it exists at present must be overthrown from the foundations with all its superstructure of maxims & of forms before we shall find anything but disappointment in our intercourse with any but a few select spirits—I wish to ask you if you know of any bookseller who would like to publish a little volume of popular songs wholly political & destined to awaken & direct the imagination of the reformers. I see you smile but answer my question.
—Percy Bysshe Shelley, 1820

Side 1: Wouldn't it be nice?

 Track 1: May 4, 1970, 2:15 a.m.

"I'M NOT SURE YOU'RE UP TO THIS—I'm sorry, your name. What is it? Martin Alan Porter?"

She doesn't look up from the screen. I'm a distraction.

"Call me Pepper."

One with the computer terminal, fingers flying on the keyboard—sprays of keystrokes, slowing, accelerating, waves synced with the riffs and rhythms in her mind—she's fully connected, hard-wired to the vast, all-powerful mainframe computer system arrayed behind the glass wall in the university data center.

The young woman stops. She brushes strands of hair from her face, loops them behind an ear, picks up a pencil, taps the table.

"Pepper." She raises an eyebrow. "You're kidding."

I've pulled up a folding chair, timidly located it across the wide table from her in one of the University of Michigan computer labs. I'm nervous about getting too close—she *is* intimidating. I'm here because she's got something I want—*the password*, the completely unauthorized underground skeleton key to the computer lab kingdom representing complete freedom and unlimited systems access, available only to the elite, the elect.

It is a blow against the Empire.

How cool.

The problem?

First, she's a *girl*, the only one in the smart boys club that is the computer science department. Second, she is stunningly *gorgeous*—

this is no Dobie Gillis smart girl *Zelda*.[1] She uses no makeup, which is fine by me—I ask you—what's not to like about getting back to nature if you're this smart and foxy? Third, she has a *reputation* as a monster programmer and again, she's got that password—*she* hacked the password.

She asked about my name. I adopt a casual, off-hand story-telling manner, "It all started with my dad. See, he's an old baseball ..."

"You strike me as the type who's all for tearing down walls and making things happen as long as it doesn't interfere with your comfortable honky life. Or golf game."

"Huh?"

"Are you *committed*?"

"To what?"

She sighs. "Look, I can tell you're pretty smart and you *have* been recommended. We've had those two classes together—"

It's true. She was the one sitting aloof in the back of the classroom, not part of the scene, yet somehow shining with an aura of inaccessible brilliance. It's evident she's much smarter than me. One time, a visiting professor asked some bizarrely tough questions and on the fly she created an algorithm so new and unexpected, so clearly correct, he was forced to concede even a *girl* might have a shot at a career in computer science.

The fact that she—this woman—even acknowledges my existence is cause for jubilation.

But her question—her accusation really—is valid. *Am* I committed? And to what?

She returns to the keyboard, playing the keys, intensely, artfully, lost in her programming, her coding. She's probably skulking about in the online bowels of the administration mainframe checking my transcript, verifying my technical worthiness. From an olive drab rucksack festooned with embroidered rainbowy peace signs and Vietnam War Moratorium buttons, she removes a black notebook about the size of a clipboard—riffles through it, places it by her side. Reading upside down, I see that she's consulting an elaborate handwritten table

---

[1] Later, she'll tell me that mentioning her appearance and relating it in qualitative terms and referring to an early '60s black and white TV comedy in which a very smart but goofy-looking female character is named Zelda, indicates that all is lost.

containing both alpha and numeric information. I cannot discern its purpose. With a slender finger, she follows the x and y axis locating multiple mysterious glyphs and sums.

I say nothing. I want the password.

Freedom.

The password. She cracked the code and bypassed the standard measly computer system time allotment granted to students, thereby establishing a completely open world where time does not apply, where information is free, nothing is restricted, where I can make that computer get up and dance, make romance—a new computerland Oz. She has enabled a happy hippie world of peace, love, rock 'n roll—it's the world I want to live in—it will be the land of me.

Pepper land.

This whole bootleg password business is, of course, an underground operation. I've been, as she says, recommended to her by a grad assistant computer lab rat—a haggard hippie known to be a supporter of subversive technical activities and politically radical causes. The guy heard me singing some of my songs at an Ann Arbor open-mic dive—liked my music—became familiar with my programming and apparently deemed me worthy.

She sits back in her chair, pinching the bridge of her ever-so-slightly ski-jumped, delicate nose. Two turquoise bracelets skid to the sleeve of her ropy earth-toned sweater. A decision is imminent.

A smile runs across her face, rippling to the most exalted reaches of magnificent cheekbones. She reaches across the table, shakes my hand with a sure-handed but feminine grip. "Sorry. We haven't been introduced. I'm Susan Frommer. But my name is Sooz."

I know that. Everybody knows that. She's telling *me*.

Wow.

My pulse quickens. Sooz slides a small slip of paper across the table, her long fingers pressing on it—not quite willing to hand it over—stops mid-table. I reach—our fingers not quite touching. The slip contains the password.

"I am willing to give this to you, Pepper Porter, only if you resolve to work to *change the world* with this knowledge, this gift of *time*." She pauses, lets the gravity of that resolution sink in, a slight tilt of her head silently inquiring—am I up to the task?

Her piano black hair hangs below her shoulders, shiny and lustrous as a Breck girl's, parted in the middle framing cheekbones high and sculpted, sometimes marble, sometimes butter. Her almond eyes a shade beyond bottle green, then the angle of the light changes and there's a glint of gray-green. Her makeup-free skin mixes strawberries and cream with a field of windy, waving summer grass. Her mouth is wide and her toothy grin, when granted, reveals a gap in her two front teeth, a gap I hear she swears never to fix. Why would she? She eventually will tell me that she is not defined by some male idea of female perfection.

The slip remains fixed on the table under our fingers. A hint of that slightly crooked smile crosses her face again. With all the resolve in my body I firmly state I will indeed work to change the world—what every nineteen year old should hope to do.

She says, "Put everything at risk." Her voice lowers. "No fear, uncertainty, or doubt."

Sooz releases the password.

The guitar pick in my pocket—a worn, blue slice of celluloid I always carry—vibrates, hums, and rattles. This almost never happens. It's a *sign*. Of what, I don't know. But I smile.

I am admitted to a shrouded, skull-and-bones, secret-sharing society—a victory that forever changes my life's direction. Now, I have private, unlimited access to one of the largest and most advanced academic computer systems in the world. I suddenly have my own mainframe computer—like my guitar, I can pick it up anytime and play.

A new world.

I thank her extravagantly. That smile flickers again, like a firefly on a summer night. She resumes work. I leave, mission accomplished.

In my room, I exult and crank tunes—appropriately guitar heavy, pointing to the sky heroic, celebratory. My headphones burn 'til the gray dorm dawn.

Finally, I sleep.

I dream of guitars, memory, and disk drives.

And Sooz.

Later that day, Kent State happens. Horror, anger, four dead in Ohio. Sooz, running with a political crowd, marches in the streets, carrying signs, singing songs. I'm there, I sing, I march, though I'm only a satellite, a minor moon.

Her fuse, however, is lit.

 Track 2: Summer 1970

A MONTH OR SO LATER, by a stroke of cosmic synchronicity, Sooz and I find ourselves as counselors at old Camp Annawanna, way up in northern Michigan, the place where my brother Dave and I spent many a goof-off July, sunburned, bug-bitten little kids. Hadn't been back in years. Sooz, it turns out, is a veteran camper and counselor.[2] I never knew.

At Annawanna, guitar in hand, I'm the cheerful, long-haired, bandanna-wearing, kids-on-my-shoulders, guitar-strumming, song-singing, swimming-lesson-giving, sailboat-instructing, tall and storky Pepper Porter the Pied Piper camp counselor.

Sooz is something else.

She and I begin our real relationship the second night, before the kids arrive.

I'm in search of a Fanta Grape soda. Moseying up to the pop machine, lit by a pool of yellow bug lights over the back door of the dining hall, I see Monty the Camp Director perched on the porch railing plinking on his guitar, serenading Sooz with "I'm a Girl Watcher." Though I'm still intimidated by her—amazed that she, of all people, is here at this camp—I have the brains to see that she, giving me a *look*, is a damsel in distress and needs someone to perk up and say, "Hey Sooz, don't we need to get that *thing* done in the girls' cabins?" So I do. And she says, "Yes, we do indeed!"

We scamper off.

She grabs my Fanta, guzzles it, says, "Damn, I love this stuff"— thanks me profusely, curses weird Monty. And that's that—Sooz and I become subterranean allies.[3]

---

[2] On seeing me on day one, as we're cleaning cabins, Sooz says, "Well, well, Pepper Porter"— she remembered my name!—"here to do your bit to save the children?" I grin, say something incoherent, try to look cool. I fail. She smiles.

[3] Monty and his co-camp director, a perky older chick named Susie with a blonde flip perm,

Turns out this icily brilliant programmer—this girl who is distant and inaccessible—is everybody's favorite counselor, the one every kid wants to sit next to at bonfires or in the dining hall.[4] She works hard, is very serious about her job—seeking out problems, trying to undo the damage of snippy camp cliques, healing homesickness with jokes and giggles, taking oppressed, lonely and shy little girls under her wing with a hug, then holding their hands, walking them around the leafy camp on the big sandy bluffs of Lake Michigan—Sooz with her little flock of reassured, freckled and adoring followers. Tall and summer-brown with long arms and graceful hands like a dancer's—she talks with her hands—Sooz is head of the tennis program, endlessly tossing fuzzy balls to the littlest kids, hitting easy ground strokes to the big ones, running disciplined drills with a deep well of patience.

I can't help but fall a little in love with her.

Though of course she's nice as pie to the camp's directors Monty and Susie, Sooz says, "I have *nothing* in common with her" and "That guy's gonna get himself into some serious *girl trouble* some day." Soon after the Monty the Girl Watcher Incident, she tells me she *despises* them. She backs off a bit, says, "No, maybe *despise* isn't the right word, that's too harsh." But Sooz questions everything they and, for that matter, we as a culture are doing to the kids—she says that she is there to try and counter what is happening to the children—*they* are just training them to be cogs in the machine, little capitalist drones, little consumers of all the crap our society dishes out—"Don't you think so, Pepper?" Then she waves her hands and runs them through her slightly frizzy hair,[5] trying to smooth it out—"What kind of world are we inheriting?"

I listen earnestly, feeling stupidly inarticulate.

I'm nineteen. I know what I want. I don't know what I want.

---

had been actual members of the Doodletown Pipers—one of those fine singing groups of the '60s with twenty guys and gals in matching outfits—maybe gingham, maybe polka-dots or maybe even quasi-hip turtlenecks, singin' bland as Velveeta cheese tunes. Parents loved 'em—"Gosh, aren't those kids nice ... why can't you look like them?" As a result, Monty and Susie both wear perpetual perfectly legal smiles—he likes to whistle songs like "Winchester Cathedral" or "Music to Watch Girls By," and she is a Lawrence Welk Champagne Lady in training.

[4] I want to sit next to her but am not allowed. Boys and girls are strictly segregated.

[5] Summer heat leads to frizzy hair with its embarrassing split ends, quite a problem for many older girls at camp. Sooz doesn't care. She says, "I'm not a Breck girl, for chrissake."

So there are two sides of Sooz. Side 1—the Mary Poppins, corn-fed camp counselor everybody loves and—Side 2—the shadowy, fiercely intense Sooz that nobody at Annawanna knows but me. In a rare off-duty moment, she shows me her big army surplus duffle bag in which she's brought issues of that politically radical mag *Ramparts* and a big envelope full of carefully preserved underground mimeographed sheets—meeting flyers, newsletters, scholarly papers with terrible statistics, speeches, quotes and other damning evidence against the evil military/capitalist establishment, the Empire.[6]

We begin a routine of illegally skipping off to the beach late at night, long after lights-out for the campers. We go way down the beach, far away from the ears and eyes of Authority. We sit and talk and laugh on the still-warm sand under skies so dark that the starlight mirrors and ripples on the gentle waves of the big lake. I hope to impress her in some way—*any* way. Computer technology just doesn't seem to fit as a subject of conversation and since I'm sure there's no way I could score too many points there, I pretty much avoid it. So I bring my guitar, I sing songs—I make up revolutionary anti-establishment tunes.

They're lousy.

She recommends I stick to programming.

This is when I discover that she has a snorty sort of laugh—it's so unexpected that I'm convinced she's riffing on Jonathan Winters or that chick on *Laugh-In*. But she isn't. It's just her.

She tells me about her parents—old school New York progressive left-wingers. Her dad teaches history at CCNY, her mom a secretary for the United Federation of Teachers. They took Sooz and her little sister to antiwar events back in '64 before it was the thing to do—they would've taken her to Mississippi on the Freedom Rides if she'd been old enough. But wherever there were workers' rallies, boycotts, and local elections—the Frommers were involved.

So I tell her about the time Dave and I almost drowned right here at this very camp all those years ago—how we went sailing when we shouldn't have with a storm rolling in—the best time for little

---

[6] For the record, my birthday, November 5, 1950, and draft number, pulled in the Official Lottery on December 1, 1969 (fall semester, freshman year) was a lucky 310. I was relieved. I was guilty. I went on with my life.

knucklehead hotshots to take a boat out. This gets her attention. She tells me to go on.

Dave is ten and I'm almost twelve, summer of '62, a year after our little brother Elliot was killed, but I don't lay that on her—I didn't expect to get into all this anyway.

*   *   *

It's late afternoon and I tell Dave, "C'mon, Davy boy, let's get out there before this storm hits ... it'll be the sail of our lives!" The western sky is getting pretty dark and the wind's picking up, waves building—perfect sailing weather. And why not? We are Annawanna-trained sailors.

Dave and I push one of the little wooden daysailers into the surf, make it out past the break, fly out into Lake Michigan, a speedboat wake trailing behind us.

The lake is wild. Already a mile off shore, screamin' and shoutin,' we need to come about and head back in. I'm having trouble, can't make it happen. Dave says, "C'mon, just jibe it"—turn the boat with the wind rather than into it—a far riskier maneuver in high winds. Cocky little Dave says, "Let me do it, whatsa matter with you?" I tell him to shove it—I know what I'm doing. So I jibe. But I time everything wrong and we flip, throwing us into the hissing waves.

We're smart enough to have our life jackets on—the fat orange kind that gets heavier the wetter they are—and we're lucky enough to be able to climb right back onto the boat bottom and grab the centerboard. The little boat is turtled—upside down with no hope of righting—the heavy sail and mast now pointing straight at the sandy lake bottom, maybe thirty, forty feet below.

The waves heave and the wind picks up. The swell batters us. The centerboard, slick and slippery, is a fluttering flag in the wind.

Between waves, Dave yells, "We can't die out here, Pepper."

"No, not here, not now." Another big whitecap rolls over the boat and slaps us in the face.

We drift in the wind-driven current down the beach—we're still about a mile out and the big lake is midsummer warm but with a storm coming in, we can only see the shore when we roll over the peaks of the waves. The high dunes are dark green, striped with white sandy chutes, stretching off far to the south. Soon they're lost in the mists. It's obvious that we will travel a long way before finally being driven into shore.

It begins to rain.

I holler, "Wouldn't be good for Mom and Dad, would it—another dead kid."

"Two more dead kids."

"Be awful."

"Elliot would've been a good sailor I bet."

"Better than you."

"Better than you."

"Creep."

"Jerk."

We bounce and drift for a while. Distant thunder is now close, lightning crackles out over the lake. I count the seconds between the sound and the flash, figure it's only three or four miles away. I interlink my arm with Dave's and we arrange ourselves more securely around the centerboard. I wish that we were back at camp, washing dishes or something boring.

A whip of lightning cracks overhead, scares the hell out of us. We hang on tighter to the slippery centerboard.

"Gonna be fine."

"Yeah."

I start singing some camp song. We sing together until we can't remember the words.

We blow farther down the coast.

Dave asks, "Think they're coming?"

"Yeah, they're coming."

"Maybe they don't even know we're out here."

"They do. They'll come. Just wait."

We wait some more. More thunder. More lightning.

"Where are we?"

We've blown pretty far down the shore—the camp's fire tower on the big dune is beginning to disappear. I say, "I think we're off the state park now." It feels like we're shipwrecked off the coast of some foreign country.

Dave asks, "What if Mom hides all the pictures of us if we die out here? Like she did with Elliot."

"She won't."

"Maybe she will." We slide down the trough of a really big wave. "We'll be dead, gone. She'll forget us," he hollers and his voice cracks.

"They won't forget us. And she never forgot Elliot. Don't be an idiot."

"You're the idiot."

The tip of the mast, arrowing straight down into the lake, begins to scrape the hump of a sand bar, the current and wave action jamming it into the soft bottom. The little boat begins to pivot on the mast's new fulcrum and with the waves and wind, we began to flip upright, slow enough so that Dave and I are able to stand on the centerboard, grab the gunwales and pull, helping right the ship. She comes all the way over, jerking, the sail snapping. We scramble into the open cockpit and Dave grabs the tiller while I find the line of the boom, cinching it as fast as I can. The Porter boys—Team Porter—quickly turn the boat toward shore. With Dave at the helm, we ride the wild surf and careen up onto the beach. We pull the boat up as high as we can and collapse on the wet sand.

Soon, a sharp whistle sounds through the crashing of the lake. We sit up. Three or four camp counselors are running down the beach toward us. I look at Dave, he looks at me. We shrug. We hug. Then we stand up and face the music.

*   *   *

Sooz has her knees pulled up under her chin, her eyes a little misty. She touches my hand.

"We were stupid kids. But we survived. Lucky."

"Mmm."

We watch the stars for a bit.

"Elliot. Another brother. Do you want to tell me what happened to him?"

I never told anyone that story, really. I mean, sure, I think about it all the time and it runs in my head like a broken record and I wish it didn't happen the way it did.

I tell her. The bike, the skid, the whole bit. It's been so long, a lifetime ago, a different era, and yet it's still right there. In my head, details seem to waver, then solidify, burned into a groove, people, faces—time slows, time stops. Memory is a funny thing—it's not all digital ones and zeros. It flows off the chart, slips, fades, and then comes raging back when you least expect it. Virtual memory.

But the outcome of this story is always the same.

I tell her that Dave told him that he could do it. Elliot is smiling as he pushes off from the top.

I tell Sooz that I didn't mean to get into all this.

Sooz holds my hand. We're quiet for a while.

After all that, I try to lighten the mood. So I sing her a song I've had in my head for a few weeks—it's a half-baked dreamy ballad, but it's got a nice melody and she listens with a smile I'd never seen before ... anywhere.

Things are different after that night.

A few nights later, still early in the camp season and apparently having decided that I'm worth the trouble, Sooz fervently reads favorite passages to me on the beach late at night, long after lights-out—*The Greening of America, Soul on Ice,* the *Port Huron Statement*[7]—flashlight in hand, she rubs her tanned toes in the cooling sand, burying them, seeking warmth. I listen and say yes, four-dead-in-O-hi-o.

Sooz, her flashlight dimming and the moonlight playing on her hair, stops reading, sits up straight with thin-lipped, grim determination. "One day, Martin Alan Porter, maybe our computer technology will make a difference, but we have to change the world *now*, make it a better place. Yes, we can—yes, we must bring power to the people," and she says, "Pepper, I think you could be wonderful." And, with a suddenly sing-songy voice from a song I can't quite place, she whispers, "You could be won-won-wonderful," touches my cheek making my hair stand on end, and I think, *Jesus, it's just her hand,* and she tilts

---

[7] The *Port Huron Statement: Agenda for a Generation,* was written by Tom Hayden in June 1962 and is the founding document of the radical Students for a Democratic Society—the SDS. It begins: "We are people of this generation, bred in at least modest comfort, housed now in universities, looking uncomfortably to the world we inherit." Fighting social injustice and war—Sooz's two great causes. Idealistic and naïve maybe—the document refers to goals of selflessness and generosity and the desire to replace power and privilege with "love, reflectiveness, reason, and creativity." It's like a beautiful song.

her head, smiles, looking again for something that maybe isn't there but I hope is, and I am ready I am ready and then she says, "I don't know I don't know," turns back to her book and reads another passage from the *Port Huron Statement*.

She stares out over the dark moon-sparkling lake and in a sepulchral voice says, "All the gods are dead, except for the god of war."

And I think, *who is this girl?*[8]

A shooting star streaks across the southern sky.

Later, she brightens up, says, "You know, maybe we could sing together, you and me, at the talent show next week."

I perk up. "You think so?"

"Yeah, let's do it, it'll be fun, it'll be Sooz & Pepper! We'll do some campy songs, liven this place up." She punches me on the shoulder and I consider it—Sooz & Pepper, Pepper & Sooz—and then I agree. "Yeah, okay, let's do it," and we sing a bit of "Yellow Submarine." Then she says, "Yeah, yeah, that's it! Maybe there's hope for you after all." We fool around with a couple more tunes, promise to practice and come up with an act. Things quiet down.

I'm nervous. I waste time, flat on my back under the stars, my fingers run up and down my old guitar's fretboard weaving a new melodic line sweet and clear, putting it off—putting off the moment of truth. I finish on a lovely densely packed chord that rings in the wood of the guitar and lights up that smile again.

That's it.

I put the guitar down, take her by the hand and we move our blanket up into the hidden dunes where there are only shadows and the strange semaphore of softly sparking fireflies to shine warm light on my second time ever, only my second ever, ever.

She, however, has been here before. A year older, she senses my inexperience, she *knows*, brings me along with her, guiding, slowly, slowly, smiling my name—me, my name, she says it—*Pepper, Pepper*, not in a rush of passion but calmly, quietly, gently and the mound of sand beneath the blanket patiently shifts and wind whispers through the beach grass. She holds my hand, mouth on mine, slowly slowly,

---

[8] When she said it—"All the gods are dead," I couldn't place it. It's from *Soul on Ice*, by Eldridge Cleaver, 1968.

her strong tennis legs around me, pulling me to her, and her skin—her skin, dunes of coppertoned satined skin—I'm inhaling intoxicating airs, am imprisoned by her breasts, firm belly, thighs, and the grains of sand in the hidden places beneath her ear, in the curve of her neck, are now in my mouth, now in hers—we laugh—her hair mixed with mine and her breath, secret to everybody but me, right there right there and I wonder how did I get here—here!—this inaccessible world—am I worthy and what does she think and then a hoot owl hoots above us, we look up, we smile—together, and if that firefly could speak, she'd say this is how it should be, this is *it*. And then Sooz murmurs *we could be something, Pepper Porter.*

Tonight, for her, I don't think the earth moves, I don't think choirs sing. But for me, it's a night forever etched in my mind.

She has taken me to a new land and I don't want to leave.

From then on we're on the beach again and again, many nights reclined against big logs around a distant old bonfire pit watching the two-in-the-morning summer smear of the Milky Way over the lake. We roll scrawny joints from her summer stash—an old black leather tobacco and pipe case she keeps well hidden in a worn peace sign–embroidered shoulder bag. She takes deep drags and holds it firmly in her lungs, reclined on her side like a Buddha with a lopsided gap-toothed grin and a goofy horsey laugh.[9]

One windy night she asks me, snuggling in her camp sweatshirt with her head on my chest, "What do you want to be, Pepper Porter?" Before I can answer, she says, "Never mind—*what* are you going to be?" I realize that, coming from her, I'm entering treacherous waters. I have no good answer—I'm only nineteen and I don't know where I'm going or where all that Ann Arbor computer stuff might lead. IBM? Burroughs? What do I know? So I riff some nonsense about graduating with a degree in something ... get a job, maybe go to work in Dad's bank, find a wife, two kids, a dog ... and buy a Buick.

I immediately realize I have made a serious mistake.

She sits up and glares at me, running her hands through her hair,

---

[9] Sooz told me that she had refused to have braces to close the gap between her two front teeth. "My teeth are fine ... and natural—why should I allow society and its paternalistic, sick demand that women look a certain way, dictate something about my body, tell me that *that* is a *flaw*, dearie, and needs to be fixed? They're my teeth. It is a matter of principle."

mussing it up like she can't believe what she just heard and begins talking fast, crazy gusts of words spewing like a fire hose. She hollers, "Daddy's bank? Daddy's *bank*? Just another dismal drone dumped in a sea of desks on a fucking leather chair? Are you just going to push pencils and move Establishment money around, opening and closing boring accounts for pathetic suburban train daddies feeding more and more data to government computers so they can watch us and tap our phones and do who the fuck knows what while you hand out bank calendars and free toasters for the rest of your life ... while there is so much suffering in the world—and while there is a state of declared war between the people and the government? There is! Did you know that?"

I didn't know that.[10]

She says, "Yes, war is declared. A couple of months ago. SDS is revolutionary, the lines are drawn."

She takes a breath and slows down. "Now, I might be able to make a difference in the straight world with my technical abilities—you too. You're good. Hell, you could get a job with IBM—talk about the evil heart of the Empire—but I think all that might have to wait a while." The wind picks up. She looks out over the black lake. "What are they going to say about Pepper Porter when they write the Book of Revolution?"

I have no idea. It's my own revolution that concerns me.

I ask her, "But what if you're wrong? What if there's no revolution?" I think that it's possible that her desire for all-or-nothing, seemingly pure perfection and her certainty and lack of moderation, is a flaw that will bring her—or maybe even us—down some day.

Rumblings of distant thunder roll across the water, waves starlit and luminous as foam begins to build. The stars sink beneath a growing cloudbank in the west, rising like a dark aurora over the lake.

"There's always a revolution going on somewhere, Pepper Porter—pick one."

And I think that she is a psychedelic rainbow kite flying fearlessly,

---

[10] On May 21, 1970, following the invasion of Cambodia, Kent State, and everything else, the Weather Underground Organization released a statement recorded by Bernardine Dohrn saying that a state of war existed between the People and Amerikan imperialism. The Weatherman intended to lead white kids into armed revolution.

strung out over the churning lake in a howling storm, and I am just managing to hang onto her thin string of high-grade hemp. I can't reel her in, so I let her play it out, hoping her line won't break, sending her spinning out over the lake, gone and lost forever.

Or maybe I'm the kite, strung together with a spindly cross of thin, junk wood with cheap twine, folded over lousy yellow paper flying with a short tail making me aimless and lunatic, diving and circling wild ass and blubbering crazy like a stuttering Porky Pig—and Sooz has my string in her strong female fist and I know that she just might let go at any moment—or she could reel me in.

A sudden storm is blowing in. Over the rising crash of the wind and waves she hollers, "What do you care about Pepper Porter, I mean, what do you really *care about*?"

Pause.

"Music. My guitar. Computer stuff, coding." Then, "Entropy!"

It just pops out.

She looks at me funny. A monster wave rolls up the beach, soaking us. We skitter to higher ground.

Then I tell her about the day I discovered entropy, that memorable moment in high school physics, just before Christmas break senior year, when Dr. Thompson, with heavy oven mitts, holds a bubbling beaker of boiling water high above his head. In a dramatic Latinate cadence, he tells us that soon the water in this beaker would cool to a lukewarm room temperature, and "that simply and elegantly illustrates how everything—everything—in the entire universe—the entire universe, people—tends to deteriorate and lose distinctiveness, differentiation, the stuff that makes life interesting. Don't you see ... and that, my friends ... is high *entropy*. Entropy! What a word," he cries. "Entropy! Savor this word, let it roll around on your tongues and lips and then say it again. Entropy!"

There are some snickers in the room, but then, as if his boiling beaker is some holy chalice he intones, "Behold!" He sets the beaker down on a tripod perched on the big black-topped lab table in the front of the room. The good doctor stands back, silent. We watch the bubbles quietly disappear from the beaker. Dr. Thompson says, "Hear me—now look at this entropic beaker in a social context. As I cleverly predicted, the beaker and the water it contains have reverted to a state of blandness, a state of sameness, and as all closed systems must, it has reverted to a state of high entropy."

Or is it low? I tell Sooz that I may have this whole thing wrong—entropy is a slippery, chancy concept and there are forty-seven different varieties—thermodynamic, social, and informational—who can keep track?

Doc Thompson speaks in subdued tones and everybody hangs on his words, he is fervent. He says, "But you kids, I implore you to understand that as we arrive at the close of this most chaotic year, 1968, this *annus terribilis*," trilling his r's like a Shakespearean Henry V orating on a classroom stage, "where there have been many forces allied against you demanding that you conform and be silent, to you I say avoid the fate of the bubbles! Do not be like these bubbles and disappear, reverting to a stale vapidity, as some of my colleagues would have you do." He pauses, thinking—he's about to go off the syllabus. "When you leave these hallowed halls and go out into the open system of our nation—yes, it is an open system despite what you might think—as you go out to make your way in this world, I look to you to comport yourselves in such a manner that ensures the continuation of differentiation, crazy ideas and even a little chaos. Do battle with the forces of entropy, do battle with it and win! Fight the good fight. And let me know how it goes."

Doc Thompson finishes and the classroom is hushed. It is December 1968.[11]

"Sooz," I say, "I don't know, I just don't know."

A crooked smile spreads on her face.

Over gusts of wind speckled with lake spray, I tell her that I sure as hell don't want to end up like one of Doc Thompson's little bubbles and disappear into some great societal lukewarm miasmic stew.

That's when she jumps me—laughing and yelling over the wind, "You are one weird but cute skinny little shit, Pepper Porter!" She climbs on top of me, loudly claiming that she could kick my ass and pin me in a heartbeat—she straddles my chest with her tennis-strong thighs, clamping my hands to the sand with her face leaning

---

[11] Doc Thompson retired at the end of that school year, June '69. The last anyone heard of him, he had a little place in Key West, raising cats and chickens.

close to mine, long fronds of her hair brushing my cheeks, grinning a teeth-gritting leer, hissing goofy-accented like Natasha Fatale—"I am trained in dark and mysterious arts, yes I am, dahlink." She plants a hard deep kiss on me, long and wet. It is stunning, thrilling. I break her grip on my hands and pull her to me.

And like Grace Slick says in one of those songs, flying Jefferson Airplane on time in People's Class, Sooz says, "We can be together Pepper Porter, we can be together," and we are.

The rest of the summer floats by in a hot and delicious sexy haze, but I begin to wonder how it's going to be when we both return to Ann Arbor to resume our normal student lives amid twenty thousand other kids, academic pressures and the ever-increasing bad news from the real world. A few times she and I make runs into town for various official camp purposes—Monty the camp director has long since seen the error of his ways with her, treats her with a grudging respect and me with a polite distance. In town, we pick up newspapers and see that the war continues to go badly—the bombing of Cambodia leads to a wider, expanding war—and antiwar militants, the Weather Underground, are indicted in Detroit. When she reads that, Sooz, her hair in a ponytail and still in her camp tennis whites, hands me her ice cream cone, folds the paper and stifles tears. I hold her close, she breaks down in angry sobs. We sit on a shady bench. Our ice cream melts.

During the final week or two of the camp schedule, as departure arrangements are made—I'm heading home to Chicago for a short break before returning to Ann Arbor again—Sooz tightens up, is quiet, obviously troubled. On the grim day we actually leave, we're standing in the little bus station in Traverse City, tickets in hand— she's bound for Ann Arbor, me, Chicago. She can't afford to go all the way home to New York, though I've been trying to convince her to come with me to Chicago, an idea she's firmly resisted. She tells me that I should not be surprised if she isn't back at school in September. In the waiting room, we read a story in the paper about the University of Wisconsin's Army Math Research Center being bombed, apparently by radicals, protesting the university's ties to the military.

She says, "Pepper, I'm so very late. It's a state of war."

"But *you* don't have to ... it's crazy ..."

"If I don't, who will?" She grabs me by the shoulders and says, "Come with me. The two of us—come with me."

The pick in my pocket begins to jump furiously.

I'm not prepared—she's way beyond me. Sooz feels responsible for the world. Me? My borders don't go much farther than Ann Arbor or Chicago and my guitar.

The pick's still twirling. My hand goes to the outside of my jeans pocket to quiet it down.

"I can't, Sooz."

She takes a deep breath, says she understands.

Maybe she does.

I don't.

My bus leaves first. Before I get on, there's a long kiss amid diesel fumes and bus engine racket. But she holds me differently—harder and with a kind of desperation, like she is about to jump off a cliff. I know enough not to ask too much. I tell her to be careful. She looks into my teary eyes and says, "Don't forget that we can be together, Pepper Porter, don't forget."

As the bus pulls away, she waves and disappears back into the waiting room.

I don't forget.

 Track 3: Three years later—May 4, 1973, 3:00 p.m.

T HE PLEASANT AND POWDERY IBM executive receptionist, in her crisply creased, white cotton blouse and blue suit, hemmed perfectly at the knees with sensible low-heeled black shoes, shakes my hand with a papery grip and graciously motions for me to follow her through twin heavy glass doors.

"We've been expecting you, Mr. Porter. Please, right this way."

Yes, since Sooz left, they've been expecting me. I have slid into the groove of great expectations—I have found the on-ramp to the rat race.[12]

We emerge into a hushed mahogany hall, thickly carpeted in

---

[12] I could be a winning rat.

grays and whites flecked with subtle company blue. Somber tomb-stone paintings of current and past chief executives, most of them dead or dying, hang on the wall. I know that I am walking a short splin-tery plank of life that could crack at any moment and all would be lost again.

In a precise and professionally cadenced voice that is Dictaphone-toned, the executive receptionist inquires of my health and if I had any trouble finding this brand new glass-and-steel, fifty-two story monu-ment in the Loop that looms over the algae-striped Chicago River like a blank-faced castle of the military industrial complex. I say some-thing about "L" stops, transfers, bus routes. In the process of speaking I notice that I am strangely anesthetized, numbly running through what has become a programmed interview routine. Amazingly, I am *in demand*—a college graduate with technical talent—despite the fact that these are certifiably tough times. I have done the rounds with all the big computer players—Honeywell, Control Data, Univac, and Burroughs. I am also anguished to say I have cut my hair to a short-ish but certainly not daddy's businessman-length. Perhaps it is this newly sedate length of hair that enables me to say the right things and ask my intelligent questions and look them all in the eye. Though I am under the influence of no foreign substance—uh oh, here we go again—my brain has begun to multi-process and cycle simultaneously through well-traveled and diverging corridors of central processing's main memory.

To wit:

1) A recently generated mental subroutine pops into the computer room of my mind—*this* is the big one, *this* is I B fuckin' M—and it's my fourth and probably final interview. Going to work for IBM? How could *that* be a mistake? It's your life we're talking about. Sit up straight and pay attention.

2) I perceive the nice Dictaphone Lady pressing the elevator but-ton for the twenty-seventh floor with a well-manicured slender finger and the shiny gold doors sliding shut, revealing a handy full-length mirror that shows just how far I've come. Here I am—tied, suited, briefcased, staring at my father's face. His steel-gray buzz-cut hair morphs to mine—floppy and basic brown, under control and combed in a thousand ways gracefully across my forehead, cut to cover only

the top third of my oh-so-sensitive ears in the aforementioned attempt at buttoned-down dignity. There's no mistaking the slender Porterian filial face, though my father's is filled with the lines and currents of experience and responsibility. I see the wide thin mouth that wrinkles sideways firing verbal zingers, along with the heavy-duty eyebrows arched in the middle, so useful in questioning glances. And the nose. It's large. Ringo and Pete Townshend large. Today, however, it's the eyes—his eyes say *you are on the right track son,* but my eyes stare back at me—brown, haunted, hunted.

Today's the day—are you going to do the right thing?

My eyes say *this* ain't you—flee!

My head says, get the job.

The executive receptionist is blind to all this. She and I contemplate the illuminated numbers flicking on and off in filmstrip sequence as we rise higher and higher—my ears pop. I find myself again taken somewhere else.

Here—looking for *it.* I am threaded between six silver strings stretched and tuned tight across a painted sunburst plank of space-age contoured wood that ring, rattle, buzz and jangle in my head, kicking off magnetized electronic signals that stream in a torrent through rows of glowing vacuum tubes. I am blasted through speakers, fat cones of black paper, and I fiddle with the tone control in my head because that song is back—the one that keeps playing on the turntable of my mind, the one from the beach all those years ago—and I need more bass, more treble, more reverb, more dwell, more gain, more volume and more volume. But then, the above-mentioned subroutine 1) kicks in and I perceive I'm being introduced to someone. A question has interleaved my personal multiprocessing, state-of-the-art operating system, and I find myself handed off to the IBM Regional Vice President of Corporate Data Processing Services who, like the carpet, is grayish and bluish amid vapors of Aqua Velva aftershave. We shake hands manfully and I am touring the IBM Regional Headquarters Data Processing Center System Support Division of the Midwest Financial/Manufacturing and Distribution District—MFMADD. I nod pleasantly as we walk through the big computer room because I am here to get a job.

Here it comes again—the howling whir of the big mainframes

forces the flowchart of my mind straight back into the infinite loop of her—Sooz:

Input.
Who?
Sooz.
Status.
Gone.
Process.
Repeat.
Branch.
Gone?
Yes.
Sooz is gone.

Long time gone, but she sends postcards. Postcards! Never signed, but I know it's her. Just two or three a year, but they keep coming. Generic photographs—a view of Newark, the Portland skyline, *Greetings from Miami* postmarked St. Louis, a library, city hall, a Holiday Inn. Like smoke signals from the front—*I'm still alive, still here*—though I know she's in trouble, on the run. I see it in the papers, a Weather Underground bank heist gone very bad in early '72. Cryptic and weird, many say nothing but tell everything of her state of mind. From Maine, Albany, Denver, D.C., California. Obviously coded—was she practicing on me, joking? In a firm hand—"Maggie's Farm," "Bad Moon Rising," "Kick Out the Jams," "Purple Haze," with sprinkles of a reassuring word or two—like *love* or *together*. She's keeping the connection open. I should forget her.

But I can't get her song out of my head.[13]

The plastic VISITORS badge falls from my lapel, skittering across a square of clean white tile on the raised floor in the data center. I reach to retrieve it, my fingers touching the cold laminated surface and I drop into another hidden do-loop. I see *her* at the system control console, intense, driven, and beautiful, then I see her up against some distant wall marching to the sea, flying around crazy in a post-Woodstock rain while an army of guitars and stacks of amps career

---

[13] *But c'mon, get a grip, man! Look what's happened to her! She was a million years ago.* And yet …

between my ears, making me smile hallucinatory like some '60s art film but she's right there again—produced by the sound of the click of a time-sharing terminal keyboard or the smell of the sterile arctic data center air or the mechanical clatter of a thousand-lines-a-minute printer. All conspire to throw solenoid switches in my brain, causing me to be seated comfortably, spinning at 33-1/3 on an old Jefferson Airplane record, and I do not come back until her song is over.

But fear not. VP/CDPS observes none of this. I am right *there*, with it, in the moment. I am what he hopes me to be—smart, charming and perfect for the position.

VP/CDPS shows me the data center's monstrous twin IBM System 370/155s, new and state of the art, roaring in a metallic water-cooled and well-ventilated whine. So cool. I groove on those big tape drives' stutter-stop spinning loops of loose tape, suspended free behind showy glass in invisible vacuum columns. The unseen tiny and amazing read/write heads of the storage units flip out in a marvel of precision engineering, flying low over marching ranks of disk pack platters reading and writing and strafing bits and bytes in perfect patterns. We discuss new and exciting virtual main memory technologies—memory that isn't really there, we just think it is—and I nod and offer reasonably intelligent commentary because I do in fact know something of this. Before she disappeared, Sooz burrowed like an electronic time-sharing, time-stealing mole deep into similar machines back in Ann Arbor, hunting and gathering and searching and learning and striking blows against the Empire—the Empire of the military industrial complex. She went off to do something about it, do what she thought was right. I didn't—I burrowed deeper into the Empire.

I am with another vice president. *The Man.* The Vice President of Systems Programming Architecture Services and Operating Systems Support. VP/SPAS/OSS and I are discussing my college thesis—*the systems and channel level handling of bisynchronous data communications in an IBM OS/VS2 370 environment.* He speaks in admiring tones, asking the questions he should. Then the big one, "Mr. Porter, where do you want to be in five years' time?"

I zone out.

Through the floor-to-ceiling glass window of his office I see the silent traffic on the Michigan Avenue drawbridge and the stony white cornices of the Wrigley Building—workers in the windows taking calls, making calls, typing memos, drinking coffee. Past that, far off in the lake is the lonely, Victorian city water intake pumping station glinting in the lowering afternoon sun. I've wondered what it would be like to stand on its parapet looking back on this big city skyline rising in the west, seeing this great Chicagoland and all its crazy stories. Like viewing the city from Mars. While I am zoned out, my face does all the right things—brow wrinkling, chin rubbing—no cause for alarm.

Sitting up straighter and going for the big finish, I sing my spot-lit, well-rehearsed, number-one-with-a-bullet answer and VP/SPAS/OSS is blown away. Inadvertently, I finger the guitar pick in my pocket and my answer is a song of dedication and a humble willingness to learn, be trained, be a company man, come in early, go home late, advance up the ladder of middle management where the sky is the limit.

The pick in my pocket has plucked the strings on a certain guitar that has been lost and gone so many years, disappeared soon after nine-year-old Dave skidded his bike on the gravel at the end of the driveway, crying, screaming, racing past me into the house because there'd been a terrible terrible accident—little brother Elliot is dead. Elliot is lost and I ... we ... will never be the same again. Questions were not asked. And there were no answers. Elliot was not discussed.

For many months the house was shrouded in a cloud of mourning. Our parents moved about like ghosts, quiet, melancholy, and the slightest thing could set off a downward spiral of grief—a bit of music, a stray photograph, a family portrait, a toy, his room. But time eventually lightened the load and like the railroad tracks that seem to disappear and end in the distance, we carried on.

And Elliot's guitar—an old one I let him use—was hidden away, never again to be seen or heard.

Time passed and Dave and I grew up. But we didn't forget.

VP/SPAS/OSS slides a slip of paper across the table to me. On it, a number is written. "An excellent offer son, a handsome salary—we feel that we can use a fine young man such as yourself in the future we are creating here at IBM."

I look at the number. Large. A well-compensated, bright future.

Do I take the job?

Lit up like landing lights at O'Hare, the runways cross—blue lights one way, red ones the other. The pick in my pocket twirls, vibrates. Sympathetic strings in my brain quiver and ring and here at the crossroads, the answer is evident.

Like Sooz jumping off her cliff, I jump off mine.

Q & A

Q: Well, this has worked out well. Here we are—what? Eight months later? You stupidly spurn IBM, turn your back on a particularly lucrative career from the largest computer company in the world—Jesus!—and now that band you started has gone up in smoke.

A: Oh man, yeah, that last gig was a disaster. One of the soles on my platform shoes broke—

Q: A three-incher if I'm not mistaken—with glitter—

A: —and my hair caught fire and somebody doused it with beer and Porky's owner wouldn't pay us … and the drummer quit—Gravity Moose is a dead duck.

Q: You burned the blue streak in your hair right off. But you looked stupid in platforms—made you ten feet tall. Jesus.

A: (…)

Q: And now you've got no band, a Mickey Mouse job at a screwy little record store on Clark Street in Chicago, a cold crappy apartment and the rent is due.

A: (…)

Q: Should've gone with IBM.

A: I just couldn't do it. Get this—VP/SPAS/OSS calls me every once in a while still sniffing around. Amazing. But all that computer stuff reminded me of her anyway, it was painful …

Q: Please. *She* doesn't have anything to do with it. What, is this some coming of age tale, some *girl* from school disappears and you don't have the balls to actually grow up. So, let's mess around and play that rock 'n roll music—

A: Absolutely not. And she was not just *some* girl. She was *magic*.

Anyway, there's a lot at stake here—like what to do with my life, the future of American popular music—it's balls out man—

Q: Or the future of all bisynchronous data communications. Whatever happened to that?

A: (…)

Q: Your parents, what are they …

A: Shaking their heads, but you know what? They're mostly great.

Q: That's not where this tale is going.

A: No, it's not. Look. If I went with IBM I could've changed the direction of all mainframe computing and positively influenced the gross national product for the next twenty years and …

Q: Bullshit. So, you start a band and sing your little songs.

A: That's it.

Q: (…)

A: (…)

Q: Now what?

A: I've got it figured out.

Q: What.

A: Dave.

Q: Your brother.

A: The alive one. Yeah, that chick of his dumped him and he's moping around—time for the brothers to get it together just like it used to be. I think he's the karmic key …

Q: Karmic key?

A: See, I've got all these songs ready to go—they're *unusual*—I liberate him from school and away we go. See, I'm going to zig when everybody expects a zag. My music, with the right band, can change the world 'cause …

Q: Jesus.

A: … I got a line on a record label around here that's down on their luck—they need somebody like me—us.

Q: You're nuts.

A: But wouldn't it be nice?

Q: (…)

A: (…)

Q: And her?

A: I dunno. Probably never see her again.

Q: You condone what she's done?

A: Officer, I have no direct knowledge of what she's done.

Q: (…)

A: Sometimes, if you're really committed and you're responding to a superpower bombing the hell out of an agrarian society like a typhoon of steel, maybe you've got to do a little bad to do a lot of good. I don't know. It's murky.

Q: No absolutes?

A: In her world, I think there are—she's completely digital, not analog.

Q: What?

A: Ones and zeros. On or off. Right and wrong in her highest sense. All or nothing. Hegelian dialectics, Goethe's cosmic dualities.

Q: Please. But the world, is it digital or analog?

A: Haven't figured that out yet. She said digital is the future. I think she's right. Love that stuff.

Q: How about a revolutionary, wholly political tune? Can you write one?

A: I've tried. They stink—*c'mon brothers and sisters, we're marchin' to the sea*—nobody cares about that stuff anymore.

Q: That's true. It's a new world. Now she's an outlaw.

A: Tragic. She was the one that could've changed the world with that talent of hers, changed the way things are done—invent the new, throw out the old …

Q: What happened to her?

A: Wish I knew. Gone underground.

Q: Where's that?

A: Could be here. There. Anywhere.

 Track 4: January 1974

THREE IN THE MORNING. Dave and I are zooming up Interstate 55 to Chicago. I have liberated him from his downstate liberal arts country club—Newton College—he's a business major—*why not?*—*the safe approach.*

His longtime girlfriend—the very lovely and highly desirable

Marilyn—has dumped him and that, reportedly, sent him into a funk that made him very receptive to my phone pitch:

Me: Hey man, I'm starting a new band.

Dave: What? (Much background noise. Stereo. Unidentifiable band.) I can't hear you.

Me: Turn that thing down!

(Scuffling sounds, silence.)

Dave: Okay. What.

Me: Hey man, I'm starting a new band. I need you.

Dave: Again? Mm. I dunno.

Me: Without you, I'm nowhere. Only you understand my songs.

Dave: But I don't.

Me: Blow this semester off. Do you good. Help you forget Mari—

Dave: Don't say it!

Me: Sorry—it'll be like the old days, but better. You know, rockin' our asses off …

Dave: Yeah!

Me: We'll be back—Dave, remember our search … for *it!*

It.

Elusive concept. Hard to define. We always know it when we find *it,* or when *it* finds us.

Dave agrees to run away with me because he remembers those times in the garage when *it* happened—musical nirvana, sublime and pure—soul-stirring sparking guitar gusts of sound, crazy and out of control. But maybe he agrees because he wants to forget.

Interestingly, Dave has revived his on-again off-again interest in Eastern philosophical thought—my clever appeal to the Zen-like concept of *it* also helped close the deal. (It occurs to me his very unbusinessey Eastern intrigues may have contributed to his breakup with Marilyn.) To minimize any opportunity for reconsideration, I drive down there to personally escort him up to the big city. A hands-on approach works best.

David. Dave. Number One Brother. Bass guitar. Kazoo. If Brian Jones were alive and not strung out, he'd look like Dave.[14] Or Dave would

---

[14] Brian Jones, founding member of the Rolling Stones. Known for all that thick blonde hair,

look like him—the Porter family golden boy. Me? I got the nose—
he got the looks from Mom—angular face, knockout girly-blue eyes,
eyelashes that don't quit, long blonde hair that Barbie would love
to have.

But what flows through the rocks and stones at the bottom of
his soul?

Memory speaks. The Elliot story. It was Dave.

The two of them riding bikes down on the hill by the railroad
tracks in Hinsdale summer of '61. Nine-year-old Dave and his buddies allow six-year-old Elliot to tag along with the big kids—he's
just learned to ride his new red Schwinn Spitfire—the kid thinks he's
pretty cool. They ride to the secret summer place of forts and hideouts,
imagined battles, clubs, and crazy schemes. A slalom course marked
by little rocks is set up on the sidewalk that runs down the hill, Deadman's Hill—the turns compress fiendishly tighter and tighter close to
the bottom—the course ends right before hitting the street that runs
along the tracks and a speed racer has to be able to stop fast, naturally
part of the fun because long, heroic skids are highly prized. When a
nervous Elliot finally makes his run, egged on by Dave and the guys,
he loses control at the bottom. There's a long, black skid mark off the
curb that ends under a car at the bottom.

"It's all my fault!" Dave, screaming all night long.

We pull off the highway for a middle-of-the-night pit stop at the
Funk's Grove rest stop on northbound 55. The stench in the men's
room is overwhelming. I bail. Dave makes an appallingly extended
visit.

The parking lot of the rest stop is empty, the world is home in
bed, asleep, an alarm clock set to go off in just a few hours, sleepers
dreading the moment when they will be switched on, Monday morning life lit up, the hamster wheel of the day rolling again. I am out
here on the banks of the concrete river that slices through the Great
Corn Desert. The trucks and cars that roar up and down the road in
a torrent during the day dwindle down to a skimpy stream at night,
with the howl of a single truck blasting by, one northbound to Chi-

---

his state-of-the-art getups.

cago, then another southbound to St Louis, big Macks and Peterbilts, serious highway stars—the whine of tires and diesels dopplering off across the disappearing two-lane blacktop, curving with the soft rise and fall of the flat land, the gentle breathing of prairie earth Illinois. Lights appear down the road, off in the distance, single yellow-white eyes flickering away to the south, growing to two distinct sixty-mile-an-hour amphetamine-fueled pupils. An empty flagpole stays ticking in the wind, rises from the middle of a winter-dead garden surrounded by bricks in front of the restrooms.

The sharp staccato of a truck's horn snaps me out of my fog and haze. I look up. A million stars light the black dome of the sky. To the west, a faint, fuzzy patch of light is hanging low over the dark horizon, silver-haired ragged and out of control—a mysterious traveler from the emptiness of interstellar space on its journey around the sun, doomed to return to the blackness of the universe, where even the interstate won't go. It's that comet we've been hearing about. Kohoutek.

I wonder what it'd be like to ride the comet, ride it bareback.

I wonder what it'd be like to see her again. Sooz.

Dave reappears and we're back on the road, wheezing along at a stately and energy-saving fifty-five miles an hour.[15] He fiddles with the radio, pulling in long-distance AM stations—New York, New Orleans, Denver—signals that have bounced off flocks of buzzing ions up in the atmosphere, charged and electrified by that long-haired silver visitor from deep space. But it seems only Tony Orlando songs are abroad on the airwaves tonight. Dave mutters darkly, gives up, slumps in his seat, tries to sleep.

Up ahead, the road begins to curve. The Dixie Truck Stop—the midway point on the road between Chicago and St. Louis—looms in the darkness, lit up like a space ship marooned in the dead corn stubble and dirty snow. Don't need gas, so we motor on under the overpass that is probably the highest point of land for a hundred miles in any direction. Flatlands.

Sulfurous shafts of light of the on-ramp drop from spindly hooded light standards lined up like a newly landed one-legged army from

---

[15] We are driving Otto, our aging VW van. Yes, I know it's a hippie cliché. But our mom loved that van and named it. So it goes.

Mars. In one of the pools of light, there's a hitchhiker standing on the roadside gravel, thumb out. I slow down to have a look.

Dave says, "Oh shit, no no *no*, we aren't picking anybody up. Might be an escapee from Joliet for chrissakes."

Historically, Dave is the cautious type. His Eastern serenity comes and goes.

I say, "If he is, he's headed the wrong way." I slow down a little more. "Man, middle of the night, out here in the sticks. C'mon—let's pick him up."

"No fuckin' riders, man. Let's just go."

The hitchhiker is in a long coat, tall and rock 'n roll skinny. He's got straight blonde hair hanging down to his shoulders from under an Ahab-dark, broad-brimmed hat—the sort an old preacher might wear. There's an acoustic guitar case in his hand with a big yellow smiley face sticker on it. As we approach, he is sepulchral, unsmiling. In a hallucinatory slow motion, the frames of this strange film unfurl and my eyes lock with the guy's and I forget about the road ahead—Otto drives himself. There is something about this guy.

Now, my policy is that candidate riders smile at the prospective ride provider—me—times being what they are, the energy crisis, the economy and all,[16] thereby at least making an attempt to minimize any understandable uncertainty, exhibiting friendliness and projecting an unthreatening demeanor such as—no, *I am not the Boston Strangler, I am not straight out of that Doors' song—killer on the road—I am not going to stick my knife right down yo throat.*

We draw even with him, his eyes retreat into shadow. His mouth forms the words, "Have a nice day!"

I heed Dave's recommendation and pass him by—the weirdness is too heavy.

Dave shudders, turns, watches the stranger vanish on the dark sea floor of the prairie.

We zoom on.

Dave can't sleep so he produces a tape, sticks it in the player that sits on the black rubbery floor in front of Otto's stalky stick shift. Turns it way up. The new Yes.

---

[16] Gas at $.50 a gallon, 10 percent unemployment. Holy smoke.

We rock.

We drive more.

He turns it way down, "You really fucked up not taking that IBM job, didn't you?"

Jerk.

He says, "And I knew that your stupid Gravity Moose glitter thing would die."

Creep.

"Yep, looks like good old Dave is going to have to save your skinny ass once again." He roots around in the McDonald's bag at his feet, snarfs a cold French fry.

Cosmic Dave, seeker of Eastern wisdom, bringer of patience, humility, and wide-eyed wonder, has vanished. I make a mental note to add to his serenity by making my pristine copy of *Jonathan Livingston Seagull* conveniently available once we get to my place in Chicago.[17]

"No, Dave. Things are going according to plan. You're here and the new band—the one that will surely take off, is coming together."

I pause for dramatic effect and then ask, "Do you remember Brian Hawgrim?"

"Fuckin' Hawgrim?" Dave bashes me on the shoulder and we nearly swerve off the road.

I tell Dave about the recent reappearance of Brian A. Hawgrim— my childhood playground nemesis, a menacing presence who also happens to be an excellent keyboardist—actually *accordionist*, to be specific. That disastrous last gig at Porky's Rooftop—a joint out on the far southwest side of Chicago, hardly more than a taco stand and a bar located in an industrial moonscape under towering heaps of factory slag and tailings of God knows what. Yeah, my platform heel broke—sending me crashing into a couple of the amps, tipping them and a few foaming beer bottles onto drummer Harold. He scrambled for cover, drumsticks and cymbals flying. I lay there on what's supposed to be the stage at Porky's, sparks flying from broken amp tubes and shattered light bulbs. I was, frankly, quite comfortably prone amid the flattened amps and dripping beer, staring at the crappy ceiling.

---

[17] *Jonathan Livingston Seagull*, by Richard Bach, 1970. Metaphysical birds. I once got a date by telling a girl that I'd read it.

Obviously, Gravity Moose was on its way to extinction.

A guitar, still slung across my waist and plugged into a still operational amp, started to squeal a stringy sort of electronic feedback from the alcohol and smoke-stained speakers. The noise was fairly impressive so I stayed there, on the floor, relaxing, thinking about new musical directions. If I tilted my guitar to the left, the feedback shrieked higher, if I angled it right, it howled lower.

New explorations in electronic music. I felt like John Cage.

Harold the drummer noticed the smoke rising from my hair and kindly doused the rising flames with a beer. I thanked him.

Brian Hawgrim appeared over me, looming with his customary disgusted look. "The hell are you doing, Porter?"

"Hello, Hawgrim. Nice place, Porky's, don't you think?"

I narrowed my eyes, raised an eyebrow, started to get up. He actually offered a hand, pulling me off the sticky stage, and I limped with my broken heel over to the bar with him, stuffing my sweaty satin shirt back in my jeans, feigning nonchalance. Tony Orlando came blasting over Porky's sound system. People screamed. They changed the station.

Hawgrim—shoulder-length, mop-water hair (thinning rapidly) pulled back in a stringy ponytail—took a bottle of Hamm's from the bartender, sprinkled beer on my still smoldering hair. He handed the bottle to me, peered at me through wire-rimmed glasses, a beat-up "Four More Years" button pinned to his jean jacket next to one that says "Support Our President."

"Porter, you've hit a rough patch with this band of yours, Gravity Mouse."

"Moose."

"Right."

He told me how he had a new business venture and handed me his card:

Brian A. Hawgrim, BA, LS
Legal Advice and Insurance Sales

"BA, LS—?"

"Bachelor of Arts and Law Student, Pepper.[18] Actually, I'm start-

---

[18] Rule of Salesmanship Number 3: always use the prospect's first name as much as possible—

ing law school next year. In the meantime, I'm offering quite a nice range of insurance products that could lay the foundation for your future, and I'm here to tell you that you need to think about that future, Pepper Porter." He warmed up, started waving his arms, his head cocked to one side, peering at me earnestly through his glasses that lay just slightly crooked on his nose. He had to shout over the sound system. "Ever contemplate what you'll be doing twenty years from now, Pepper? Depravity Goose seems to be entering a period of, shall we say, reassessment and reevaluation, my guitar-playing friend. You're in last place, the cellar, a hundred games out of first place and the season's almost over. And yet, I believe I could be of some assistance. Pepper, I specialize in recognizing the insurance needs of college students, current and otherwise. Naturally. Pepper."

He noticed my waning interest.

"Pepper, you need to be aware of one of my other ventures." He handed me a second card out of his wallet, this one creased and stained with cheerful musical notes printed on it:

The SwingTones
Wedding Music For All Occasions
B. A. Hawgrim, Bookings

"Weddings? You've got a wedding band?"

"Absolutely. I play the accordion and our friend Ricky—remember him?—is a fine drummer. Grandma needs the 'Tennessee Waltz' or 'Lady of Spain'? We got it."

"Accordion? Are you kidding?" I choked. Beer entered my nasal passage.

"Don't laugh, man. It's a fine and noble instrument. Hey, with my big Baldoni squeezebox and Ampeg amp, I kick 'In-A-Gadda-Da-Vida's'[19] ass. Can sound just like a Hammond B-3 with a Leslie—a 707 taking off. Or I can sound like Myron Floren and make the old folks happy."

---

people love the sound of their name. Hawgrim shared this with me later.
[19] Iron Butterfly, 1968. Eighteen-minute song with a twenty-minute drum solo. Heavy organ tune.

"But what self-respecting bride would hire you guys? I mean, you look, er, well, you know."

"Check this out, man. How do you think I got through college?" He shoved an 8x10 glossy photo of the evidently clean-cut Swing-Tones into my hand. Baby blue tuxedo, yellow ruffled shirt and a slicked-backed ponytail disguised Hawgrim surprisingly well.

"Perhaps we can do business, Pepper Porter. Perhaps we can do business."

Dave howls. *"Accordion? Are you kidding me? And he's selling insurance?"*

The thwack of a swarm of the interstate's winter expansion joints bumps loudly, rattling the van like we have a flat.

So Hawgrim and I talked about the SwingTones and some of their latest gigs—weddings with brides collapsing drunk in the parking lot, dresses torn and tattered, stuff like that. After a while, he finally got to the point. He said he had some new music of his own and it was time for him to go for it—the choice was insurance sales, law school, or rock 'n roll—or maybe all of the above.

Then he said, "I want to join your band."

Dave says, "How can you even consider him, after all the shit he put you through?"

Hawgrim's most spectacular offense occurred in sixth grade during an all-school talent show in which I had been dragooned along with two other short, shrimpy saps, compelled by our dia-bolical teacher to form a trio, don green brocade dresses, wigs, and high heels and lip-sync the McGuire Sisters' "I'm in the Mood for Love." Admittedly, I deserved the abuse, but his back-of-the-gym heckling—which earned him a string of detentions, and his subse-quent humiliating theft of my then girlfriend—the much-admired Lynn R., who kept real-time boyfriend standings on her home-room desk—five names inscribed in girly script in regular rota-tion—that was it. The day after the talent show, I was off the chart, gone. And Hawgrim was perched with a leer at the top. He and his hoods beat me up on the playground, cigarettes stuck behind their ears.

They called me Boo Boo.
Dave says, "Jesus."

 Track 5: Saturday night

A FEW NIGHTS LATER, back home in Chicago, Dave and I are at a Moose Lodge on the northwest side—it's a wedding and the SwingTones are playing. We are auditioning Brian Hawgrim.

Dave and I are at the bar, trying to act like we're supposed to be there, smiling and nodding to people, trying to maintain a low profile, hanging out. The SwingTones are set up on a little mound of risers over in the corner behind a dance floor, amid a minefield of white-draped tables with dark blue and orange Chicago Bears centerpieces for *him*, pink orchids and lace for *her*.

The SwingTones play. They're pretty good. As advertised, Hawgrim plays "Lady of Spain" and "The Tennessee Waltz," everybody does the Hukilau.

Dave and I drink. Stanley the bartender is most accommodating, supplying many well-made Tequila Sunrises. Dave finds a flowery, half-drunk chick named Gloria. They disappear into the crowd.

The evening's going along blandly well, people becoming thoroughly liquored up, when Hawgrim pulls a rock 'n roll rabbit out of his double-knit powder blue tux. The SwingTones begin this musical tour-de-force by stomping through "In-a-Gadda-da-Vida," with Hawgrim belting out the vocals over the stone cathedral timbre of his fancy Baldoni accordion juiced up through his big amp, lighting a fire under the shrieking, well-oiled wedding crowd.

Midway through the famous thudding drum solo performed by the SwingTones' *percussionist*—a big fuzzy-haired guy named Ricky, one of Hawgrim's old playground hoods—*budda budda budda bup, bup bup*, mysteriously, Hawgrim begins to croon, "*The stars won't come out, if they know you're about, 'cause they couldn't match the glow of your eye-yi-yi-yis.*"

With a pulsing, hard-driven percussive *thomp* running at ninety miles an hour, the SwingTones fling open the hood of Tony Orlando's "Candida," a middle-of-the-road harmless pop ditty, rip out the wimpy two-stroke, throw it over the side and install a brand new

Chevy V8 with hotrod headers, a rumbling exhaust generating maximum rock 'n roll horsepower.

Hawgrim! The clever, twisted bastard!

The wedding comes to a skidding halt a few alcohol-soaked hours later as the bride grabs one of the Chicago Bears centerpieces—a plastic football and a Chicago Teddy Bear—triumphantly drags it outside like road kill. In the freshly snow-plowed parking lot, in an admirably athletic motion, the formidable bride punts the plastic NFL football, her shoe flying off her foot fluttering over the cars and mountains of snow like a crazy pink pigeon. Up go her arms. Three points! Cheers erupt.

As the crowd bellows the Bears fight song, she climbs to the top of a parking lot snowbank with the little sweater-clad, football helmeted bear in one hand, beat-up bouquet in the other. She plants the little bear on the peak and, standing like a shaky Sherpa, spins around and flings the bouquet into the happy mob below. Then she and her pink taffeta bridesmaids make snow angels in the black and white gritty piles until a cab arrives to whisk the happy couple away to their new life.

I stand in the Moose doorway watching the rapidly deteriorating scene, worn out and half drunk, wondering if I'm about to do the right thing—invite the evil Hawgrim to join the band. The security rent-a-cop is corralling the crowd back into the Moose and I'm heading back in myself when two dark shapes fly by, catching the corner of my eye.

Two enormous crows alight on a billboard atop the building next door, flap their wings and get comfortable. Like countless other structures around the city—three-flat apartments, cheap furniture showrooms, or Household Finance offices, the building is three stories of weathered dark brick crowned with a concrete parapet and a black iron fire escape scaling down from the flat tar roof. The billboard is a large, well-lit car dealer sign hanging on the wall facing the Moose— *Morrie Stunkel Ford*—*Where You Always Save More Money*. Heavyset Morrie has a Nixonesque five o'clock shadow and a single eyebrow, a slash of black crayon stretched from temple to temple. His smiling face, and thus the entire sales effectiveness of the billboard, is nicely enhanced by a nifty, state-of-the-art, 3-D representation of his outstretched hand, ready to shake on your great deal.

My head spins. Then Morrie winks at me, his hand reaches for mine, and the black crows, like Heckle and Jeckle, begin a cane-twirling song and dance—"Tea For Two."

The Tequila Sunrises have taken hold.

When the little Chicago Bear mascot, perched on top of the snow pile, yells at me, says he's looking for a job in Mayor Daley's office and do I know anybody who knows somebody, I know it's time to act.

I stand in the main entrance to the big ballroom. Hawgrim is carefully laying the big Baldoni accordion to rest in its black case, purple plush like a coffin. Ricky the drummer, sweaty and exhausted, has a big cymbal in his hand. He sees me and grins, putting it on his head like a Chinese hat.

This is it.

"Hello, Hawgrim." I loosen my already loose tie, stand there with my hands on my hips trying to look authoritative yet casual, surveying the pile of amps, instruments, and cases. He wipes a sweaty strand of hair from his eyes, smiles and extends his hand.

He says, "Hey, man. Glad you could make it. What'd you think?"

"I thought it was a provocative juxtaposition of the sublime and ridiculous, of the high and lows of our American culture today, symbolizing how we have lost our way. And if we are to survive—as a culture, you see—we must band together, musicians united as one, together, attempting to change the world. With our music."

Hawgrim looks at me with a smirk. "Have you thought about your insurance needs, Porter?"

"No."

"You should."

"You want to join?

"Yeah. Let's do it."

And with that, the lineup is complete: Dave on bass, vocals, and kazoo, Hawgrim on keyboards (actually accordion) and vocals, Ricky on drums, and me—guitars and vocals. We begin rehearsing like madmen almost every night in the musty basement of my record store employer—Gramophone Records on Clark. We learn my tunes—all originals—and then we record a two-song demo on my new little cassette tape recorder.[20]

---

[20] Song One: "Ants Are Cool." Song Two: "Burgers in Benton." Re "Ants Are Cool"—here's a quote from an interview with *Rolling Stone*: "Pepper Porter: That tune came out of Dave and me hanging in our backyard, lying on those plastic woven-webby sort of lawn chairs

Dave asks, "Excuse me. The band name, please?"

Hawgrim says, "Yeah, what the fuck?"

Ricky just smiles and twirls his drumsticks.

I say, "We are Pepperland."

Puzzled stares.

"Because I think it sounds cool. And it's my band."

Amazingly, everyone smiles and agrees.

We practice and rehearse, rehearse and practice. We get gigs—Pepperland plays bars, dumps, and dives. People begin to like us.

Lazlo Toth, owner of Gramophone, my scraggly chain-smoking boss and longtime record industry expert, listens to us. He taps his toe night after night, silent and enigmatic. But he keeps coming back. One night, he becomes a hero. He pulls me aside and says, "Pepper, my young friend," he waves a copy of a record company promo he received in the mail, stabbing it with a crooked finger. "I have two words for you—Checkers Records."

Track 5.5: Monday

Postcard. This one from suburban Chicago—Hinsdale, my hometown. All it says is, "Technology will set us free."

Is she closing in on me or something?[21]

Track 6: February

Harrison Creach finishes his recording session with Shine and the Funkolas around five in the morning, takes a deep drag on a Kool, though he is trying to quit for the seventeenth time. Bobby

---

positioned over a big anthill with a magnifying glass. We were fascinated with the amazing civic spirit of those ants, caring for each other, watching out for their children, teaching them, just like in that old song. But unlike us, ants clean up their little city, clean up their garbage. But then we accidentally burned a few ants up when the sun came out and blazed through the magnifying glass, torching a few drones. We were devastated.

RS: A metaphor for our times, indeed. You must have been shocked.

Me: We were never the same again."

[21] She has somehow found my latest address. How does she do it?

"Shine" Washington and his large platform-soled, spangled leather and dashikied entourage have finally cleared out, leaving him alone in the worn Checkers Records studio on South Michigan Avenue. They had been reasonably well behaved—instruments, equipment, and building still intact. Creach smiles, surveys the small collection of old amps, mics, and music stands arrayed around the room amid the debris, cigarette butts and bottles of the night. An abandoned roach on a clip lies in an ashtray, thin and spindly like a dusty ancient scroll. He relights it and takes a drag. The weed is lousy, mostly seeds and stems, but it smells good. The stained tweed top of one of the old amps is still warm to his touch, its hot vacuum tubes cooling and softly exhaling electric fumes after a long night of pushing sound through four ten-inch speakers. The amp's fabric is worn away to the wood frame on a spot near the loose leather handle, accelerated by a cigarette burn ringed by ancient beer from a forgotten session or gig at the old Club Zanzibar.[22] Creach sighs happily. He is back in the game again—Checkers Records, almost given up for dead, is alive again. New owners, new money, new life. Creach is looking for talent.

He sits down at the old Kimball upright, touches the yellowed keys—a few notes from an old tune he used to play during his touring days, a smooth legato phrase with thick harmonics, ninths and thirteenths, out of style, timeless. Creach gets up, walks out of the studio singing something about *funk, uuhunhh—funk funk-o-sicle, yow yow yow yow yow yow, funk, uuunhh—funk funk-o-sicle*, flicking a cymbal on the drum set on the way out.

The faded and peeling institutional green paint of Checkers Records hasn't been touched since Little Norman and his Dukes of Soul painted the place one weekend in 1964 to repay an advance from the company that was hanging over their heads. The building's windows have long since been plugged with thick glass blocks as the neighborhood declined—the Robert Taylor homes, the projects, rose a few blocks away casting a long and heavy shadow on the little two-story studio. The metal front door on the street has had a buzzer for years, replacing Mrs. Robinson, the last receptionist who was mugged on her

---

[22] 13th and Ashland Ave. Creach, then known professionally as "Papa Spo-dee-o-dee and his Orchestra," were the house band for a stretch in the early '50s, purveyors of romantic rhythms for your dancing pleasure. Replaced by Muddy Waters.

way home one day in '67 and never came back. The rusting and twisted security grille guarding the entrance sometimes rattles in the dry wind off the street, catching flying newspapers and dead city leaves.

Back in his office, Creach pulls the old glass ashtray from the long-gone Zanzibar out of its periodic hiding place in the bottom drawer, feet on the desk. Smoke fills his lungs, menthol and nicotine's deep warm fingers satisfying an old need. A reassuring old friend.

He sorts through the night's track sheets trying to decide if he hears a hit. It comes down to "Funk-o-Sicle," "Chocolate Bloop," or the very interesting "Jive Kangaroo." Creach heard about the Funko-las from his old friend and past bandmate E. Rodney Jones, now the venerable dean of Chicago black radio on WVON, 1390 AM. Jones's career took off when he left Checkers back in '59, just as Creach and Checkers began the long spiral downward in the '60s fueled by lousy decisions, bad luck, and alcohol. Creach hung on through different and indifferent owners, long hitless streaks.

Creach knows exactly when Checkers last had a top forty hit—he wrote the tune and produced the record. November 1962. Little Frankie and the Cat Daddies, "Who's Yowling at My Window?"[23] The Cat Daddies made a few more records, even opened for Sam Cooke once at the Flame in Detroit. They played Southside clubs and ballrooms but it was the disastrous "Gospel" tour that Creach booked for the decidedly un-pious Cat Daddies that nailed their coffin—whiffs of inappropriate behavior with overly attentive female fans. They split up when seventeen-year-old Little Frankie went back to work for his father's fuel oil business—on the run from an irate choir director.

"Who's Yowling" got some local radio play with WVON, spread to St. Louis, Detroit, and Philadelphia, peaked at number nineteen on the national pop chart. Not bad. Looking back, Creach was proud. He and the label made a few bucks. Little Frankie and the Cat Daddies didn't come out so well. Frankie and the boys signed away everything in a contract, got screwed. Checkers owned the master tapes. That's the way it was.

---

[23] The Cat Daddies were mostly alumni of Creach's old traveling band, session pros. Checkers and Creach paid union scale for studio work. The B-side of "Who's Yowling" was "If I Was a Three-legged Cat (Would You Still Love Me?)".

Creach pours a new cup of coffee and concludes "Jive Kangaroo" has the best shot at the charts—it's got the *groove*. He thinks that he'd better clean up the studio.

Instead, he begins to doze.

The phone rings. Creach opens one eye and looks at the phone, then the clock. Still before six. He rubs his face and takes a deep breath. It is a matter of personal pride that no matter what time the phone rings, he will answer it politely and professionally.

"Checkers Records, Home of the Groove—Harrison Creach speaking, how may I help you?"

"Creach, you smooth-talking motherfucker! How did those goddamn Funkolas do this past evening?" Jones's voice is disk jockey smooth and rich and dark gold—the inside of a charred oak cask of resting bourbon.

"Jones, your language—please." Like an old bandleader habitually respectful of an audience, Creach always speaks courteously and with a dignified smile. He knows that Jones is about to go on the air on VON, morning drive time. It is 5:51, nine minutes to air. Creach relaxes back into his chair and lets Jones do the talking. He pinches the bridge of his nose, eyes closed.

Jones says, "Oh yes, pardon me, Sir Harry. May I enquire after your health this fine winter's morning?" Jones likes to riff in a jive British accent.

"Still dark, my friend."

"Do we like what we heard last night? How about that 'Jive Kangaroo' bullshit?" Jones trills the "r" in kangaroo.

"I am reminded of a Salvation Army band on LSD."

"Creach, you and I are old school, my good sir, and I am inclined to agree," he loses the accent. "But goddamn, I think I hear a hit there, at least regional." Jones gargles coffee, coughs and barks at an assistant.

"'Jive Kangaroo' is indeed impressive. And actually, I thought that 'Funk-o-Sicle,' as performed, had a certain rhythmic appeal that might enable a crossover to white kids, maybe even get us a shot at WLS, or those FM cats at WXRT or KSHE down in St. Louis."

Creach stretches the phone cord to the coffee machine in the hall.

Jones says, "I agree. And I know those stoners at KSHE. And LS? Sirott's a little shit and Lujack's a bastard.[24] But here's why I called. Listen, I need a new, preferably unknown, cheap but competent white band for a tour this brother of mine's putting together. Downstate sunshiny brotherly love bullshit this summer—you know, black bands, white bands, funk and rock, everybody loves everybody or some such wholesome shit. Some unusual venues, a couple festivals, too. You said you might know of some acts like that."

"Unusual venues?" Creach reaches the pot and pours himself a cup. It is 5:54.

"Yeah, gig at a big ass goddamn nudist camp down by the big river. Ha! You believe that? Anyway, you cats at Checkers Records—you'll get to put out some records—and you *know* I'll play them." Jones puts the phone down and noisily blows his nose. Then he picks up again. "Excuse me. Man, I gots to go. Thank you so much for your time." He hangs up.

Creach swivels his chair to the stack of cassette demos rising neatly on his credenza from would-be recording stars. At the top of the pile is a tape that is labeled in a way that screams *white band*:

      Band name: Pepperland

      Contact & Bookings: Pepper Porter. (312) 929 1793

 Track 7: Meanwhile ...

MY BROTHER'S BEEN READING the *Jonathan Livingston Seagull* that I left lying around. He's now telling me he is *one* with Chiang the guru gull who exhorts young Jonathan to ever-greater heights and unlimited feats of wonderfulness. Cosmic Dave, a hazy smile on his increasingly rock 'n roll star face, has reread *Siddartha*, claims he is the unwavering sidekick Govinda—he is him and all this is that and, thanks to the liner notes in a Yes album, is reading a fat book called *The Autobiography of a Yogi* and has taken to meditating, playing weird koto music on the stereo, drinking funny tea, eating

---

[24] Bob Sirott and Larry Lujack. Longtime disk jockeys on WLS, "The Big 89," in Chicago.

brown rice, and has given up Froot Loops. He's traveling a well-worn longhair path.

He says he is a *Seeker*. He says I should meditate.

I say hell no.

He says, "You dumbshit! If you're ever gonna fuckin'—no, no. I'm sorry, I'm sorry. Oh my brother." He smiles blissfully, recovers a graceful state. "Please forgive me. I am merely suggesting this."

Cosmic Dave tilts his head ingratiatingly, resumes his own inner reveries.

But I close my eyes and think about what it would be like to stand inside my electric guitar—right inside the slab of heavy dark mahogany, pressing my hand to its wall like a blind man, fingering the grain of the wood layered and wavering like a great river's ancient sediments laid by stately muddy waters one over another, my head just underneath the stamped steel of the bridge and the arrowing silver strings. In that tiny chamber smelling of dense wood and ancient oils, lit by a stream of flashing firefly electrons, I'd lay my head against the lamppost of the pickups—the coiled copper wires winding around a creamy white plastic bobbin, encasing a dusty old black magnet pulling at the strings strung overhead like telephone wires, humming a howling hurricane. I'd be swept up in the blue electric winds and be blown through old, fabric-sheathed wires spewing in a torrent down past maxed-out volume knobs and then sent spinning out of the guitar, through the twisted cable to a vast stack of guitar amps fat with current, washing me into a sea of glowing vacuum tubes, waves of sound—D's, G's, C's, and F sharps gathering in a riptide of chiming treble, jangling and pushing out through twelve-inch speakers, heavy magnets diaphragmed with shiny silver domes, coned with thick, black paper faced by silver-sparkled grille cloth, and then Madison Square Garden high, moving acres of sweet smoke-fragrant air, flying above many thousands of people, ears tuned, ears alight, eyes closed, pink tulip petals of sound showering softly through the sweeping glare of monstrous Super Trouper lights. They would hear me and I would play for them and make them happy.

And they would say that's a Pepper song. That's one of his—that's

Pepperland. And the things I did would matter and change their lives for a long time.

I think—how nice.

I quietly open my eyes and see Dave still meditating cross-legged on the beanbag chair by the apartment's front picture window. He is at peace. I am at peace.

And I haven't thought of her since I read the paper this morning and didn't see any mention of her.

The phone rings. Hawgrim tells me that we have just been booked as the opening act on a short string of downstate Illinois gigs in a mere one month's time—somebody cancelled and we are in the right place at the right time to open for Pavlov's Dog, a noted up-and-coming St. Louis band that has actually signed with Columbia. *Columbia!*

I stand in triumph!

When asked how this miracle occurred, Hawgrim says, "Ricky."

"Ricky?"

"He's connected, man. He's deep. He was in 'Nam, you know."[25]

"Wow …"

As I speak, the beat-up, grayish sheet that has been tacked to the window frame falls from the window like a magician's cape on a vanished sawed-off lady exposing me to the dark street lit by the orange glow of the mercury lamp at the corner, snow flurries swirling high amid the naked trees in the light. My reflection, dark and distorted in the ancient wavy glass, stares back at me.

On the other side of the street, there is a man in a long, black coat, guitar case at his feet. The guy waves.

I wave back.

"Hey, doof." Hawgrim—he's still on the phone. I thank him for the good news and hang up.

The guy on the street is a rock 'n roller, maybe a little younger than us, maybe about as tall as I am but with that long blonde hair hanging to his shoulders from under his flat-brimmed black hat, he's got that weird, old-timey preacher sort of vibe we saw out on the road.

There's a smiley-face sticker on the guitar case.

It's the hitchhiker from 55, the Dark Stranger.

---

[25] Marines. May 1969, Hamburger Hill. He doesn't want to talk about it. Ricky *knows.*

I stand at the window. I look at him, he looks at me.

"Dave."

Dave, barefoot, walks to the window, stands next to me.

I whisper. "It's the guy."

The apartment is silent.

A shower of thick snowflakes, blown from trees by a gust of wind, rains on the Dark Stranger. He removes his hat, shakes it off and brushes snow from his shoulders.

Dave says, "Jesus, I think he looks like Elliot. Like he would've."

He does.

I grab my boots, hopping around on one foot yanking them on, falling into the beanbag. Out the door without a coat, I skid down the front stoop stairs and slide into the street.

He's gone. No trace. Next to me, a fat rat emerges from beneath a parked station wagon. The rat, calmly and with a confidence that only a Chicago rat could have, regards me with disdain, turns and skitters up the middle of the snowy street toward the lights of Clark Street. I follow the rat. There, in the middle of Wrightwood under a streetlight, almost a block away near Clark, standing in one of the inches-deep tire tracks, is the guy, guitar case at his feet.

The rat turns and disappears up an alley.

I approach the guy, following the ruts in the snow.

The Dark Stranger reaches down, picks up a handful of snow. He makes a snowball, flips it up and down in his left hand like a baseball, a pitcher waiting for the sign.

I am sixty feet away. I stop.

If I could actually remember exactly what Elliot looked like, if I could remember the little details of his six-year-old face, I would. But I can't. It's only from photographs long hidden in family albums that I pull out when nobody's looking that I have a clue—the hair, the blue eyes, the high forehead. Artificial memory. No portraits, no pictures on the wall—he's gone, hidden away, obviously saving my parents from the reminder, the unimaginable horror of the death of a child. But me, I'm okay, I did fine, I recovered. I was not damaged.

And so he has remained the little kid in the first-grade class picture, front row, second from the left sitting on the linoleum floor behind the little sign—Miss Pearson's class, 1961, big crooked grin like he was still learning how to smile, well-combed blonde hair and a little bowtie all spiffed up for picture day, and he looks like ... he looks like ... he looks like *this*.

The Dark Stranger calmly tosses his snowball, hand to hand. He's got no gloves, his fingers are long and slender—the hands of a piano player. Elliott hated piano lessons. That was then. Maybe this is now.

Standing right in the middle of a Chicago street on this strange snowy night, he peers at me hard, looking for a sign. I have no sign to give him.

He winds up with a high pitcher's kick and lets the snowball fly and it's coming right down the pipe, hard and fast and if I had a bat I'd hit it out of the park, but I have no bat, and then it curves and it's coming at me so fast I have no time to hit the dirt. The Dark Stranger nails me right in the chest, letters-high, right in the heart. His snowball is well packed and hard. It hurts.

I look down, and the remains of the snowball dribble to the street. I look up and here comes another pitch, this one aimed higher. I duck and it flies by my head.

He's got a good arm.

The Dark Stranger, though he has another snowball ready to go, motions for me to have a go. He's grinning. Crookedly.

I have no gloves. The snow is wet, perfect snowball material. My hands are freezing. The wind picks up.

I wait for the Dark Stranger to give the sign. He calls for it high and inside. I wind up and make my pitch.

It lands ten feet in front of him. He looks disappointed. I'm embarrassed.

I try again.

This time, it's closer but still feeble. Though he has every right to, he doesn't gloat.

I try again.

My hands are warming, I'm forgetting the cold. I stare at him, try to imagine *him*. Maybe I'm nuts and this is crazy. I make a new snowball.

Dave appears, taps me on my shoulder. He hands me my coat, offers gloves. I decline. We both stand there in the snowy street like the pitcher and his coach, considering this Mickey Mantle monster cleanup hitter, deciding on the perfect pitch. It's bases loaded, two outs, bottom of the ninth, seventh game of the World Series.

Dave murmurs, "Fast ball, high and tight, kid."

I wind up and let it fly.

It's a good pitch, sailing down the street, perfectly thrown, right in there—it's gonna be all over and everybody'll go home happy.

The Dark Stranger, black coat flying in the rising wind, picks up the guitar case and, wielding it like a lumpy Louisville Slugger, swings for the fences and my snowball splatters in a snow globe explosion lit by the glow of the street-lit Chicago night.

Instinctively, all three of us raise our arms in triumph. We're all in an ecstatic rounding-the-bases, home-run trot, though our feet remain rooted in the street and we move not an inch. The cheers die down.

With his hat, the Dark Stranger carefully cleans the black guitar case, starred with the remains of my snowball.

A bus appears behind him at the corner on Clark. The guitar case is returned to the street by his feet and with an extravagant swoop of his hat and hand, it's clear that the guitar is for me. He turns, races to the bus and is gone.

I turn to Dave. Wordlessly, *what the fuck?*

Back at the apartment, thawing out and dripping on the floor, we both sit there and contemplate the mystery guitar case on the floor between us.

I open the case.

 Track 8: Later that night

"YOU SURE IT'S THE ONE?" Dave whispers, bug-eyed as I hold a beat-up, dusty Felix the Cat guitar, *my* Felix the Cat guitar from a million years ago. "C'mon, how can that be? *This* is your guitar?"

"This is so *weird*. Yes, it's the one. What the hell?"

I turn the half-size plywood body of the guitar over and study the scratched and faded back, the painted black and white Felix, crazy red-tongued cat mouth gaping, eyes closed in Saturday morning ecstasy, cartoon hands stretched wide in a ta-da!—"Here I am, dig me, that's all folks, let's learn to play guitar"—balloon pop of fizzy freedom. I look carefully at the top of the cat-black headstock and find the small, curved dent in the wood—the Elliot dent. I had let him fool around with it that summer and he made me teach him a few easy chords. Screwing around with it, somehow he dinged it pretty bad. I yelled at him. Weeks later, he was gone.

And on the back of the guitar is a remnant of my former little self—a carefully inscribed "P.P." in red Magic Marker, a thick line of black underscoring the letters in a careful hand, recording some long ago day in my life when I began to care deeply about stringing a few notes and words together, seeking some secret sound that I was convinced could only be heard coming out of that guitar's round wooden sound hole with Felix cheering me on. Or Elliot.

"Okay, I give up. How'd this thing get here?" I look at Dave. "Is this *Candid Camera* or what? It isn't my birthday, you know."

"Hey man, this is freaking me out, too. I know nothing."

"It disappeared years ago. Mom always said some plumber must've stolen it out of the basement since it was so valuable."

"Ha! That's what she said about my baseball cards."

Our eyes meet. Mom!

"No, no. This isn't Mom," I say. "This isn't her style at all. She'd wrap it up nicely with a bow and a mushy card and take pictures of me opening it. And Dad would just yell and say music hasn't been the same since Spike Jones and His City Slickers."

"Yeah. Spike Jones. Dad." Dave grins and shakes his head.

"No, I don't think so. I just don't know. It's a mystery."

"Something strange is going on, man."

Dave, still wrapped in his blanket, yawns loudly and drifts into the kitchen to make a peanut butter and jelly sandwich. I take Felix to my room and sit down on the bed and start to play the old guitar. It's in perfect tune.

My fingers find familiar shapes on the dark, worn wood of the fretboard, grooved and scalloped—old simple chords open up and ring on the sturdy silver strings still sounding clear and honest, like a letter from home. Felix leads me down some old pathways not followed in years, trails that had been long overgrown with big bombastic weeds and undergrowth treacherous with too much attempted fancy junk masquerading as sophistication. Felix railroads me back onto square-ribbed stuff that is direct and uncomplicated—three chords—verse-verse-chorus and out. And then three more of the same chords. Like the unheard music in the bushes from an ancient poem—go, go, go, said Felix the guitar cat.

Wandering, my head on Felix's shoulder, the wood ringing and vibrating and the guitar's body humming, the bare bones of new music appear—the antenna of my mind picks up a simple song, crackling in from somewhere, skeletal and vague, it twirls for a while in my head then vanishes but appears again a while later, changed, better, then not as good, fleeting, then it becomes magic. My eyes are deaf and my ears see.

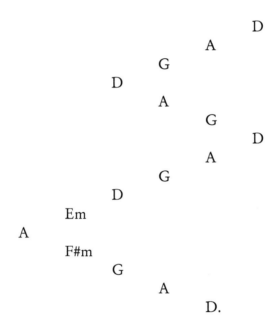

That night three new songs gush out, pouring through Felix and scribbled on paper. Clearly, Felix has been modified—an investigation of his innards reveals a tangle of wires, mysterious electronic switches, capacitors, and strange gizmos mere mortals dare not touch. When plugged in, Felix is amazing.

I fall asleep with Felix carefully laid in his case next to my bed.

I'm dreaming I'm a DC-10 on final approach to O'Hare on a warm and windy day swooping low over the lakefront, Wrigley Field to my left. The Cubs are losing again but everybody in the stands looks up, waves happily. I smile a metallic jet smile and zoom away across the city. On board is a huge entourage of rock 'n roll stars with shades, scarves and silk, tearing my insides apart like a Hyatt hotel room, tray tables down and lusty chicks fully reclined with seatbelts completely unfastened—everybody's swilling Tequila Sunrises and smoking spliffs the size of cigars hazing my interior like a hash convention in Tangier, smoke spilling out my windows flung open by Miss February in a fetching stewardess uniform while my cottony contrail spews and drifts behind my engines, snaking behind me like a Bugs Bunny hookah dream of Arabian nights. Then a humpbacked 747 flies up to me flapping its wings like a pelican with a bulging beak full of a hot and bitter peyote tea. The 747 is Keith Richards with a dark head of bird's nest hair, trailing a long scarf of leering lips and tongues with huge aviator sunglasses perched on the nose of his flight deck that project kaleidoscopic views of Sooz, beaches, big black hats and mainframe computers shifting scenes like a psychedelic Viewmaster. Keef the 747 asks me if I'd heard the latest Tony Orlando song. Then he grins, adjusts his sunglasses and flies off with Felix slipped under his big aluminum wing, singing "so long sucker, it's a gas gas gas!"

I wake up wide-eyed in a sweat.

I jump out of bed, banging my toe on the cinderblock bookshelf, blindly trying to locate the light switch in the dark.

I open the case. Felix is still there.

My little black notebook lies open on the floor, scrawled lyrics and chord progressions from the night before filling the last few pages. I try them out, picking my way around the words and music, amazed that they still make sense—the feel has not been lost in the night. But I decide not to take any chances. I set up my cassette recorder on the bed. With the door closed, I quickly record demos of this new material, plinking away with Felix still feeling the energy. The new stuff will not be lost now.

Later that morning, just as I am about to walk out the door and head to work, the phone rings. It is a Mr. Harrison Creach. In soothing and courtly tones, he inquires if Pepperland would be interested in auditioning for Checkers Records.

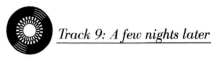

OUR LITTLE BAND is set up in a two-storied room about the size of a three-car garage. It's stained with ancient smoke, grimy acoustical tile paneling the walls and sturdy wooden chairs are carefully arranged in a broad C-shape, a grove of tall shiny microphones planted like bamboo shoots in a corner surrounded by weedy black music stands. A large window, with heavy curtains drawn, is centered high on one wall, apparently the upstairs control room, lights glinting through the fabric gaps. A row of old amps—some Fenders, big ones and little ones, an intimidating Marshall and an ancient Gibson—are lined up along a wall next to an old upright piano. Big JBL speakers hang from all four corners of the room—they look new.

The studio smells of tobacco and weed with the dried and faded tang of alcohol-stained leather and tweed, and is warmed by the wavering heat of glowing vacuum tubes in ceramic sockets—a musically inspiring combination.

I have dictated that the band show up for this galactically important audition in unconventional rock 'n roll attire—dinner jackets, both white and black over whatever. Under his beautifully tailored white jacket obtained from Goodwill, Dave has chosen his best lolling red tongue Stones t-shirt. Hawgrim has a purple ruffled shirt open at the neck, displaying a bit of hairy chest under his black coat. Ricky, our large, bearish, 'Nam vet drummer, is nicely attired in a bright yellow t-shirt spangled with blue sparkles under a long-tailed black tuxedo.

Me? Under my white dinner jacket, also acquired from Goodwill, I am spiffy in my big candy-apple red bowtie and crisp white shirt.

My thinking is this—sartorially, we zag when everybody else zigs.

We have not yet met Mr. Creach. I look at Dave, Hawgrim, Ricky. This is it. We nod as one, straighten our dinner jackets. I adjust my tie. We are completely set up and ready to go.

The bright overhead lights of the studio are extinguished, a single little fat lamp with a fringed lampshade on a doily-covered table in the corner that I hadn't noticed remains on, lighting the room with a dim forty-watt grandmotherly glow. The little red and blue "on" lights of our amps shine like little jewels.

The speakers up in the corners begin to hiss and crackle. A familiar series of noises emerge above electronic white noise—it's our demo tape. I hear my reedy voice, the count-off, a snappy one-two-three-four with the click of Ricky's sticks and "Burgers in Benton," the first tune on our tape, crashes into the room.

I think it sounds phenomenal. Though the sound is muddy and raw—it's a lousy cassette recording—the big studio speakers pump us up bigger than life and the loud guitars chime, the keyboard and drums swirl. Hawgrim grins, Ricky winks, and Dave appears serene.

I try to imagine the song, newly recorded in eight deep tracks coming over somebody's radio on a hipster station in real FM stereo with no static at all—somebody hearing the song for the first time through a big Pioneer, Sony, or Marantz receiver, the biggest stereo in the frat house with monster dorm speakers pointed out the open window serenading the green college quad on a warm and windy spring day, the exposed papery cones of the black woofers shuddering with bass and drums, silvery tweeters sparkling and kids stopping, staring, smiling, the guy with the big stereo is writing a paper on Chaucer, *Aprill's shoures soote* and the *swich lycour* in his *veynes*,[26] and he's feeling the music, understanding, measuring and judging, wondering who the hell *is* that?

The taped tune careens to a halt with Dave's ecstatic off-mic rock 'n roll hollering over a big three chord punch-out ending that is absolutely bombastic with Ricky's rumbling thunder underneath—and then the speakers go silent. We all smile knowingly, a little surprised.

Not bad.

Then the control room curtains slide open. Two men, dark shadows, sit under lights illuminating them from above and behind. It's hard to see their faces.

"Good evening, gentlemen. My name is Harrison Creach." One of the shadows delivers a crisp salute while leaning over the intercom's clicking, crackly mic. He speaks slowly, with professorial pur-

---

[26] The guy probably got a C on the paper. But he would've bought our album.

pose—his voice is dry, a bit raspy, hoarse and lower register, an older black voice with, I hope, secrets and wisdom. We all sit up straight, instinctively.

"It is a pleasure to welcome you to Checkers Records, where we are recording a new musical future ... right here on the South Side of Chicago." He turns from the mic and says something to the other shadow. He starts to cough and then flips off the intercom, holding up his hand in a pardon-me gesture. "Excuse me, boys." Coughs again. Recovering, "I do hope to get to know you all better. Perhaps ..." he pauses for dramatic effect, "Pepperland will tune in, turn on, and be the bearers of glad musical tidings." Mr. Creach chuckles.

We are all looking up to the control room window, its lights shining down on us as if the sun is streaming through a rose cathedral window. Our upturned faces are a painting from one of the Old Masters, maybe Rembrandt—woody darkness surrounding pale faces bathed in rapturous light from above. It's only the Checkers control room, but we know that we are being offered a shot—just a shot—at entrance to an exclusive club. My heart is thumping like a big bass drum. We await Mr. Creach's word.

"Gentlemen, that selection we just heard ... what is it called?"

"That was 'Burgers in Benton,' sir," I say.

"Young sir, I wonder if you'd use that mic right there in the center, the better to hear you with, my dear."

I comply and speak clearly into the fat microphone suspended in an elaborate cradle hanging from a big chrome boom. "Sir, that was 'Burgers in Benton.' An original."

"Certainly was, as you say, *original* ... no doubt about that." Mr. Creach's voice on the intercom was sharp and magnified, piercing the studio. He clicks off. Then clicks back in. "And where is this Benton place ... *where the burgers are so fine*?"

I say, "Downstate sir, middle of nowhere. George Harrison's sister lived there. George visited there in '63."[27]

"Is that a fact. Well, how about that?" He mumbles something to the other shadow in the control room. Then he says, "Excuse me boys, but I'm coming down there."

---

[27] True fact.

Everybody stands up, at attention. Dave adjusts his shades, folds his arms calmly over his bass. Hawgrim squirts a breath freshener in his mouth while Ricky stands parade dress behind his drums. I feel like we are about to meet our Ed Sullivan, keeper of the keys to a change-the-world kingdom, the doorman holding a big door wide open, allowing access. Mr. Creach—*Starmaker*.

The lights go back on and the big padded studio door opens and Mr. Creach strides in, confidently, a General MacArthur on our little band's beach. Mr. Creach, sharply attired in dark slacks with a crisp crease, a well-pressed white shirt with an open, button-down collar, no tie, and wiry reading glasses perched on top of his head, selects the chair closest to me and sits down. His black shoes are well-shined, elegant, socks pulled up tight.

"Please, everyone, have a seat." Mr. Creach regards me with a smiling raised eyebrow. Whistles. "God*damn*, I like bowties," he says, eyeing the big red one under my chin. He has a close-cropped goatee that looks jazz-catty to me, a graying, understated Afro sprinkled with salt. He looks around the room, gets up, introduces himself to each of us, shaking our hands. He turns to me, says, "You know, I can't remember the last time I saw a rock 'n roller ... with a bowtie. And that cartoon guitar—how the hell you make it sound like that?"

Before I can attempt to describe the modifications made to Felix, he says, "No, don't tell me. I don't need to know."

Mr. Creach turns his attention to Hawgrim. "But this goddamn accordion ... you boys might be the whitest band I've ever seen."

We shift a bit in our chairs.

"Frankly, you boys are a little unusual, but I'm used to that, hell, I spent the other night with a bunch of jive kangaroos. But I tell you what, that tape of yours, while certainly loud, muddy and screwy—man, where'd that kazoo come from?—I think it has a certain ... odd-ball melodic appeal." He looks up to the control room. We hear distant laughter from behind the glass. "Makes me want to have a burger in ... Benson or wherever the hell it is." He strokes his chin and looks suspiciously at Dave, eyeing the Kazoosh hanging around his neck like a strange medieval implement of torture.[28] "Perhaps we'll talk

---

[28] Dave invented the Kazoosh, ™ an ingenious adaptation of the old-style harmonica holder—

later about that thing around your neck, son. In the meantime, I'm sure you've got it under control."

Mr. Creach sits there, thinking, still rubbing his chin. He says, "And one other thing, your harmonies are rather tasty, that's fairly evident … even on that shitty tape.[29] You two are brothers, so that makes sense." He turns to Dave and me, leaning back on the hind legs of the chair. "Something about brothers singing together, kind of seamless, eh?" We nod like "well, shucks." Then he looks at Hawgrim. "You're in there, too, aren't you son?" Hawgrim instinctively pulls out his business card. He hands it to Mr. Creach. I hold my breath.

Mr. Creach pulls his glasses down from the top of his head. "Insurance sales *and* law student?"

"That's *prospective* law student, sir. I'm waiting to hear from a few schools."

"God*damn*." He whistles admiringly. "But this band is your real job, is it not?" he says, his voice low and conspiratorial. Hawgrim is about to begin his thirty-second insurance pitch but stops as I glare at him.

Mr. Creach stands up, smiling, and says, "All right, enough of this bullshitin' around. You boys ready to play us a tune? I'm just going to sit over here at the piano and make myself comfortable. Any time you're ready."

The unidentified dark shape in the control room becomes a bit clearer as I step up to the main mic. The shadowy and likely male person leans back in his chair with his hands together, forming a bejeweled church and steeple at his nose, rings on every finger, slowly swaying from side to side—his large, round glasses glinting in the light each time he swivels to the right.

---

a rickety loop of wire around the neck holding the little instrument. The Kazoosh™ holds a kazoo firmly in place at the musician's mouth along with a harmonica—thus enabling Dave to play either kazoo or harmonica and his bass at the same time. Further, Dave's innovation allowed him to add a third device—usually one of those birthday party paper blowouts and horn that would be played rhythmically. The paper blowout sometimes had a big PEPPERLAND sign on it for further band identification—other times it simply said, "*BANG!*" or "APPLAUSE." The Kazoosh™ produces both a memorable sonic and visual effect.

[29] "Burgers in Benton" is a non-stop vocal duet, me lead, Dave harmony on top, then Hawgrim a fifth above on the chorus. It's not bad.

Dave and Hawgrim arrange themselves at their microphones, play a few habitual tuning riffs on their instruments, resettling their shoulder straps. Dave resets the Kazoosh around his neck, adjusts his shades and then Grouchos his eyebrows at me. Ricky kicks his bass drum a few times and whips off a quick, tight roll on his snare. He twirls his sticks, salutes and smiles. I take a deep breath and count off.

We proceed to play the best "Ants Are Cool" in recent memory—Dave and I sing like two cool cats outside a newly stocked fish store on a moonlit night. And Hawgrim pumps his big black Baldoni squeeze-box like an LSD-crazed Myron Floren and, despite the fact that Dave blows the end off his paper blowout in the big finish—the *BANG!* disintegrating in a blast of cheap pink and yellow paper debris—he holds it all together and his kazoo solo rocks and despite Ricky—a jumping jeep in four-wheel drive on a bad road—breaking two drum-sticks and knocking over his big ride cymbal in a garage band frenzy at the end of the second chorus, the song shudders to a halt, everybody stopping at the same time on the same or similar notes.

The room is dead quiet with only the electric hum and buzz of hot guitar amps and magnetic pickups. Mr. Creach's jaw hangs open. Dave pooches his lips out, scrunching his face and pumping the air with both fists knocking the Kazoosh out of whack, "Thank you, Chicago!"

A new voice crackles over the studio intercom.

"Hell *was* that shit?"

Mr. Creach, still seated at the piano, announces, "Introducing one of the *Good Guys*—Mr. E. Rodney Jones, Program Director of WVON Radio, 1390 on your AM dial."

A few seconds later, the studio door bangs open and a portly little black man in a white suit and a wide purple tie sweeps into the room, a big cigar in his hand. He has a thick bushy beard and a fat, though receding, Afro—he and Mr. Creach are about the same age—old, fif-ties. He strides into the center of the studio puffing on his cigar and observes each of us carefully.

"What the fuck is that song called?" Mr. Jones's voice is sharp and fast and he sounds a little higher pitched than he does on the radio—he speaks in a very practiced, natural cadence sprung from years of internal time signatures disk-jockey jiving over song intros with split-second timing.

I begin to babble about how the song was originally called "Ants Are Cool," reviewing a long ago summer afternoon in the backyard, observing an anthill by the driveway, but Dave stops me.

"What my brother is trying to say, sir, is that, over time, this song has evolved from a goofy song about ants ..."

"... into a cry of longing for love, symbolic of our society's repression of the individual and our innately human need to create, despite the overwhelming ..." Hawgrim the bullshitting student is rolling.

Dave looks at me and shrugs. We let him go.

"... entropic nature of modern American life. Today, 'Aunts Are Cool'—that's a-u-n-t-s, is a ..."

"... jive-ass song about aunts and, I tell you what boys, I think I hear a hit!" Jones makes his pronouncement.

A stunned silence.

Then Mr. Jones yells, "Hold it! I need to think." He begins to pace slowly around the studio, one hand up calling for silence, deep in thought.

The only sound in the studio is the hiss of my amp and the occasional commentary from Dave's stomach, the remnants of a Big Mac. Dave whispers, "Pardon me." Hawgrim calmly picks up his cigarette from the ashtray and relights it even though it is still smoking. He blows a perfect smoke ring that drifts slowly to the tobacco-stained ceiling. Ricky pulls a small black notebook and pen out of his dinner jacket pocket and scribbles something in it. He winks at me.

Mr. Creach plays a tune on the piano—it is something soft, slow, and candlelit, distantly familiar.

I can't stand it any longer and decide to chance it and break the silence. I clear my throat and say, "Excuse me, Mr. Jones, but did you say you think you hear a, er, did you say a *hit*?"

"Call me Jones." He raised his hand again, signaling for quiet—Mr. Creach stops playing, closes the keyboard cover and leans back on the old piano, his face expressionless. Jones circles the room chomping on his cigar that appears to be unlit.

Hawgrim says, "Pardon me, sir ... Jones ... please allow me to re-light that cigar." He walks confidently over to Jones who has stopped pacing, facing the back corner of the room, flicks his Bic. Jones is in some sort of trance, rocking back and forth on his thick white vinyl platform heels, hands folded behind his back, cold cigar between his teeth.

Jones turns, snaps out of it, surprised to see Hawgrim and his mighty Baldoni offering a light—but he accepts. Hawgrim bows slightly, grins, and returns to his assigned place, slinking backward, a humble servant departing the king. Jones takes a big puff of the revived cigar, stares at Hawgrim. He points the cigar at him, says, "You know, very interesting what you said about that song and the entropic nature of American life, young sir, but fuck a duck—that tune doesn't have a lick of entropy[30] in it." Everybody looks admiringly at Hawgrim, who shrugs it off. Jones goes on, "But I tell you what, it's so nice, I gots to hear it twice!"[31]

So we run through the song again and then again. Finally, Mr. Creach goes up to the control room to play everything back—they'd been rolling tape the whole time.

When Creach leaves the room, Jones says, "Do you know who that man is, boys? Do you have any idea? *Sheeit.* 'Course you don't. That sombitch Creach is *Cool Papa Spo-dee-o-dee,* a living legend and yet a sadly forgotten founder of the Chicago musical scene! Used to play bass and piano for some of the best rhythm and blues bands in this city. And before that, well, sheeit—he was playing music in this town long before you little shits were little shits. You pay attention to what that man says and he will take you far."

Up in the control room, Mr. Creach flips on all of the control room lights. Everyone, including Jones, gazes on high, reverently awaiting guidance from the altar.

Mr. Creach comes on the intercom.

---

[30] Review: High school physics with Dr. Thompson and his lesson: *The Day I Discovered Entropy.* In physics, "as entropy increases, the universe and all closed systems in the universe, tend naturally to deteriorate and lose their distinctiveness." Applied socially, entropy has to do with the tendency of things to revert, over time, to chance, chaos. So, *low entropy* is a state of order, with little differentiation, like a lukewarm bathtub, like bland people in gray. *High entropy* is chaotic, diverse, differentiated. Or is it the other way around? Anyway, I wrote a paper about it for that class. Thompson liked it. I hadn't thought about it when I wrote the song.

[31] A Jones WVON catchphrase.

"Let's have a listen to that last take."

Dave and I look at each other grinning, jumping out of our skins—this is so *great*!

The rest of that ecstatic night is spent going through "Aunts Are Cool" countless times, Cool Papa Creach making suggestions, tightening things up, making cuts and additions—things I had never thought of—changes in tempo, melody modifications, adding to the chorus, filling out the bridge, lyric changes. I am more than willing to go along. He is almost ready to cut the kazoo solo, but Jones stands up for Dave, saying it's at the heart of the song, a key part of its charm. But it's Cool Papa ("just call me Creach") who says, "Maybe we should change the title to 'Your Aunt is Cool.' I think that has a better sexy ring to it. Don't you think?"

Which launches Jones on a riff about the importance of the title and its ability to hook the DJ, give him—or her—the ability to riff and jive, play with the intro. We all nod enthusiastically, yeah sure, whatever you say! So we give the intro a nice twenty-two second instrumental space before Dave and I come in with the vocals. Over the last take, Jones demonstrates a scat-style radio jock intro—*dee-da-pan-de-bop-a-bop-be-bop and it's thirty degrees below zero in sunny Chicagoland*—that nestles in those twenty-two seconds perfectly, ending precisely at the moment our vocals pop from the speakers to launch the tune.

Dave and I shake our heads in wonder.

"Your Aunt is Cool" is in the can.

By one in the morning, we have reworked, reviewed, and recorded "Burgers in Benton." Our stylish dinner jackets are long gone, thrown in a heap over guitar cases and chairs. My hair is sweaty, stringy, and in my eyes, and Dave, Hawgrim, and I are clustered around the main mic, headphones on, three hardworking rockers ready to johnpaulgeorge the "Burgers" chorus one more time—*where the burgers are so fine*—when Creach comes over the intercom saying, "I think we've got it boys, that's it. Good work. We're done for the night."

Then I think—what have we just done? What has actually happened? We have magnetized two of our best songs and they are now stored on somebody else's inch-wide 3M premium tape on some machine up in that hot little control room. I'm a little uneasy, a little pit of paranoia striking my stomach, a burning churning flame. Checkers Records will send us home, *thanks but no thanks*, two months will go by and then one day I will be coaxing Otto down a potholed Chicago street, nearly out of gas and just a buck in my pocket, gritty snow-pile remnants of winter still hanging on in the tire-black dirty gutters and I'll have the radio on WXRT-FM, and a velvety-voiced female jock—the one I always listen to—will admiringly and wondrously announce a new band, an amazing new band straight out of the corn-fed Midwestern heartland right here in Chicago with a completely new sound, a sound so original and fresh, honest as good old American dirt and here they are—*the-who-knows-whats*—and a raucous chiming tune will come on and it will be our song, *my* song played by a bunch of studio imposters that sort of sound like us even right down to the kazoo and accordion, but no Felix, and it just won't be right, it would not be right, it would be slick and sanitized and I would be stunned and shocked and Otto and I would run blindly right through a couple of stop signs, roar right across Halsted, horns honking, people shaking their fists and I would be wide-eyed and oblivious, pounding on the steering wheel—*they stole my song! they stole my song!*—and then I would plow into a boxcar-sized pothole and Otto and I would come to a screeching halt right there in a broken asphalt canyon in the middle of the street with Otto's dented Volkswagen hubcap rolling away lazily, swirling in circles until coming to a halt in the gutter in front of a failed fish store.

Creach interrupts my paranoid reverie. He asks if we would be available to join him at a place he knows to discuss *business arrangements*. Now.

I say yessir.

 Track 10: Later that night

SOON, WE FIND OURSELVES IN A BIG, black leathery booth at the downtown Playboy Club, served by a gorgeous, black-haired Bunny named Kitty, supplying endless Tequila Sunrises while perfectly executing the Bunny Dip. We are terribly impressed and I think—*Sooz would be appalled by all this.*

Kitty purrs, "Don't you gentlemen look nice in your dinner jackets!"

But what could be better for young rock stars? We have found part of *it*—hanging out in the Playboy Club with a record exec and a famous DJ, and we are talking about a *deal*.

Steaks and lobsters are delivered. Platters sizzle. Kitty winks.

Jones says, "Eat up, boys, you worked hard tonight."

And *they* are buying.

Cool jiving jazz, played by a trio of tuxedoed, distinguished-looking black men, rustles quietly around the dim cavern of the Club—it's Oscar Peterson and his trio. Gorgeous runs of piano choral chords, laid carefully over a big woody bass line that is sometimes plucked, sometimes bowed, marked with muffled drums and subtle sparkling cymbals, mixed with the clinking of heavy silverware, glass, and china.

Dinner and chitchat end.

Creach sips his ginger ale, puts it down, then slides the tall glass and its very nice souvenir-quality Bunny coaster aside. He folds his hands on the table in front of him and smiles reassuringly at me. "All right, Pepper."

But the jumpy jazz stops and, after polite applause, Oscar Peterson announces that some tenor sax player I'd never heard of will be sitting in with them and *wouldn't-we-please-welcome-I-don't-catch-his-name*. Enthusiastic applause ripples across the room. Both Jones and Creach look surprised. They smile—they know this guy and they turn to the bandstand. A man the size of a linebacker steps onto the little stage in the corner of the room. He's dressed in a green plaid sport coat, turtleneck, and porkpie hat and has a pencil thin mustache. The rose, chrome, and azure of the stage's small spotlights glint off the big man's brassy horn as he launches into a solo vamp, the group laying out as he touches high clear notes, trilling and bleeting then diving to obscene low honks flapping and farting, falling and flowing, speaking the bebop jive language of saxophones. Then the quartet breaks into a new tune—up-tempo, jittering and stuttering, chords on the piano clanking in some dissonant free jazz thing, like four voices traveling in different directions in a key I'd never heard of. The quartet skitters and rolls—the drummer drops muffled thumping bombs, punching his pearly black bass drum on strange off beats, snapping his tight snare. The man holds his horn in tight, curving and caving his body like a question mark.

Creach leans across the table to Jones and says in a lowdown, admiring growl, "Lockjaw!"[32]

We listen and groove. The tune ends.

Then Creach pulls out a pen and, taking a paper cocktail napkin, begins to scribble on it, drawing boxes, lines, and arrows—a music biz flowchart. Turning to me, Creach says, you see, boys, we're going to sign you up because we'd hate to be wrong and because we think you've got a hit here, a hit that we could break right here in town, it's a good tune, it's a charming tune, it's a happy tune in these unhappy times and old Jones here will play your record on his radio program on his radio station and he will guarantee us air time and he will interview you boys live on WVON Chicago drive time home of the good guys and then we will send you out on the road and *goddamn!*

And I am saying yeah, saying yeah. Dave is saying yeah, yeah, yeah. And Hawgrim dunks a fat chunk of lobster tail into his little boat of melted butter and Ricky slices into his Porterhouse and winks.

Creach points to his napkin diagram that explains how the money goes 'round and around—it goes in there and comes out here—think of Checkers Records as your bank, boys. We'll take half and you'll take half and they'll take half and you'll maintain complete creative control, Pepper Porter, you too Dave, you too Hawgrim, you too Ricky, and we'll publish your tunes—let's do it now because time's a-wastin.' Are you ready, Pepper?

And I start to think about that nightmare of the radio station with the imposter band playing the imposter tune and me and Otto skidding across Halsted, horns honking, fists waving, crashing into the derelict fish store one hubcap short.

Lockjaw swings into a new tune—blowing a ballad, liquid lines flowing in a trance from his horn, low, sad, and sweet.

Creach smiles.

I look and feel brain-dead, addled and over-Sunrised—eyes glaz-

---

[32] Eddie "Lockjaw" Davis, tenor saxophonist from New York, born in 1922. Creach, on bass, played a few Chicago dates with him in the '50s, the London House.

ing over with all this big talk. And then my shoulders begin to turn into massively high brick walls looming high over my head sprouting cartoon eyes and ears, staring down on me, both walls becoming vast watchtowers with voices, booming low voices thick, deep, slurred and undecipherable like a record slowed to 16 RPM in a paranoiac swamp.

And then Dave says, "Pepper!" looking at me with a clear-eyed glare.

I say, "Pardon me, uh ... Mr. Creach, Mr. Jones, but would you excuse us? My band and I need to talk."

"Of course."

Everybody stands up and we climb awkwardly out of the booth.

We make our way through the Club looking for the men's room. Hawgrim says he thinks it's that way, Dave says no no, it's this way, over there. Then we lose Ricky. So we wander around in the darkness, searching, swimming upstream through gentle warm currents and eddies of spectacular Bunnies of the night all drifting by slowly, smiling, balancing trays of drinks and sizzling blood-rare steaks—blondes and brunettes in green satin, pink satin, white satin, and even one or two rare and ravishing redheads in black satin—it seems that we have explored all possible reaches of the Club before finally finding the men's room—a manly hutch with more dark wood, mirrors, and marble, smelling of aftershave and talcum, presided over by an older gentleman in a tuxedo.

Ricky is already there.

Ricky leans against the sink chatting with the attendant like they're old buddies. He greets us, "Hey."

Dave, Hawgrim, and I line up at the urinals like ducks in a row. The attendant resumes talking to Ricky.

"So is there a problem, Boo Boo?" Hawgrim addresses the wall, chomping on a Jones-supplied cigar that is stuck in the side of his mouth like a tough guy movie gangster. He turns to the sinks and begins a fastidious hand washing routine. Dave is silent. All conversation comes to a halt.

Ricky hands me a towel.

Hawgrim says, "Well?"

Before I can answer, Dave erupts, "Right! WHAT THE FUCK'S

THE MATTER WITH YOU? Goddamnit man, like you've been telling me—this is *IT*! And here these guys are handing *IT* to us on a Playboy Club platter, which is very nice thank you very much and here's Pepper," —he's rolling, mewling, and simpering—"Oooh, mister record company man, I'm Pepper Porter and I'm just not sure I want your contract because oooh I dunno maybe I'd be selling out to *the man* or my Felix the Cat guitar might not approve or WHO THE FUCK KNOWS what you're thinking and oooh nooo, I'm too much of a wussy DUMBSHIT and oooh nooo it might not be the right thing, ooooh I just don't know ..."

Silence. The sound of the ladies' room toilet flushing filters through the walls and Dave is breathing heavily. I sigh.

The attendant calmly cleans his glasses.

Then Hugh Hefner walks in with a pipe clenched in his teeth and a nice purple paisley formal jacket, his bowtie undone.

We all stand at attention. He says, "How're you boys doing? Having a good time?" He looks around the room a bit doubtfully. "Everything okay?" We nod eagerly. "I tell ya, if there's anything I can do for you, let me know." He attends to the matter at hand but speaks to us, facing the wall. "Man, that Oscar Peterson is a *real gone cat*. Don't you think? I'm always here when he plays the Club."

Hawgrim says, "You're absolutely right, sir, he is some *gone cat*! Yes, we're having a great time, aren't we boys?" Everybody agrees. There is an awkward silence broken only by the sounds of mechanical and human plumbing.

Hef turns to the sinks, smiling through his pipe and re-tucking his slacks.

"That's just outta sight. Uh, excuse me." He quickly washes his hands and splashes a bit of the complementary men's cologne[33] on either side of his neck, elaborately relights his pipe, puffs up a feathery cloud of sweet, dark tobacco. The attendant hands him a towel.

"Thank you, Mr. Roosevelt. Well ..." He dries his hands vigorously and has a better look at us. "Do I know you boys, I mean are you, uh ... right, didn't we meet at the Mansion last month?"

We smile helpfully.

---

[33] Brut by Faberge.

"Oh, I remember, you boys are Hawkwind, right? Yes indeed, a fine … what do you say? … *progressive* band." We allow Hef to reach his conclusion. "That was some night, wasn't it?" He pauses and considers whatever happened that night with a satisfied and wistful smile.

We can only imagine.

Then he takes another puff and says, "Well, we'll have you all over to the Mansion again next time you're in town, eh?"

Everybody—"Okay!"

"It'll be *some* night. Now you boys just take care of business, all right? Mr. Roosevelt here will make sure you're taken care of." He murmurs something to Mr. Roosevelt and vanishes.

"Hawkwind!" Dave whistles reverently. "Man, Hef's really misinformed. I mean, they're so weird!"

"That … was a brush with greatness, men," Hawgrim breathes reverently.

"And he thinks we're rock stars … whoa." Dave leans back against the wall next to the hand dryer, spent.

But then our attention turns to Mr. Roosevelt, who says, "Don't worry boys, your secret, whatever it may be, is safe with me."

We relax and take a collective deep breath.

Mr. Roosevelt continues. "But I will say this." He stands in front of the mirror and straightens his dapper red velvet bowtie. In a driedout, near whisper, he says, "You know, I am authorized to offer each of you complementary Club Keys, free passes." Turning to me he says pointedly, "But goddamn, I don't think I will until you boys get the hell back out there … and do what needs to be done … unless your big ass record company execs have flown the coop. Now scram!"

Another toilet flushes next door in the ladies' room.

It all becomes clear—our meeting in the Playboy Club men's room is a *sign*, as was Dave's tirade and our seemingly chance meeting with Hugh Hefner that was most certainly preordained, and I am indeed being a whiny, wishy-washy wuss and that I need to get the hell back out there to Creach and Jones and sign up for our rock 'n roll destiny—this is *it*.

I fish my last five out of my butt-curved wallet and press it into Mr. Roosevelt's hand, thanking him profusely. He gives me the free passes.

I give Dave a big hug with a theatrical *ha!*—and everybody follows me back out into the dark of the Club, scrambling like four lost stooges arguing about the location of our table—this way, no that way, admiring many a satin-clad Bunny, and then, spotting Kitty with a tray of drinks, we follow her bouncing white cottontail back to the booth.

Jones is alone. Kitty dips and serves him another Manhattan. I stop in my tracks.

"Where'd Mr. Creach go? Did he leave?" A cold shiver freezes my heart.

Oscar Peterson's piano still sparks in the dark and Jones uses his Bunny stirrer as a drumstick.

"No, no. He just went over to talk to Lockjaw. I think they're at the bar."

The boys climb back into the booth, Dave and Hawgrim giving me a don't-fuck-it-up eye as they slide past me. Ricky winks. I turn and see Creach walking toward us, relaxed and confident, cigar in hand.

"Well, well, well. The band has returned." Creach puts his hand on my shoulder and leads me over to the bar, saying *Pepper come with me,* and he sits me down, tells me that if he were me, he'd be nervous, too. And then, as Oscar Peterson launches into an ocean of swirling chords and runs up and down the piano's keys with a rumbling drone of bowed double bass underneath—Creach pauses and tells me, "That's 'Green Dolphin Street,' son, you know that tune?" I don't know that tune. So he buys me another drink, we sit and listen. At critical moments he points out what Oscar Peterson is actually doing in a solo or how the bass and drums did something they shouldn't have, but *that* is what makes the tune what it is—a bit of unexpected *art*. And all the time, I am nodding, saying yeah, listening, but also trying to practice what I am going to say when "Green Dolphin Street" ends.

And Creach grooves.

When the tune does end and the applause dies down, he looks me in the eye and, hesitating, says, "We all have to be a little insane, a little nuts to do this, trying to make a living selling records, these plastic platters full of tunes and maybe it is a bit of a vicious game but goddamn it is a mighty fine vicious game because we get to play music and do exactly what we love. We may fuck up but we get to play music. And isn't that something? I tell you, isn't that something?"

Yes sir, it is.

So it all begins. Three weeks later our first single is released (mostly in Chicago, Detroit, and St. Louis) on Checkers Records: "Your Aunt is Cool" b/w "Burgers in Benton." We are interviewed by E. Rodney Jones on his morning drive-time show on WVON—it's a soul station, but so what—Creach sez *it's exposure.* And there is a small bit on us as "a local band to watch" in the *Reader,* a Chicago hipster rag, featuring a new publicity photo of us in our unexpectedly cool dinner jacket/ hip t-shirt getups, including Dave with bass and kazoo and me with bowtie and Felix the Cat guitar. The shot has an appropriate *rock 'n roll flash look* but we are just *accessible* enough for a *broader marketing appeal.* Sez Creach.

And we are about to take off on that little downstate tour opening for Pavlov's Dog.

Side 2: Volunteers

 *Track 1: Thursday morning*

THE DAY BEFORE WE LEAVE, out of nowhere, I get a letter—a *letter*—from Sooz, postmarked Chicago, no return address:

> *Dear Pepper,*
> *It's time.*
> *I need your help.*

Last I'd heard anything specific, spring of '72, she was on the run, a fugitive from the law, wanted by the FBI. I find out about it standing in the main library in Ann Arbor, flipping through the *Chicago Tribune*—a stone cold spike shoots right down my throat. I'm shattered. The front-page article says there'd been a bank robbery in upstate New York and somebody got hurt. The paper says that the bank heist was a Weather Underground operation—the radical group committed to the violent overthrow of the US government, ending the war in Vietnam, changing the world, changing everything. And there she is, one of five alleged young perpetrators. I stare at the defiant mug shot, dug up from an earlier antiwar protest arrest. I fold the paper, put it back on the rack.[34] I go back to my room and cry.

I stand by the apartment front door with the little pile of mail fallen from the slot reading her letter, my bare feet freezing on the cold wooden floor. It's a shivering, sleety morning after a hot, sweaty rehearsal.

This time, the letter is signed—*Grace Slick*.

I'm stunned. In my hand I am holding a message direct from the underground, not some weirdly reassuring postcard, but a let-

---

[34] Her mug shot is proud, haughty, sexy. She is above it all—it's like they've arrested Greta Garbo.

ter from somewhere close but somewhere far—direct word from the Revolution, whatever that means. My own personal Patty Hearst has reached out, poked me with a cold blue steel Uzi. I don't know what to feel about this new reality—elation? Exhilaration? Suspicion? Fear? Love?

All of the above.

The letter says she's been in Chicago for "a while now," that she's feeling a bit safer, more secure these days. It's like we're in a Hollywood B movie—maybe the heat's off and she can now peek through the dusty window blinds in her on-the-lam crummy hideout and try to be sort of normal—to contact me. *Me*. She wants to get together. Like that song, or maybe not. And she says that she's made some big mistakes and she really did say that one of those mistakes was abandoning me[35] after that great Annawanna summer. I read that and a little shiver runs through me.

Makes me smile.

She gives a phone number—it's a phone booth somewhere in the city that she uses. She says she will be at the booth this Thursday at 3:00 p.m.—she hopes I can call. *Call. Please call.*

Today. *Today* is Thursday.

Sooz signed the letter in a schoolgirlish hand, small and timid like she is hiding in the back row of a scary math class, don't call on me, please don't call on me—which is not like her at all. No class was scary to her. Sooz's real signature is confident, sometimes with little cartoon explosions popping out of the twin O's in her name. Before she went underground, anything from Sooz was an extravaganza—fizzing with personality, an old-time circus poster with crazy doodles. This isn't normal. But then, being underground isn't normal.

I drink some coffee. I watch TV. I get Felix out and work on some tunes.

I should tell Dave. I shouldn't tell Dave.

I decide to tell Dave.

I quietly nudge Dave's door open, a few fingers of incense tickle my nose. The room is cave dark, his earth-tone sheets hung over the window. I fling them aside, providing a close-up view of the next

---

[35] Honest, she did.

building's brick wall. His bed has the usual mound of clothes—clean, just unfolded—rising like a volcano in the middle of an ocean—jeans, sweatshirts, socks, underwear, maybe part of a blanket—I can't see him, but I can hear him snore—he's in there somewhere.

"Dave." I give the mattress a little bounce. Perhaps he's meditating in a new prone pranayama position.

"…"

"Dave. Wake up."

The pile of laundry moves, rustling at both ends.

"Dave. You up? I got a letter from Sooz, you know—*her*." I bounce the bed again.

"…"

Then the mound of fabric flips open where his feet should be and Dave's disembodied head appears next to me—a hairy bowling ball with bloodshot eyes. I yelp.

Dave's head stares at me thoughtfully. "Good morning, oh my brother."

Then the head says, "Sooz? Another weird postcard from that Susie whatsherface—the technically brilliant bank robber radical on the lam, wanted by the FBI—who, oh yes I believe it's true, is also brother Pepper's true summer camp love? *That* Sooz?" Dave yawns.

"Yes. Her. No. A *letter*."

"That chick's nuts." He leans up on his elbow and rubs his hand through his wild bed-hair. He coughs. "No, I'm sorry. That's unfair. I must not be judgmental … maybe *you're* nuts." Then, in a blur of naked skinny legs, hands, and feet, he scrambles to the other end of his bed, assumes the lotus position and says meditatively, "Chick needs enlightenment."

"Dave. Get some clothes on."

He shrugs.

I tell him about the letter. He abandons the lotus and pulls some clothes out of the heap, spreading them around him to get warm.

"Jesus. You can't meet *her!* I mean, what the fuck?—she's *wanted!*"

"Oh, man. I have to call her—don't you think? What would that hurt?"

"She's a fuckin' fugitive for chrissakes!"

"She needs me, she needs a friend."

"Who're you, fuckin' James Taylor?" He closes his eyes and leans his head back into the corner.

We sit in silence for a minute or two. I'm waiting him out.

Then, like flipping to a completely different radio station, Dave wipes both his hands over his face, keeps them there and through his fingers says, "Pep."

"What?"

"It really happened, didn't it?"

"What happened?"

"C'mon man, you did *see him* right? Him! The guy! The Felix stranger guy! That snowball fight the other night. I'm not crazy, and he fuckin' nailed you, man, with a snowball!"

"He did."

Dave lowers his hands from his face and looks up at the ceiling. "He really did look like Elliot, you think?—but shit—fuck a duck." He exhales loudly, blowing his cheeks out, struggling. "This is ridiculous." His face is lined with the indentations and creases of the laundry he had laid his face on all night—his eyes are wide-open, trying to hold it all back. "And that guy was left-handed. Just like Elliot."

The guy *was* left-handed. I nod, but the analytical side of me says, "C'mon, it couldn't be, I mean really …"

"Could be our cosmic inner eye, man, the one we *really* see with."

"I want to believe it."

More silence.

Dave wipes the corner of his eye and points to the ceiling. "That crack up there's getting worse."

I go and get Felix.

"Here, look at this."

Dave takes Felix in his hands with respect, one hand on the neck, the other on Felix's body. I point to a little rip in the wood—it's less than an inch long at the base of the headstock—a worn gash of naked wood uncovered by the ancient chipped black paint, evidence of damage done, a hidden fragility that I always had to be aware of.

"See that? Elliot did that. He was so little, kindergarten! He was fooling around and somehow that happened. I don't know how he did it, but he did it."

Dave sits up straight on the bed and holds Felix gently.

I say, "But here's the thing, he came to me and told me he did it. He told me! He said 'I'm sorry Pepper, I didn't mean to.' Jesus! Little Elliot. And like a big jerk, I yelled at him."

"We all have our crimes," Dave says slowly. He flips Felix over, thwangs a big flamenco-style E chord, letting it ring, and then, lifting Felix to his ear like a rock 'n roll conch shell, listens to the silver strings vibrate with their strange echoes coming from somewhere deep inside the guitar's dark body, floating and airy then decaying slowly. Nods admiringly. "Felix sounds amazing."

"Felix is the ear that I hear Elliot with."

We smile.

"And that chick? Just do the right thing."

Good old Dave.

 Track 2: Thursday afternoon

A T A FEW MINUTES TO THREE, armed with a bunch of dimes, I duck out of Gramophone and zip across the slushy street to the pay phone in the Parthenon Diner. Some salesman-type in a wrinkled raincoat and plaid hat is using the phone so I do an I-need-the-phone pantomime. He ignores me. I sit down at the counter. An abandoned *Sun-Times* is there, its headline says, "*Watergate Indictments Expected.*" I riffle through the paper, relieved to find no pictures of Sooz—mostly just Haldeman, Erlichman, Nixon, and Cubs spring training shots. And why would there be a picture of her in there? I'm just being paranoid. The guy hangs up, leaves with his vinyl valise, looking depressed—he must not've gotten the order.

I grab the phone and dial.

A female voice picks up on the second ring.

"Mmyellow." The voice sounds like a receptionist at a dentist's office. This is no crazy rainbow kite flying in the wind. Maybe I have the wrong number.

"Uh, I'm looking for ... *Grace ... Slick ...*"

"This is she. May I ask who's calling?" There it is—calm, confident, still tinged with summer camp—it's her.

"Uh … this is … *Marty Balin*."[36]

"So nice to hear from you … Mr. Balin. Perhaps we could meet later today. Are you available?"

I am available.

"Do you know the Chicago Public Library, the big one downtown on State Street?" Her voice has a bit of gravel in it, a bit lower than I remembered it. But it's Sooz, no question—the way her voice rises delicately at the end of a question, polite and firm, insistent. She tells me she'll be at the library for a while around five that afternoon in a study carrel on the science and technology floor. She looks forward to seeing me. Before I can say anything, she hangs up.

Things at Gramophone are slow, so Lazlo agrees to let me off at four. I hop on a southbound 151 bus on Clark and head to the Loop. Traffic's light—it's almost rush hour and folks are beginning to head home, outbound—I'm traveling upstream. So I sit alone toward the back of the bus, my head leaning against the sleety rain-spotted window, bouncing, staring out at the passing storefronts, lights beginning to come on in the late afternoon—I'm beginning to see my own reflection in the window's glass, wavy and out of focus, raindrops blowing to the rear, splattered all over my mirrored face. After twenty minutes or so, the bus stops at a light in front of the big, modern, rusted-on-purpose bronze of the IBM building—I know this place. I see myself, deep in thought wearing a dark overcoat with a leather briefcase, hurrying, twirling through the revolving door, spinning and then spitting out inside the big corporate glass and marble lobby into an elevator, up up and away.

What am I doing?

The bus moves on, wheezing slowly over the Chicago River, crossing into the Loop, big tires whining loudly over the drawbridge—in a fleeting moment of panic, I think maybe I should bang through the emergency exit window and jump out into the dirty dark water below the grated see-through surface of the old bridge—I'd hang on to an ice floe and float downstream to the Mississippi, then build me a raft and disappear in the Delta thickets of the old muddy river escaping from myself, Elliot, and all those years ago.

---

[36] The *other* lead singer of Jefferson Airplane.

We cross the river and I don't jump.

It's around four-thirty when I push through the old brass and wooden doors into the hushed quiet of the big central library. I'm early. The science floor turns out to be one of the sub-basements, far below State Street, sunken amid the ancient coal tunnels of subterranean Chicago—the cramped elevator is a groaning hydraulic lift that descends slowly and unsteadily, finally opening its doors with a rattley gasp at the bottom of the shaft. The room smells of old paper and damp heat, the ceiling is low and laced with dusty white-painted pipes traveling in all directions, faint gurgling sounds among the endless rows of green metal shelves packed with book spines of aged dark red, scholastic blue, and serious brown. A long line of softly buzzing fluorescent tubes marches over me to the far reaches of the wavy wooden floor, disappearing like a funhouse of barber's mirrors. I step on to the deserted main aisle, my boot heels unavoidably clomping on the hard floor. The end caps of the shelving network are carefully labeled with its alphabetical range of subjects—*atomism* to *azeotropic*, *Bernoulli* to *Bohr*, *dynamo* to *entropy*.[37]

I am amazed that there's an actual *entropy* aisle—how thermodynamic is that?

I stop in front of that cosmic aisle and feel the heat of the room flow over me. At the end of the narrow line of bookshelves, up against the wall, right where all knowledge and lore of *entropy* would be, somebody in a dark coat with a white knit hat over a thatch of short blonde hair is bent over a small, built-in desk. I begin to walk quietly toward entropy, my steps echoing awkwardly. When I get to within fifteen or twenty Dewey decimal points of this person at the study carrel, I stop, pull a book off the shelf and pretend to regard it with keen interest. The dark figure, a woman, looks up. I don't think it's Sooz—this person seems older than me, maybe a little craggy, hard to tell. I have scared the hell out of her because she quickly grabs her books, throws them in a bag, disappears around the other end of the aisle, elegant black coat flying behind her like a cape. She flees down the hall and I hear the elevator ding. I am alone again.

But the woman has left a small book open on the little desk, a Bell

---

[37] Dewey Decimal System: Science; heat (entropy) 536.

System Technical Journal from 1928—*Transmission of Information.*
I leave it there and explore the rest of the floor, finding no one. So I
go back to the entropy desk and sit down with this abandoned document. It's open to a page discussing the absence of information, the
cost of information, chaos and uncertainty—it's like a message from
Doc Thompson run through a mechanical confusability machine—it's
dense and archaic. I try to understand, but I'm too distracted.

Was that woman Sooz?

At five o'clock, I hear the ding of the elevator door, I put the book
down and listen. I hear nothing—no steps, no rustle of a coat. A few
moments later, the elevator dings again and I hear the door close. The
elevator whirs up and away.

I go back to the technical journal and read until a voice on the
intercom announces closing time.

Sooz does not show up.

I check out with *The Transmission of Information.*

So I leave on the 151 bus—again crossing the bridge over the half-
frozen dirty water of the dark river.

 Track 3: Thursday evening

THE 151 RUNS NORTH on Michigan Avenue between the spot-
lit bone glow of the Wrigley Building on the left and the stone
gargoyles of the old Tribune Tower on the right, both guarding the
southern entrance to the Magnificent Mile, the *Boul Mich*—massive
gates opening to Chicago's swanky street of the consumer, domain of
capitalist tools, and mindless minions of the Man.[38] It's dark and the
earlier sleety drizzle has turned to light snow, glazing the sidewalks
full of people in dark winter coats rushing out of office buildings,
heading home, retreating to hotels and bars, hailing cabs, waiting at
cold stoplights and windy bus stops. Traffic is bad.

The bus is packed, people standing, hanging onto the gray plastic
straps in the aisle—sad-faced women, secretaries and clerks toughing
out the lousy economy, probably worrying about their jobs—some of

---

[38] That's Sooz talking.

the men are Sooz's top-coated and pin-striped, gray-faced train daddies marooned on the bus heading north along the lake to the glamorous Gold Coast, Lincoln Park and the cliffs of condos on Sheridan Road. I give up my ripped vinyl seat to a well-dressed older lady, tailored and permed, probably a legal secretary from a white-shoe firm, who looks at me with a mix of disgust and fear when she sees my hair falling out from under the oversized newsboy hat I borrowed from Dave. When I stand up and see myself in the mirror of the wet windows I can see her point—it's a *look*, a rock 'n roll look, dark, a bit menacing, a little mysterious, hair out of control, the look of an outsider,[39] but with a closer look in that weird looking-glass, I can see the glint of sorrow in my eye as the bus bounces in a big pothole and I grab a swaying strap—*she* stood me up, *she* didn't show, and who knows? Maybe this was it, I'd never see her again.

Maybe that's good. Maybe not.

Or the cops would run her down—Sooz would be holed up in a dingy cold-water flat over a fish store in a crumbling neighborhood on the southwest side, *come'n get me, coppers*, her face plastered all over the papers and she'd be on TV escorted from the paddy wagon to Cook County jail by some big gut Chicago cop with a shit-eating grin on his face like he'd just bashed a kid at Balbo and Michigan at the '68 convention, and there'd be stories in *Rolling Stone* written by Hunter Thompson or Mike Royko in the *Sun-Times*, and she'd be defended by William Kunstler who'd make impassioned statements to the press about the innocence of this poor lower-upper-middle class girl and besides these deeds were, in fact, necessary, required, that she is, in fact, a patriot of the highest order and that we all should be like Sooz, be like Sooz, we all should have done what she had allegedly done, all in the name of peace and love and then some radical priest would come to get her released, speaking outside the courtroom under the klieg lights while Allen Ginsberg would mantra and meditate, calming the crowd while demonstrators marched, singing songs and a-carrying signs—hooray for Sooz!—and I would sit glued to the TV in my little cold apartment, *News at Ten*, looking for some sign that she remembered *me*, that I am still part of her life

---

[39] Rainy, mirror-y windows always made me look better than reality.

even though her life, it seems, is a complete disaster area, a million miles distant from the sparkly waters of Lake Michigan and sandy love in the dunes. She is my Chicago One.[40]

I'll never find another one like her.[41]

The bus inches up Michigan Ave and then grinds to a halt, stoplights endlessly cycling in front of us while we sit gridlocked, missing the green, then waiting through multiple reds, horns honking, clouds of winter exhaust spewing and people crossing the street against the light, weaving through the frozen traffic. Another 151 is right behind us, waiting, and the big bus windshield wipers slap the time away, a steady mechanical beat ticking in my head—*click click smear*—*click click smear*. I am hanging on to that personal plastic strap with both hands, my head leaning morosely on my wrist, staring at the city snowflakes blowing down the boulevard, Jefferson Airplane tunes running through my head—the ones with Grace Slick singing lead, a repeating random bunch of clips—*one pill makes you larger but we can be together while his leather chair waits at the bank and the white knight is talking backwards*.[42] I don't care that I am going to be late for rehearsal—sometimes there ain't nothin' you can do.

I am standing next to the driver with a clear view of the street ahead and the sidewalk. First in line at the Michigan and Pearson stoplight and stopped cold right in front of the old Water Tower. The bus steams and stamps.

People hurry in front of my landlocked bus trying to get across the street, the eastbound yellow light getting stale, about to grant us a northbound green—at last there is a clear shot ahead of us, open black pavement for a block or so. Then, a sleek, green Jaguar XKE makes a desperate dash eastbound across Michigan—the bus lurches, then stops—I swing on my strap, stutter stepping elbow to elbow with everybody else—the Jag is trying to beat the light but a few pedestrians

---

[40] Not to be confused with the famed *Chicago Seven*—Abbie Hoffman, Jerry Rubin, Tom Hayden, et al—veterans of the Democratic National Convention of 1968 who were charged with inciting the people to riot. They were acquitted in 1970.

[41] But I had gotten over her. (Yeah, right.) Who knows what she's done or how many guys she's had since then? Until her letter showed up, I hadn't thought of her in at least twenty-four hours. On the other hand, maybe Dave's right. What am I doing? She's not a part of my life, hasn't been forever. Only that one summer. Get a grip, for crying out loud. And yet.

[42] From "White Rabbit," 1967, "We Can Be Together," 1969, "Lather," 1968.

are already crossing as the yellow goes to green. The white *walk* sign is lit and the crush of the crowd surrounds the snazzy car. Horns honk—the Jag is stuck. But then I see some tall guy take command—he's trying to clear a path—Moses parting the endless stream of people to let the car through and straighten things out—like Western Man—from chaos, create order.

The bus begins to move ahead and I duck down to look out the snow-speckled side windows to have a look at this citizen traffic cop—a beanstalky guy in a long black coat. He's waving his broad-brimmed black hat, directing cars and people—his scarecrow straight blond hair hanging like straw on his shoulders and as we pass, in slow motion, our eyes meet through the commotion and wind-whipped snow—both of us wild-eyed, staring and knowing—it's the snowball guy, the Dark Stranger.

He turns and runs.

He runs up Michigan as the bus gains speed, rocking and rumbling—I duck down so I can see him through the windshield—he's just ahead of us, outrunning the bus, dodging shoppers in front of the gray marble of Marshall Fields, skidding on the slick sidewalk, crossing Chestnut Street, jumping over a huge black slush puddle, speeding past the diagonals of the immense crossed black girders of the John Hancock building. The bus makes a stop for passengers, people get on pushing me farther back in the bus and I lose him—he disappears in the dark, though I suspect he's turned the corner up at Oak Street but it might just be street reflections of mute mannequins in the sparkly plate glass of Bonwit Teller.

The bus rolls again.

Then I see him—yes, he did turn the corner at Oak and as the bus comes to a halt at the Oak Street light, I see him dash into the Playboy Club. I make a snap decision—*what the hell, he's out there, or something*. I squeeze to the front door of the bus, bumping past people, briefcases and handbags—*sorry, excuse me, terribly sorry, yes ma'am, sorry*—jump out onto the sidewalk, almost losing Dave's hat in the stiff blast of wind off the lake.

I stand at the corner of Oak and Michigan, look east up that genteel street, a quiet avenue lined with bare trees underneath a stone bluff of old residences overlooking the raging automotive rapids of

Lake Shore Drive, the black lake beyond. Behind me, back down Michigan, a sea of bobbing heads and hats, people walking fast trying to be somewhere else. My bus roars away, coughing fumes. Then the other 151 pulls up at the stop, some folks getting on, some getting off. I turn and head for the Playboy Club, despondent, hoping I still have that complementary club pass in my wallet from that crazy Creach and Lockjaw night.

I do.

Hands stuffed in my pockets, looking straight up through the wind-whipped snow, the beacon at the top of the old wedding cake of a building—a hooded, endlessly seeking searchlight that shines only to the north and east out over the big lake—turns a few cycles through the flying snow. In my pocket, I rediscover the little technical journal, *The Transmission of Information*, its corners starting to make a small hole bigger.

I hurry into the Club.

I hand over the pass and am provided with a complementary sport coat, allowing me to comply with the dress code—it's a nice understated plaid that is only a bit too small.

The place is jammed with business types, side-burned and trousers flared—maybe conventioneers in from Peoria or Des Moines whooping it up in good old Chi-town. Some of them have dates. The girls sit with them tippling drinks, laughing at their jokes.

Bunnies float by greeting me politely.

I wander around, but see no strange long-haired guy. A piano plays jazzy standards and a jumpy thing that turns out to be a Stevie Wonder song—the music bounces around in the tobacco-dark haze amid the glittery golden tubes of light that hang like stalactites from the wooden and stone ceiling. The place is smoky dim.

I have a seat at the bar.

A Bunny in blue named Dina—with a blonde Jane Fonda in *Klute* shag do—appears in front of me and, in a voice that is an octave too low for normal girls, she asks how she can serve me. Fortunately, I have enough cash for a Tequila Sunrise, which she produces quickly, looking me straight in the eye as all Bunnies are trained to do. She glides away with a knowing smile, probably wondering what the hell I'm doing here.

A few swigs of the Sunrise clears my mind.

I open the little technical journal and place it on the bar and start reading, embarrassed that here I am, sitting at the bar in the Chicago Playboy Club, surrounded by wine, women, and song and I'm attempting to read something as dusty and weird as *The Transmission of Information*. But the book feels like some sort of connection to Sooz—maybe that was her in the library poring over it at the end of the aisle of entropy or maybe I'm just nuts.

But why did she run out?

I hold the book above my head, fanning the pages, hoping a note or something might fall out. Nothing.

I fan it again. A small slip of white paper floats to the bar, almost lands in my drink. I snag it. The hairs on my arms stand on end, as if it's a hieroglyphic message from the beyond. It's a penciled jagged lightning bolt, or maybe an electrical charge sign like the Commonwealth Edison logo, but filled in with rainbow colors—crisp, fine-lined, and perfectly drawn, all the colors within the lines, angled diagonally across the little note. There's no signature or anything else—just this rainbow slash. Maybe it's the Sooz equivalent of a yellow smiley face.

Dina places a small dish of mixed nuts in front of me.

"We don't get many rock stars in here," she says sweetly as she begins mixing a Harvey Wallbanger for somebody. "Have a nut."

The Sunrise is loosening me up. I stick the note in my jacket's inside pocket and try to concentrate on Dina, but am still under the lightning bolt's spell.

She asks, "Are you somebody?"

I cough, straighten my undersized plaid jacket, unused to such a question. "I am indeed a rock star. Haven't you heard my record?"

"I'm sure that I have." She delivers the Wallbanger to some guy down the bar, returns and begins pulling a draft Schlitz. "What's it called?"

"'Your Aunt is Cool.'"

"Excuse me?"

I say it again and she smirks. "Is that aunts with a 'u' or just ants? No, no, wait a minute. I think I heard that the other night on the radio ..."

I sing a few bars.

"Right, right!" She cracks up and hums along, spilling a little Schlitz on the floor. "That ... is a funny song—and you're cute."

It occurs to me that this is the very first time anybody—let alone a Playboy Bunny—has told me she likes my music and thinks I'm cute. I'm speechless.

I have another deep gargle of my drink. Dina disappears.

Then I think—a *funny* song? Appalling. All wrong. It's like it being on *AM radio*. I am misunderstood.

I pull the rainbow slash out of my pocket, stare at it.

Dina returns.

"Excuse me, but what exactly do you mean, *funny* song? Evidently, I have failed ... to *communicate effectively* with you." I drum my fingers on *The Transmission*, drain my drink.

"Oh ..." she waves me off. "Not at all. So what's your name, Mister Rock Star?"

Another first. Nobody has ever asked me that question in that particular context before. "Pepper ... Pepper Porter."

She repeats it a few times dreamily, like a late night FM disk jockey. With *her* voice, *Pepper Porter* sounds very nice. "You *are* cute, Pepper Porter." Then she puts both hands on the bar in front of me and asks if I want another drink.

"Thank you very much. And you're cute, too. Yes. I would like another Sunrise, if you would be so kind."

Soon, she slides a fresh one in front of me and I drink deeply.

I wave my hand professorially and turn to the second page of my book and say, "Okay, listen to this." Dina stands in front of me, prim and attentive as a Bunny could be. I clear my throat. "*In any given communication the sender* ... that would be me ... *mentally selects a particular symbol* ... that would be a chord, a note on my guitar ... *and by some bodily motion, as his vocal mechanism, causes the attention of the receiver* ... that would be you, Dina ... *to be directed to that particular symbol* ... uh, blah blah blah, uh ..." I'm losing her. "Oh hell. I have failed. My song has failed."[43] I slump my head on the bar.

---

[43] *Transmission of Information*, by R.V.L. Hartley. From *The Bell System Technical Journal*, July 1928, liberally abridged, adapted, and garbled.

"For Lord's sake, what are you talking about?" Dina looks at me and gives me a punch on my shoulder. "Pepper. Buck up! You have not failed. I like your little song."

My *little* song?

I moan, regretting all the scientific gibberish. "Oh, man. Please forgive me. It's the tequila talking." I close the book.

"Believe me dear, you're a peach compared to the rest of this crowd."

Behind me, a purple Bunny with a tray full of sizzling New York Strips and fat baked potatoes glides by—a distinctly comforting and strangely reassuring scent. Dina nods at her.

She excuses herself and vanishes.

I place the rainbow slash on the bar in front of me. I am reminded of my trusty IBM flowchart template, a handy translucent green plastic tool, a means of designing and flowcharting systems and applications by hand—an oval for this, a parallelogram for that, lines, arrows, and boxes. It occurs to me that this rainbow slash is an IBM symbol for a *communication link*.

The piano player announces that he is taking a break and somebody flips on the Club's sound system—it's Oscar Peterson's "Green Dolphin Street," Creach's favorite tune, the one we heard just a few weeks before at the big record label/band meeting.

Dina returns.

I ask her if she's seen this tall guy come in with a long dark coat, big hat and stringy blonde hair. She leans close to me, and looking side to side like she's afraid of being overheard, whispers, "No."

Then I begin to tell her about being stood up by this amazing chick from my past, oh, this girl's an engineering genius and you wouldn't believe …

Dina stops me and says, "I think you need to visit the men's room, freshen up a bit."

I sigh, ask for very specific directions—I tell her I might need a trail of breadcrumbs to get back.

"Tell the attendant that Dina sent you."

"Thank you."

I open the door of the men's room, walk in a little unsteadily. I'm fine, completely coherent. Except for Mr. Roosevelt, who smiles knowingly, looking over the top of his spectacles, the men's room is empty.

"Dina sent me."

"Well, well, well. The return of the rock star." He's folding a small stack of white hand towels. "Son, what's it been? Couple of weeks? I sure hope that you've got things figured out a little better than the last time you were here." With a small courtly bow and a crisp gesture to the line-up of urinals, he said, "Please. Be my guest."

He ignores me while I do what I came to do. I approach the sinks and take in the full-blown Playboy Club mirror view of me and my shortish, green plaid blazer. I'm storky, a little uncertain. I turn on the hot water, lean up close and look me in the eye—I'm a whistling and hooting conventioneer in from the sticks, away from the old ball and chain—or I'm an entry-level member of the IBM batch processing, remote job entry, HASP operations systems software utility team—or I'm a washed up mid-level manager with a mortgage hanging over my head still grimly hoping for a shot at my own Shangri-La—or I'm a sappy rock 'n roll kid with a useless bit of graphic design in my pocket.

Mr. Roosevelt hands me a fluffy white towel, then a comb, then a bottle of *Aqua-Velva*—to freshen up. He offers a green bottle of *Brut*. I decline—that's the scent of my father.

He sits back on his tall stool, regards me carefully.

I feel it appropriate to stand at attention.

Hef does not walk in.

"You get the record deal?"

"I did, sir. I mean, we did. We've got a song out, it's on the radio, only WVON so far."

"Excellent."

"Had a little thing in the *Reader*. We're hoping for some play on WLS next."

"It would appear that you are doing all the right things."

"Thank you, sir."

Two guys walk in and he greets them warmly. Urinals flush and faucets flow. He straightens his black bowtie and courteously hands them towels, inquires of their evening's progress. They give him a few damp, crumpled bills. They walk out and he sighs.

"I see guys like that all the time. They're not *looking*, they're not watching, just out for themselves, climbing the corporate ladder; they don't *see*, don't you see." It's a statement, not a question. "You need *eyes* … you got *eyes*?"

"I hope I do, sir."

He resumes folding the towels, straightening things up.

I relax a bit and am now leaning on the counter, feeling that I have somehow gained Mr. Roosevelt's acceptance.

"Isn't that Oscar Peterson *something*?"

"Sir?"

"Oscar Peterson, on the piano, his trio, you were here that night, with Hef, Lockjaw, all those cats."

"I was. 'Green Dolphin Street.' I'm in the know, now." He raises a bushy eyebrow, and like a muted horn whispering a staccato riff, I say, "I am a hep cat."

"Indeed you are … indeed you are, yeah," extending the word, a bowed bass note smooth and low. "I believe that big stuff is going to happen to you."

Then, like everything is settled, he brightens and says, "Come with me, young sir. I need to escort you to your table."

"Thanks, but I'm at the bar. My drink … Dina."

"Never mind about that. Your drink and Miss Dina will be fine. You come with me."

I follow him through a sea of cottontails, blue and brown three-piece suits to a remote nook, hidden away in the mahogany and brass—a small table for two with a fresh Tequila Sunrise in a bulbous glass with an orange slice impaled on a plastic Bunny stir stick, a dish of nuts, and a small, wavering candle in a warm pool of overhead light.

"Your table, sir."

"There must be some mistake, I'm just a kid and I really don't belong here and I'm only here on a free pass …"

Mr. Roosevelt will hear none of it, shaking his head saying, "All you gotta do is the right thing young sir, just do the right thing." And then he excuses himself and disappears in the darkness.

I sit there awhile, sipping my drink, sucking on the orange slice. Why am I here?

A sparkly purple Bunny enters this hidden hutch in the warren, gracefully approaches my table, her tray expertly balanced—her hair is short and blonde in a conservative sort of cut—curls and ringlets hanging seductively around her face.

"My name is Grace."

I feel my veins transform and restring themselves with warm wires that pulse through my body, the blood flowing, sparking and pumping. My heart is a big bass drum and each beat is a pulse of exhilarating electrifying sound washing over me with five hundred watts, a million volts, arrowing out of monster speakers aimed right between my eyes taking me somewhere else, taking me deep inside my soul, which is where the real power of music and rock 'n roll lives and breathes. Sometimes it's not a sound that does this, but a thought, sight, or a person. This is one of those times.

Sooz.

A deep and royal curtsy, a radical and completely unauthorized variation of the Bunny Dip—her free arm spread long and graceful like the white wing of a Lake Michigan gull on a bright and windy summer day, or the tail of a crazy kite over the dunes wild and free.

She tells me she had indeed left me that book at the library but didn't stay—sort of freaked out—and she followed me up Michigan Avenue on the 151 behind mine to make sure I had no tail and she saw me get off the bus and she knew, just knew that I would come, and I sputter, "How, how did you do that, how did you know, I didn't see you"—and she smiles and whispers, "Tradecraft dear, tradecraft." Then I place the rainbow slash on the table, smooth it out and look up at her, she puts her hand on mine and looks through me with her deeply mascara'd Bunny eyes and says that she trusts me, asks if I trust her and I say yes, and I want to hold her again and take her away to some safe place and she says this is a safe place, that she is safe here and she says, "Do not worry, Pepper, don't worry. Technology will set us free."

 Track 4: Later that night

"HERE. DRINK THIS. YOU NEED IT."

Grace/Sooz pours me a big cup of black Bunny coffee, tells me that I've had too many of those Sunrises—she's been watching me. I plop three bunny-shaped cubes of sugar in the brew, stir vigorously, grinning like a madman because she is *here*—right here within perfume wafting distance, glorious and sparkly in her purple Bunny suit, wrapped up like a cellophane Easter bunny basket cut up to here and down to there, for big boys only. She tells me to pull myself together—we have things to talk about.

I say, "Talk to me."

"Know that this is *not* the real me, the real woman. This goes against everything I stand for, but it's necessary. I know you understand, Pepper."

"Of course I understand."

"Nothing's like it used to be."

"I know."

"I wonder if you do. Drink your coffee."

I drink.

"So much has happened to me, there's so much I need to tell you, so much I need to do."

Her face is focused and intense but thinner, her cheekbones sharper than I remember. Maybe it's the Bunny makeup, the Bunny rouge at work. She leans back gracefully to peer out of our little rabbit hutch—her slim wrist arched, encircled with little black and white starched fake cuffs with long fingers splayed on her hip in perfect array. Her movements, slow and deliberate, beautifully choreographed in Hefner's busty ballet.

"I need to go check my tables. But I'll bring you something to eat. Don't worry, it's free—they like me here."

The coffee's hot and scalding and it burns my tongue, I drink it anyway because she poured it (which is an intimate act for which I am grateful), but I suspect she's right—maybe I don't understand. Like where does Bunny Grace end, where does Sooz start? Or the other way around? And the FBI?

Yikes. No, really.

I sit at my little dark table in the little dark room like a long-haired Sam Spade looking for clues.

I swizzle cream into my coffee. The whorls of white cream blend with the black brew and both are changed—like Sooz and Grace evaporating, disappearing into the bland sameness of the cosmos.[44]

---

[44] Once you pour cream in your coffee, that's it—you can't un-pour it—it's changed forever. Time's arrow flows one way.

She brings me what she says is a defective Bananas Foster.

"See, the bananas are starting to brown a little and somebody screwed up that bit of whipped cream. Right there." She points. "It either goes to you or the garbage." The old Sooz gives me a lopsided grin, the gap between her two front teeth is wonderful.

"Looks good to me. Have some?"

"No. Look Pepper, we need to talk."

"Come back to my place tonight."

"Don't be ridiculous."

"I hide out there all the time. So does Dave."

"I'm sure that's true but, look … I get off in exactly two hours." Her professionally manicured hand is again draped artfully on her magnificent hip, atop one of those never-ending legs. She tells me to meet her at this diner at the corner of Rush and Bellevue, a few blocks away.

"I'll be there."

Then with a quick, yet clearly against-Club-policy Bunny kiss on my forehead and a slow alluring swoop of a long finger right through the crème covering the caramelized fried bananas of my Foster, she touches it to her lips like a magazine cover I can't quite place but know intimately, turns expertly on her spiky heels and vanishes in a glorious swish of cottontail.

After turning in my no-charge plaid sport coat and retrieving my own coat from the charming hatcheck Bunnies, I slip them a buck each and emerge from the smoky Club a new man, energized and ready for whatever the hell is next. I stand at the corner of Michigan and Oak sucking in a lungful of cold air that I blow out in a cloud. The snow has ended, the night wind is gone, leaving the sidewalks and trees of Chicago coated with an inch or so of slushy city snow. A few stars are now dimly visible above the city lights, and the apartment buildings that stretch north up the mostly deserted Lake Shore Drive stare blankly out over the black frozen lake. Only a few headlights and taillights shine on the wet pavement of the Drive.

I kill time sitting on a snowy bench in front of a high-priced toy store on Oak, hands stuffed in my pockets, feeling warm and in control. Blobs of wet snow hang on tree branches like ornaments, ready to fall in the slightest breeze. I could be one of those blobs. Or not. And she's the wind.

My head's clearing.

A cop patrols his beat on the other side of the street in his blue-black winter coat and ear-muffed hat. He regards me carefully. I sit up and try to look respectable, whistling and looking down the street like I'm waiting for a friend. He walks on. I decide to find the diner.

The Acropolis Diner is simple, lonesome, drenched in greenish fluorescent light like that Hopper painting. I'm just a guy waiting for a dame. I look around—there are only a few other people here, an older couple, a few old guys nursing cups of coffee and dabbing at pieces of pie arguing about Nixon, Watergate, and Patty Hearst. The waitress seems to be glad that I'm not talking to her. She calls me "Babe," keeps my cup full.

The all-night jock on WLS comes on the diner's radio, jives the time and temp, *Straight-up midnight on the Big 89, 34 slushy degrees on a beautiful snowy night in Chicagoland [cue jingle] double-u el ess, in Chi-ca-go! And when oh when is it ever going to be spring, and we're going to get boogular—yeah!—hey!—and here's our number one one one hot hit.*

It's straight-up midnight. She appears across the street.

Grace/Sooz waits a minute or so as the light cycles a couple times, crosses the black street, now wet with melted snow. She's wearing stylish boots and a blue woolen knee-length pea coat, a loosely knit long white scarf wrapped a few times around her neck, matched with the wool hat that covers her short curls like a globe. A large bag is slung on her shoulder. She walks in, and as the door closes behind her, quickly scans the joint, glides over to join me.

I start to get up.

She quietly suggests that we move to the booth in the corner away from the line of windows, near the restroom and an *Employees Only* swinging door. She selects the side of the booth that faces the street, slides in across the cracked vinyl.

She whips her hat off, shakes her hair free. Her off-duty makeup is toned down. She looks worn out.

"Pleased to meet you. Grace Kelliher is the name."[45]

---

[45] She tells me she came up with *Grace Kelliher*—"Grace" because of Grace Slick, of course, up against the wall and all that. And "Kelliher" because it's sort of like Grace Kelly, which makes no sense in a cultural context, but there you go. But how'd she come up with some sort of ID,

We shake hands.

It's been a few years. Things are a little awkward. To be expected.

She orders a salad, some yogurt, and a large glass of grapefruit juice, tells me that the Club is dead serious about Bunnies maintaining proper weight. She says she's in good shape but confesses that she's forced to wolf a steak or a cheeseburger every once in a while—it's unavoidable. I agree that she looks good and she smiles. In a voice that sounds years older than either of us, "Tell me how you're doing, Pepper. What's happening in your life?" Eyeing my hair, "You obviously aren't working for IBM."

So I tell her how, thanks to that password she hacked—the password of unlimited time—I got all kinds of programming practice, aced Michigan's computer science department, graduated *cum laude* but maybe screwed up, turning down offers from a bunch of the biggest computer companies in the world, IBM included, to have another shot at this rock 'n roll stuff. See if I might get lucky in the search for *it*—the real *it*.

She's not surprised.

"The endless search." Another smile. "Let me know if you find it."

I tell her about the band, Dave, Creach, our record, our little tour—*tomorrow*.

She's impressed.

"A tour."

"Can you believe it?"

"Where, how long?"

"Just a couple dates, downstate. One at SIU, so, not really a *tour*."

"Yeah. That's great." She pats my hand.

"Thanks for your postcards."

"Communication is so important."

The cook tosses something on the grill and it sizzles like a live wire. I lean against the side of the booth spinning my spoon slowly on the tabletop. She concentrates on her salad.

"The papers said you drove the getaway car."

Like she's been through this a hundred times in her head or with

---

Social Security number and all that? "Not too tough," she says, "I've got friends." And how'd she get the Bunny job? "Simple. I just walked in the door. It's great cover, don't you think?"

who knows who, she tells me how the bank job was a complete screw-up, an incompetent disaster, and yes, she was the driver and yes, the bank security guard was killed but it wasn't her and she hates guns, hates the feel of them, and she did not carry, and yes, that's contradictory with the idea of the Weatherman fomenting armed insurrection, and so what, she still hates them but goddamnit we needed the money, we needed funding in order to do our work which was supposed to be ultimately good work and then she says that sometimes you've got to do evil in order to accomplish a bigger good and she says it'd be best if I not know all of the details of the whole thing, no need to drag me into this any further than necessary.

Necessary?

Then she tilts her head to the door, points with her eyes. The beat cop I saw on the street walks into the place and gives a loud hello to the waitress. He glances at everybody in the place, takes his hat off and sits down at the corner of the counter on the other side of the diner facing us. He looks like one of my old scoutmasters—portly, with a few inches of gut hanging over his belt, losing his hair—he seems like the sort who would help you get your campfire started in the rain. The waitress slides a cup of coffee to him without being asked. He takes out his reading glasses, reaches for a newspaper somebody left a couple of seats away, settles in.

Sooz/Grace smiles, and with both hands, reaches for mine—it is wonderful. Her hands are a little cold and she rubs my knuckles, massages my clammy palms affectionately—like she is thawing out and things are going better but then it occurs to me that this handholding thing is merely a stage prop for the cop's benefit.

She leans across the table, whispers, "Don't worry. I'm probably already dead."

She pushes her plate aside, signals the waitress for a cup of coffee.

I ask, "What's it like? I mean, your life?"

"You get used to anything. But if I could turn back the hands of time, I'd tell me to not get in that car, to not let myself be convinced by them. I'd immediately run like hell, go directly to the nearest bus station and go home, or to Ann Arbor. Or camp." The waitress brings her a cup. She rearranges herself in the booth and daintily daubs at her eyes with the napkin. "I want my life back."

I take her hand. I have no clue how I'm supposed to handle this.

She says, "The reality is that my life has changed forever—I am now underground and will be—I don't know, forever? Or in jail. Or dead. Or both. Who knows?"

Silence. Radio static. Silverware clinks.

She straightens up and pulls herself together, blows her nose with a napkin. Then she says, "But I've got a plan."

I pull out the rainbow slash and flatten it on the table between us with *The Transmission of Information* placed to the side.

She stirs her coffee and looks right through me. "Like I said, technology will set us free, Pepper dear."

The cop at the counter hacks loudly and stands up—he's headed our way, hiking his pants. Without shifting her intense gaze from me, Sooz/Grace gracefully snatches the rainbow slash and stuffs it in the shoulder bag that was propped at her side. She holds my hand and we look like a moony young couple grabbing a late night bite.

The cop nods at us, pushes down the grimy little hall to the men's room. The radio warbles. My coffee is cold.

Sooz/Grace relaxes slightly. "Great little book isn't it? I'm so glad you had the brains to pick it up in the library. My bait."

She opens the tech journal, flips through it, stopping and scanning for her favorite parts, like it's a greatest hits album. "You know, this is important stuff."

"Yeah, horrendous stuff, too. You always were more of a hardware engineering type than me."

"Pepper." She reaches into the shoulder bag and pulls out a big manila envelope. "Look," a fat sheaf of papers bound in a cheap blue plastic cover slides onto the table. "I've been working on this for a long time. Years."

"On the run? How can you do that?"

"You can do anything anytime anyplace when you're a fanatic."

A toilet flushes loudly in the men's room. Grace/Sooz pauses, stuffs the document back in the envelope. The cop, surreptitiously checking his fly, emerges, walks by, straightening his belt, walking away.

She breathes again.

The document slides out again and she swivels it around so I can read the title: *A Means of Sharing a High Speed Communications Channel.*

She tells me that before she left school, she'd been working with a couple of graduate engineering students. They were working on wild and strange new technologies—*networking* technologies that connected not only computers, but actual people together, and "No, this isn't some sort of government project funded by Dow Chemical—Jesus Christ, no, this is something different. There are people out there working on wondrous new things—tools—that will enable the people to compute and communicate and, if we hurry, Pepper, if we act now, swiftly, we can help bring these tools to the people before the corporations and even the government knows what hit them. This is all about information flow, information flying around free and easy, information for the people. Real societal change. We can do this. And I need your help."

And I'm thinking about that crazy kite of the old psychedelic Sooz flying in the howling storm over the gray steel waves and how I'm struggling to hold on to her string, and here she is again tugging at me, pulling me in. She's flown back into my world through a window I didn't even know was open.

She gulps her coffee, black. She says, "It will be computing—of, by, and for the people. And this," she holds the document in both hands like a precious stone tablet, "is part of the revolution."

It's the old Sooz talking again.

She opens the paper and takes me through a couple of her detailed diagrams and flowcharts—my old flowchart slashes, little lightning bolts of transmission, connecting boxes everywhere—"You *get* this, right?" And I sort of did. It could be very cool.

She's telling me, "Pepper, are you with me? Pepper, can you hear me? It's an elegant algorithm and look—it's … it's part of your battle against the fierce and arrayed forces of entropy. Remember? Entropy? You told me that on the beach all those years ago. How could I forget?" Smiles, twirls one of the curls in her new blond hair. "And we're doing just what your old physics professor asked that we do—go out and make things happen—out with the old, in with the new."

Quietly, she says, "There is a professor of computer science and electrical engineering at the University of Illinois, head of the department. Quite important, quite connected with this sort of thing. I need you to get this to him."

"Me? Why can't you do it?"

"I can't just show up, walk into his office by myself. I need an intermediary, a colleague. And you're it." Pause. Eyes locked with mine. "I trust you."

"What's he going to do with this thing?"

"He'll circulate it in certain very brilliant circles, float it around, ask for comments and then you will get the feedback and we will work on this further ... and ultimately—get it built."

Whoa.

"There's not a moment to lose. When can you do this?"

I'm a little flustered. "We're leaving on our little tour tomorrow, first thing. I ... I dunno."

She slouches in the booth, carefully regarding the look on my face.

"You can either play your music and write your little songs—or you can help change the world. What's it gonna be, Boy?"

"How about both?"

A *yeah, right* look.

Then over my shoulder I hear the WLS jock jiving about some new band in town with some new song ... *the phone lines are open so call me and tell me what you think!* Then a jangling tune crackles over the tinny radio speaker and it's like I had just plugged myself in and blown a 50-amp fuse—electricity flooding every one of my screwy little circuits. I stand up wide-eyed and ecstatic.

And to everyone in the joint and to no one, I yell, "That's my song!"

Sooz is cool and quick as she grabs my arm, firmly pulls me back down into the booth and tells me to put a lid on it. The cop looks up from his paper, sits up straight and shifts on the stool like a hoot owl spying a luckless mouse. His hand drops to his side, twitching on his black nightstick. The old guys at the counter look over their shoulders and laugh. The waitress cranes her neck at us suspiciously, asks if everything is okay over here.

Sooz smiles dreamily at everyone saying it's *our song*. Not to worry. She nods politely.

And I groove, trying to listen, hearing everything, amazed. I look at Sooz.

"Wow, is this really *your* song?" She listens. "It's nice."

"Your Aunt is Cool" ends and an ad about carpeting comes on.

"Let me shake your hand." She shakes my hand firmly and with purpose, like I'm some business client or something. "Congratulations, kid. You're changing the world."

"What?"

"No, no, it's fabulous that your song's on the radio." Shakes her head. "I'm sorry—I shouldn't have said that. It's great. You've worked so hard." Sooz tries to get me to smile, backing off a bit. She takes hold of both my hands—now her hands are cold.

More diner sounds—some news about Patty Hearst, more Watergate stuff, hockey.

I say, "I forgot I had told you about all that entropy stuff back at camp."

"Good old Camp Annawanna. That was a wonderful summer. But sometimes I thought you were a little weird." Her mouth tilts in a crooked grin, she raises an eyebrow. "But, given how things have worked out, I suppose I was even crazier than you."

I don't say anything, but I think that she probably is right—she is crazy—but I'm not sure if I care. How crazy am I?—injecting a discussion of *entropy* into a dreamy night on the beach with a girl like her, turning down IBM. What was my problem?

I go on. I did it once before and I decide to do it again. "I think it, entropy I mean, really does have something to do with me … and with you."

She leans across the table with fire in her eyes. She whispers excitedly, "Of course it does! Of course it does! It has to do with all of us … it's the spinning down of things." She stops, searching for the concept. "It's stuff … going to hell, it's the growing sameness of life in America and … and it's the reduction … it's the reduction in … I don't know. Call it *magic*." Sooz is rolling. "And you know what, Pepper Porter, it just occurred to me that that is exactly what you've been doing all this time with this music of yours—and that band. And your life. You've been hunting for magic. And that is exactly what I'm trying to do with *this*."

She picks up her fat sheaf of paper and shakes it.

"This—it's just a small piece of a cosmically complicated puzzle, but if it ever gets built, the whole thing, I mean—all this crazy hardware and coding, the network, the computers—it'll all be like magic itself. You won't be able to tell the difference!"

Ghosts of the old computerland Oz-freedom thing glimmer in my brain.

She sputters a bit, then drives it home. "The difference between this and magic will be ... *indistinguishable!*" She slams her hand on the speckled Formica convincingly. I jump.

"So. Pepper." She has become an expert at leaning across the table and looking deeply into my eyes smiling that smile, again trying to close the deal, but this time, she's looking through me. "Will you?"

"Sooz. Or should I call you Grace?"

"You can call me Sooz," she whispers. Then she sits up straight and places her document on the table beside her carefully folded, now warmer, hands, waiting for whatever I've got to say.

"Well then. There's one song that I don't sing for anybody. It's unheard—unplayed—nobody knows it but me. It came to me on one of those beach nights way back all those years ago ..."

"... yes—"

"... right, it came to me after I saw you making such a difference for all those little girls ..."

"... just doing my job ..."

"... and—and after we made love for the first time, when we lay there on that sparkly windy beach, you in my arms, quiet and content, not a word needing to be spoken and our world, as far as we could see, was at peace."

Her body relaxes, her eyes are getting a little wet. She rests her head in one hand, smiling. She says, "I believe I know what's coming."

"Did I sing it to you back then?"

"I think you did, but go on—it's wonderful."

"It's much better now."

"I'm sure it is."

And I begin to softly sing for her that one song from my own great, lost, un-made album—"Dreaming's Done," ending the tune in a quiet threshold of a dream surrender. In my head I hear jangly guitars, swirly keyboards, and vocal harmonies that are airy, soaring, and spine tingling. She must hear the same thing, because when I finish, her hand disappears under the table and quickly finds my knee and her fingers slowly spider up my thigh that is rapidly becoming very warm and glowing like a night on one of our summer beaches. Her Revlon red lips curl upward, subtly puffed and ravishingly pouting, a not-so-faint hint of a Miss February and everything about her that has haunted my head all this time.[46] She tilts her head inquiringly and wipes a tear. Or maybe it's just my imagination.

Then she asks, "So will you help me?"

"Yes."

 Track 5: Middle of the night, Thursday

A
N HOUR LATER, we're walking up Wrightwood from the bus stop, arm in arm in the middle of the snowy street—pussy willow tufts of snow drift down from the black bare trees—it's a dreamy city snow globe, shaken gently by somebody's unseen hand.[47]

"What'll we do if your brother's awake?" Sooz wraps herself around me whispering in my ear about how much trouble we're gonna be in for being out so late, maybe we'll be grounded, "Do you think maybe, Pepper, huh? This is so *college.*"

I prefer not to think about Dave at this moment.

I turn the lock and, as quietly as possible, open the door, stopping just before its well-known squeak point—I listen, now holding her tight with my right arm as I lean inside. Silence.

Her tongue explores my ear, snaky, swampy wet and lizard hot. Then she Greta Garbos slowly deeply madly, "I am a *Bunny*—a Playboy Bunny—the *real thing*, Pepper darling, and I am here for *you.*"

She's toying with me. And she knows what she's doing. My own humble self has been on the rise since way back in the diner—the old

---

[46] I know this is sexist and wrong. But I couldn't help it. That's what I thought.

[47] It occurs to me, as we walk on the street, that this scene was not unlike that of the cover of Bob Dylan's second album—*The Freewheelin' Bob Dylan*—shot in New York City on a winter's day in 1963 when he was just a young folk punk from the Midwest on the make, with his willowy hipster girlfriend hanging on, just before he hit it big.

dream of her now physically present—the feel of her skin, the smell of her breath, and every move she makes sound a lush chord at the reptilian base of my brain.

The apartment is quiet, softly humming with only the distant buzz of the fridge down the hall in the kitchen, the hiss of the radiator in the front room. A whiff of cold pizza and the faint scent of baloney sandwiches meet my nose. The coast is as clear as it's going to get. She follows me, softly padding down the hall to my room.

In a silent way, hushed with the swish of sheets and the hiss of heat rising from an old radiator under tall windows with shades rolled high, ancient with chipped paint and city lights visible through cracked glass, we produce shadows that lay themselves across the bed like flimsy ghosts. Sooz feathers and arches her back above me, the gentle pale half moon of the smooth and fiery soul of youth slowly and softly rising and falling over mine. My hands follow the curves, rifts, and valleys of her body, slender and strong there, puffed and pillowy there. She is a stunning vision. Then she descends and her fingers encircle me firmly, pulling gently, pushing harder, her mouth seeking mine, her tongue hot in my throat. Her hand guides me and I slide inside her; she hovers over me like a warm cave that consumes and protects me, and I rise to the pearls and diamonds of her pendant breasts and pull her to me and then her hair frames her flawless face, swaying above mine in time with our unheard song—two diverging and soaring melodic lines slowly and inexorably coming together, eyes closed in a knowing ecstasy that washes over the both of us simultaneously in the effortless rhythm of radical love.

Still. Night sounds flow in and around my room, dark but dimly lit with the always-on dome of light that drapes the city.

Aftersmile.

Early morning delivery trucks rumble a few blocks away on Clark. A garbage truck turns a distant corner, metal cans clang in a dirty frozen alley. Winter rats run. She breathes softly, sleeps lightly. Her slender arm crosses my chest, her head rests on my shoulder, nearly submerged in the covers, and I'm staring out the window watching the shadows of a tree waver on the bricks of the building next door reflecting silvery pools of night light that have nested on my bed. We are braided together in the bed beneath a heavy weight of blankets, and I think about how she must run and never stop and how it was so good then and how it's been such a long time, such a long long time and now it's still before the dawn and what must she be dreaming?

She must be dreaming of that big fat technical treatise that she has placed on the dresser next to my hairbrush and beat-up wallet and used bus transfers and two guitar picks (the One and one that's broken) and nickels and dimes and the Brut aftershave that I got for Christmas but haven't used yet. Felix reclines patiently in the corner, listening.

She must be dreaming about how she and that plan of hers are going to change the world and how she's going to have to remain underground but somehow live in plain sight, and how she is going to somehow find the money to get somebody to build a device based on her crazy technology and it will astound everyone and that's where I come in, but I'm not sure exactly how.

She must be dreaming about staying one step ahead of her pursuers, whoever they are, and how that cop last night was just one more in a long line of jittery paranoid encounters.

And then I dream about how, in a few hours, Pepperland will be on the road heading south on the great concrete river. I dream about how we will get to play music and maybe things will be happening on stage, truly happening, and we—Dave, Hawgrim, Ricky, and I—will reach one of those rarely visited, rarely documented indescribable places on the map where the music all comes together, where that magic—the magic Sooz talked about—happens, where Dave's voice and my voice, his guitar and my guitar twine together in tight wavelengths aligning like oscilloscoping sine waves. Dave says it's a perfect satori of sound and it hardly ever happens.

Sooz shifts cozy in the covers. She pulls her leg up higher, knee bent across my waist, the flesh of her inner thigh rubbing achingly *right there, oh boy, oh boy,* and she reaches up and softly kisses my neck and with the dreamy fog of sleep still fluttering on her lips murmurs, "Sing that song for me one more time, Mister Rock Star."

The marvelousness of it all—she's *here,* right here, cottontail under cover.

So I pick up the tune where I had left off a few hours before, whisper singing, marveling about the unforeseen beneficial effect it seems to have on this girl. Sure enough, soon as I get into it, her head disappears between the sheets and underneath the snug blankets and slides slowly down to where her warm hands were already engaged, softly fingering and strumming the most ecstatic personal chords I'd ever felt.

What a song.

The radiator under the window clanks. A new supply of hot water surges up from the basement while my own heating system fires up again, it having been in a ready-to-go, no-way-to-turn-it-off position all night.

The mound of blankets that is my Bunny in the bed is a range of low wooly foothills rising to the gentle summit of her head. They ripple and pulse in a silky slow-motion dance. Underneath, her liquid lips are locked gliding and pulling me in and out of her mouth where her tongue rules the warm and wet coiling darkness with slender fingers deftly flicking and kneading—I me mine myself, dribblings of delight in blanket-muffled moanings.

Down the hall, Dave thumps into the bathroom and turns on the shower. I freeze, wide-eyed. I raise the covers—a gloriously curvy, creamy, and salacious sight greets my bloodshot eyes.

"Sooz! My brother's up!" But she is undeterred, continuing in her slow oral tango. She angles for the kill and I flinch—a gasp stuck in my throat. I remind myself to breathe.

"Mmmmph ..."

It always takes a couple minutes for the water in the shower to heat up and Dave usually goes to the kitchen to put on a pot of water for his weird tea. I hear him approach.

My door swings open—enter Frankenstein. Dave, fright-wigged and bleary eyed, mumbles, "So, you're alive, eh?"

The large hump in the middle of my bed is motionless. Dave regards it suspiciously.

He says, "Hell were you?"

Brightly, I say, "Oh, jeez, is it time to get up already?" I smile and yawn with a smooth nonchalance. "Yeah, I guess I needed a night of quiet contemplation, you know, getting my head together before we hit the road. You know, man?"

I feel a barely perceptible but unmistakable chomp of teeth. I grin at Dave.

He whispers, "She's here, isn't she," his eyes on the hump.

I shrug innocently.

"Yeah, well, fuckin' Hawgrim freaked when you didn't show."

"He'll live."

He surveys my room. I raise my Bunny-free left knee and assume a casually relaxed pose, arms behind my head. Dave arches an eyebrow.

"Okay man, get your ass in gear. We've got to pick up those clowns in an hour. And there's traffic and weather to worry about."

He bangs a hand on the door in an up-and-at-'em sort of way, says, "I know nothing," returns to the bathroom and his shower.

Under cover of Dave singing in the shower, Sooz scrams. She makes it clear that nobody needs to be aware of her existence and certainly not know what she looks like or where she is or anything.

I hesitate. "He's my brother."

"Yes, I know, but you just never know about these things. How do you think I've lasted all this time?" She punches me in the chest and gives me a look. "This is serious, buster."

I don't say anything, but she sees through me, says, "He knows, doesn't he."

"Only that I got your letter. Nothing else."

Sooz, looking like one of her programs didn't compile correctly, dresses quickly and asks that I find time—make time—I must read her paper and then call her at this number at three o'clock on Saturday. It is time to act.

"I will."

She pulls her boots on. "Where are you going to be?"

"Benld. Way downstate. Some motel. Then SIU Edwardsville."

"Right. You told me."

But at the front door, she lays one last big wet kiss on me. Then she pulls away and lights up with a thousand-watt smile. *We're going to change the world! Bye!* And with her unbuttoned peacoat flapping and white scarf flying down the stairs behind her, she takes off and vacates the premises.

I close the front door. From the big window, I watch her try to run down the slushy sidewalk in the gray morning light. Sooz waves as she twirls a pirouette around a little old lady walking a short-legged city dog. I wave back and once again wonder if I'll ever see her again. I have no idea—she might get picked up, run down by J. Edgar at any time, *come'n get me copper!* And now I'm in the thick of it.

I scan the apartment, looking for evidence of her visit, anything she might have forgotten, a hairbrush, a tube of lipstick, a stray strand of blonde hair, anything sure to tip off my brother. Looks clean.

Her Plan, still encased in its big manila envelope, sits on the top of my beat up purple-painted Salvation Army chest of drawers. I pull it out and see that she's included a mimeographed copy of the *Port Huron Statement*, ready for my personal and provocative reading.

She never gives up.

I hold the Plan in my hands and I drift back into Sooz Land. I flip through its flimsy pages. It's an inky link back to her. I raise the sheaf to my nose and breathe deeply. Mostly it's just dry and papery, but I'm sure that there is a faint whiff of her, an evaporating mix of her non-perfume, the real Sooz, her skin, hair, and even her breath—*her!*—mixing with the exotic lavender flowery tang of Bunny Grace.

I fan the pages again and this time a small sheet falls out. It's another rainbow slash with a phone number and her signature, the real one this time. I stash it in my wallet.

I resolve to keep the Plan near me at all times. And I will read it and become an authority. I won't let her down. I stuff it and *The Transmission of Information* into my duffel bag, throwing underwear and socks and my bowtie on top of it. The Plan is safe.

Side 3: Highway 55 revisited

Track 1: Friday morning

WE ARE DRIVING. Southbound.
  Dave looks over at me and says, "What's this?" Out of the knapsack stuffed between the two front seats, he pulls a rainbow slash. "It was on the floor in the hall this morning." He holds it up to the sunlight, admiring it.

Uh oh.

"Just a thing from the store. You know Lazlo and all that head shop stuff."

"Yeah?"

Hawgrim, who's been reading the *Wall Street Journal* and providing occasional admiring commentary about the life and career of Ronald Reagan, leans up from the rear and says, "Gimme that."[48]

He peers at it through his wire-rimmed glasses, turning it over, examining it closely.

"What, are you some fuckin' commie pinko fag, Boo Boo? This is clearly a variation on the symbol of that crazy Weatherman radical bunch of nuts."

"Get outta here."

"I didn't just fall off the turnip truck, man. You an SDS sympathizer or something? Or maybe you just think it's *pretty*. Hell'd you get it?"

---

[48] Hawgrim, despite his appearance, was former secretary/treasurer of the University of Illinois chapter of the Young Americans for Freedom (YAF). He battled clouds of suspicion amid hints and allegations of the existence of a beer and weed slush fund, as well as liquor store kickbacks in the heady days after the Nixon landslide victory in 1972. He was exonerated when, with the revelation of secret tape recordings of key conversations, it was proven that what he did was merely wrong, not illegal. He served out his term with prudent distinction. It should also be noted that Hawgrim lives at home with his mother in a very nice house in Hinsdale and drives a Porsche 914. No, really. It is also rumored that his rather formidable and influential mother (stay tuned for her) somehow arranged his avoidance of the draft despite a very low lottery number. I'm not offering editorial comment on all this. I'm just presenting information.

I snatch it away from him.

Hawgrim eyes me skeptically and returns to the *Journal*.

I need a diversion. I remember that I heard our song on WLS in the diner—our song had actually been played on big time radio!

I make the announcement—"I heard it with my own ears—WLS, around midnight!"

Dave hoots and hollers. Hawgrim says I must've been hallucinating and Ricky grins and says yep. Dave quickly tunes it to 890 on our AM dial yelling shut up shut up as an ad for Virginia Slims comes on, followed by Coke (*I'd like to teach the world to sing...*), then McDonald's (*you deserve a break today...*) and Morrie Stunkel Ford (*where you always save more money*)—everybody waiting until the end of each ad and then howling foul obscenities at the radio when another ad starts. Dave pounds the steering wheel and Hawgrim throws a McDonald's bag at the radio. A Tony Orlando song comes on and there is more vile language.

"You sure you heard it, Boo Boo?"

So we drive, Otto plowing along at 55 on 55, as fast as he can go, and we listen and listen until WLS starts to crackle and fade.

We never hear the song.

"You must've been stoned," Hawgrim snorts.

The boys fall asleep again and Dave twirls the dial in search of toonage, surfing the airwaves, picking up low-power rural stations that come and go with farm reports and country music. He finally turns it off and looks at me.

"Goddamn, I sure hope you know what you're getting into, whatever it is." Then beatifically, he murmurs, "Let those with eyes hear, those with ears see."

So maybe he's saying everything's gonna be alright—or maybe not. Then he puts his right hand out and touches my shoulder. He turns the radio back on. We drive farther.

 Track 2: Friday afternoon

WE FIND THE GIG PLACE in Benld, a winter brown farm town far from anywhere, which inexplicably seems to be able to attract small crowds to actual concerts with actual name bands. The promoter is said to be a wizard.

We're on for a sound check. The roof of the nearly empty high school gym is an arched roof with big curved wooden beams rising high over an old wooden floor. Little birds flit around like hopeless prisoners with nowhere to go. At our appointed time, we set up our equipment in front of Pavlov's Dog's monstrous gear and tune up. I stroke Felix's neck, touching the little Elliot dent like I always do, that pick in my pocket. We launch into "Freakout in Coal City."

"Freakout," a recent composition that deals with the socio-economic anticipation of our touring downstate Illinois coal country, has a revolutionary freak out middle part, a bridge, that hangs on an extended E chord. Usually we come upon the big E chord and everybody trades twelves,[49] soloing, then handing it to the next guy, each building on what went before. We consider it quite innovative. First, Dave thumps *arpeggios* on his big Fender Bass, then Hawgrim holds the Baldoni in a Leslie swirl of jazzy eighths and ninths, reviving ghostly figures of Doorsy organ solos in my mind—weird scenes inside a rock 'n roll gold mine. And then me on my own E chord, not the easy one down on the open bottom of Felix's neck, the one ringing all six strings flying free and loose—I'm on the E chord high on the neck holding three silver strings tight with one finger, the E itself snug in the middle between the fifth and third—and the song is happening. I mean it is really *happening*. Everything is coming together like pieces of an impossible puzzle that keeps drawing you back because you know you're almost there—all the pieces are right in front of you, so you know *it*'s in there somewhere. And when *it* happens, it's a spine-shuddering, freezing hot chill that somehow plugs you into a strange invisible power source that flows within you and without you simultaneously in all directions, through your ears, fingers, through your toes, through your mouth and eyes and straight up out of the top of your head and the hair on your arms and the back of your neck electrifies—a science fair Van de Graaf generator[50] that's invisible to

---

[49] Twelve bars or measures, each. 1-2-3-4 … that's a bar.

[50] You know, the silver-domed machine that makes your hair stand on end in a sci-fi frightwig when you put your hand on it. Amaze your friends.

everybody but you—if you're lucky your band mates can see it and feel it. If you're really lucky, *everybody* can see *it* and feel *it*.

My turn to blow on the twelves, I grip the worn wood of Felix's neck and set my feet wide apart, ready to accept the feeling. Felix is in tune, so well in tune, never before as in tune as he is at this moment and my fingers fly and know where to go—not too far and not too fast, arrowing directly to the right place on the little map of Felix's fretboard. And Dave notices. There are only a few people in the gym—some Pavlov's Dog guys, the wizard promoter—a slightly older guy in dark glasses with brown hair on his shoulders, a thick mustache, and a long black leather coat with platform shoes—and the fairly relaxed-looking sound guy in the back of the hall at the sound board who keeps giving us the "okay" signal. Dave turns and faces me, wide eyes egging me on.

But my eyes are on Felix as he does something unusual. I watch as sparking wires of current, clear and crystalline and powerful fling themselves from Felix's little black body straight to Dave's big sunburst bass, making a strange connection—wiring us together—and then a splash of rainbow colors flies between us and we forget about everybody else in the gym.

It happens.

I keep going on my E beyond my twelve bars, riffing percussively, moving higher on the neck, hitting notes that I don't usually go for but are now weirdly available, notes that may have seemed wrong a week ago are now right. Everything I know is right, nothing I know is wrong. And I keep going. The band is roaring.

Then a new, third microphone appears between Dave and me. I hadn't noticed it before—I'm sure it wasn't there a minute ago—certainly it hadn't been there in that first chorus. But now, in the middle of the bridge in the middle of the stage there is a new mic. It's a very beautiful vintage sort of microphone, one of those silvery old-style fat radio mics with a fine vaguely automotive grille—a '57 Chevy Bel Air on a thick heavy stand. The Dark Stranger stands at this mic, almost shoulder to shoulder between Dave and me, his Lincoln black coat and hat perfectly creased and pressed, his long hair shining and clean, softly curled at the ends, tucked behind his ears in a glow of cornflower blonde, draped on his straight and strong young shoulders.

The whole thing is very normal—there is no shaft of light, no shower of snowflakes, no nothing. But it is Elliot—Elliot!—I'm sure it's him, has to be, grown, high cheekbones angular where there had been little kid pudge from ancient snapshots—but how do you know your own brother, who's a million years gone and you can't even remember his face, you can't even remember what his little kid voice sounded like and you can't even remember what color his eyes were because they only took black and white photos and stuck them in the back pages of the family album. I don't know how you remember him but somehow you do, or you think you do.

But there *is* a shaft of light—I was wrong—I'm sure there is. And it shines down on the three of us on that small stage in the gym, a little round silvery pool of theatrical light, a single streetlight in the middle of a dark field. And I look up for its source thinking this is very *Hollywood* and how did they make this effect happen way out here in a gym in darkest downstate Illinois—maybe that sound guy is amazingly good.

Elliot, the Dark Stranger, a guitar slung in front of him—it's one of my old ones, a beat-up sparkle-red Sears Silvertone guitar I abandoned years before, thinking it archaic and hopelessly clunky, but he seems to be able to make it or anything look cool. His eyes are closed as he takes the solo—he riffs, improvises, building, gaining intensity moving higher on the neck, then crouching over the guitar almost crushing it, legs splayed then jumping straight up, picking hand reaching high—he makes that guitar sound like nothing I'd ever heard before—and he isn't even plugged into an amp. Dave, blissed out, eyes on the Stranger, is in one of his Yogi Bear trances. And the kaleidoscope eyes of our guitars, like twin Roman candles, are still flowing and seeing between us. Elliot the Stranger is slashing his high E chord, but it's like he is coming at it from someplace else—an E chord from Mars, from a place on that guitar's fretboard I'd never been before.

We get to the chorus and the three of us—Dave, me, and Elliot the Dark Stranger step to the big silver mic—three on one, like Brian, Carl, and Dennis in a seamless three-part harmony, Beach Boy wonderful, crisp, high, and clean as only brothers can. We don't miss a note, didn't forget the words, and we never sounded better.

And then I am flying high up among the gymnasium's tethered

climbing ropes, exercise rings, and folded up basketball hoops. I am a cedar waxwing fluttering in the dusty rafters looking down on the little band in that light—the three of us, washed in airy sound so beautifully clear. Dave's bass shakes the old wood of the roof, the drums and Baldoni dancing a fabulous frug, and the guitars—me and Elliot the Stranger's guitars—ring in pulsing perfect harmonics that I, in my little bird body can both hear and see. The song seems to slow ... down ... and I can see ...

each ... note ... spiraling ... up ... from ... the ... stage ...

... and present ... itself to me in simple ... but chaotic order in a key ... signature I can clearly ... see and a light that I can plainly ... hear. This E chord from Mars hangs in front of my little feathered self and I fly in and around it, the notes vibrating happily in their weird tablature of light, and I weave the vanes of my elegant feathers into the chord's elevating fabric, noticing that note is green, that note is bluish, that note is brown and that note is silver and gold. It all seems perfectly normal. Elliot the Stranger looks up at me, hesitating, and I fly away ... satisfied.

Then the song ends. Perfectly. And there is no more third mic. Dave and I are out of breath—sweating, hot, grinning and glorious.

Harrison Creach walks out of the shadows in the back of the gym. The only sound is the electric hum of the amps and his two hands clapping.

 Track 3: Later that afternoon

HARRISON CREACH, looking like an old school ring-a-ding-ding, four-in-the-morning after-the-clubs-close-Sinatra, by way of Sammy Davis Junior crossed with Sly Stone, standing in the shadows behind the sound board next to a pommel horse, his gray-flecked Afro seeming a bit more global than usual and his platforms a tad taller, looking completely out of place in this corn-fed high school barn of a gym, beckons me over, touches my arm, looks me in the eye and calmly says, "I saw it."

"Saw what?" I am holding Felix's neck in my hand, his little body close.

"It. *It*! I saw it. Goddamn!" Whistles softly.

Did he really see that third mic up there, us playing like we'd never played before? Did he see me fly away up into the rafters like one of those brown birdie gym prisoners looking for a way out?

"Oh, young Pepper Porter." His delicately fingered old bass fiddle playing hand is on my shoulder. "I saw further evidence of what you and I have talked of before, that strange musical magic that occurs only once in a blue moon. It's that sweet ... I don't want to call it part of that mojo that you rock 'n rollers riff on but have no idea what in hell you're talking about, but it's part of what makes all this downstate country-ass bullshit worth it, you see?"

I'm too flustered to speak.

He says, "You boys had it going *on*, sounding quite righteous in that last number."

"Man, we did."

"So who *was* that? Who was at that mic in the middle?"

Speechless, my heart picks up the pace, an accelerating metronomic tic.

"That never happened to you before, did it."

"No, sir."

Up on stage, Dave, Hawgrim, and Ricky are slapping hands and butts, laughing and bullshitting, hairy Ricky twirling sticks like batons from Jellystone Park, even Hawgrim looks happy. Then some little skinny guy with two fat black cameras slung around his neck goes up to them and begins snapping pictures.

I decide to tell Creach.

"I think it was my brother, sir, my other brother. Killed in an accident a long time ago."

"Mmm. Makes sense. I'm not surprised."

"But I dunno. I'm probably just nuts."

"Most natural thing in the world. Rare—but natural."

With a faraway glint in his eye and slipping into his venerable jazz cat tone, thick and well-cadenced, deliberate like a walking bass line, he says, "I'd be up on the bandstand with that big bull fiddle of mine and sometimes, when the band was really laying it down, swinging hard, me and Bloop, he was the drummer, you see—Sunnyland Slim's band, you understand, he and I would be locked in so tight, so right, so nice and, well, you know what I'm talking about." He fishes a white handkerchief out of his hip pocket and quietly blows his nose. "Damn cold. Excuse me." He blows again, folds the handkerchief, stuffs it back in his pocket.

"See, sometimes it'd be just a sort of feeling that something or somebody was guiding my fingers, that I could do no wrong, that all the wrong notes were right and all the changes were opening up in front of me with new licks lit up like the Fourth of July right on the chart, and I'd be shining in some glowing down-home light that would just surround me, making me feel like I could fly. Some nights it was just the light, others it felt like somebody."

I look into his eyes knowing exactly what he is talking about.

He shakes his head and says, "Hell, I'm not going to get into the who and what just now. Suffice it to say," he returns briefly to his Queen's English accent, "whenevah it happened the music just kept getting bettah and bettah." Coughs. "Yeah, maybe you think that's just some hokey bullshit but I know that the old folks know. Old folks would talk about things like that on summer firefly nights. And sure enough—those things happen, even in this plastic age, though there are indeed forces afoot working hard to wind that shit down. And now I know that you know. You do know, don't you?"

Yes, I say, yes.

"*Magic*, my friend. And we get paid to experience it ... or *perhaps* experience it. What'd I say? I believe you and I have talked about this."

We stand there silently, admiring the floor.

Creach says, "But you know what, I'd do it for *free*. Hell, I'd *pay* to do it!" He takes his handkerchief out again and wipes his brow. "And these people here ..." He scans the gym, swinging his arm like a city slicker impresario, suddenly there are more scraggly long-haired roadies that look just like me, older even, climbing around on the stage messing with mics, amps, cables, and lights. "They might feel those things, might see something once in a while, but I kind of doubt it. Unless they're blowin' weed or hung up on some crystal ship or something. Which is okay with me, you understand, and I been there, but I tell you what. It just ain't the same." He looks me up and down, seriously considering me and what I am all about. "But today, just now, you got *it*, young sir. And this is not some goddamn wise old Uncle Remus jive here. Hell no."

Then he flips on his non-musician, non-bassman tone, his not-kidding voice of learned wisdom. "Do all you can to keep that magic with a capital M, that old enchantment, the contrary-to-fact jump'n jive jack juice. Tell me, what was his name?"

"Who?—oh, Elliot."

He pauses, breathing noisily through his nose, eyes trained on mine.

"Elliot. Well, don't you lose him or *it*, Pepper Porter—try your *goddamndest* not to lose *it*. You and that crazy cartoon cat guitar of yours, there's something there, I don't need to know the what and who and how, I just know that something's there and that is good enough for me and I believe it ought to be good enough for everyone around you. And furthermore, I don't exactly know what you've got to do not to lose *it*. Whatever it is, I recommend you do it. Do not be just another unmagical cat."

I'm trying to think of something to say but he waves me off and tells me he's just happy as hell to see that *something* inexplicable went down up there and at least he still has the eyes to see that sort of strange and beautiful thing.

Inexplicable is good.

Then he says, "But I have good news, which is why I'm here." He blows his nose again. "Our little record, 'Your Aunt is Cool,' is beginning to get some airplay in St. Louis, KXOK, big AM station."

I nod, hungry for more.

"Now the greater Benld metropolitan area is within reach of that signal, so I thought that I'd better hustle down here and listen to the drumbeat of the natives—and, of course, see you boys in action. And I have actually been getting phone calls about you boys. This is good. This is all very good."

"Mr. Creach, sir, that is amazing news but ..." and I steel myself to speak up, voice the concerns that have been stewing in the back of my mind, "I wonder if this record of ours is getting airplay for all the wrong reasons ..."

"Because it's funny? Indeed it is. Catchy, too."

"But isn't that a wrong reason? I think it's a problem."

"It's a *first class* problem then. Hell's the matter with you?" Creach pauses and softens a bit. "Don't get hung up in some artistic funk and mope around whining that your art is misunderstood. Believe me, I know about that."

He looks past me, says, "Excuse me, Mister Rock Star, but it would appear that that photog over there is in need of your presence for some very valuable and might I imagine free promotional photography. Now you run along and give the man what he wants. Don't you worry about a thing. Cool Papa Spo-dee-o-dee will take care of everything."

The photographer says, "Okay, if you gentlemen would be so kind as to ... oh excuse me, uh ... who are you? Oh right, Felix the Cat boy."

He's a weedy little guy with greasy shoulder-length black hair hanging out from a red bandana, a stringy long beard like the Chinese Zen master on *Kung-Fu*. With baby blue and burnt orange suede desert boots poking out from under his purple floral bell-bottoms, a black cowboy hat on top of the bandana and a beat-up olive drab army surplus jacket with a zillion pockets stuffed with camera junk, lenses, little yellow boxes of Kodachrome, he seems to have just walked the plank of a hippie pirate ship.

Dave says, "Oh, sorry! Yeah, this is my brother ... Pepper Porter, this is Ralph—Ralph, Pepper. Pepper, Ralph. Ralph's from St. Louis."

Ralph says, "Call me Flash."

"Hi, pleasure ..." I stick out my hand just as he turns back to the boys with his big Nikon at his eye. Dave grabs my hand and drags me into the group. Flashy Ralph starts snapping pics, rapid-fire, barking directions.

"Dave, you look killer, just fantastic. Hey, tall guy with the nose, yeah you, what's your name again, uh Peter! ... behind Dave please. Okay, let's move all of you over there up against the stage so we can see the drums ... Dave in the middle. Oh yeah. Great shot, great shot. Uh, Peter, can you look a little better, uh ... well, okay ..."

"It's Pepper."

"Right. Oh, these will be great. Okay, Dave, thanks a lot!"

Then Flash tells us that there are some unbelievably fantastic photo backdrops just outside the gym and that if we are willing he'd be pleased to keep on shooting and he'd make us look like Foghat, Savoy Brown, and Uriah Heep all rolled into one. He mentions some St. Louis weekly hipster rags and radio stations and says he could guarantee we'd get picked up, absolutely. So we zip out a side door and follow little Ralphy who, as soon as he gets outside into the cold and gray behind the gym and begins stomping through the crunchy snowless winter weeds, pulls a little scraggly joint out of one of his many pockets, cups his hands in the wind and lights up. He passes it around and we all pull deeply, happy to be out in the cold clean air. The sun bursts through the clouds and I can actually feel a bit of warmth on my face. Flash the Photog forgets about the roach and quickly lines us up against the chipped mottled brick wall of an old railroad storage shed that is close to a set of tracks that stretches into the distance. He wants to take advantage of the light.

So we pose like glib glam rock stars without the eye shadow in front of the shed's old brick wall with the faded green and white Illinois Central sign, Flash the Bulb having us look bored, no smiles, then menacing, then laughing, all the time focusing mostly on Dave who, I freely admit, is the best looking guy in the band—he's the Davy Jones that the girls want to flirt with, to take home. This is not new. Then Ralph the Flash moves us up the hump of rocky ballast to the twin train tracks where he says he wants to go for a ramblin' man sort of look—we're bluesy hippie hoboes headin' off down that lonesome road lookin' for the next highballin' redball freight, feelin' bad and blue. Hawgrim makes Ricky lie down on the tracks like a creosote cross tie, a big furry damsel in distress, he, a rock 'n roll Snidely Whiplash. Dave and I hiss and boo him but Ralph says, no no no—too much Monkees, this ain't no hard day's night. So we go back to being grim, pouting, and cool. And Ralph snaps his shots.

The sun slips back behind the clouds and the cold wind ends the shoot. Everybody turns tail, flees back to the gym. I stay out on the tracks that are laid on a little man-made rise arrowing across the frying-pan flat Illinois prairie. I feel drawn to the scene. Windblown American dirt, the good earth. To the north, the land is frozen topsoil, black and fallow brown, flecked only with random stripes of dead grainy snow fanning out from me to far away groves of bare trees sheltering remote farms, ramparts around little stockades. A distant coal mining rig rises against the horizon like a ship steaming across an empty sea. I stand in the middle of the shiny rails, stare down the uncurving line, the tracks not wavering from their parallel march to the west, heading to the big river and St. Louis. Then the sun breaks through again, sinking below the dark blue cloudbank in the west as it begins to set.

I shade my eyes and see the point on the horizon where the rails fuse in a long V, the vanishing point where the two tracks I stand between, separated by the deep black of the sturdy old railroad ties, appear to meet and end. But like Mom always told me, I know that the tracks do not end—nor do they come together—they only look like they do. It's an illusion. And life, too, is somehow an illusion that does not end. Think of your brother. He did not end.

But I don't know. It's a mystery.

And then at the tip of the V, a figure appears, someone walking toward me, a crosstie walker like an old blues cat where the Southern crosses the Yellow Dog in the lonesome hot Mississippi Delta. Far down the line, a farm truck makes its way over the tracks at a crossing. The truck pauses on the tracks and then moves on. The figure is gone and the V reappears.

The wind blows. I head back into the warm gym.

And I miss her some more. Elliot too.

Q & A

Q: Strange times in downstate Illinois, eh? What was *that* all about?

A: You mean the third mic thing, right? Oh, man, I dunno. Very weird. I haven't even talked to Dave about it yet. Not sure … did something really happen or was it just me? Or was it just the music?

Q: Could've been. Just the heat of the moment, the band was kicking ass. One of those times it was all coming together.

A: Yeah, but all that Dark Stranger stuff in the last few weeks—the snowball fight, the bus thing—

Q: And Felix.

A: Oh man. *Felix!* That's just bizarre. But here he is.

Q: You're a completely rational human being with no history of excessive weirdness, other than the usual teenage offenses.

A: Right! I'm okay, just a normal kid.

Q: Let's not get carried away.

A: But what the hell?

Q: I don't know. Let's move on.

A: ...

Q: So. Harrison Creach.

A: He's my man. But I went through those little paranoid suspicious episodes about him ...

Q: Indeed ... why?

A: Plenty of reasons to get paranoid in these plastic days. Hell, I dunno. It's just the way I am. I get myself worked up ... needlessly, I guess ... I'm sure I was wrong. See, I am really hoping that he'll be this inspired source of great wisdom from the college of musical knowledge.

Q: And Hawgrim tells you you're a dumbshit—

A: Yeah, but what do you expect. Hawgrim. Anyway here's Checkers Records, you know, obscure little Southside label with a weird past, they sign us up. I dunno. And that E. Rodney Jones DJ cat. Like, what do I know about the record business?

Q: Zero. Zilch.

A: Nada. So what's an average rock 'n roll kid like me supposed to do?

Q: Just sing yer songs, son ... and hope for the best.

A: That's right ... but Creach sure looks like he oughta know what he's doing—old, kind of distinguished. Don't you think?

Q: What, so because he's an old black guy, you think he's naturally endowed with a cosmic handle on everything?

A: Uh ... no ...

Q: And here's Checkers Records, a crappy little has-been failed label, once known for their screwy novelty records including Creach's own immortal "Do You Like Tractors" recorded by Scratchy Fenwick and His Itchy Zoot Suiters. In the '50s! You think he knows what he's doing in today's world? Rolling the dice, man.

A: It'll be okay. He's a good guy.

Q: "Don't worry, Cool Papa Spo-dee-whosit'll take care of everything."

A: I hope he does. Right now, I just wanna make my music.

Q: You're using him.

A: And he's using me. Everybody uses everybody.

Q: You're still suspicious.

A: Maybe I should be. A healthy paranoia.

Q: Speaking of being used, there's that chick. You're nuts. She's gonna be hauled off to the hoosegow one of these days and then what?

A: I was wondering when you were going to ask me about her.

Q: What if she's playing you for a fool—she could be using you! I mean, you could end up in a heap o' trouble boy. I'm just sayin'.

A: You think?

Q: Could be. You don't need this.

A: Love is never wrong.

Q: Haven't I seen that on sappy dorm posters?

A: It's the *yes* of rock 'n roll.

 Track 4: Friday night

T HERE ARE NO visitations on stage that night, no third mics, and no cedar waxwings. Though we don't reach those out-of-our-heads unbelievable heights of that mystical sound check and the presence of *it* cannot be confirmed, we rock the joint and we are damn good.

Tonight, it's Dave's kazoo.

Or maybe it's Dave's kazoo, his Kazoosh, and his suddenly mysteriously improved bass guitar musicianship *and* his under-appreciated all-American studly good looks that light everything up and steal the show. But one thing's for sure—those fresh-faced farm girls, those frizzy-haired hippie chicks from the Greater Benld and Tri-City area, all decked out in their finest freakery—squiggley em-broidered bell-bottoms, knotty macramé vests, painter's pants, and sky-high platforms—are left slack-jawed, salivating, and screaming for more when we wrap up our little thirty-minute opening act set for Pavlov's Dog.

"Freakout in Coal City" rocks. "Windblown American Dirt" rocks. "Burgers in Benton" is a huge hit and "Your Aunt is Cool" leaves 'em stunned, hootin' and hollerin' with lighters held high. They've never heard anything like that down on the farm.

Dave. He's been electrified with his hair on fire—or plugged into some new wavelength, sprouting some new weird antenna siphoning signals from some cosmic gas tank, drawing people to him—like Flashy Ralph—who's drawn in like a summer bug to Dave's new hundred-watt light bulb snapping shots before the show.

We scamper from the old high school stage—*thank you Benld!*—forbidden from doing an encore by the promoter—and roar into the stinky boys locker room, struttin' and screaming and slappin' asses. Ralph follows, flash bulbs popping. Pavlov's Dog and a bizarre assortment of hangers-on and who-knows-who are in there tuning up, lying around—they nod at us through a buzzing amphetamine haze—*hey man, where'd you get that amazing guitar, man* and *I dig that bowtie* and *whoa, that freaky accordion, far out, dudes.* I sit down on a wooden bench in front of a row of beige gym lockers, feeling good, feeling wiped out.

Dave pops the top off a beer that some fat guy with a beard and cowboy hat and *KXOK Good Guys* t-shirt hands him. He sits down next to me and says, "Man, what was *with* you tonight—you were fuckin' on fire! Unbelievable!" He takes a long swig, wipes his mouth with his sleeve, says, "Jeez, this is shitty stuff!" He grins, puts his arm around me. "But hey man, all those chicks out there, hanging on the stage? They *wanted* you, man!"

"Bull*shit*, they wanted *you!*"

"Like you were a rock 'n roll god, for chrissakes! And the guys? Man, those kids just wanted to *be you.* I tell ya, none of them have ever heard or seen anything like you and Felix before. It's like you were channeling the pranayama and going in and out of every chakra known to man!"

I channeled the chakras right back at him. "I was going to say the same thing about you, man."

He pauses with a distant Dave look in his eyes. "This is very cosmic."

Then Hawgrim starts playing "If I Were a Rich Man" on the Baldoni and all of the Pavlov's Dogs and their weird vaguely Russian-looking entourage begin dancing around the locker room, beer cans balanced on their heads like a bunch of Cossack rock 'n roll fiddlers on the roof.[51] Ricky thumps around the room, a happy dancing bear snapping the thick fingers of his outstretched paws. Everybody sings.

But Dave and I stay on the bench. I ask, "Dave. Did you see or maybe feel anything ... unusual at the sound check? I mean, when we did 'Freakout,' did you see, uh, or feel anything out of the ordinary, or was it just me?"

"Sri Yogi said there'd be days like this."

"But what does Sri Dave say?"

He drains his beer, carefully puts the empty on the beat-up tile floor, leans forward with both elbows on his knees, hands clasped in deep thought.

He speaks quietly, confidently. "We're lucky to have receptive oceanic minds, man. Because cosmic whales like that, like the sound check 'Freakout,' that was no little fish man ..."

"Dave ..."

"... and I ... am not surprised. It was like that snowball fight—he was there, he wasn't there. The more I know, the less I know." He takes a deep breath. "I am the cosmos ..."

Good old Dave.

"... and *you* are the cosmos."

I say, "But *it* didn't happen again tonight."

He thinks about that.

"No. But we came close. And we must always be *seeking it*. And don't you want to get back out there and do *it* again?"

"Hell, yes." *It's* out there somewhere.

"And you know what, those kids *believed* in us. *We* believed in us."

We smile.

Creach appears, tapping me on the shoulder. He says, "Telegram for Mr. Porter."

---

[51] "I'd never have to work hard, ya ha deedle deedle bubba bubba deedle deedle dum. All day long I'd biddy biddy bum, if I were a wealthy man! Hey!" A classic Hawgrim Swingtones wedding tune. He had become an expert at playing this tune on the Baldoni while balancing a bottle of wine on top of his head, perched precariously just behind his newly receding hairline. The wedding party always went nuts. This eventually becomes a crowd-pleasing part of the band's set.

"What?"

"You have a telegram. Here." Ceremoniously, he places it in my hand.

"Nobody gets telegrams anymore."

"You just did, my man." He smiles like he knows something.

I tear open the flimsy little yellow envelope thinking that maybe Aunt Gladys died or something.

DEAR ROCK STAR STOP HAVE YOU READ THE PAPER YET STOP STUDY HARD STOP HA STOP CONSIDER THIS A DATAGRAM STOP 0000110111011001001 STOP HA HA STOP THERE WILL BE A QUIZ STOP DID YOU SING MY SONG TONIGHT STOP LOVE STOP GRACE STOP

"Who's Grace Stop?" Dave is reading it over my shoulder. "And read what?"

"Jesus Dave, it's nothing, don't worry about it." I quickly fold it up and stick it in the inside pocket of my sweaty white dinner jacket.

His eyes narrow and he flicks his eyebrows. "It's *her*, isn't it?"

The locker room performance of *Fiddler on the Roof* ends with a crashing klezmer chorus followed by all of Pavlov's Dogs loudly clearing out of the locker room for the stage, fired up and thoroughly juiced, amped, and high. The place is empty except for our little band.

Creach pats me on the back, halting any further discussion of the telegram, and loudly gathers our little band together for he has an announcement to make.

Hawgrim swings the Baldoni off his shoulders, lights a cigarette, says, "This place is a dump."

Ricky says, "Rock 'n roll sounds best in a dump." He paradiddles on a gym locker like it's a beige metal tom-tom.

"Gentlemen. I congratulate you on a most sublime performance this evening. May I say that each one of you performed at or, dare I say, *above* your abilities. I, for one, am most impressed and gratified, as was your audience here in the fair city of Benld." He's rolling, orating most impressively, enunciating the 'l' and the 'd' of Benld quite clearly, rolling them out on his tongue. His white handkerchief is in his hand like Louis Armstrong without a horn. "And I believe you are at the beginning of a transformation."

Hawgrim says, "Here, here!" Ricky spins a drum roll on a bench.

The crowd noise down the hall from the gym builds. It's a chant—*arf arf arf,* as the Dogs thud drums, twang guitar licks, and ripple organ riffs in noodley rock 'n roll warm up.

"While I am not exactly sure what got into you boys tonight—" Creach shoots an inquiring glance my way "—you will be pleased to hear that your little record—our little record, 'Your Aunt is Cool,' B-side of 'Burgers in Benton,' is now enjoying a little airplay on a fine, fine radio station in St. Louis, KXOK, 630 on your AM dial."

And there is great rejoicing, much twisting and shouting.

He goes on. "I understand that it may even become one of their *bubbling-under pick-hits*, particularly after your outstanding performance here this evening. You see, that rather large gentleman who was so enjoying your impromptu reprise of selections from *Fiddler on the Roof* just now, was Fat Phil, sole proprietor of the graveyard shift most nights on the station but, more importantly, assistant program director. I believe he likes what he heard."

There is more rejoicing.

Outside in the gym, Pavlov's Dog rip into their set with everything they have. The building shudders with a subterranean cannonade of amplified rock 'n roll. The crowd goes nuts.

Creach speaks louder trying to reach above the din.

"But may I say a bit more on this transformation that I alluded to. You see, you boys are going into what may be a rough patch." He pauses and blows his nose. "Excuse me. Now, everybody sit down."

We all sit down.

"Here's the straight dope, boys—your song is starting to be played on top forty radio yet I know that you don't exactly see yourselves as part of that, shall we say, *milieu*." He extends the word into three or four syllables, drawing it out like a long Slinky, his voice dropping nearly an octave.

Hawgrim helpfully translates for us and says, "He means we think we're hipper than AM radio."

"Thank you so much, Mr. Hawgrim." He dips his head in a courtly bow. "But don't let that get you down, bum you out, so to speak. Airplay is airplay, and if people like your music, even for the wrong reasons, that's good ... so shut up and let it happen."

Hawgrim says, "Sir, I have no problem with wrong reasons, sir."

"I knew that, Mr. Hawgrim, I knew that you would have no problem."

He continues, slowly and deliberately. "But as I said, just sit back and relax. Whether you know it or not, you are probably on the right path. See, I once had a song called 'North Dakota Love Call,'[52] a song that was white as your lily white ass, but you see, I knew my audience and I knew what they wanted and so ..."

Creach goes on about the importance of being serious, but I zone out thinking about Sooz's paper. I haven't touched it, haven't read it and have no idea what's in it and here she's going to quiz me about it for crying out loud.

The Plan is safely nestled in the bottom of my fat duffel bag, waiting for me out there in Otto.

Then Creach says, "But enough about that." He pauses for dramatic effect. "You will be happy to know that a certain Englishman has made discreet inquiries with me about this happy little band. It seems that this gentleman has expressed a deep interest in offering his international record distribution services to you boys. His name is Rodger Slothwell and he is affiliated with Terpsichorean Records, which, I believe, is a small yet plucky English record label. He is going to rendezvous with us tomorrow night at your gig in Edwardsville. I will be pleased to make the introduction and offer any advice I can on the subject."

We all stare at Creach as a shrieking guitar solo stabs our ears. Then, as if on cue, everybody rocks out and cheers. Dave, Hawgrim, and Ricky head out to the gym and the blasting Dogs, but I stay in the locker room with Creach.

He says, "That telegram. I know you'll do the right thing, son."

How does he know?

How do I know?

I spend the rest of the evening on a pile of wrestling mats that smell like thirty years of gym class. I'm working my way through her paper. It's incredible.

---

[52] "My darling if you and I could snuggle and smooch/ it would be really swell/because the Dakota wind is cold as hell ..."

*   *   *

A digest and commentary:

> <u>The Network of the Future</u>
> *Controlled Statistical Arbitration: A Shared Media Access Methodology*
> *By Martin Alan Porter*
> By *me*. Not Sooz or Grace. *Me*.
> What's she trying to do?

> *Section 1.A*
> *The network is a shared communication facility between locally distributed computing stations. It is a passive broadcast medium with no central control.*

She says her network is an *unrooted tree*—a great tree of life to which everybody and everything is connected. The network is a tree because there are branches everywhere—it's thick, giving the cool green shade of *bandwidth* with every leaf and twig being equal with only one path between me and anybody else—one path between Sooz and me—simple *connectivity*. The tree is unrooted because I can join the network anywhere—it can be tapped like a sugar maple for its sweet sap of speed and it will extend and grow from any point.

And nobody is in charge.

Like our generation.

But making my way through her pages, I've lost the map and am in trackless territory, leaving my little world and entering hers, sailing offshore in a leaky boat where the winds might shift crazily and where big waves get bigger and cosmic pressure blasts like the volume on a hundred-watt amp turned all the way up. And yet, I calm myself as I read her steady, confident, and warmly elegant words of cool technology, winds that waft over me gently ruffling my hair, soothing my cheek. Like she used to do.

> *Section 1.B*
> *Coordination of access to the network for datagram broadcasts is distributed among the contending transmitting stations using controlled statistical arbitration.*

I stand shivering in a dark length of cable lit dimly by passing streams of charged electrons—cold fragments of Sooz's statistically controlled datagrams. Then I see little personal network stations strung out in the distance like a long string of Christmas tree lights— each light a voice waiting to speak, ready to banish the black sound of silence, contending for a little chunk of time on the network, a little air to breathe which is all that I need and with peace, love, and understanding, we'll share the land and the wine, and share the free flow of her deep river of electronic bandwidth. I feel better.

Section 1.C

With carrier detection we are able to implement deference: no network station will start transmitting while hearing carrier. With deference comes acquisition: once a packet transmission has been in progress for network end-to-end propagation time, all stations are hearing carrier and are deferring: the network media has been acquired and the transmission will complete without an interfering collision.

The carrier is a silvery electronic Frisbee flung low and fast along copper corridors of wire passing little wide spots where Sooz's *peoples' computers*—actual computers built for *one person*[53]—are tapped in, listening with invisible bunny ears ready to talk but courteously waiting, deferring, avoiding the unpleasantness of speaking at the same time as other stations, causing messy data collisions where everything falls on the floor, countless ones and zeros lost and scattered in disarray. When the little bunny ears hear the carrier zip by, when they detect the presence of this strange little electrical UFO—the carrier—when they see it scream down the wire at impossible speeds bound for somewhere else on the network—the computers see it effortlessly hauling a string of frames full of those bits and bytes like little boxcars of data on a high-tech express—the bunny ears back off waiting for the invisible high ballin' data freight to pass by, gone like a train. They wait until they can't hear the carrier whooshing along the wire anymore, the sound of its trailing frames—datagrams—mere echoes leaving only a white noise of hissing electrons natural to the wire and their own polite circuit board selves. And I'm feeling good.

But then the streamlined train of ones and zeros reappears on the

---

[53] Sounds crazy, I know.

horizon where the tracks converge. It's a sunny day and I'm standing on a remote railroad crossing in the middle of a flat prairie with the sign dinging wildly as the train gets nearer and nearer, blowing its horn which sounds strangely similar to the riff in "Louie Louie."

I turn to get off the tracks, but I see Dave and the Dark Stranger there on the country road, safely distant from the whistle-blowing train, holding balloons, wearing party hats, and tootling little paper blowouts. Behind them, also waiting at the crossing, is Creach at the wheel of a yellow '62 Buick Electra 225 convertible with the top down, wearing a mostly green and pink Hawaiian shirt, bad-ass shades, with a martini in hand and cigar FDR-jaunty in his teeth. But Sooz is seated fetchingly on the tonneau cover of the white pleated Naugahyde back seat like it's a parade, looking like a homecoming queen, waving at me like Marilyn Monroe on the first *Playboy* cover. The train's a comin.'

Before the train of paranoia runs me down, I shake myself awake. The image of the dream begins to fade.

I read another page.

But my eyes close again. Then, my hallucinating sleep-deprived brain resolves that I will not be a sap and follow her around blindly, letting her use me, derailed from the band, chased down by G-men and dragged in for questioning under suspicion for fraternizing with you-know-who about who-knows-what. I resolve not to be a rock 'n roll bug on Sooz's personal high-tech windshield.

But what do I know? I'm asleep.

*   *   *

At three in the morning, after the cleanup and the load out, I find myself in a cramped room for four at the very economical Royal Crown Courts and Motor Motel—free local telephone and color TV. Now I can't sleep. Dave and Ricky are knocked out. Hawgrim is off cavorting with a couple chicks—adoring fans. I'm reading the Plan with a flashlight.

The phone rings.

I fumble with the phone and my flashlight falls on the floor of the motel room.

It's Sooz. "So. The Plan. What do you think?"

"How's your reading assignment going?" She sounds like she's middle-of-the-day wide awake, a professor patiently working her way through a long agenda, checking on a slow learner.

A Three (Two) Stooges snoring chorus shakes the thin walls of the Royal Crown Courts and Motor Motel, conveniently located on Highway 4 just south of Benld. Creach has installed us there saying *don't worry about a thing, boys*. Pinkish parking lot lights seep through the frayed brown and orange drapes that won't quite close. I sit up on the board-hard bed with the phone at my ear and hair in my eyes. Ricky and I won the coin toss, opting out of the creaky cots. The room is overheated and reeks of cigarettes, Mr. Clean, and the natural vapors arising from rock stars with dirty socks and beery breath.

Ricky, after dropping a couple quarters in the noisy and rippling Magic Fingers bed massage meter, is a mound of comatose hairy drummer flesh rising and falling with each gasping snort. Dave sleeps like he's dead, flat on his back with his hands peacefully folded across his chest as if he's holding a funereal lily—he and Ricky have a remarkable two-part snoring harmony thing going.

I mumble, "Ooooghhh ..."

"Pepper, my dear, yes I know it's the middle of the night but I just got off work and ... hey, you're a rock star ... you're not supposed to ever sleep."

I stifle a yawn, shake my head and try to sound intelligent.

"So have you read it?" she asks cheerfully.

"It's brilliant. But we need to talk." I'm whispering trying not to wake the snoozers.

"Yes, it's good. I know. But I need you to *understand* it ..."

"I do, but ..."

"And you're going to have to *pitch it*. But it's okay, it's okay. Don't worry."

Then she goes on to tell me about a Dr. Ivor Flarf, professor of engineering, computer science & cybernetics at the University of Illinois in Champaign.

"Don't you remember him? He visited Michigan a few times when we were there, ran a few symposiums."

"Flarf?"

"Flarf."

"Flarf, Flarf—yeah. Wasn't he German or Austrian? Maybe Hungarian? Hard to tell. Had one of those Hollywood European accents."

"Exactly."

"We called him Colonel Klink."

She tells me that the U of I is one of the very few locations in the country[54] that is a node on the ARPANET, an obscure government-funded computer network—an internet of some big time universities like Harvard, USC, Stanford, and MIT. But more importantly, the military weapons labs are plugged in—Ames, Livermore, Aberdeen, and that mysterious think tank, the Rand Corporation.

I shudder in a cold sweat. "Whoa Sooz, you're not talking about, uh, doing anything we might regret later—"

"No, no. Of course not." She sighs.

"Didn't Rand practically invent the Cold War, the military industrial complex?"

"Look, I am trying to do the right thing here—Marx would say that I'm revolutionizing the instruments of bourgeois production again—it's history, part of another step on the road to revolution, for heaven's sake."[55]

Sometimes the long-buried cuddly camp counselor in Sooz rises to the surface, saying things like "for heaven's sake."

Then she tells me that Herr Doktor Flarf is one of the key engineers involved with making the big experimental data network work. He is heavy into the bits and bytes, engineering the down and dirty of the networking technology that runs the ARPANET and is building all sorts of crazy communications contraptions right there in Champaign—not that far away—maybe even in his basement. Or his garage. Sooz says that there will ultimately be lots of little networks that feed big ones. And that is what she—we—are interested in.

"This ARPANET thing's going to be big someday, Pepper—*if* they let it out of its Pentagon cage—it could be for everybody. What

---

[54] Less than fifty back then.

[55] She lifted that from *The Communist Manifesto*, by Karl Marx. By inventing something fundamentally new, Sooz, I think, is attempting to help accelerate societal change—help move it along the process of change that is history—which is inexorably moving toward revolution. There was a big argument back in some econ class—being an agent of change didn't sound like a bad thing, revolutionizing the means of production and all that.

I see are the little people, us, you and me. Now? We're all disenfran-
chised, we have no power. But with *this*—*this* is power. Remember the
password? That—was *power*."

A fond memory—a closed world thrown open.

"What I'm talking about is empowering people—if the people
have their own computers and networks, they can control their own
information and power is distributed, not centralized ... think of it,
Pepper. Today we've got these monster corporate computers behind
glass walls, glass houses guarded by *men* in white coats with clip-
boards. You know those guys ..."

I did. I almost became one of them.

"And we used to beat the system right under their noses."

"It was great ..."

"They never even knew ..."

I lay there smiling.

"And still the only way for anybody to use a computer is if one of
those *men* consents to *allow* you to connect via some supervised hard
wire straight in to *his* computer. And *he* decides what you can do with
it! Computers should be used for, not against, people. But with this
it will be anybody to anybody connectivity, no hard connections and
nobody is in charge—we will tear down that glass wall! And if people
can do that, then society really changes and the possibilities are endless. It blows my mind." She pauses to get her breath. "It's big—it's
like Gutenberg, going from parchment to print. Now it's taking the
analog world and going digital."

"But what could you actually *do* with your *own* computer. And a
network?"

"I don't know ... people will figure it out. Just a small matter of
programming, software." I hear her scrunch her shoulders like she's
coming in for the kill. "You're a musician, Pepper—maybe you could
make music on a computer or write on a computer. Be insanely creative! Hell, maybe you could even connect to libraries over this thing,
do research, search for data, information, knowledge—it could be
freed from its corporate prison! And who knows?—maybe someday
you could even borrow a book—maybe you could even—*buy* a book
using your own computer—on a network! It could happen."

I sit back and consider the implications. "Is *this* really you? I mean, buying and selling stuff—on a computer? So commercial. Sounds like Frankenstein capitalism."

She's considered all this. "Yes, of course—*what have I done? It's alive!*" Then, softly, slowly and carefully, "Like anything, it's a double-edged sword—good and evil, ignorance and knowledge. It's inevitable and unavoidable. Progress. Part of the sweep of history."

"Time's arrow."

"Yes. What I have here helps *enable* that future. Creates possibilities for good."

"So that's what change the world means."

"That's it. So what're you waiting for?"

"Sooz."

"What?"

"Why have you got me as the author?"

"You're worried about *that*?" A grim laugh. "Look, you wouldn't really be aware of this, but one time I met Flarf in a receiving line at some departmental reception—did you go to that? Around Halloween, '69?"

My arm starts to fall asleep. I shake it out.

"Anyway, *that* was an experience, let me tell you. Old school prima donna. But he's got this very high-end government security clearance so he can work on this exotic stuff. It's like he's the Werner von Braun of computers. Lord knows what he did in the war."

Then she launches into a Soozean rant about war criminals from the last war serving as high-level government advisors during this war. "Here's Dornberger, chairman of Bell Helicopter. And Jesus, look at von Braun, head of NASA! He built those goddamn V-2s that blitzed London—probably built them with slave labor—and of course we firebombed the hell out of Germany and then Hiroshima and now it's My Lai and—and did you know that it happened again, to the survivors in '72? Again! They were relocated and ... goddamn ARVNs." She takes a breath. I hear her tapping a fast beat with a pencil or pen on a table. "It never ends, Pepper! Who stops it? Who finally changes it? We've got to ... transform us—and society."

She's *good*. Gives me goosebumps.

Sooz takes a sip of something. "Okay, here's the deal—Flarf is an unbelievable male chauvinist, a terrible misogynist, an anti-woman pig and, in that receiving line, at that reception? He came *on* to me, I mean he really came *on!*"

"You're kidding."

"No, right there in the line! So I firmly pulled both his hands off my butt and I sputtered something ... I tried to be dignified ... nobody else noticed and he just laughed it off—*ach, such zee spitzfires zey have in Ahn Ahrboor! Jah?* Spitfires! Like I'm ... Chita Rivera!"

She seethes on the phone.

"Damn!"

"I'm much better dealing with male manipulation these days."

I imagine her in her satiny Bunny suit shutting down some clown in the Club.[56]

"I really thought I might get tossed from the class ... I didn't, but I was the only woman there and I was frozen out, ignored while some idiot boys sucked up to him. Flarf scribbled a few nonsense comments on my papers, gave me C's ... though I knew they were good. I aced the stuff he couldn't argue with—after all, numbers don't lie, most of the time anyway. Ended up with a lousy C minus."

"I'm sorry. I got an A."

"Of course you did."

Pause.

"So Pepper, if I whisked in there with a paper like this, Jesus, he'd laugh, toss it in the trash and bark that girls don't do engineering or math and then he'd try to get his hands in my pants while demanding that I get him a drink, his goddamn slippers, and heaven knows what else."

"And if it's me and *my* plan, then it's okay, he'll listen."

"Yes. But I'll be with you as the grad assistant, secretary, adoring girlfriend—you name it, I'll be it."

"Will he ... uh ... remember you? I mean ..."

---

[56] And here's Sooz, in her delectable Bunny costume, the ultimate degrading symbol of male domination of women, somehow striking a blow for equal rights. Yes, I see the contradiction and so does she. But she sees it as a tool, a turning of the tables—a weapon of the empowered woman.

"I'll be unrecognizable."

"A visual aid, shall we say?"

"You cynical boy."

"But I'm not in your league, this level ..."

"You will be soon. We'll go over it all in detail and I want you to look for holes in it. But for now, I am your ... instructor."

It's an appealing image. "So we pitch it, leave the paper ... do we leave the paper with him?"

"Yes. It's okay. He reads it, is intrigued and introduces me, us to the next level."

"Which is ..."

"People with money. And this is where we come face to face with the capitalist system. We'll have to be very careful not to be corrupted. But there will of course be some serious technology vetting. Who knows? He might be the one to help me build a test bed."

I try not to think about Flarf and Sooz in a test bed.

She says, "I know it'll work."

"But could he just steal your technology and call it his own?"

"He could but he won't. He's a respected academic, an engineer at the top of his field. He may be a twisted pig but he does have some scruples. He *is* known for that."

"You sure?"

"No. I mean yes. There *is* trust out there. You know these engineers, those kind of guys, scientists, it's kind of a small world. And in that little world everybody trusts everybody—peer review and all that."

I do know that world. And it is a strange and bizarre little subculture full of oddballs, geeks, and weirdos. Look at me.

I say, "And you trust me."

She seems surprised. "Of course. Yes." Pause. "Do you trust me?"

I hesitate. "What reasons do I have not to trust you?"

"C'mon Pepper, let me count the ways ... number one, I'm a fugitive from justice, I'm on the lam, underground ..."

"Sooz ..."

"... two, I just reappeared in your life out of the blue under rather mysterious circumstances with a completely new identity and three—

or is that four—I shove this crazy pile of engineering gibberish in your hand with your name on it! That enough for ya?"

"Sooz."

"Oh, and I've asked you to drop everything and run off to change the world with me, on some wild technology goose chase."

The motel room is suddenly quiet, a gulf of silence between snores. An eighteen-wheeler roars by out on the highway shaking the windows and then the whine of its big tires trails off in the distance.

"Okay, here it is. I'm tired of being alone, an outsider, totally isolated." I can see her running a hand through her hair, thinking. "I need you, Pepper Porter ... you're my way back." For the first time, she seems to bend a little, and her voice, always a source of strength, for a moment cracks ever so slightly.

"Oh Sooz ... back to what? Normal life? I don't think I know what that is. Sometimes, normal is crazy."

"And crazy is normal—and I've been very crazy, or normal ... I don't know which. But now I just want a life where I can be free again. I don't know if that can happen." She pauses. There is just the quiet hiss of the line. "Pepper, I've loved you since that first night on the beach all those years ago."

And I let that word, love, hover in the air, singing with all the soft electrostatic noise of the phone connection—it's a word I had long ago given up associating with her, after she vanished underground.

"But you left, disappeared ..."

"There were even more important things I had to do. It was unfair of me to expect you to understand back then, to just go along with all that. So I left. I think I was wrong. I was wrong in a lot of ways ... but I'm right about this."

"The Plan, your technology."

"No, I meant that I'm right about you. Trust."

And I think about her in that Buick convertible waving at the railroad crossing, and me standing on the tracks while a freight train of datagrams barrels down on me, horn blaring and Creach puffing on a stogie, and I think about doing my goddamndest. And I think about her being alone and isolated.

So I stand up on my hind legs and say, "Yes, Sooz, yes. I'm with you. And I love you."

And she says, "Oh, Pepper," with a dreamy middle of the night satisfaction, a slow, sleepy *that's it that's it that's it!*—her voice lowering and lilting as if her head is on a pillow next to mine. And my distant storms recede and a warm wave rolls over me—I sink my head into my lumpy rubber motel pillow on my side of the phone line.

She goes on. "All this might take ten years, twenty years or more! I don't know. I have to learn patience." She stops and considers that. "There's not a moment to lose."

And once more, I marvel at this girl.

There is silence on the line, I hear her switch the phone to her other ear.

"Sing my song for me again."

I croon the tune in a hoarse whisper with a backup of choiring snoozers.

I finish and she murmurs, "Oh, so won-won-wonderful."

Then the phone scrunches like she's holding it between her ear and shoulder, hands free.

"Pepper, do you know what I'm doing right now?"

I say that I am trying very hard to imagine what she is doing as she coos and sighs and tells me that last night, that amazing night, is still *right there* in her mind and that she has been thinking about me ever since and that she is very, very wet *right now* and that she imagines me gliding in and out of her mouth and across her coiling tongue and that I am the one keeping her going, that I am the one giving her new hope and that she is thinking about me … *now*.

I shift myself under the covers, revved up hard and wet with my ear glued to the phone and a dusty dry mouth with my heart booming like a big bass drum and marveling that she really did say "coiling."

Her breathing accelerates rapidly, little cries as her voice flutters in a silky queen of the night coloratura cadence and then she erupts in ecstatic volcanic tones, so loud that I am forced to pull my pillow over my head so the boys won't wake up.

The phone is quiet, hissing.

"Sooz …"

She recovers slowly. "Oh, Pepper ... that was ... you were ... glorious."

"Sooz ... did you really ... "

"Oh yes ... oh yes, it was real. And you and I ... we're going to be together—and we're going to *come* together ... you and me, again. Don't leave me alone."

Then in a pillowy, luxuriously relaxed voice she whispers, "Good night, my love. Try to sleep."

Sleep? After that?

"But when will we talk again?"

"Don't worry ... I'll find you." She sighs and murmurs a serene, "Bye."

It's four in the morning and after that phone call I'm left high and dry, wide-awake with no decent way out—certainly not with these clowns in the room. I get dressed and sneak out of the stinky room. Get my head together.

Across the road, a gas station, dark and deserted. The twin towers of a grain elevator—blank-faced country skyscrapers—rise next to the motel on the edge of town. I walk a mile or so into the flatland dark along the two-lane blacktop slicing arrow-straight through snow-speckled fields, westbound. I stop. Far off, low on the horizon, silver-haired Kohoutek shimmers, a fuzzy pendant of light amid a bright dome of stars.

I finger the guitar pick in my pocket, smooth and body-heat warm. It twirls, vibrating like a high E string. Been a long time since that happened.

A & Q

A: Trust.

Q: Is that a new song?

A: Maybe. I do, you know, trust her.

Q: If it helps to say that, then fine.

A: No, like I've been saying, this is it.

Q: Love's easy, trust is hard.

A: I've never known anyone with such an amazing sense of commitment, moral purpose.

Q: So idealistic. But perhaps you are being naïve? You run into her two or three days ago and you're ready to run off and join her circus ... and you've already got your own circus. Don't you think that is moving rather quickly?

A: I'm committing to something here.

Q: This is good, this is good. We're making progress. But you're suddenly going to get smart and be able to pitch that thing?

A: Exactly! Have you seen that paper? *Controlled Statistical Arbitration* ... Jesus. I'm good, but I just don't know if I can be what she wants me to be ...

Q: ... and live up to her expectations.

A: Right.

Q: Natural insecurity. Nothing to worry about.

A: I'm worried about worrying. This is a fork in the road.

Q: So take it.

A: I don't know. But something tells me that what she's got is important and if she doesn't get it out there and get it in front of the right people, the future of all data communications will be changed forever—for the worse!

Q: You made that up.

A: But I wanna believe in her.

Q: Does she believe in you?

A: Sure seems like it.

Q: And what about your brother?

A: Which one?

Back at room number nine, I jiggle the knob quietly, attempting a silent reentry.

Hawgrim has returned, in bed, innocently asleep.

All is normal—choiring snore boys and the scents of men, locker room fresh. But the Plan—it's not where I left it—at least I don't think it is—it's at the foot of my bed flipped open and sprawled on its spine. But the radical *Port Huron Statement*—which I hadn't touched—is half out of the big tan envelope on the floor next to my duffel bag, like a burgling snooper had been trying to stuff it back—and was interrupted.

Everybody looks angelic. The snores continue.

Track 5: Saturday morning

B RIGHT WINTER SUN streams in the big storefront window of a little diner in downtown Benld. The band is crammed into a worn red Naugahyde booth waiting for a late Saturday morning breakfast. It's five to ten the morning after. Creach told us he'd meet us here at ten. Miraculously, we're all here.

I brood and wonder who's been reading in my bed. I'm wired.

Hawgrim slurps coffee and fiddles with the fancy new TI mini-calculator he bought a few days before for only fifty bucks—"goddamn things were over a hundred last year!" He announces that the little electronic wizard—"Look! It's got a memory!"—will help him close insurance deals.

He looks at me. "One always needs an unfair advantage."

Usually wordless Ricky is reading some strange sci-fi paperback—something about androids and electric sheep. He says, "We need to go to San Francisco before it's too late." He returns to his book.[57]

Dave is in a daze, stirring his tea, half asleep. "Strange times," he intones. Then he sneezes elaborately. "Ah-aah-ah-ahah—*flarffff!*" Everyone stares—the sneeze is clearly not bona fide. It's a hidden message sneeze.

"Would you please repeat that?"

Dave complies theatrically. "Heh-heh-eh-eh-*fl-aaa—a-a-r—ffff!*" He blows his nose daintily on a napkin. "Excuse me!"

Hawgrim raises an eyebrow.

Ricky says, "Bless you!"

Dave gives me a look.

So Dave knows.

Then Creach enters the restaurant and, after a dignified little bow and cheerfully charming good morning to the little old lady at the cashier, strides up to our table accompanied by someone who obviously isn't local.

---

[57] It's that Philip K. Dick book, *Do Androids Dream of Electric Sheep?* Ricky's deep. I read it, couldn't get into it.

The man is short and babyfaced with a shaggy Sgt. Pepper-era McCartney moustache, a little pudgy and older than us, maybe thirty or so. Peering through round wire-rimmed Lennon-style glasses and with a slight upper-class overbite, he has the look of an English public school boy who always knew he was smarter than those really good-looking other boys anyway. He's completely underdressed for the bitter prairie winter with only a light brown tweed jacket and a long tartan scarf twirled a few times around his neck that's noosed with a skinny black tie that looks like something my dad used to wear. His starched white-on-white striped shirt with French cuffs and conservative bronze cuff links go quite nicely with his crisply pressed brown slacks and snazzy Italian shoes. A smoldering cigarette with a long precarious ash hangs in his hand in front of him, upturned like Peter Lorre in *Casablanca*.

Regular folks in the diner sit up and take notice—stagy whispers of commentary, including one or two that may have been insulting barbs, float around the place.

With a bit too much morning perkiness, Creach says, "Good morning, boys! Everyone's looking so fine today. Ready for another day on the road, are we?"

I'm not sure that I am. She needs me.

Turning to his guest, he says, "May I present Mr. Rodger Slothwell, Esquire.[58] He has traveled far and wide and this morning comes to us all the way from London! England!"

Dave perks up immediately. Ricky grins. Hawgrim reaches for a business card.

I shake Rodger Slothwell's hand, stand up and excuse myself from the table. I ask Dave if he has any spare change. He fishes some out of his pocket, drops a little pile in my hand. Everyone stares as I slide out of the booth. But Creach smiles and tells me to do what I need to do. As I dash from the table, I hear Slothwell say, "I've gotta coupla quid here, mate! Wotya need?"

I find a pay phone in the back hall of the place between the men's room and the cigarette machine, just a phone on the wall in a little silver metal enclosure and an armadillo cord on the receiver. The hall

---

[58] Pronounced *Slow*-thwell.

is cold since a door is propped open to the outside and a delivery guy is bringing in a load of Wonder Bread and boxes of cigarettes. The long distance operator comes on and I tell her I need to make a station-to-station call. She tells me to deposit ninety cents for the first two minutes.

It rings and rings and rings. I lean my head into the cold phone, drumming my fingers on the cold steel and start talking to the phone, talking to myself, head down, eyes closed. *Sooz pick up, pick up, answer the phone, it would be very nice if you were there right now, please answer, please answer, please answer Sooz.*

There's a tap on my shoulder.

Dave says, "*What* are you doing?"

"Making a phone call."

He rolls his eyes. "To who? *Her?*"

The operator asks, "Shall I keep trying, sir?"

"Yes, please." I look at Dave. "I have to do this."

"Do what?"

"I gotta get a hold of her."

"Why?"

"I just do."

"'Smatter with you? Try again later. This Slothwell guy's important."

The operator comes back on saying, "Sir, no one seems to be there."

Dave says, "C'mon. This guy's *British*."

I thank her, say I'll try later.

The place is busy and the aroma of coffee, bacon, and cigarettes hangs in the air in an eye-level haze. Outside the joint's big window is a big old oak tree—I think about her unrooted tree again and Sooz trying to make the whole thing work, all by herself.

"Dave." I grab his arm and pull him over to the lunch counter. We sit on a pair of swivel seats. He twirls around once and then faces me, suspiciously. He has an unbuttoned beat-up flannel shirt on over a yellow t-shirt with a glitzy design—*Everybody's a Star* in blue sparkles. His hair is pulled back in a ponytail.

"What?"

"I've got to get back to Chicago. Now."

"We *are* going back tomorrow, after the gig tonight."

"No man—now. I need to get back there."

He considers that and tries again. "Yeah, so we go back tonight after the gig."

"No. I mean *now*. What's one lousy gig?"

He slumps over the counter. "Jesus, what the *fuck*? It's her, isn't it—I heard that phone call." He shudders. "What was she *doing* during that weird song you ..."

I can't help but smile, then, "She's got something so big you can't believe it. Earth shaking."

Creach appears behind us and puts his hands on our shoulders. "Is there a problem, gentlemen? Perhaps I can be of some service?"

"Fuckin' Pepper!"

"Mr. Creach, sir, I need to get back to Chicago, like now, sir."

His hand remains on my shoulder and he smiles patiently. "Is there a family problem?" His gaze is fixed on me. Behind him, I see Slothwell holding Hawgrim and Ricky in rapt attention.

"No family problem. I just ... need to."

"Fuckin' Pepper, goddamnit, I can't believe this, *you're* the one who ..."

"Now David, I'll handle this." Creach gets between us and politely pulls Dave up off the stool and points him in the direction of the booth. "Please. Go and have a seat with the boys." Dave leaves, glaring at me, muttering.

Creach sits down on Dave's stool. He is his usual immaculate self—crisp gray-flecked goatee neatly trimmed and a black turtleneck under a dark brown houndstooth sport coat, maroon double-knit trousers with a knife-edge crease. A bit amused, he eyes me over his black-rimmed glasses and then fishes around in his pocket and pulls out his car keys. "Charlene's out there on the street, gassed up and ready to go.[59] You need wheels?" He places the keys—a black leather

[59] Charlene is a 1965 Marlin-blue Buick Electra 225—a Deuce and a Quarter—with plush black interior, power steering, air-conditioning, and power windows. Very luxurious, though the rear windows sometimes didn't work. A survivor of many savage Chicago winters with 110,000-plus miles on her and as clean and well-maintained as Creach could manage, Charlene is showing her age, looking faded, tired and run-down—a collection of city dents had been valiantly hammered back to a reasonable approximation of the original shape, and then coated with primer and paint like cheap makeup.

fob with a dangling enamel Buick logo—on the counter in front of me. "You got wheels."

I stare at the keys and see a wave of guilt and remorse coming at me. "Is your cold better?"

He smiles. "Yes, thank you. My cold is better. But what's going on here?"

"Well, Mr. Creach, I wasn't even thinking about your car. This isn't necessary."

"Then how the hell were you planning on getting back up there?" A very slight hint of agitation creeps into his voice as he pours a little cream into Dave's coffee cup and stirs. "That van of yours sure as hell ain't going anywhere and we, you do have an *obligation* tonight. You—and your band."

Then I tell him that there is something important going down in Chicago *right now* that has to do with the future of all human communications and that she has only reappeared in my life that Thursday night, only two days before and that I am astounded and completely overwhelmed by her and that she needs me right now and that if I don't get to her right now I don't know what will happen to her, me, and the future which keeps slipping farther and farther into the distance. While I say all that he's still placidly stirring his coffee, the spoon tinkling the sides of the cup like a ticking clock. Or bomb.

Creach sighs, "It would appear then, that you are doing your ... what'd I say? ... your *goddamndest* right now." He lays the spoon down, smiling at the waitress as she walks by. Then, like he's testifying late at night on his big bull fiddle, running down a long bass solo in some Southside dive he says, "Music. Women. Women and music. Music and women? It's a problem." Creach shakes his head. "Mr. Porter, come with me. Let's go hear what this English cat's got to say."

I think about it and decide.

I grab Creach's keys, thank him profusely and run out the door, dodging an old pickup as I cross the street.

Charlene, plush as a rich man's coffin and shabbily luxurious, reeks of a thousand old cigarettes. An exhausted air freshener shaped like a Christmas tree, creased with age, hangs from the rearview mirror. I adjust the seat, think about it all again, reaffirm in my head that I'm still doing the right thing, turn the key.

Charlene tries to turn over, struggling. Nothing. I turn the key again. *C'mon.* The big engine works to get going, almost starts almost starts, then nothing. *C'mon, c'mon. C'mon.*

I try again.

Charlene fails.

I try again.

Dead.

I punch the steering wheel.

I look up. Across the street, Creach and the boys in the band are watching. I try to ignore them.

My hand returns to the key.

Then something changes inside Charlene, the air, the vibe, the feel.

In the passenger seat, where just moments ago there was nothing but a new carton of Kools, is the Dark Stranger, silent, imposing in his spooky Bible-black coat, black hat, his blonde hair in a ponytail. True fact. There he is.

Up close, his coat is finely tailored and the fabric is woven in a thick, faultless brocade that speaks of a distant past that has been appropriated to the here and now, a coat as at home in an old weird America as on a tear-down-the-walls rock 'n roll stage. That hat, wide-brimmed with a low crown, has a slight, top hat sheen.

A guitar case is between his legs. Felix. His hands rest on the case's black shoulders, keeping it close. His face. The Dark Stranger's face is pure, cheekbone-chiseled and his skin as unblemished as a cameo portrait. His eyelashes don't quit and his nose, in profile, is familiar and comfortingly prominent. I decide that he really does look like Elliot.

And he is here.

And I am staring at him.

His eyes are on Felix, a relaxed smile on his thin lips.

Sitting on the sofa-soft front seat of Charlene, the only sound is my breathing, air pushing through my nostrils, breathing in, breathing out, rhythmic, fast and steely tense. I can't hear his breathing. I notice that the car's miasma of tobacco is gone, replaced with something faintly sweet, warm summer floral.

Now another man might've been cool, calm, and collected, quietly engaging this physical presence—or dream, Shakespearean spirit, figment or hallucinatory relapse—in a discussion as to the nature of reality and the relation of our physical world to that of pure thought, spirit or mind, then maybe drawing him into a discussion of nineteenth-century transcendentalism or postmodern metaphysics. Don't get me wrong—that would've been a good idea. Or another man might've asked simple questions like, *hey man, how'd you get Felix* or *what was with that weird snowball fight up in Chicago?*

But as Dave would say, *WHAT THE FUCK?*

The only sound in the car is me, streaming and spewing loud, fast, and out of control—"Are you my brother? *Are* you? And if so *why* are you here, what's it all about? Are you really *here*? Am I *completely nuts?*"

I continue.

"I'm so so very sorry it happened how it happened all those years ago, so horrifying and mindblowingly awful that I've never gotten over it and neither has Dave or Mom or Dad, but the damage is done and Dave is damaged I know it's true and the damage is real for all of us and unrecoverable and it's right here every second of every day and this is unbelievable and are you really *here*? Sorry, I've already asked that. Or maybe you're only last night's weed and alcohol talking or some bizarre and sappy Psych 101 relapse and subsequent release of repressed distant but just below the surface memories, virtual or otherwise, and you are what I want you to be."

Poor Elliot, I knew you well.

I just don't know.

There's my breathing again.

The Dark Stranger says nothing. He looks me in the eye. His are deep blue, I think they're Mom-blue, but far away.

He arches a finely shaped blonde eyebrow.

Now, such a gesture can say a lot and prompts many questions. For instance, how high is the eyebrow raised? Is it a single pulse? Is it a staccato series, Groucho goofy, or a sustained, questioning ironic arch? I'm talking about reading and measuring amplitude, frequency, and period—the never-ending attempt to master the inexact and analog science of the oscilloscope that is the human face.

His eyebrow is lifted in a sustained arch, and I think it is of the gently ironic variety because the gesture is not combined with a flattened grimacing mouth that transmits a you-dumb-shit whatsamattayou message. His mouth is slightly pursed in a kind of oh-come-now-really are you still hung up on that smirk.

But maybe not. I try so hard to *see* but my synapses and neurons are flashing at a zillion megahertz per second and I'm overloaded and I just don't know.

We sit there awhile.

I speak up again. I tell him that that sound check was *it*, everything, a pinnacle. As if he doesn't know. It's something I know.

He smiles his smiley smile.

And with that Harpo grin on his face, lightly drumming his hands on the top of the guitar case in a kind of you-got-it send off, he opens the car door with an odd airlock kind of whoosh. The Dark Stranger gets out and disappears.

Just like that.

My ears pop.

But Felix remains. Creach's carton of Kools is still there.

I'm breathing pretty hard.

Across the street in the diner, I see everybody—Dave, Creach, Hawgrim, Ricky, and even Slothwell—wordlessly watching through the big plate glass window.

I try Charlene one more time.

Nothing.

I give up. I sit there for a few minutes. Lucidity and logic return.

That's it.

Then, after carefully removing Felix from the passenger side of the car and locking it up, I cross the street back to the diner, dodging another pickup. I hand Creach the keys. He pats me on the back. I stand in front of the booth.

Dave's face silently screams *what the fuck was that all about?*

Everybody else looks a little embarrassed.

I apologize for the strange interlude.

Creach re-introduces me to Rodger Slothwell who gets up and hands me his card. *Managing Director, Artists & Repertoire, Terpsichorean Records. Muswell Hill, London N10.*

"Rodger Slothwell at your service. A pleasure. May I call you Pepper?" I apologize again for running out. He waves it off, sits back down, and motions for me to sit next to him. Creach pulls up a vacant chair.

Slothwell, his hands warming around a nice cuppa tea, looks quite comfortable and self-assured.

I take an immediate dislike to him. It's as if Slothwell has doused himself in some sort of formula that has all the ingredients guaranteed to annoy me. Maybe it's his perfectly coiffed hair and the way he holds his head, constantly tilting one way or the other as he tries to underline a point or answer a question in a way that is hipper than you, or smiling ingratiatingly while he uses your name just a few times too many. Or the way his hands are constantly moving, making a point, drumming or fiddling with his well-manicured fingernails. Or maybe it is his voice that, despite the always-appealing hard-day's-nightness of a British accent, is clipped, squeaky, and metallically grating. And he insists on calling us "dudes." Or maybe it's his rancidly sweet cologne.

It all bugs me.

My thoughts return to what just happened in Charlene. Then Sooz, out there somewhere.

And I'm ecstatic, I'm depressed, I know exactly what I'm doing. I haven't got a clue. I'm brilliant, I'm an idiot. I know. I don't know.

Slothwell is saying something.

He says, "Well, Pepper my mate, I think you and I are going to get along just brilliantly." His thin lips spread into a toothy grin, revealing a set of small off-white teeth that are slightly out of alignment. "You know, I caught your *show* last night. I was able to *slip in undetected* and I must say that I was *most* impressed. And the bloody hell of it is, I am simply *astounded* at how *full* your sound is!" He speaks slowly and deliberately, placing great laborious emphasis on certain words and phrases, like an Oxford don lecturing about the economics of fourteenth-century English shipbuilding. But I begin to listen more closely, reluctantly beginning to nod and smile as he proceeds. "And the bloody hell of it is—you're only a *four-piece band*. I found myself thinking that there had to be *somebody else* up there!"

A laser beam shoots between Dave and me.

"Are you quite sure there was nobody else up there on that stage with you?" He laughs. We all laugh. "Have you got somebody hidden up there?"

We all shrug. A friendly chuckle.

"But your songs are simply *marvelously melodic* ... and ... and ... and they *kick arse!*"

Everybody agrees. "Yeah! We kick arse!"

"You dudes sound like no one else. And may I say, that I find 'Your Aunt is Cool' to be a breath of fresh air in today's rather stale musical landscape? May I say that, dudes?" He looks around for agreement. "It is a seriously good bit of songwriting, Pepper. And that unusual guitar of yours. So unique! And the bowtie!"

"Thank you very much, Mr... *Slowthwell*—"

"Please ... call me Rodger." He says, *raw-ja.*

"Sorry. Rodger ... I'm curious. Do you find, it, the song I mean, uh ... to be *funny?*"

This question puzzles him. He glances at Creach whose face says *I don't know what he's talking about.* Slothwell replies, "Of course not."

I am beginning to think he isn't so bad.

Over Creach's shoulder, I notice two rather good-looking farm-fresh girls with dark wavy hair parted in the middle, apparent high schoolers attired in what must be their glam best platforms and embroidered bell-bottoms—maybe they're twins—standing over by the cash register looking at us. They are whispering to each other, giggling. I smile at them and they walk over. I realize that they had seen us last night and they are *actual fans*, girls whose only connection to us is the music.

We had actually reached out and touched their young minds.

Then Hawgrim says, "Girls, girls. Hey babes!" He pushes Dave out of the booth, scrambles up and kisses them both, deeply. Then he turns to us with arms around each and says, "We met last night. This is Sunshine ... and this is Luna."

We say hi.

"Go on, Rodger. We're listening." Hawgrim drags over another chair and sits down. One of them, I think it's Sunshine, is on his lap and Luna is draped around his shoulders. Hawgrim tries to look cool.

Then Luna, I think, whispers, "Hi, Dave!" He winks at her. I look at him inquiringly.

Dave innocently mouths, "What?"

Then we spend an hour discussing Slothwell's career. Creach kicks off the discussion, asking, "How about you tell us about Terpsichorean Records and yourself, Rodger?" So Rodger tells us dudes the tale about how he had plucked many lucky bands from obscurity, the Thamesmen, the What, Nigel and the Pub Crawlers, and launched them into the British top of the pops ozone. We had all heard of the Thamesmen, they had had a couple hits during the early British Invasion, "Don't Cross the River (Without My Heart in Your Pocket)" that had a great catchy hook and I could still hear the chorus, and I remembered the What, but not even Ricky knew of the Pub Crawlers and he knows all the obscure bands, American or English. Or Irish, German, Dutch, or French.

Sunshine and Luna are apparently bored and get up to leave. Hawgrim has a brief unintelligible discussion with them and out they go, waving at us through the plate glass window. Dave appears crestfallen.

"Pepper, Nigel and the Pub Crawlers are one of my very recent projects." He sips his tea. "The *Melody Maker* wrote them up a bit last month." He looks to Dave. "David, I think you'd like them—glam, progressive *and* trad English folk rolled into one! *Brilliant*." Everybody nods. "You see, dudes, most bands never *make it* because of three things—terrible songs, poor focus, and *bloody awful songs*."

We all agree. Creach takes off his glasses and cleans them with a napkin.

Slothwell tells us that he thinks Hawgrim is an excellent musician. Who'd've ever thought to use an *accordion* in a *rock* band? *Brilliant!* So imaginative and so powerful and so *expressive*. And then he marvels at Ricky's steady, booming yet delicate heartbeat and he wonders out loud what *sort* of drumsticks Ricky uses. He thinks they sound *rather* like telephone poles, so *fabulously huge*.

"And Dave, may I say that your stage presence, your appearance, voice and … and your … dare I say … *flash* … add so much to the band." Slothwell then goes on and on about Dave's magnetic rock 'n roll personality so much that it gets to be a bit uncomfortable. Hawgrim turns to Dave with a what-the-fuck look on his face and Ricky smiles his usual knowing smile. Slothwell very obviously digs Dave, who is spellbound. While I certainly think that my brother is cool, terribly hip, vital to the band, and a chick magnet, Slothwell's adulation seems kind of crazy and I am becoming re-annoyed.

My bloodshot eyes drift out the restaurant's window. That big oak tree is standing right above Charlene's parking space. Its shriveled brown leaves from last year are still hanging on. Its big roots are buckling the sidewalk. No sign of the Dark Stranger. And then she's back on my mind again.

I am a psycho.

Creach steers Slothwell back to the subject at hand.

"Yes, sorry. Quite." Slothwell gets down to it and says, "On behalf of Terpsichorean Records, I am pleased to be offering you a one-year recording and distribution contract for the United Kingdom and all countries of the British Crown Commonwealth and dependent territories."

Silence.

Hawgrim guffaws, "We barely have US distribution and we're talking about the UK?" Everybody stares aghast at him. Creach looks hurt.

Slothwell says, "I should very much love to be a part of the musical future that you dudes are creating. Yes?"

I look at Creach. His nod and his eyes say *okay with me, man*. I look at Dave and *don't fuck this up* is written all over him.

I say, "Okay."

With everybody laughing, smiling, and slapping backs amid wild promises of stardom from Slothwell and me wondering if I'm doing the right thing, we leave the diner and head to the cars for the drive to the next gig. Creach stops me and asks if I want those keys back, saying I don't look so good—"you look tired, young sir"—and that if I leave it'd be a problem but he, we, would survive. I say no—I'd better play it all out, after all, I can't let my brother down.

Creach asks, "Which one?"

"Good question."

Then I remember that I've got a three o'clock phone date that afternoon with Sooz, though she hadn't reminded me of it during our chat. I know she wouldn't forget that.

By the way, when Creach got back into Charlene, she fired right up.

Track 6: Saturday afternoon

WE'RE DRIVING, back on the road with Dave at the wheel, heading farther downstate through the dead furrows of flatland corn, farther down big old 55 to the gig on the SIU campus in Edwardsville, a suburb of St. Louis, another night opening for Pavlov's Dog. Dave has the eight track blasting serious toonage—the new Yes album again—and Hawgrim and Ricky are loudly playing gin rummy in the back of Otto, slapping cards on an upside-down sizzle cymbal that rattles and buzzes over every bump. Ricky is clobbering him. This outrages Hawgrim since he always figures that he's the smartest guy in the room. He claims Ricky's cheating.

"What was the deal with Creach's car?"

"He was going to let me use it, that's all. Didn't start."

"But what *happened* out there?'

"Probably nothing."

Dave raises an eyebrow and I say I don't know.

"You didn't have Felix when you ran out the door, and you came back with him."

"Strange times." I shrug.

We drive some more.

Then he says that he can't figure me out. *Do I wanna be a rock 'n roll star or what?* I say I do. He turns the stereo down. "Then what the fuck's your problem?" But before I can answer he says, "I know what your problem is—it's this *Susie Creamcheese* chick, that's what it is, man, and like I said before, she's going to get you and maybe the whole bunch of us in big trouble. So what the fuck, man?"

"Don't call her that, man. And I didn't go, did I."

Hawgrim says, "Girls, girls, easy ... easy."

And so, talk of Sooz is now in the open and that's that.

Dave begins to huff and puff. "So let me get this straight ... you were ready to completely jump ship this morning, crawl back to her on some sort of *pussy-whipped* mission to save the world but here you are, graciously consenting to stick it out for ... Jesus ... yet another gig on this measly yet CRITICALLY IMPORTANT TOUR OF TWO GIGS?"

"Fuck off. But yeah, you got it."

"And we are so grateful to you, Pepper, my oh-so-wise and talented brother!"

It occurs to me that the 33-1/3 RPM LP of my life has developed a skip that could make my psychic tonearm and needle jump to a parallel groove on the record—from the groove of *IBM Junior Programmer* to *Rock 'n Roll Band* to *The Mission of Sooz*, three completely different experimental and probably self-indulgent concept albums with just about anything capable of shaking my spinning mental turntable off its rocker—like hearing her voice, a smarmy British record label executive, the smooth tones of Creach, the ecstatic guitar solos of Dark Strangers, or old Buicks—any of that could make my needle jump. And there is no evidence that these record grooves would ever converge.

We drive some more.

After a while, changing the subject, I say, "You know what? Creach *sees*. And he *hears*. He saw everything at the sound check." I lower my voice, "He saw the third mic, like it was some splash of light or maybe a cosmic intersection of psychic consciousness. And he said he'd never heard us play so well."

"Whoa."

"I don't know."

The road underneath our wheels whines—a stretch of swollen expansion strips and cracked concrete rumbles below us like jungle drums. Ricky steadies the cards on his cymbal. The day is still bright and the sun is warming my side of Otto. Brown-slatted snow fences stenciled *State of Illinois* patrol the farm fields, racing along the side of the flat and unbending interstate.

"Yeah, he saw the whole thing and he told me that he's been there, too, he's had strange stuff like that happen to him on stage, you know, back in the day. And he told me to do my *goddamndest*. Keep *it* happening."

Dave whistles. "Do your *goddamndest*. See? This whole thing is transcendental and we are plugging in to … our brother … or something." He thought more about that, marveling. "That's why you're still here ... you're doing your goddamndest. Man. And so are we all. Or are we just nuts?"

Hawgrim, from the back, says, "Both you needledicks are crazy—but it's a catch-22—you have to be crazy to do what we're doing. We're all bozos on this bus." He discards the ace of clubs—always a dumb move—and goes on, "But as I see it, you two think too much. All this metaphysical experience stuff? Shit, we just had a great gig. It was one of those fucking great nights. That's it. Nothing more, nothing less."

Ricky takes the ace and gins.

"Bastard." Hawgrim tosses his cards on the cymbal. Ricky smiles his beatific smile.

"What about Creach? He told me he was right there, saw something, felt it, heard it."

"Fuckin' Creach. C'mon, he's just using you, manipulating you, Boo Boo, building up his talent base, praising you, building empathy. Make you feel like, *yeah, I've got the power!* It's simple management 101." His voice is dry, authoritative, like he's in a district sales meeting. "If he can wring a little more psychedelic *frisson* out of one of his *artistes*, all the better for him. Simple as that."

We all consider the word *frisson*, marveling that Hawgrim came up with it. Hawgrim says, "Hey, I'm pre-law." A half-mile of countryside rolls under us. A string of Burma Shave signs come and go. Ricky shuffles the cards and begins to deal.

Then I say, "I think you're dead wrong, man. Your problem? You're too much of a three-piece-suit wearing, brief-case carrying, insurance-selling, young Republican tool of the system."

"Fuck that. I am indeed a tool of the system. Someday, you'll all work for me."

A hail of verbal and physical abuse rains upon Hawgrim. Ricky grabs Hawgrim's head and delivers a brain crunching noogie.

Dave says, "But back to the issue at hand. You took Creach's somehow sharing our onstage experience as the A-OK to skid off the road and run back up to her to do who the hell knows what? Whatsamatter with you?"

My tonearm jumps again and I ask, "What time is it?"

Ten minutes later we pull off the highway. It's quarter to three and Dave is gassing us up at a big truck stop an hour or so north of St. Louis. We're paying an outrageous $.50 a gallon. I'm inside among the truckers, standing in front of the Hostess display rack, a package of Twinkies in one hand, a pair of cupcakes and their cream-filled goodness in the other, trying to decide. Hawgrim, his thinning hair still showing evidence of the noogie and warily eyeing the place's burly clientele, appears behind me and mutters, "Long-haired rock 'n roll bands aren't exactly the people's choice around here, eh?" He sees what is in my hands. "How can you eat that shit, man? Do you know what they put in them? Jesus."

"I'm hungry. I need a jolt of sugar. We rock stars live hard. You oughta know that."

"Indeed. That's why little chicks like Sunshine and Luna are so important, very valuable service providers." He grabs a bag of granola-something and smugly waves it under my nose and says, "But I have something I need to talk to you about." Lowers his voice, goes on conspiratorially. "I know the bottom-line reason why you were going to selfishly ditch us out here in the wilds of downstate Illinois." Lowers his voice again, "Bad form by the way, old chap."

I turn to him skeptically, upset that he even knows anything about her existence. But it's my own fault, making such a grandstand play that morning.

I say, "Sorry."

"Perhaps I can be of some assistance."

"What?"

And so Hawgrim assumes his entry-level insurance sales-trainee persona[60] and proceeds to tell me that he has also deduced a number of facts.

"Pepper, my friend. May I call you Pepper? I'm kidding, of course." He chuckles. "But seriously ... Pepper, I'm simply putting two and two together here and could be way off base, but it would appear that your, uh, friend has a few ideas of a technical nature that

---

[60] Basic Sales Rules 1, 2, 3, 4, 5, 6, 7, and 8. (Ref earlier footnote re Rule 3): Smile. Establish good eye contact. Confidently outline your prospect's problem. Confidently describe your solution to the prospect's problem. Seek agreement. Attempt a trial close. Get the order. Leave.

may be in need of advocacy or perhaps may benefit from the attention of someone with a bit of business acumen. You're a smart guy, so you know that."

"I don't know what you're talking about."

"Now, now. We're two men of the world." He sniffs. "I freely admit that I just happened to have a casual glance at that very impressive document of hers on your bed last night." He flicks his eyebrows menacingly. "But what I found much more interesting, more provocative perhaps, was that other document—the *Port Huron Statement*, radical *manifesto* of the *lunatic* fringe that just so happens to have her real name inscribed on it—*Susan Frommer*, I believe?"

My heart is pedal to the metal and my skin crawls.

"That name is of some *note*, I believe. And the other name that your charming brother rather cryptically communicated this morning, cryptic but recognizable to a man such as myself. Flarf? A Dr. Flarf perhaps?"

"So what?"

"As you may recall, Pepper, I am a recent graduate of the University of Illinois and strangely enough, I have had the pleasure of the good doctor's acquaintance."

"How could you know *him?* Champaign's huge."

"I'm well connected, even at curiously high levels. But further, I have deduced that your friend is going to be seeking money … investors for some sort of venture based on her ideas. Pepper, I believe I have access to such resources. However, there is the small complicating factor regarding your friend's … uh, background, some minor inconvenient details." He shrugs. "But I'm sure that these can be minimized. Though I could be wrong."

"Fuck off, Hawgrim." He has opened up a creaky door in my head and barged in on this new little secret world inhabited only by Sooz and me, huffing and puffing like the big bad wolf—he's trying out the furniture, sitting on this and bouncing on that and who knows what he could or would do with his little bit of proprietary information—Sooz, Flarf, her plans. The FBI. He could fuck it up.

He smiles and opens his little bag of unpurchased granola. He pops some in his mouth chewing thoughtfully. "But Pepper, my friend. Seriously. I can help. If I may, I'd like to review that document of hers.

Like I said, I know people with the money and the contacts for this sort of thing. Introduce me to her."

The big clock over the lunch counter says three o'clock.

"You aren't getting near her. And I've got to make a phone call. Now."

As I turn to the bank of pay phones down the hall that leads to the truck stop showers, most of the phones marked for "Professional Drivers Only," Hawgrim barks, "You tell her that you've got friends, man. And she needs guys like me. She needs friends!"

I wave him off, nauseated that he seems to know so much, kicking myself for letting it happen and realizing that I had just encountered a new version of the old Hawgrim. It is junior high all over again.

I find a phone with a quarter in the coin return and, believing that to be a good sign, inject some dimes and dial. Her number begins to ring and ring. No answer. I don't wait for the operator to ask. I hang up, surprised and worried. A paranoid chill wraps its arms around me.

Flashy Ralph meets us at the loading dock of the SIU auditorium waving a big white envelope. He's agitated, saying he thought we'd never get there. While Hawgrim and Ricky start to unload Otto, he drags Dave and me to a tall desk next to the big garage doors. The envelope is stuffed full of photos.

"Dave, Peter, you gotta see these pics from yesterday and last night."

"It's Pepper."

Holding a big eight-by-ten black and white photograph close to his chest, he says, "You're gonna dig 'em. I developed all this stuff this morning. This one is from your sound check yesterday. One of my best ever." With a dramatic wave of his hand, he says, "Look at *this*."

The photo is beautifully composed, like a painting from the Italian Renaissance, halos and everything. It'd been shot from behind our backline of amplifiers, the camera facing the two big super-trouper spotlights that were rigged on a couple of platforms at the back of the gym shining on us like two exploding super nova headlights. Dave and I are at the center of the frame facing each other, guitars gripped in our hands, faces lifted to the rafters, each of us silhouetted by one of

the spots, our hair wild rock 'n roll coronas exploding with the electric
energy of "Freakout in Coal City." Between us on the stage is a hazy
shade that is vaguely transparent, but bright, tall and slender like a wavering spear of burning grass, both ends of the shadow are tapered but
the middle is slashed with the rough outline of what could be a guitar
like a bolt of lightning that also pierces both Dave and me. So maybe
it's more like a surrealistic Dali.

Dave shivers and touches my arm.

"Yeah, I don't know what happened with this weird area in the
middle. Sometimes you get lucky and stuff like that happens, seren-
dipitous flashes of magic." Flashy Ralph is very pleased with himself.
"But goddamn, doesn't it look cool?" Dave and I are stunned, silent.
"Look closer. See?"

Dave and I are both lifted from the stage, both caught airborne by
the camera, floating gracefully as any Nureyev arabesque, the flutter
of my open coat, beautifully curved and breaking free of the pull of
gravity while Dave is suspended above the stage, his big bass angled
rakishly toward me like a divebomber, and he, a sharp cheekboned vision of rock 'n roll perfection.

"There's more where that came from, boys." Ralph begins flipping through his stack of shots, placing them carefully on the desk
while we marvel. I pick them up and have a closer look while Ralph
ogles Dave, blowing smoke up his skirt with complements and vague
promises of getting us into *Rolling Stone*.

Fabulous pictures. They make us look better than we have any
right to look. Ancient innumerable and eternally hopeful teenage attempts to have heroic action shots taken of me, Dave, and long-van-
ished bandmates masquerading as John, Paul, George, Ringo, Mick,
or Keith were hopeless failures, doomed dorky love in vain. But these
are worthy of any Madison Square Garden, London, or California
rock 'n roll gods. I smile and jump another groove. I begin to believe
that maybe all this could turn into a steady job. But then I think—just
pictures, just shallow pictures, only rock 'n roll, and I notice I am
starting to think like Sooz.

Then I jump back again. *Hell with that*. Those shots are magic.
They *are* rock 'n roll. They are real and they are me.

Ralph also has glossy contact sheets, pictures not yet enlarged, arrayed in time sequence with a photo lab feel. He hands me a small eyepiece like a jeweler's magnifier and I scan over his photographic chronicle of the rest of the night's concert. I pause over another particularly good one toward the end of our set, taken from the back of the hall near the sound guy's big board. It's an arty shot, the camera off-kilter and overhead stage lights popping starry sparkles with each of us blurred in soft focus musical mayhem. But it's the figures in the foreground that stop me—heads, shoulders, hair, people in profile. There is Creach. There is the sound guy.

And leaning against the wall is Sooz.

 Track 7: Saturday evening

B UT I'M NOT COMPLETELY SURE. It's a young woman in cinematic profile, dark shadow-lit, back-of-the-hall light, blonde hair mostly tucked in a white knit hat like she had just blown in out of the cold night, a beautifully tailored black peacoat draped on the elegant curve of her hips, hands in her pockets, leaning languidly, suggestively, gorgeously—I'm getting carried away—against a wooden rack of round bars that climb the wall, another mysterious gym class instrument of modern teenage torture. I blink a few times and then shift my eye on the little scope, trying to focus just a bit more, zeroing in on this woman.

Is it her?

Her hat is pulled too low.

I look for more.

Ralph had shot a slew of pictures in rapid succession, a long string of stagy scenes from the strange shifting of the camera's oddball point of view, like a rock 'n roll silent movie. It's evident that he was going for a fashion-model *Blow-Up* David Hemming/Michelangelo Antonioni sort of thing, angular and provocative, maybe depicting the futility and loneliness of modern twentieth-century life, contrasting the shallow bourgeois music hall show on stage, garishly lit up beyond any reasonable necessity with the solitary faces and figures shadowy in the background, the searching haunted souls in the crowd symbolizing the masses, the camera looking from here, looking from there, jarring like a Warhol soup can or a psychedelic album cover. But I could be wrong.[61]

I move the magnifier across the contact sheets. The pics were shot from the back of the gym and the possible Sooz chick had drifted from the camera's view. It looked like the song ended. Could've been "Your Aunt is Cool" or it could've been "Burgers in Benton" which, not surprisingly, was a particularly big hit with the crowd that night. They'd all been there, they knew what I was talkin' about—*biting burgers with my buddy in a Buick in Benton, hey!*, just up the road. Started singing along.

It's the last frame, the show is over, lighters are lit—amazingly for us!—held high by waves of arms drifting in the currents of a dark smoky sea, the photo channeling the dreamy energy and the up-lift of the rock 'n roll tide. And there she is, no doubt about it this time—lower right corner of the frame, below the points of light—hat off, blonde short-haired off-duty Bunny Sooz, confident, her lips caught in mid-sentence in what looks like a serious conference with Creach. Two worlds that I had thought unbridgeable, completely disconnected, weirdly intersecting only in that strange railroad dream. My body shakes and rattles while my un-breathing mouth hangs open in a one-eyed gaze fixed on Creach and Sooz.

Then Dave grabs my arm, breaking the spell and, amid a chorus of palm-slapping hey mans and right ons with Flashy Ralph, I snap back into reality and we begin the load-in, setting up all our stuff—piles of amps, drums, and guitars—on stage, once again in front of Pavlov's gear. We're still buzzed from the night before and from the meeting with Slothwell the British weenie. Our energy is way up, our confidence as a band gone through the roof.

But I'm freaked and spooked about Hawgrim. He and I haven't spoken since the truck stop Twinkie/granola incident that afternoon. However, newly professional, I resolve not to let that mess up the music, kill the vibe.

So we do our sound check on stage in the big double-decked auditorium. It's the biggest hall any of us have ever played in. A full-

---

[61] *Blow-Up*. What a movie. No—it was a *film*. 1966 London. How cool was that? And Vanessa Redgrave, too. Man oh man.

blown balcony stretches up high and far away, the building's architecture with smoothly curving interior walls of sandy-colored brick gives the place a modern, clean and sleek feel. A huge Southern Illinois University–Edwardsville round metallic medallion with some Latin motto looms above us.

The disembodied nasally voice of the sound guy, the same guy from the night before, crackles over the sound system like the Wizard of Oz and says, *Okay dudes, let's do this.* After methodically testing every last mic and amp connection—vocals, drums, keys, amps, and monitors—he says, *All right, let's hear it.* I count off "Freakout" with a here goes nothing look at Dave. He smiles his beatific *I am the cosmos* smile.

We get to that part, the bridge of twelve trading but it's normal, a *new normal*, no doubt about it, the tune is now on a higher level but there are no fireworks, no weirdness, just good, competent musicianship, our level of play now distinctly higher. I sing the words hoping for another spontaneous and combustive incarnation of the Third Mic—or something—though my eyes and mind are wide open, scanning the room for her. But she isn't there, just empty seats and bored roadies, a few college kids, the sound guy up in the back amid his knobs, dials, and sliders.

Though I hit all the notes and play all the chords, my head is somewhere else, ruminating on what that photo must mean. She's here, she's not there and why didn't she tell me she had followed us and why doesn't she just appear and then I remember that she's not like everybody else, that she lives a shadow life and, like she said, I'm her way back, her way-back-machine. Or so I think.

The sound guy hollers, *Excellent, we're done* and we split and begin killing time before the show, crashed in a big windowless community dressing room in the basement below the auditorium stage, its whitewashed cinderblock walls plastered with old posters of campus theatrical productions like *Bye Bye Birdie, West Side Story,* and *Death of a Salesman.* Big mirrors lined with Hollywood light bulbs hang on the wall above white Formica countertops, where collegiate stars and starlets, hopeful Tonys, Marias, Conrad Birdies, and Ann-Margrets have worked hard at becoming fabulous and beautiful.

I noodle on Felix, reclined on a neon orange and aqua Naugahyde couch.

In a corner behind the snack bar, Dave props his head on his duffle bag and reads his beat-up *Siddhartha*.[62]

Hawgrim roots around in his briefcase. Ricky snoozes on another sofa.

The big IBM clock on the wall ticks.

After awhile, Pavlov's Dog and their entourage shatter the peace and sweep into the room with easy confidence, their sound check finished. And then guys and chicks and chicks and guys—sometimes it's hard to determine gender difference with the hair, eye shadow, glitter, and rouge—drift around the room, lighting joints, grooving, spreading the invisible fumes of mellowness.

Hawgrim flops down on the sofa next to me, admiring the view. He says, "Next month, we'll have our own entourage." Then he pulls a small brown bottle out of his gig bag and rattles it like a maraca. He flips it to me like a baseball. Amphetamines. "Peace offering, man. Keep you going, fuel for the fire. Medicinal purposes, of course."

I say no thanks and toss the bottle back to him. He pops a couple in his mouth and swallows, no water. He smiles and says, "It's a hard life."

Then he leans closer with his arm up around my shoulder and murmurs, "Rule number ten of salesmanship is to always be persistent, never give up."

I look at him, my guitar noodlings taking a sudden aimless and dissonant 12-tone tack.

"Pepper, my friend, your earlier rather firm, yet puzzling, hesitancy to accept my offer of advisory assistance to that fair damsel of yours—"

I stop noodling. "Look man, she's doing just fine without you."

Hawgrim tries another approach. "I get the distinct feeling that

---

[62] Dave says I'm Govinda, the earnest, ascetic, puppy-like sidekick (though I dispute that) and he's Siddhartha, the noble, charming, and handsome seeker of wisdom. Creach is Kamaswami, the businessman teacher guy, and Ricky is like Gautama the Buddha, sometimes at least because he hardly ever says anything—he just smiles. But Hawgrim is the black snake that bit the beautiful and amazing courtesan Kamala, killing her. He says I'd better watch out. That spooks me and I tell him to keep reading and report back later.

you are fuckin' out of your head with this chick and have lost all sense of proportion. What makes you so sure about her? I mean, what if somebody was to, you know, become, shall we say, uncomfortable with her, uh, her ... *terrorist* past?"

Hawgrim, his natural Hitler Youth rising to his seedy surface, has banged my psychic door open again and begins barging around in the china shop of my mind, getting close to the central crystal pedestal on which Sooz is positioned, vulnerable and innocent in a shaft of my mental light. He sees things he shouldn't see. This pisses me off.

"What the hell do you think you know anyway?"

"I know who she is, I know about her past. I'm just offering to ... facilitate things."

"Bullshit."

"Have you thought this through, man?" Hawgrim revs up, his head and shoulder in a half-shrug that says he knows more than you do. "I mean, those Weather freaks made fuckin' bombs, tried to blow up the Pentagon and instead blew up themselves in that place in New York. They do all kinds of crazy shit. Are you completely blind to that?" He rattles his amphetamine maraca again and his voice gains speed as the drugs take hold. "Is she fucking with you? Just because she gives good head and is a great lay you're ready to put it all aside and validate her get-out-of-jail-free card? Man, is there no right or wrong, no absolute? I am pre-law, you know." He sits up straight, head twitching like a sparrow on a fence scanning the room that's filling up fast with delectable worms. "Man, look at that fox over there on the table. Jesus Christ, what a fine piece of ass."

"Fuck you, Hawgrim, and fuck the horse you rode in on. Fuck your fuckin' pre-law insurance sales bullshit and ... just stay the hell out of it." I jump up off the couch, one hand strangling Felix's neck, the other running wildly through my hair.

"Methinks I struck a nerve. Man, think of all the guys she fucked in the underground, even now ..." rubbing his chin thoughtfully.

"You asshole."

And yet. Not that I am some dumbshit Galahad preserving her honor or anything like that, though that has a certain appeal. Not that in the last few days I hadn't thought about the black and white and shades of gray, and sometimes had trouble with it all. Not that I could put it out of my mind and change the channel just like that. Though that's exactly what I try to do. I flip my psychic antenna to the Sooz I know and the Sooz I want her to be and the Sooz she says she wants to be and her dream of changing the world and her dream of being free and my dream of being part of that future and I think—is that really my dream? And like my little old song says, dreamin's done because she entered that warm little hutch in the Playboy Club and I sang for her and everything changed. Is that it? The static of doubt sometimes sneaks in and ruins my reception.

Hawgrim says, "Just sayin' ... and hey. Let's have a good gig." He gets up, buzzed and scattered, and wanders off in the direction of the chick on the table.

Then the lead Pavlov Dog, a scarecrow skinny guy with blue-streaked black freaky hair and an all-black stage get-up, wide bell-bottoms, and crushed velour shirt with embroidered silver penta-grams, comes up to me and eyes Felix. "Nice guitar."

I shake his hand. It's like a dead fish. Quietly, Pavlov says, "Hey, man. Dig your music."

"Thanks, man. Dig yours."

He points to his throat, whispering something about saving his voice. He turns and vanishes in the crowd. It's a nice gesture. I start to calm down.

A stereo blasts Motown. Fat Phil from KXOK shows up again and begins handing out *KXOK Good Guys* t-shirts. He puts his arm around my shoulders and like a kindly uncle says, "Dig your music. That Aunts tune of yours? You might have a hit on your hands, son." He hands me a t-shirt, grins, and asks me if it's "aunts" or "ants." I am about to explain when somebody starts singing "If I Were a Rich Man" like the night before and Hawgrim and Dave jump up to join the sudden kosher conga line winding around the room. Fat Phil hops in line, too.

I don't.

I grab a Busch Bavarian from a tub of ice and crack it open. There are new bodies on my sofa so I sit on the cold floor in the corner and open the Plan, returning to where I left off the night before. I figure why not? Everybody knows about it now.

Ricky appears above me, moon-faced and frizzy-haired, in a

KXOK t-shirt, un-tucked and hanging over his big gut and ripped jeans, a pair of drumsticks sprouting from his hip pocket. Smiling gently, he leans down and says, "You know, I saw it, too."

"Saw what?"

"You know, *it. IT.* At the sound check yesterday."

I lean back on the scratchy wall and stretch my legs out on the floor. "Yeah?"

"Yeah. You can see a lot from behind a drum set ... by observing, I mean. I've seen a lot."

A little peace and serenity flows from him into me. I put the Plan down, relax a bit and gaze around the room—bodies strewn everywhere, the conga line snaking between over and through them. I cross my legs in a meditative way and say, "It was wonderful. But I just don't know what it was, man." The line passes in front of us. I let them go by and then say, "You should see the pics Ralph took."

I space out and again think of her in the back of the room, all that time, right there.

Ricky squats down in front of me, an oddly floral scent floating about him. "I know. You just gotta keep going, man."

We both nod at each other.

"Don't let him get you down."

"Who?"

"Him. *Him.*"

"Hawgrim?"

He puts a big hand on my shoulder, leaving it there like a fluffy pillow. "Don't get off the track." Then Ricky smiles, stands up and turns away, carefully placing the beer can on his head. He rejoins the cast of *Fiddler On the Roof*, artfully twirling a drumstick in each hand and spilling no beer. Later I see him kibitzing like old buddies with Fat Phil.

Then Creach appears, smiling and confident, and makes his way through the crowded room. He catches my eye, winks, and says, "Time to go."

We're in the hall, then climbing stairs.

"You were talking to her last night!"

"Who?"

"Her! Uh, a friend of mine, there's a picture, back of the hall."

Puzzled. "I talk to a lot of chicks. You expecting someone?"

I let it go.

Minutes later we're standing backstage waiting. Fat Phil taps me on the shoulder and I almost don't recognize him. He's more in charge, more a figure of power, like he lost a little weight, his ratty t-shirt replaced with an open-necked striped shirt, plaid double-knit pants, and a snappy blue blazer, the sort that Creach might even wear. He pops a little white pill in his mouth and says, "This is bigger than you think, kid." He shakes my hand and has another look at the crowd. Then, to everybody he says, "Rock your asses off, boys."

The house lights are still up in the auditorium while a beach ball bounces around the crowd and the sound system plays Doobie Brothers' tunes from their second album—*whoa-oh-oh, listen to the music, whoa-oh-oh, listen to the music.* Dave closes his eyes, breathing deeply and murmuring *the bliss of the heart cannot be stated in words.* Hawgrim flashes his eyebrows at me and trims his fingernails, nervously chewing on a toothpick and Ricky, with drumsticks stuck in his bushy hair like a headhunter, winks, juggling three dirty tennis balls that he found somewhere. I touch the Elliot dent and wonder if she is out there.

Fat Phil says *go!* and we hit the stage—me and Dave plugging into our amps, Hawgrim setting himself up behind his keyboards and strapping on the Baldoni, Ricky climbing onto the drum riser, sticks twirling, tennis balls bouncing away behind the curtains.

The Doobies tunes hush, the lights in the hall go off and immediately whoops and cheers skitter up and down the aisles and it's dead dark except for exit signs and the jewel lights on our amps glowing like little blue and red stars. Lighters flash like summer fireflies in the crowd, flaring, blinking, then snapping shut, dovetail joints begin to burn and the sweet smoke of finely cut grass begins to float, wisps from Aladdin's rock 'n roll lamp. The crowd revs up in waves of happy chaotic noise, stomping, stamping, and hands being put together. Ricky smoothly tests his drums, booming and rolling across his mic'd toms, cymbals, high-hat, and snare, while Hawgrim and Dave whip off loud gut-shaking licks. With Felix in hand I turn from my amp to face the audience, but after the bright fluorescence of backstage and the sudden blackout, I am a blind man in need of a rock star seeing-eye dog. Then a soft touch on my arm guides me to the center stage mic and time slows like a turntable spinning from 33-1/3 to 16 RPM and, as I stand in front of my microphone adjusting the stand with Felix slung Clapton-cool behind my back, and as the big lights bloom from the side of the stage and from the back of the stage and as the monster spots from high overhead light up on me as Ricky kicks off the splashy drum intro to "American Dirt" and, as I now seem to be seeing and hearing it all in slo-mo, I notice something different about the crowd as I smile and greet them—*hey SIU!*

Like scraggly birds on a fence in front of the first row of red felt theatre-style seats, leaning on the stage at my feet are wide-eyed faces, expectant, jostling for elbow room, happy, laughing, shouting, drumming hands on the worn wood of the stage floorboards in front of our fancy big black sound monitors shoulder to shoulder in a loud long-haired crush. There are college kids, almost identical in their parted-in-the-middle shaggy hair, and I realize that they all look like me. I mean *really* look like me, because a lot of these kids are wearing white shirts with red, blue, or green bowties just like mine, and there are kids with Felix the Cat t-shirts and even dinner jackets, and they are hootin' and hollerin' my name. I see other kids with blue cowpie hats just like Dave's yelling his name, and there are even some girls screaming for Hawgrim although they could've been those Sunshine and Luna chicks from Benld—it's hard to tell and they're probably drunk—and then with Ricky's drums and Hawgrim's Baldoni and my brother standing next to me thumping bass and the entire first three or four rows of kids going nuts, hands reaching forward like starving fans looking to me because I have something they dearly want and dearly need—news from the front, word from the land of rock 'n roll, broadcasts from some place called Pepperland—I begin to play and dig into Felix's six silver strings. As the sound takes me floating in a comforting puffy cloud I know exactly what to do and I know that I can give it to them because they are already giving it to me, forming a perfectly symmetrical mandala, a perfectly efficient transfer of energy—a give and take balancing act just like old Doc Thompson's second law of thermodynamics—and the energy level grows and grows and becomes self-sustaining, limitless and impossibly perpetual and anti-entropic, and the band plays on and the kids even know the words to "Your Aunt is Cool" and the kids are alright.

And it goes like that the whole gig.

The Pepper Porter look-a-likes, the Dave cowpie fan club, the Hawgrim chicks and the calls for Ricky drum solos—they open up my head, climb inside and set up camp, and we play our goddamndest and we do indeed rock our asses off. Creach, standing in the wings with one of his big stogies, a fat cheroot smoldering in his teeth, watching and appearing serene and confident with Rodger Slothwell at his side who is grinning and holding another one of his Peter Lorre cigarettes in his upperclass hand, with a very slight nod of his head, motions for me to go farther—go *furthur*[63]—and take this crowd with me. And I understand and I do.

After it's all over and we're outside buzzed and whooping it up on the loading dock, piling our gear in Otto, and after Slothwell reaffirms his fervent commitment to us pledging Terpsichorean Records' undying support in the British Isles and all Dominions of the Commonwealth as per our verbal and gentlemen's agreement saying *right on, dudes,* and after Creach congratulates us all saying that Fat Phil is going to be all over our little record and is hungry for more, I grab Felix's case and wander down the campus sidewalk looking for a little solitude and dark fresh air.

Creach calls out, "Mr. Porter."

I turn, still juiced and amped up.

"Lovely evening, young sir." Pleased, he relights his cigar. "And remember what I told you."

"You mean about my goddamndest?"

In a Cab Calloway showbiz sort of way he jives and grooves in his low-down on-stage voice, "Music and women. Women and music." Smiling, "We'll meet again. Soon."

I jive right back at him.

But despite the fine groove of the glorious night on stage and the unbelievable display of sudden crazy fans—those kids who had somehow grabbed a part of us, made it their own and run off with it—a grim gloom rises on my other horizon. It's the darkness of Hawgrim and everything he could, would, or might do to her. I decide right

---

[63] Author Ken Kesey, accompanied by a lunatic bunch of proto-hippies including Kerouac's *On the Road* buddy Neal Cassady, drove a psychedelically painted school bus across the country in 1965. Its destination was painted just above the windshield—*Furthur.*

then that I could be, should be, must be with her, and that any doubts he may have tried to plant in my mind are evil and aggressive mental stink bombs designed to increase my paranoia and bring her crashing down. I shuffle those foul cards to the bottom of my mind's deck, throw them on the floor and move on—but even so, Hawgrim is on the loose and I believe that he is capable of great treachery.

I look up and breathe deep. The late winter stars flicker bright in the cold night. I walk on. Not far away, under one of the matching campus streetlights, I find a stone ledge that contains a line of bushy evergreens, a hedge guarding some big classroom building. I put Felix down and hop up. It's hard and a little lumpy but it feels good to rest my bones. Some kids mosey by, flying high stoned and happy. Then something flashes over my head, something small, dark, and fluttery—a bat! In winter! Then another. And another. Bats—strange and rare, and I think them creepy harbingers of the shadows I feel building. They circle above my head a few times like they are listening and watching, little inky spies on some twisted mission, and then they skitter off toward the loading dock.

Then a cold wind kicks up and a wave of ancient dead leaves rattles in the street, streaming in front of me as if somebody had flipped on a giant fan. I look up the street into the wind and under a huge old oak tree still festooned with the dried brown remnants of last year, a car is parked—a big one, like a police car, idling, exhaust drifting in the now steady and stiff wind out of the west. The car's headlights flash once, then twice, and then again, short short short long and then short long long long, like a coded rhythm signaling something at somebody. I look around. But there is nobody else—just me and just the car. The headlights flash again in a different pattern and then stop.

I think about it and wonder if I am about to be mugged. Or maybe it's just a bunch of harmless potheads or maybe I'm just missing something.

The car door opens and someone tall and slender in a long dark coat gets out, closing the door quietly, carefully placing the car keys in a shoulder bag, then turning and walking toward me with a confident pace, an elegant fashion-show stride with boots clicking on the sidewalk one in front of the other in a clipped well-trained single file. A woman. I stand up. She passes under a streetlight and stops, maybe fifty yards away. The wind flutters the hem of her form-fitting coat and I catch a whiff of a sweet floral scent, probably not hers but so what? She lifts a hand to her head, holding onto her white knit hat as another gust swirls up, carrying more leaves and winter grit.

"Pepper!" Her voice echoes like a *Stella!* on the empty street as she stamps her feet on the cold concrete in a hot flamenco and she cries again, louder, "Pepper!"

"Sooz!"

And as if we are in a hopelessly romantic and corny love story movie, we run to each other, arms wide open, catching and twirling, spinning and laughing, lips in a deep lock not caring that we're not on a beach somewhere but are marooned on a March-gray college campus in downstate Illinois. I lift her off her feet and place her on the long ledge—she thrusts her thigh between my legs and our mouths are tongue-entwined, my hand on her cold cheek, the other below her bell-bottomed hips.

We come up for air. I ask, "Why the dramatic entrance?" and she says, "For fun!" Her hat falls off and we take a breath and then restart. After an age, the kiss softens and slows like the end of a smoky jazz cat solo and then our lips part and our foreheads touch in a glorious smile of peace and love. It feels so good.

We're both still breathing hard when she whispers, "Pepper, we've gotta go. *Now.* We've gotta go, Pepper."

"Where?"

"Flarf."

And I don't hesitate. I say yes and we run to her car, jump in and we tear out of Edwardsville.

Side 4: She's a rainbow

 *Track 1: Later Saturday night*

WHITE CASHMERE turtleneck sweater draped loose around the perfect curve of her neck under the sleek black peacoat I saw in Ralph's photos with blue-jean bell-bottoms over dark leather boots—she doesn't look like an enemy of the state. Her platinum blonde Bunny hair relaxed and free—the tight curls of her satiny cottontail get-up softened and brushed back, and the complete absence of her fancy makeup allows flashes of the old summer Sooz to rise to the surface, replacing her working state of Grace. I reach over, put my hand between her legs, kiss her neck while she tries to keep one eye on the road. She resists. She gives up, we screech to a halt bouncing up on the curb in front of a chemistry lab as I crawl across the big seat and my lips cover every inch of her fabulous face as she very deftly keeps one foot on the brake. I allow her to put it in park.

After a few minutes steaming up the windows, I sit back and she puts on a pair of glasses with big elegant wire frames.

"I need them when I drive, particularly at night."

I think they look great on her, studious and no nonsense like the mousy librarian in the movie who morphs into the knockout bombshell, bowling the boys over—she's a movie scene running backward. Flutters her eyes. "Don't you think Doctor Flarf will like them?"

I say yes.

She says, "Let's go."

We drive.

We emerge from the campus and at a deserted stoplight Sooz reaches her hand to my cheek and breathes, "Pepper." I take her hand and kiss it, amazed yet again that she is where I am, right there, right here. I hold on.

Empty suburbia, dark fast-food joints, gas stations, and funeral homes.

"How come you don't play my song at your gigs?"

"So you *were* there."

"Both nights. And you guys are *good*. So good. And I saw all those kids with the bowties. Unbelievable! Can I be a member of your fan club?"

"Why didn't you tell me you were there? Why all the sneaking around?"

"I'm so happy that you're starting to make it. Aren't you excited?"

I tell her I'm ecstatic and that the music is really happening now. I tell her about the sound check, which is, as I think more and more about it, a hugely important moment although it still remains a mystery.

She looks a little skeptical … though trying to be supportive.

"Who or what do you think it is, the third mic I mean?"

I hesitate. She'll probably think I'm nuts. "I think … it's Elliot, my little brother, or something."

She looks at me wide-eyed and funny.

"These are strange times. Remember I told you about that Dark Stranger guy and my guitar Felix and how he mysteriously reappeared?" She nods and then a creepy feeling that I'm forgetting something important opens up the bottom drawer of my mind. I go on. "And you come back in my life? Ever since that guy showed up, miraculous things've been happening—the band really gets going, we've got a sort of hit record—it's like *magic*."

"I've been thinking about this—your dark stranger person … your little brother or … whatever? This is *very* bizarre." We drive in silence for a bit waiting for the interstate to appear. "Look, I'm very much an empiricist, a show-me-the-data realist—but this makes no sense at all." She gives me a look. "Not that I think you're crazy, but this is so fascinating, weird, and unexplainable—it's a commentary on the nature of reality."

"Unreal reality?"

"How do we really know?"

"This could all be a dream."

"I thought dreamin's done."

At the next stoplight, she puts the car in park, leans over and tells me everything is going to be all right, yes it is, plants a big wet kiss on me, this time her hand down where it counts. Since there isn't anybody else at the light, we cycle through a few hot greens and heavy reds. Finally, she leans back calmly smoothing her hair in the rearview mirror. I clear the inside of the, again, very steamed up windshield with my sleeve.

We move out again.

The big old interstate looms in the distance with traffic flowing across the overpass like a gasoline-powered river, we speed up the on-ramp to I-55 northbound.

Sooz handles the big rental car like a pro—it's a new black Ford Galaxie with power everything, including the windows, which I can't resist playing with. She tells me to cut it out but notices my admiration for her driving and says, "I've had plenty of practice driving fast cars you know." She checks her rearview mirror again, turns in her seat performing a quick scan of the following traffic, eases in and then pins the cruise control at fifty-seven miles an hour, just over the annoying new gas-saving national speed limit. "Fifty-five is so slow. But there's certainly no need to stand out around these parts." Cautious. "You and me? We're happy, law-abiding citizens—a perfectly normal couple out on a late Saturday night drive." She looks at me doubtfully, "Not that you look the part." Then she orders, "Fasten your seatbelt."

I ask her, "What was all that headlight flashing stuff back there?"

"Oh, I was just trying to send you a message in binary.[64] You know, digital code. Didn't work, did it."

"No. I'm analog."

"I love when you talk like that."

We have a high-tech laugh.

Sooz flips on the radio. "No FM in this thing." Like she cares. "But I did hear your song this afternoon on the local station down here! KXOK?" More supportive support. "I really like the hard hitting way it deals with the plight of women and the poor in our male-dominated patriarchal society." She gives me a look. "I'm kidding. Really. I'm very proud of you."

I am very happy about that.

---

[64] It's the gut language of computers that tells the machine what to do. The ones and zeros. 0011 1010 or 0101 1110. Stuff like that. I would've needed my little old assembler handbook to figure out whatever it was she was trying to say. She never did tell me. I wonder if I'll ever understand my own internal machine language.

We're floating on a well-upholstered, gas-powered sofa rolling down the highway, the road beneath the big Galaxie's wheels very distant, very quiet. It is nicely bland. Like a Velveeta cheese product.

"So that really was you in that picture talking to Creach?"

"Yes. He and I had a very nice chat. Couple, actually. Man of integrity. You're lucky."

She says she decided to follow me downstate the morning after our glorious reunion—she figured that since I was going to be at least within a hundred miles or so of the U of I and Champaign, she'd whip in, pick me up, train me, and we'd go see Flarf—it'd save time—and time waits for no one. So, with her veteran camp counselor's innate sense of order and planning and after renting the car (she said that's easy, you think I don't have a real ID or a credit card?), she found Benld and then Creach, and asked his permission to shanghai me after the last show. Then we'd drive like hell, stopping only for coffee and truck stop breakfasts while she would direct me in a crash training course on the ins and outs of controlled statistical arbitration, preparing us for what she hoped would be a meeting with the good Doctor Flarf, a chance to give him the technology pitch at his home the next day since she had reason to believe he'd be around on a Sunday.

She says she certainly didn't want to appear at our gigs like some groupie chick and risk screwing up the vibe of the band, distracting me. But more importantly, she didn't want to broadcast her existence too much anyway, though she had had a good feeling about Creach from the little I told her before. So she layed low, standing in the shadows, but couldn't resist that middle of the night phone call. "I had to do it … you know … after your concert, I was so proud of you … and it made me hot. I had to hear *my song.*"

I think about the strange power of that song, the effect it has on her, the phone call and then I think it better to put it out of my head for the time being, save it for later because something is beginning to stiffen uncomfortably.

"So what does Creach know about all this?"

"Nothing … and everything. I don't know …" She pauses, drumming her fingers, her long nails clicking on the plasticky Ford steering wheel. "As soon as I tracked him down in that gym in Benld I got this strange sense of déjà vu, you know? It was kind of like I had been there before with him … and you … and he knew I was coming and knew the reason why. I don't know, probably just another one of your weird unexplainable things."

She may be empirical, cool and analytic, but I know that she's got her own magic bubbling right below her hard-wired surface.

"Dave would say it's all very cosmic."

"Would he? And what would Pepper say?"

I look out the window at the flat black fields, a few lights of remote farms flicker on the dark horizon, a distant foreign coast. Then, far behind us, a siren wavers in rising tones, approaching fast. Sooz watches her mirror. "Trooper." With both hands on the wheel she breathes quietly, her eyes triangulating between the speedometer, mirror, and the road ahead. "Commence waving and smiling," her voice clipped and tight, her hands strangling the wheel.

I turn, watch the flashing red lights scream toward us, cars and trucks moving aside like the majestic parting of downstate prairie waters. My pulse races, my hands begin to shake. The state trooper's cruiser roars toward us, a big Ford nearly identical to ours, a blinding lightshow stabbing my face and the back of Sooz's head. Coming after us.

The trooper flies by, vanishing in the darkness up the road.

"Jesus. I'll never get used to that." Sooz slumps in her seat, grabs my hand and hollers, "Paranoia is not healthy for children and other living things! Do you understand that, Pepper Porter? Do not give into it," trying to convince herself.

I hold her hand in both of mine. Cold.

We drive a few miles. She shakes herself out, perks up again. She withdraws her hand. "Okay, where were we?" Pats my leg. "Yes, what would Pepper say about my déjà vu thing with Creach?"

I resettle back in the black velour cushiness of the seat. "Pepper would say that he's worried about Hawgrim."

"That strange-looking accordion and keyboard player you've got? I'd be worried about him, too."

"No, really."

I finally get up the courage to tell her about my little chats with him and how he scanned part of the Plan and saw the *Port Huron Statement* with her name on it and how he had caught Flarf's name and all that and made what I thought was a bogus offer, like he was really interested in her technology and that he could certainly provide useful contacts, but gee, there's the matter of her awkward background—"What? Goddamnit Pepper!" Waving her hands. "How could you …"

"I know, I know, I'm sorry …"

"… do such a thing?"

"It was so stupid. I shouldn't have left the motel room."

"Jesus, this is bad. A simple thing, *keep it secret* and now … Christ."

I am an idiot.

She massages her forehead and scrunches her nose. "Maybe this was a mistake."

"No. It wasn't."

"Maybe I shouldn't have been so impatient and raced down here on this … lunatic mission. Or maybe I shouldn't have gotten you mixed up in this. It's just like me to be this way."

She accelerates, aggressively changes lanes, blows by a string of semis. We're hauling ass now.

"Sooz, this wasn't a mistake. We can make it work. Slow down."

I tell her that it's highly likely that Otto, with Dave at the wheel, Hawgrim riding shotgun, Ricky splayed in the back like a bear rug, is somewhere on this very road not that far behind us—Dave worrying about me and Hawgrim navigating and probably guessing that I'm with *her* headed to Champaign and Doctor Flarf.

On the other hand, I tell her maybe not. Maybe they're just wiped out after the gig, snoozing in some motel room or more likely tearing that motel room apart with a delectable throng of fanatic fans like Sunshine and Luna, and they'd just stagger back to Chicago tomorrow or who-knows-when, forgetting that I'm even gone. After all, Hawgrim does have his Monday morning insurance sales meeting and he's been telling us he's going for *salesman of the month*. What could be more important than that? She says, "What are you talking about?" I say it doesn't matter—our time is at hand and it is time to move.

We drive for many miles in silence.

I tell her that she and I need to get down with the crash course now. No time to waste, no time to worry about the outcome, the future of all data communications is at stake and we aren't going to screw it up. We're going to meet the good Doctor Flarf who I'm sure will see us and we're going to do that within the next twelve hours.

She's still pissed off and looks freaked. She's cool, but more vulnerable than I've ever seen her. I don't want to see her like this again.

"Want me to drive?"

She looks in the mirror again, hunted.

"Stop that. It's not helpful. C'mon. Pull over and we'll switch."

We pull over on the shoulder, crunch to a halt amid the scattered gravelly man-made interstate debris. By the trunk of the Ford she holds me tight while cars and trucks sail by pushing wooshing columns of air, the windy wake of the big old highway.

"Too late to stop now, eh Mister Rock Star?"

"It is."

"You dumb little shit."

That makes me feel a whole lot better.

As I merge back into the stream of traffic, I check our tail, keep an eye on the mirror.

I set the cruise control. "Now, let me have it."

For the next two hours with the dome light lit, her paper and a black notebook that she says is extremely important on her lap—*my brains are in here*—Sooz, in a very well-organized manner, walks me through the finer points of her theory of controlled statistical arbitration—how a given communications media could be shared in a simple, orderly, and mathematically elegant fashion. Any concern I may have had about her fragile state of mind quickly evaporates. She is precise, demanding, and surprisingly patient, her grasp of the subject and her encyclopedic knowledge of computing and vision of what it could be is monstrous, and I am once again awestruck by this woman. But I'm good at this stuff, too, and I trail along behind her, picking it up while she drills me again and again on her big picture metaphor of the unrooted tree, how connectionless datagrams work, and the math behind her algorithms.

I'm tired. My eyes are growing dim. Up ahead, the Dixie Truckers' Home appears, lit up like a Coney Island in the flatland dark. We swing onto the exit ramp.

And that's when I remember.

"Felix!"

I left him on the street where Sooz picked me up.

I'm pounding the steering wheel, screaming, hollering, hyperventilating in a most unhealthy way.

By the time we pull into the big Dixie lot—she tells me to park it over there by the corner of the building so we have at least two exit routes, front and back—I'm freaking out in a full-blown panic attack with Sooz trying to talk me down like I'm coming off some bad acid, and she seems to have some experience in this. I am miserable and morose, saying that I'll never write another good song never ever and I'll never be able to sing again and the little Elliot dent is gone and how will I ever hear him again and that all is lost.

She says that this is ridiculous, suggests that we go back and get him and I say no, of course not, that'd be nuts, it's been too long and who knows what's happened to him by now.

Then I say, "I'll call the police. Ask them to check it out."

Sooz is horrified.

"C'mon, it won't be connected to you. I have to try."

She says all you need is caffeine and food and, given the way things have been going for me recently, she's sure it'll all work out.

First thing in the Dixie, I make an expensive call to the Edwardsville Police Department, talk to some bored middle of the night desk dispatcher who tells me that they'll have a car go out, have a look. She tells me to call back tomorrow. I hang up the phone, kicking myself for being so stupid.

 Track 2: Early Sunday morning

IT'S AROUND TWO in the morning and we're sitting in a booth by a big plate glass window at the Dixie. Sooz asked if we could sit over *there* ... a booth with easy access to both the back hall and its rows of pay phones, restrooms, showers, and the exit to the other side of the building where the big rigs are parked. To me she murmurs that this is a strategic location. The bored hostess has no problem with that, tosses us menus, pours us coffee, leaves us in peace. Naturally, the Professional Drivers' section, the counters where service is extra quick and extra good is unavailable to us. Probably just as well.

"Pepper, there's this idea I have that I haven't really been able to articulate too well. It has to do with the notion that the more people that are connected to something, like the phone system, the more useful it is. The more valuable it is." She dumps a load of sugar in her coffee.

I'm trying to get Felix out of my mind so I say, "Go on."

"Okay. For instance, who cares about a phone system with only two phones in it? Or ten or even a thousand? So what? It might be technically interesting but not overwhelmingly *useful*. There're only so many connections that can be made in such a limited network."

Sooz, rolling again, sips some coffee, draws a picture on a napkin of lots of little telephones all interconnected in a dense maze of lines, no central point of control, all equal all free, any-to-any communications. She points to the phones. "Now think of these as *computers* instead of phones. Think *little* computers, you know, like we talked, think about one of your very own, like it's *personal*, you know? Now if there are big numbers of these things, users of this network, really *big* numbers, then the power of that universe of connections—the network becomes *hugely valuable*."

The waitress appears with our food, I snarf my plate of greasy eggs, bacon, sausage, grits, and toast—I'm starving—and Sooz, who ordered a double cheeseburger—"Hey, I'm hungry and where is it written that a girl's only supposed to eat rabbit food?"—shrugs off my raised eyebrow when I remind her that she actually is a Bunny, dunks the edge of her big burger in the puddle of ketchup next to her fries and, with her mouth full, says, "The girls at the Club hate me for this."

I shake my head in wonder.

Her mouth half full. "What? It's a truck stop!"

Sooz dabs the corner of her mouth daintily with a napkin, goes on.

She flips the pages of her notebook, finds the mathematical formula that lays her network concept out. "See? More people will want to connect because more people are connected, everybody wants to participate and communicate, wants to hear what's going on and it will multiply, the power of the people squared, cubed ... exponential growth. And we are no longer just sheep at the mercy of the corporate mainframe computer priesthood, and more people can communicate and actually use their own computers and then ..." She slams the table.

The silverware jumps. "… we can actually *change the way people communicate!* It's a fundamental, historical *paradigm shift*, from analog to digital. It'll be like Gutenberg, like …"

"The Industrial Revolution!"

"Quantum mechanics!"

"The Beatles!"

"Yeah."

"Yeah."

"Yeah."

She bangs the table again.

The waitress looks up, comes over to clear our table. "You kids doing okay?" Sooz smiles sweetly, apologizes, asks for a refill. Sooz talks quietly with Diane the waitress about how things are going at the Dixie, how're tips, are the truckers good to her, what's management like. They chat about stuff like that for a bit and Diane warms up, tells us to stay as long as we need. She likes Sooz. Who doesn't?

She looks at me. "I'm a waitress, too, you know."

"But you've got that extremely nice tail. And bunny ears, too."

She smirks and pats my hand patronizingly. "Moving right along. So this network thing, this effect I'm talking about? It's only heuristic."

"Yeah, yeah."

"Kind of a guesstimate calculation but it's also what will help get this thing built. It's numbers like that that attract *the money*. Flarf will appreciate that."

And again, she says we'll need to be careful about the power of the money to both corrupt and do good.

"I worry about what's going to happen when we're in charge."

"Who's we?"

"Us. Our generation. There's you and me. And then there're people like this Hawgrim guy. God knows what he'll grow up to be. And frankly, God knows what *we'll* grow up to be. We're not all one big happy Woodstock nation, you know. And I'm not all that sure about the world we're going to inherit. It's not like it's mapped out or anything." She swirls her coffee and says, "We'd better not screw it up."

"We'd better not screw *this* up," tapping her tome. "C'mon. Let's keep going."

I yawn.

Then she yawns.

But we plunge on further into her Plan, further into the weird arcana of Sooz's mind where she controls the direction of flying electrons, sorts it all out and hears their music, making it useful and good.

There's a break in the action as she settles back against the beat-up brown vinyl of the booth, rubs her eyes, puts her head between her hands slowly massaging her temples, thinking. I slump against the cold windowsill and gaze out into the parking lot—only one or two cars gassing up. Traffic is sparse out on 55.

I think about Felix again. It drags me down.

I say, "Let's get going."

She doesn't answer. Instead she straightens up and looks me in the eye, quizzically, like she's trying to see me with new eyes. It's an intense look, like she's trying to peer inside my brain. I sit up, too.

She raises her hand and touches me gently right between the eyes, leaving her finger there for a few seconds.

"What's going on in there, Pepper Porter?" She taps my head, leaves her finger there for a few seconds and then withdraws her hand. I close my eyes. "What is happening in Pepperland?"

I breathe quietly, find myself completely relaxed and calm, like a bit of meditating Dave has appeared in me. I probably look like a goof. But I am thinking how lucky she is to have her path illuminated so clearly.

She asks, "Is there a map in your head?"

There is. But I've spent my life trying to figure it out, yanking it from the glove compartment of my mind when nobody's looking, unfolding it, refolding it, getting it wrong, getting it right, protecting it from the gusts and storms and powerful magnetic fields all around me, then orienting it along mysterious unseen latitudes and longitudes. Music is my pole star and Sooz my sun and moon. And computers, Jupiter.

"Do you know where you're going?"

"No."

I open my eyes. She is still gazing at me very intently. She smiles and looks out the window. She stiffens.

"Pepper, that van out there looks a bit like yours, don't you think?"

It does. And it is. Otto, with Dave at the wheel, is slowly weaving through the suddenly crowded gas pumps looking for an open space. There isn't one. Then a big Electra 225 noses into the big lot like a big blue shark and pulls right up to the parking spot outside our booth, its headlights shining in on us.

It's Charlene. With Creach at the wheel.

"Sooz, here're the keys to the car. I'll pay the bill—I want you to get the hell out of here, head out the back door. Circle around and get the car—I'll meet you out by the truck pumps in a few minutes. *Go.*"

"But ..."

"Let's go!"

She grabs her coat, all her papers, hurries down the back hall. I fish around in my wallet, throw a ten on the table since I don't have anything smaller. The bill is only five bucks or so. I wave at Diane—keep the change. She nods, smiles, *thanks hon.*

I whip down the hall and around the corner just as I hear Dave, Ricky, and Hawgrim loudly push through the front doors. I know where their first stop will be. The men's room. But there's no time for me to dash through the outside door at the end of the hall. There's only one choice. So I dive in and sit down in the corner stall, pull my feet up and wait. I know it won't be long.

Sure enough, the door bangs open and my band comes in, boots stomping on the tile floor. They line up at the urinals, there are three groans of personal relief.

Dave: "Well, I don't see 'em." Disappointed.

Hawgrim: "But why the fuck would they be here? They're gone and she's pulling him by the short hairs all the way to Champaign." Voice elevating with outrage. "It's just wrong. She's a criminal. I'm gonna call the Feds. I am."

I gasp.

Dave: "You FUCKER! Leave them the hell alone, what do you care?"

Hawgrim: "Hey man, this is a moral issue and I know where I stand on it. Do you?"

Everything flushes and Dave mutters a very imaginative string of bastards sonofabitches fucking assholes all put together quite beautifully. The sinks run, noisy hand dryers blow and they leave, the door slamming behind them. Ricky never says a word.

I give them a couple of minutes and am about to emerge from my stall when somebody else comes in. Instead of heavy rock 'n roll boots clomping on the floor, the sound is lighter and slower with the click of dress shoe heels. I hear something being placed on the floor, like a briefcase. I try to see through the crack in the door but the angle is wrong. The person finishes up, then the water runs for a long time in the sink. A very methodical hand washer. After the hand drier blows itself out, a black case slides on the floor in front of my stall. The person leaves the room.

Again, I wait a minute or two. I open the stall.

Felix!

But I don't waste time being stunned out of my mind. I pick him up, go to the door, crack it open and get a glimpse of the line of pay phones on the wall fifteen or twenty feet away toward the restaurant. Hawgrim's back is to me, receiver at his ear, his hand over the mouthpiece, and Dave is ranting somewhere farther down the hall. Creach, at least a head taller than our fine accordion wizard, is quietly talking to the perfidious one. Then, with his long black bass-playing finger, I see Creach flick the phone's hook, disconnecting the call. He glances up over Hawgrim's head, sees me, and winks.

 Track 3: Early Sunday morning

LIKE HE'S DEFUSING A TIME-BOMB, Creach places the phone back on the cradle, puts his arm around Hawgrim's skinny shoulders, begins firmly walking him up the hall and around the corner into the diner, maybe lecturing him about patience, loyalty, or cosmological goddamnedness.

I don't know.

I let the door close, count to ten, open it again and bump right into a couple big square-headed farmer types in flannel shirts, scaring the hell out of me. I apologize profusely, stand aside to let them in—they eye me warily. I invite them to have a nice day and take off heading for the back door.

The truckers' side of the Dixie is stark, black, and vast, bathed in the weird orange light from a forest of towering vapor lights, misty from the exhaust of fuming always-on diesels parked in sleeping rows, some gassing up under the tall corrugated roofs over the pumps. The sky has clouded up, the lights of the Dixie produce a glow that is now a claustrophobic dome as wisps of snow flurries begin to blow in from the west. I survey the scene, heart pumping, Felix in hand. I don't see the big Galaxie—maybe she's fled completely, not taking any chances, heading for who knows where. I sprint out across the lot, weaving between big rigs, thinking she may have slipped the car somewhere out of view, snug behind a trailer.

The driver of a big Kenworth, standing by the pump while it rolls off a huge number of gallons, asks me if I'm looking for a ride or something. I ask him if he's seen a big Ford driving around the lot. He grins, eyes my guitar case. He tells me he's been six days on the road. I say good song. Do I know any Johnny Cash or maybe Merle Haggard? I say I do but have no time. He says he ain't seen no Ford. I thank him and run out into the middle of the tarmac, as big as a small airport, turning 360s, trucks roaring in and out blowing by me, scattering grit, honking horns.

She isn't here.

Then headlights flick on and off a couple times about a hundred yards away—back along the main building, next to what looks like a shack housing a pile of garbage cans and dumpsters. I stop in my tracks as the car's wheels spin and tear out headed straight at me. She screeches to a halt at my feet, flips the door open, says, "Get in the car, rock star."

I carefully put Felix in the back. She says, "Creach?"

"Creach." I hop in.

"Figures." She scans the lot. "Sorry, I've been checking the map, getting from here to Champaign."

"I was beginning to think you took off."

"Course not." She pats a monstrous unfolded map that is sitting on the seat between us, points to the center of the state of Illinois. "You are *here* and you are now the navigator," stabbing the map. "I think we need to shoot straight across on this road here, what is it?"

She pulls up to the edge of the Dixie lot and idles, awaiting instructions from me. An inbound truck rolls by, big engine screaming, gears downshifting, and air brakes squealing. I flip on the dome light, scan the familiar layout—I-55 angling thick and blue across the state, up and to the right following train tracks but avoiding each little town in symmetrical angles—towns that used to be a series of stoplights with diners, goofy roadside attractions, yellow-roofed Hornes, Stuckeys, gas stations on the old Route 66. And we are here—McLean, where the Dixie Trucker's Home lay smack dab in the middle, the halfway point on the run from Chicago to St. Louis, at mile-marker 145, barely a start on the road out to the West—Kingsman, Barstow, San Bernardino.

"C'mon, c'mon," she's scanning the vast parking lot.

"One thirty-six. Turn right here, head east and keep going."

"We're gone."

She's all business. We fly under the 55 overpass, drive into the prairie dark, motoring east for Champaign, leaving the Dixie and everyone behind. I think about the last time I'd been out here on northbound 55, right here at *this* entrance ramp—there's nobody standing by the side of the road tonight.

"So what happened in there? What took so long?"

I tell her everything, seething about Hawgrim's treachery. She shakes her head, drums the steering wheel again, nails clicking. I feel like I've just passed from one world into another, the new one uncertain, grim, and starless.

"He's going to do it, call the shoes, if he hasn't already." She lets out a big sigh and smiles weakly.

"The what?"

"The FBI, brown shoes, G-men. C'mon."

Oh man.

She resumes her rearview mirror checking. I turn around, have a look—nothing but darkness as the glow of the Dixie glimmers on the flat western horizon like a dwarf sun going down.

"One big happy family—you, me, and your buddy Hawgrim—that's us, the love generation, a generation lost in space." She flicks an eyebrow and looks at me expectantly. "Wasn't that a song or something?"

"'American Pie,' Don McLean, 1971."

"But I understand what he's doing. He's just doing what he thinks is right. You know?"

I tell her she's being quite magnanimous, considering it seems he wants to see her sent up the river, or worse. And she admits that does create a certain sense of murder in her heart for the guy, but then she says that it creates a great generational dialectic—and I say, "Wow, a generational dialectic!"—Hawgrim is simply playing his role in the social contract and so is she.

Sooz, warming up, says, "You know, it's straight out of Rousseau. Hawgrim is, as far as he's concerned, operating in his own interests as a man of property, a rich guy … you did say he comes from money, right?"

"I did. And he sells insurance."

"Right. So he wants to maintain the existing social contract that's completely unfair to workers, minorities, women, and he naturally wants to continue the rule of its law, imposing the will of his class. And I'm doing what *I'm* supposed to be doing—the state has fucked up—like old Jean-Jacques says—man is born free and yet everywhere he is in chains. Just look at that waitress. Poor thing, working hard for crappy tips, trying to keep it together, probably got a kid at home and who knows? She could get laid off tomorrow and then what?"

"Hawgrim'd say it's business—nothing personal—it's just business, like Michael Corleone."

"Yeah, the market's always right—the dead hand of Adam Smith. As I see it, the state and the corporations have all the power and the money, and that leads straight to inequality and oppression that's become institutionalized. And in the last few years, I've done my best to do something about it, tip the scales, though it didn't necessarily work out to my advantage. But now I'm coming at it from a whole other angle."

"Your technology."

"My technology."

A flash from an old class comes back. "But didn't Rousseau have a thing against science and technology? He wouldn't approve of all this exotic computer science we're talking about."

She's impressed. "Well, you're right, he wouldn't approve. And I've wrestled with that, still am."

"We don't live in eighteenth-century France. Life is more complicated here in the bad old twentieth century."

"It is."

"And this is where it gets difficult for you and old romantic Rousseau—crazy hippie farm communes aren't going to make it in Nixon's America. It's not realistic."

She doesn't reply immediately, fiddles with the heater. "You cold?" I shrug. "I'm cold." Turns the heat up. "Well, it won't always be Nixon's America. Look how he's going down right now—who knows—he might even go to prison. Though there isn't much hope that anybody better is in sight, I mean c'mon, Gerald Ford? Please. But I'm getting off track. No, getting back to nature is not the answer." Thinks. "Look, someday we're going to be in charge. Us."

"But you wanted to overthrow the government, revolution up against the wall not all that long ago. You're back in the system?"

"Yeah, well that didn't work out. That was naïve. C'mon. We've been through this. I'm coming back."

"I know I know. But look at Hawgrim. He's part of this *we* you're talking about and God knows what people like him are going to do when they get hold of the word freedom."

Sooz asks, "Who owns the word *freedom*?"

"Do we?"

"We think we do."

"It could get hijacked. By the other we. *Them.*"

"And then what."

"It'll be somebody else's America. Like Hawgrim's America."

"Could be. Then we'll be sorry. We'll have to take it back. The road goes ever on."

"Is it freedom *from* or freedom *of*?"

"You mean freedom to do what we want, freedom from the man, or the state, to leave us alone—which is one thing—or freedom from oppression by the ruling class, the rich capitalists and society's inequitable hierarchy?"

"I'll have both, please."

"That's what's bothering me. Some may choose one or the other. So where're we going with all this?" She checks the mirror and smiles. "I like it when you talk like this. We used to argue about all this stuff ... you know, me and my *comrades*." She shakes her head. "There were some crazy people around in those days. But I think they're all gone."

I squeeze her thigh, that voluptuous thigh that fills those jeans so nicely. "Hobbes said that we're either free or we've got a government and we're not free. No middle ground."

"Hobbes was nuts."

"You got a middle ground?"

"I'm doing this, aren't I? No blood, just bits and bytes. The paradigm shift. That's pretty specific. And it's very big."

"Hawgrim thinks you're crazy."

"And he thinks he's normal. And maybe he's right ... and I'm crazy. But sometimes you have to be crazy to be normal. Didn't we talk about this?"

"You're not crazy crazy."

"No, I'm the normal one."

"But he's not normal normal. He's ... crazy normal. Or is that normal crazy?"

"Or something like that." She settles back in her seat, satisfied. "Look. This is inevitable. I'm not so naïve to think that I'm the only one in the universe with this idea. Analog to digital? It's gonna happen. But it may as well be me. And you."

Revived, she takes my hand, places it between her legs and we drive on through the night.

The two-lane road is deserted and ramrod straight across the empty flat fields. Snow flickers in our headlights but doesn't stick to the pavement. I fiddle with the radio, pull in WLS from Chicago clear as a bell, even find WABC out of New York, strange signals bouncing around through the loopholes of the night's ionosphere. A Carpenters' song crackles over the airwaves.

Sooz says, "Turn it up."

"You like the *Carpenters*? I mean, I would never have guessed ... you know, the Weathermen and ..."

"It's one of my many secrets. It's good to be a little mysterious."

"A little?"

She flutters her lashes like Betty Boop.

"Nixon likes 'em."

"Then Tricky Dick and I have something in common."

So we sing "Top of the World" along with Karen and Richard and then WABC degenerates into static and some lousy local station takes over. I flip it off.

I have a look back up the road. Far behind us across the prairie, a pair of headlights, been there a while. Up ahead, the road dips into a small grove of trees. I tell Sooz to slow down as we approach—there's an unpaved gravel road amongst the oaks and poplars. I ask her to kill the lights and turn in—turn in here, turn in here. She quickly complies, wheels in, makes a deft u-turn, stops and kills the engine.

"Let's see if we've got a tail."

Hidden by the trees, we wait in silence for a couple minutes. The flurries let up a bit and the only sound is the quiet ticking of our engine, its heat dissipating. Then an old Chevy zooms by. No shoes, no Otto. We begin breathing again. The trip resumes.

That shakes me up, my paranoia being further evidence of this new world. I say, "We can't stop at a motel ... if he's made the call ..."

She thinks about that. "But I bet he hasn't. Given what you said Creach did back there, I would think they're heading up to Chicago. I think Hawgrim'll be out of touch for a while, sleeping it off, then sleep all day tomorrow ... I mean this morning. But then he might." She takes my hand. "We've got some time. What's the next town?"

I check the map. "Heyworth. It's right up here." A few lights rim the horizon and then some houses begin to appear. The speed limit drops, we slip down to thirty in a thirty-five zone and roll through the darkened little farm town at a very respectful pace. In the empty lot of a grain elevator, a darkened police car steams like a racehorse at the gate. We attract no attention and drive on out of Heyworth.

A few minutes later, Sooz checks her mirror. "Car way behind us. What's the limit around here?"

"Fifty."

The Ford's speedometer eases down to forty-five and stays there. The two headlights behind us catch up fast and then pass us like we're standing still. Kids in a pickup, Saturday night.

"Damnit. I'm really sorry ..." she talks through a yawn, "that I've dragged you into all this."

I massage her neck and she stretches and twists pushing against my hand like a cat looking for heavy petting. "Forget it. It's a pleasure being a part of a major technological paradigm shift."

She smiles.

We need to get some sleep. I study the map, tell her that we're soon going to turn right and head south to Farmer City.

"You're kidding."

"No. *Farmer City*. True fact. I'm sure we'll find something there."

Twenty minutes later we turn off the road on the outskirts of the town, tires crunching on gravel. Sooz switches the engine off in front of the little office of the Winken' 'n Blinken' Motel—the red vacancy sign blinks by the door, lighting our faces.

After persistently tapping on the window to wake up the desk clerk, a nice enough skinny older lady in a pink bathrobe, who's been snoozing slumped over a desk with a pile of cigarette butts in an ash-tray by her head, gratefully accepts the ten dollars in cash Sooz hands her and points us to room number nine—small, cold, and brownish. The room reeks of Lysol overlaid on stale smoke. The double bed has an ominously deep valley in the middle of its mattress. I find an extra blanket on the shelf in the closet and we waste no time as we strip and dive for the bed. Between the sheets, our bodies come together like two well-worn spoons, form fitting, like vintage silver in an old mahogany-warm felt-lined chest, my arms reaching around her in a protective cocoon, my hand splayed on her warm, firm belly, then drifting dreamily over the deep curve of her hip. I kiss her ear. Her breathing slows into a soft rhythm. A car races by on the road outside, its sound disappearing. We fall asleep.

 Track 4: Sunday morning

A s if an alarm clock went off, Sooz wakes with a start, sun filtering through the thin curtains. I'm only dimly conscious as she gets up, roots around in her little duffle bag, jumps in the shower. I try to wake up—nine thirty-five. When she emerges from the bath-room fussing with a pair of earrings, I see that she's in the midst of a transformation, morphing into the very model of a central-casting mousy computer engineering or library science grad assistant—

suddenly quite owly and wise with her car-driving glasses on, but with subtle provocative dashes of flash designed to make the good Doctor Flarf's pulse rise to an appropriate level of engorged yet manageable attention.

"Like this?" Her sensible wool skirt is criminally long, hemmed right at the knee. The clingy tightness of the fine blue fabric—she says it's IBM blue and she's right—reminds me of that Dictaphone lady back in the IBM building. Sooz's outfit has just enough dishiness to keep things going should the conversation falter—she ain't no executive secretary.

"I love it." I hop out of bed, jump her from behind, intent on making a terrible pest of myself. Seeing my approach in the mirror, she executes a nifty jujitsu move, flings me back on the bed, climbing on top with her blouse undone, full breasts barely contained by a lacy skimpy bra, her skirt hitched up to a more sensible and far less sedate length. It's like we're in a "Sex in the Cinema" article in *Playboy* magazine itself.

Her hand dives into my shorts, gives me a firm shake. "No time for this now, rock star. We've got work to do." She lets go, scoots her body across mine while reaching to the floor, pulling her open duffle bag to the side of the bed. "I've got something for you." Her perfectly curved centerfold-worthy ass, half hidden by her Lois Lane skirt, is arched and waving right in front of my face as she fishes around for something in the bag. I have no choice but to slide my hand right up in the warm groove between her glorious never-ending legs. She says, "Ooooh my!"

"Pardon me."

Sooz rolls off the bed and stands up proudly unfurling the only suit I own in the world. "Ta da!"

She tells me that she has taken the liberty of selecting my wardrobe for our audience with Dr. Flarf, and since she had noticed it hanging in my closet on her visit to my apartment the other night, she went back, unescorted, picked a shirt, found a tie, folded the whole thing nicely and brought the little ensemble along.

"You broke in?"

"Not too tough, dear. I'm multi-talented. Now get up and shower and shave. You can use the razor I shave my legs with." She smiles seductively, smoothing her skirt. "Don't worry. It's very sharp. We gotta look good, like computer geniuses should."

While I'm scrubbing the gigs right out of my hair, she comes into the steamy bathroom, sits down on the toilet, begins quizzing me about the contents of her paper, focusing on the high points, drilling me on my opening pitch.

"Sir, this is a completely *new* technology that will have a *profound* impact on society. It's a new kind of computer network—*a local area network*—that will enable very *high-speed* communications between host computers and new devices, small *single-user computers.* The mathematics and engineering I have devised are like nothing ever done before—it is part of the single most important change in our lifetime—an historic paradigm shift, moving society from analog to digital communications."

"Not bad. Again. Sell me."

I do it again.

"Once more. Go further."

She grills me while I shave, probing my weaknesses—the mathematics—and applauding my strengths—conceptual design and software coding. I'm getting better at this, I'm improving and I begin to think that I will actually pull it off. I am, after all, no computer slouch—hey, IBM wanted me. She says that she'll back me up and interject as necessary but that she sees no problem. I'm to get to the formulas as quickly as possible at which point she, as the math assistant, will take over, wow him with the heuristics and the calculations.

"Okay. We're ready. Let's go."

And so, dressed like a pair of very wholesome, charming, and very smart young people, we pack up the car and hit the road to Champaign.

I drive. And she quizzes me some more.

 Track 5: Later Sunday morning

"IS THAT THE HOUSE?"

Sooz checks the address, confidently folds the map of Champaign, says, "Yes. That one … yeah, that one up there must be the place." She rolls the window down. "Here. Number 909."

We're inching our way along a quiet residential street in the professorial part of town on a quiet Sunday morning, big old houses mostly built in the last century, some before the war, solid looking brick and mortar colonials, bungalows, some stucco, some with heavy overhanging Prairie-style eaves with dead winter ivy strung across the siding. It's not exactly the neighborhood where the bank president and the doctor live. Maybe it's a shade down market. Maybe lower upper middle class. More Buick than Cadillac. Some of the old wooden front porches are showing signs of age, a slight sagging, a little peeling paint. But the house of Dr. Flarf seems fit and trim, prosperous and cared for in a crisply Teutonic manner, the light snow of the night before is already neatly pushed aside where others merely hope and wait for the late winter sun. Flarf lives a few blocks from the edge of campus, away from the Greek part of town where the crappy frat houses sport their outrageous paint jobs and imaginative selections of all-weather outdoor furnishings, announcing the nonconformist conforming rebellion of their inmates. But even there, any thoughts of sixties-style revolution are on their way out as the reality of jobs and a grim economy—unemployment and high gas prices—settle on graduating seniors like a heavy gray fog laid over already thick beery and weedy hazes. The street is lined with leafless elms and oaks with roots that have heaved the sidewalk in inconvenient places. An alley runs behind the houses.

There are no other cars on the street, parked or otherwise. I step on the gas and drive past the house.

"What are you doing? That's the place, c'mon!" Sooz turns in her seat and checks the number again and said, "Park the car, this is it."

"Let's just take another look around here. You see anything that looks funny and out of place?"

"*We* look funny and out of place."

"Let's go around the block, have another look. And check the alley, too."

"The shoes aren't here."

"I certainly hope not. But how do you really know?"

I really don't want to see anything weird, like a late model black car with two crew-cut, blue-suited Feds with fedoras. Or maybe they'd be hokey hipster types with trying-too-hard sideburns and *Man From*

U.N.C.L.E. or Roger Moore turtlenecks, and maybe even a mustache. Either way, they'd be staked out behind the house or down the block or across the street, one guy's smoke trailing out of a cracked-open car window and the other guy drinking cold coffee, eating donuts, and reading the paper, waiting and watching for Sooz and maybe even for me. But that would be too much like the movies and deep down I know that it won't really be that way. But then I don't really *know*.

So we turn into the alley behind Flarf's house, cruise slowly alongside garbage cans and ancient garages that look like they were originally designed for horses and buggies. We scare a few fat cats. Some guy taking out his garbage gives us the eye. We come up on Flarf's own garage which actually looks pretty nice, with well-trimmed evergreens around the outside, empty concrete flower pots filled with snow, and some sort of room lit up on the second floor. Maybe he's up there.

"Pepper look, there's nobody back here and what the hell would we do if we saw *them* anyway? Huh?" She punches my shoulder. "They'd be all over us and I'd already be dead." Confident, authoritative. "C'mon, they're not here."

We drive back around out front and Sooz says, "Just pull over and let's do this." I park the car in front of Flarf's house and sit there.

She says, "You ready?"

I fiddle with the keys, gaze up the deserted street.

"Are you okay?" Sooz puts her hand on my shoulder, points at my head. "What's going on in there?"

"I'm not sure I can be what you want me to be."

"And I'm not sure I can be what I want me to be. Or you want me to be."

I breathe in and out a few times.

She goes on. "C'mon. You were the in-demand Michigan graduate courted by IBM—what's the matter with you? Buck up for goodness sake!"

Yeah, I think to myself. Yeah!

"Think of yourself on stage. Think of that sound check. Let's call up some of that weird magic right here right now."

She gives me a little radical computer technology pep talk, fervently asserting that someday people will look back at this moment, *this moment* as when the paradigm actually shifted. They will say that those two made the difference, they were the ones who got the ball rolling and changed the direction of computer networking, nay, all society on that cold sunny day in March 1974, right there in Champaign, Illinois.

But then she admits, "I'm nervous, too."

The flickers of shakiness I've seen in her the last few days and nights have naturally got me thinking about what it's all been like for her, how she dealt with the fear and isolation of being on the run. I don't know who she turned to when things got rough, she's held all that back so far but still I wonder and I think about the men in her life. I've read those articles in *Rolling Stone* and I wonder if it's true that there is nothing equal about the sexes in the underground, and that a girl has to be very smart and quick, otherwise she'd end up in what some have said is the natural position of women in the Revolution—*prone*.[65] But she did tell me one of her favorite lines—*I am not going to fuck you no matter how liberated you think you are.* Worked every time. And now she needs me and I need her. It's time to go.

"Okay. Let's do it."

She gathers her documentation out of the stringy macramé bag at her feet—two extra copies of the paper, a large manila envelope containing a few nice charts and graphs, and her notebook—her brains. I slip all of it into the beige vinyl valise she brought as a prop for me. She checks her fancy new TI calculator, stuffs it back in her sensible, shiny black leatherette purse that she's acquired for this very purpose. It's got a fake gold clasp and trim—"It's nice, don't you think? ... the sort our grandmothers would carry." With both hands, she elaborately puts on her librarian glasses and steals a quick look at her makeup in the rearview mirror, tilting her face this way and that in very photogenic on-camera moves, attending to a small bit of dark red lipstick on one of her front teeth.

She fishes a brush out of that purse, turns to me, straightens up my hair, dabs at my eyebrows, smoothing them down.

Sooz says, "You look wonderful. If I were Flarf, I'd buy whatever

---

[65] Stokely Carmichael, SNCC—Student Nonviolent Coordinating Committee. How could he say that? My mom would have had a *word* with that young man, let me tell you.

you were selling." With a hand on my cheek, she kisses me softly and a bit of a "Dreaming's Done" soft-focus gauzy look comes over her eyes.

I know that look.

And against every hormonal instinct and rock 'n roll sense resident in my body, I say, "No way. I'm not singing that song now. We've got work to do."

"Just testing. You passed. Let's go."

So we get out of the car and walk up to the front door, a pair of hopeful Fuller Brush high technology door-to-door salesmen, the revolutionary goods under my arm.

She rings the doorbell, a spray of yippy little dog barking erupts inside the house accompanied by an equally high-pitched feminine scolding. The door opens and a slender older woman with silvery gray hair that drapes on her shoulders, elegantly cut in a style certainly unexpected in central Illinois, stands before us. She doesn't wear much makeup but it's clear that she doesn't need it—little of the beauty of her youth has faded. The woman is bent over, holding the collar of a little black and tan yelping Dachshund that jumps at her feet. She smiles apologetically and motions for us to wait a moment. She closes the heavy round-topped door and deals with the dog.

"Must be Frau Flarf," Sooz says.

She straightens my tie. We face the door and smile professionally.

When the woman opens the door again, she's putting her hair back in order and smoothing her black wool flared slacks, a cherry red jacket over an open-necked white blouse. She assesses us—doubtfully, I think—and in what I take to be a not too heavy German accent says, "I have already been to church this morning and am not very much interesting in your freelance spiritual guidance, if that may be what you young people are here about, jah?"

Sooz speaks. "No, no ma'am. Please pardon us. We're certainly not here about anything like that. May I ask if you are Mrs. Flarf?"

The woman arches an eyebrow.

"I am Doktor Gudrun *von* Flarf, yes?"

Without missing a beat, Sooz inquires, "Pardon me, ma'am, we are looking for Dr. Ivor ... Flarf, of the computer science department? We understand that this is his residence."

"We're computer engineers."

Dr. von Flarf sighs. "Jah, jah, Ivor is here. I am his wife." She only glances at me but regards Sooz carefully as if measuring some threat level, gauging whether or not she is the good doctor's type. Sooz remains as cheery and wholesome as anybody's girl next door.

I press on. "If it wouldn't be too much trouble, we'd very much like to speak with your husband. I—we have developed some very important ideas which are described in this paper—" I hold up one of the copies. "They are revolutionary and I believe they would be of great interest to the professor in his work. I am seeking his guidance. We'll only take a few minutes of his time."

Sooz nods supportively.

Dr. Gudrun von Flarf lightens up and grants us access. A philosophy professor, Dr. von Flarf pleasantly tells us that this sort of thing happens frequently and she is quite accustomed to mistaken identities and similarly embarrassing incidents. The little yippy dachshund escapes from wherever it has been imprisoned and races into the entry hall, yapping and skidding on the nearly black wooden floor, doing his job defending the old dark and heavy plaster-walled house from nefarious and suspicious characters such as ourselves.

Dr. von Flarf attempts to shush the dog. "Schopenhauer! *Ruhe!*"

Sooz immediately goes into girl-likes-little-dog mode and kneels to Schopenhauer—"Oooohhh, Schopenhauer, what a cute little doggy woggy, dogger schmogger you are, Schopenhauer schnoopsie." This is no act. She genuinely loves little dogs and it is certainly helpful. Schopenhauer quiets immediately and begins licking her face enthusiastically. Who can blame him?

Sooz stands up with Schopenhauer curled cozily in her arms. "He's *very* cute, Dr. von Flarf."

Dr. von Flarf ruffles Schopenhauer's suddenly snoozy little head. "Well, Ivor is in his studio out in the coach house behind the *haus*. I'm sure he is *available*. He always is. Allow me to take you to him."

As we walk out the back door, faint muffled thumps of a musical sort drift across the yard. I stop and let Sooz and Dr. von Flarf walk ahead of me. I listen—big orchestral music, vaguely familiar. Its source is clearly the lit-up second floor of the detached garage—a room with piles of *stuff*—boxes, cabinets, bookcases, and what appear to be speakers in front of old leaded windows with black cross-hatched panes that ring the little structure. I catch up with Sooz and Dr. von Flarf and follow them through the door that opens into the dark garage itself. The smell of engine oil and automotive rubber hangs in the air, and a snazzy red Porsche sits on the cracked concrete floor coiled and ready to strike. Dr. Gudrun von Flarf, seeing my knee jerk reaction of awe, shrugs dismissively. "Ivor."

At the bottom of a bare wooden staircase that runs up alongside the exposed bricks and mortar of the wall, Dr. von Flarf grabs a fat scarlet brocade cord with a fringy gold tassel and pulls it firmly three times like she is summoning the butler. She murmurs matter of factly, "It's the only way to communicate with him when his music is going like that, don't you know." We wait a few moments. The rumble upstairs is silenced, the door at the top of the stairs opens.

"Ivor! So sorry to disturb you, *liebchen*, but you have visitors! Two *sehr nett* young people who have the intelligence and good sense to actually like and admire our little Schopenhauer. Unlike you, *mein Schatz*." She smiles, motions for us to go on up, like two little kids being sent off by the governess to play with a new and unknown and rather scary playmate. At the top of the stairs, Herr-Doktor Ivor von Flarf, a very large figure silhouetted by the light from his room, his face invisible to us, steps aside allowing us entrance to his inner sanctum.

Dr. Ivor von Flarf greets us formally, shaking our hands as we enter a brightly lit studio. He is large, barrel-chested, well built—if there had been a Dusseldorf football team, he would have played left tackle alongside Friedrich Nietzche, Ray's uncle. In his younger days Flarf was probably a Nordic blonde, but his longish hair and trimmed beard have thinned and whitened elegantly, leaving him with appealing movie star good looks.

He gestures for us to sit down on a low white couch, inquires if we might like a cup of tea. We accept and he begins fussing over the teapot that sits on a hot plate in the corner of the very cluttered yet strangely ordered studio. A large lab table, with an onyx top and unused metal holes for the apparatus of old physics labs, holds piles of thick books, some oversized like ancient artsy monographs—large sheets of light blue paper, circuit diagrams—lay curling at the edges, some rolled and piled next to the books like great maps of a new world. Along the walls, underneath the windows with the churchy leaded panes, is a continuous workbench strewn with electrical gear—oscilloscopes, test devices, strange black boxes, instruments with big black knobs and cables hanging from them mounted in tall gray metal cabinets vented on the sides, large green printed circuit boards lined up in wooden racks along with a handful of large, uncovered monitors, cathode ray tubes—CRTs. But in one corner of the studio are the stars of the show—a pair of big PDP 11 minicomputers from DEC[66]—side by side, tall, slender, and black with four small white tape reels like spastic spinning eyes, rows of blinking lights across their middles and a long array of candy-colored purple, red, and white plastic switches set in a dimly recognizable semaphore of machine meaning. Thick wires and cables are laid behind the CRTs, connecting them to other metal boxes, their printed circuit boards exposed and vulnerable. Soldering irons heated and resting in their sockets like hot metal pens give the air the scent of strange new science. At each corner of the room, mounted up near the ceiling is a large stereo speaker cabinet—JBL—with its grille removed exposing the monstrously large woofer—probably fifteen inches. Twin tweeter horns nestle above it. Two big reel-to-reel tape decks, a turntable, amplifiers, and other sound equipment boxes with dimly lit gauges are all lodged in an ornately carved wooden cabinet below one of the big speakers. The room is not only a computer lab—it's an audio technology lab. A subtle hiss of stereo swish fills the room and the big cooling fans of the computers surf on top of the crackle.

Dr. von Flarf hands us two dainty china teacups. "Do you prefer milk and sugar?" He offers a tray with both. Sooz accepts the milk, I decline. We thank him for his kind hospitality.

"You will notice that this room is quite warm."

We nod.

Flarf's voice rumbles like his big woofers turned all the way up, low and boomy with a bit of scratch though finely articulated. "These

---

[66] DEC, Digital Equipment Corporation, invented the minicomputer in Boston in the '60s. Back in Ann Arbor, I had worked on the earlier PDP 8 model, so seeing the new one—a pair of big new advanced PDP 11's is like seeing that Porsche in the garage. These are expensive and powerful machines—and they are in his *home*. I look at Sooz. I know that she is itching to get her hands on them. So am I.

two machines of mine provide far more heat than is necessary to heat the entire garage in winter." He sits down on his high stool at the big worktable, swivels on the chair playfully, says, "But they are already obsolete." Big grin. "Someday soon, they will be much smaller and far more capable. I suspect you know all this, jah?"

We do.

We sip our tea, he considers us. "May I say that you two make a handsome couple?" Sooz is clearly the focus of his attention. "Now, what is it that I can do for you young people?"

Flarf, with wire reading glasses perched on the top of his head, dressed in a crisply pressed light blue button-down shirt and dark blue slacks with a knife-edge crease, places his cup and saucer on the big table and crosses his legs—he has red socks, expensive-looking loafers, probably Italian.

I introduce myself and briefly review my academic background— Michigan computer science graduate, interests in mainframe operating systems and data communications. I warmly recall the fact that I participated in one of his most excellent visiting symposiums. He smiles, apologizes that he does not remember me.

Sooz introduces herself—Grace Kelliher, past student at Michigan, computer science and mathematics. She sits primly, back straight and knees together, yellow notepad and pen in hand.

So, as planned, I launch into my opening spiel—"Sir, this is a completely new, advanced technology that will have a profound impact on data communications, enabling a new kind of computer network—a local area network, a shift of paradigms from ..."

"Jah, jah, jah, the paradigm shift, analog to digital. Of course. Inevitable. But you realize, of course, that there is much work being done on this subject, here in my department and elsewhere?" Flarf glances at Sooz with his eyes darting to her fabulous legs continuously as if in involuntary muscle spasms.

"Sir, we realize that, however, what we have developed is not the network itself, but an important *enabling* technology. My paper ... our paper ... which I have right here," I nod at Sooz and she smilingly hands him a copy, "is, as you can see, entitled 'Controlled Statistical Arbitration: A Shared Media Access Methodology.'" He glances at the title page, respectfully places it on the table but leans closer to us.

"Our technology is independent of media and devices, completely agnostic. Of course," acknowledging the impressive collection of computers and exotic gear in the studio, "we envision that these networks will use what we have here and will ... will ... uh—"

"—provide unlimited connectivity to any and all devices, computers big and small, current and as yet invented. With this approach to sharing data communications media, bandwidth will be universally available." Sooz rolls beautifully, as I stumble searching for the right words. She cannot resist.

Flarf judges her, his eyebrows raised, a thin smile on his face. Sooz opens her copy of the paper to one of her flowcharts, begins walking him through a heuristic she calls Binary Exponential Backoff. Flarf scoots his stool over closer to her but it's a little awkward, so he stands up, asks her to place the diagram on his worktable. She complies. He flips his reading glasses down from his forehead.

The three of us gather around the paper, Flarf on the left, me on the right, and Sooz in the middle.

She talks about datagrams and carrier detection and deference and acquisition and she goes through the formulas one at a time telling a story, each one building on the last, building a case—

Acquisition probability: $A = (10(1/Q))(Q-1)$

Waiting time: $W = (1-A)/A$

And efficiency: $E = (P/C)/((P/C) + (W*T))$.

After half an hour of uninterrupted Sooz pitching, explaining and lecturing with von Flarf in rapt attention but a bit overwhelmed, like he's trying to drink from a fire hose, asking clarifying questions that are quickly and confidently answered, he glances at me—it's clear he's beginning to understand that *she's* the brains of the outfit. He sits down on his stool, pulls a monogrammed handkerchief from his hip pocket, dabs at his brow. The only sound is the whir of the computer fans. The room is getting hotter. Sooz and I return to our couch.

"Young Miss ... it is Kelliher, yes? This is most interesting. Jah, most interesting. Cogent, elegant, well argued and presented. And Mr. Porter—" he looks at me with a raised eyebrow "—your *assistant* ... she is very capable, is she not?" He winks at me. "Fraulein Kelliher, I know that you are not a student here at the university, but I am thinking that perhaps you are known to me. I cannot be certain, perhaps it is just one of those things, it's like we have been here before. Déjà vu as the French say." He pauses waiting for her to speak.

Sooz smiles charmingly. "Herr-Doktor, I know what you mean. It's very strange when that happens, but I'm sure that we haven't met before."

Von Flarf studies her over the top of his glasses as if she is a new circuit diagram. "Yes, it is strange. Yet, again, you are somehow familiar." He cleans his glasses with his handkerchief. "But I suppose I am mistaken." Holds the glasses up to the light. "In any event, what you young people have described is most certainly remarkable and worth further consideration." He smiles, places his glasses in a small black leather case. "May I propose that we go for a walk, get some fresh air. The heat in here is strong, no?"

Von Flarf suggests that we leave all our stuff there while we take a turn through the park just a few blocks away. He puts on a thick black woolen greatcoat and one of those *Sound of Music* Tyrolean hats— black felt, short-brimmed with little feathers stuck in the cord around the crown—escorts us out the door.

The day is still bright and sunny and has warmed up a bit, melting the night's light snow. The three of us walk down the alley and we begin a leisurely stroll on the sidewalk that rings a small park, a grassy city block with a small playground in the middle. A stream, crossed by a little stone bridge and rimmed by the papery brown stumps of dead cattails, flows from a city culvert under the sidewalk on one side and then vanishes below the street on the other.

Von Flarf asks Sooz detailed and specific questions about her ideas, probing for weaknesses, pointing out a few areas that may need closer attention or revision. Overall, he seems quite satisfied and impressed with her responses.

We sit down on a bench near the playground. For the moment, he's run out of questions. Some little kids are on the swings. The streets are quiet, just a few cars coming and going. A gust of wind whips up. Von Flarf holds onto his hat.

"Miss Kelliher and Mr. Porter. You are proposing something completely new. Something crazy! And something crazy is exactly what is needed. I know you see that. But I fear that much of the needed change will not happen from within the glass walls of computing. For example, DEC, now a very big corporation, could build a computer much smaller and much less expensive than those big machines I have in my atelier—they have the technology to do that—to build a machine that fits ... *on a desk*, and is, shall we say, personal, human. But DEC will not do it. Nein." He shakes his head sharply, pinches his nose with a bit of seasoned exasperation. "They have too much of their own legacy, their own sales revenues at stake—why bring out something crazy and new? It may affect sales of their existing machines and then their quarterly results would suffer and, and oh, it would just be too risky. Too much fear, uncertainty, and doubt! And DEC is a *young* company! You might think they would take the risk, be adventurous. You would be wrong. I am not sure that their top management even sees any reason for anyone to have their own computer." He is gesturing with his hands, very into it. "So can you imagine IBM, the biggest computer company in the world doing something like this?—ach no! They will wait for someone else. They will *not* do it! So." He turns his head, looks Sooz in the eye, speaks more slowly, emphasizing his words carefully. "It will take revolutionaries to do it—perhaps young people such as yourselves who have no problem tearing down walls. It will be a *revolution*. You see? You must be creative ... and destructive, the old must be done away with. You must be *creatively destructive*. Welcome to the revolution."

The three of us sit there on the bench considering all this. My heart is thumping.

Von Flarf pulls a small notebook out of his coat pocket, scrawls a name and phone number on a slip of paper. "You must get in touch with this man. He is well-connected politically and in the rather small high-technology community, knows many key people, people in very high places." He doesn't hand it to Sooz, he hesitates, rubs his chin. He's not quite sure he's doing the right thing. "But this man, he knows the money. Ach, the money. Always the money." He tears the sheet out of the notebook, gives it to her.

Back in the atelier, von Flarf is magnanimous in his further praise of what Sooz is trying to do. And to me he says, "Mr. Porter, I commend you in your fervent support of this remarkable young woman. Please, I urge you to continue to do your best."

Sooz and I gather our things together, shake hands with

Herr-Doktor von Flarf, thank him profusely, and promise to keep in touch. At the bottom of the stairs, von Flarf, still standing at the top, intones in his low rumbly voice, "Well done, Fraulein Susan Frommer." He shuts the door.

Track 6: Sunday noon

Sooz, wired and ecstatic, drums on the Ford's dash with both hands, looks at me triumphantly. "I knew it, I knew it, I knew it! What'd I tell you?"

"Yeah!" But I'm not so sure.

"He may be a male chauvinist pig—at least he used to be, but you know, maybe he's not as bad as he used to be … and how about that Doktor Gudrun von Flarf, eh?" Sooz is motor-mouthing. "Wow, she was really something, maybe he's scared of her. I would be. But it's obvious that right below that German movie star surface, he's a revolutionary at heart! He reminds me of that actor, you know who I'm talking about?"

I shake my head. "But Flarf knows your name. He knows who you are."

"It's von Flarf."

"Von Flarf."

"I must've misjudged him. He wasn't so bad, was he?"

"He was staring at your legs the whole time."

"I'm used to it. But '*welcome to the revolution!*' You heard him say that?" She squeals like she's in seventh grade.

"But he knows your name."

"Irrelevant." Suddenly she sounds like Dr. Spock. "He clearly wants us to succeed. Let's go. Drive."

The name thing. And that hesitation. It's just one more crack in the wall around her, it doesn't feel right to me but I start the car.

While Sooz rattles on and on about how von Flarf is like most extremely talented engineers—apolitical, fanatically dedicated to their work and oblivious to much of the outside world and how he probably wouldn't know about her background. Or, if he did, as a fugitive himself, he wouldn't care, but oh sure, there were exceptions like Einstein or Teller or Oppenheimer—I put the car in gear and we move on down the block. She speculates that von Flarf is just like von Braun who just wants to build rockets, though I remind her of how she had gone on and on about von Braun just the other night. She tells me to give her a break, let her feel good about this and besides von Flarf is the same way—he just wants to design the next generation of computers and his remembering her is simply his brain performing a sophisticated high-speed sequential search of his own local internal storage system and, unsurprisingly, coming up with correct and accurate results.

But at the corner, about one hundred yards away, I see a large car, dark, anonymous, and built of heavy Detroit iron almost identical to our own trusty Ford Galaxie except it has black-wall tires and we have white. It sits idling, wisps of winter exhaust rising from its tailpipe. I quietly point it out to Sooz as I nonchalantly execute a slow three-point U-turn, deciding it might be better that way, why take chances.

She instantly calms down and turns to check it out. "It's nothing. Just somebody out visiting the folks on a sunny afternoon. Oy vey."

"Oy vey?"

"My father. Oy vey."

She's pumped.

Ten minutes later we're sitting in a café in downtown Champaign—the Ten O'Clock Scholar—a vaguely Victorian, tin-ceilinged hang out for college kids, where granola, yogurt, and sprouts mingle with burgers, fries, and open mic nights. A vast bulletin board near the door displays concert fliers from here all the way to St. Louis and Chicago. There's even one for my band's own dates that weekend. I grab it for posterity. The board is packed with music schedules of happening Champaign-Urbana bars and roadhouses, roommate requests, and little tear-off ad sheets for used furniture and rides to Chicago, notices of fervent rallies to impeach the president, and once and for all end the goddamn war. Smells of vegetables, grease, and coffee mix in the warm air. The Sunday lunch crowd is in—bleary-eyed kids just out of bed feeling hungry, studying and schmoozing over a cup of java or Ming tea. The joint's stereo blasts Marvin Gaye's "Mercy Mercy Me" as we enjoy our romantic little table with a view of the street. Still in our pitch-the-plan garb, we stand out just a little bit. A mellow waitress in white painter's pants and a black apron drifts to our table, hazily takes our order. Sooz, still flying with von Flarf, orders her customary cheeseburger medium rare with Swiss, fries, and coleslaw. I order the same but with cheddar. There's a basket of peanuts on the table.

"What a great place!" She snatches a peanut, cracks it open, slumps a little in her chair. "So far, it's all going according to plan."

I resist the impulse to comment on her diet. What's the matter with me?

"So, the name—what name did Flarf … von Flarf, give you?"

She pulls out the little slip of paper and reads, "A Mr. Fletcher Engel—312 area code, so he must be somewhere in Chicago. Never heard of him. You?"

I shrug.

"I'll do a little research and then call him."

After her all-star performance in front of von Flarf, I'm beginning to feel a little useless, third wheelish. "Sooz. I'm thinking. You still need me? I mean, it's obvious that …"

"What? Of course I do." Marvin Gaye ends and Joni Mitchell begins. "You *must* come with—you're on board this runaway train now, Mister Rock and Roll Star. Do we have to go through this all over again?" She stumbles around looking for words. "Look, these meetings, you know, I need help, you—you're going to see and hear things that I might miss—remember you're my way back, the way back machine. C'mon, you know what I've been saying." The look on my face must be rather pathetic because she reaches across the table, takes my hand in both of hers, slows down and lowers her voice to a near whisper. "Pepper, why? What's this all about? Because you fucked up with Hawgrim?"

I look at her.

"Yes, you fucked up! But so what? We're past that, moving ahead! Got no choice. You want out, you're telling me you want to forget it all?"

The bells over the joint's door jingle and two guys in matching tan trench coats and sunglasses walk in, one tall, one short. Sooz sees them, keeps hold of my hand, murmurs, *"Shoes.* Stay cool." My body begins to tingle all over like my psychic antenna has been turned all the way up with microphones in the walls and under the tables, vivid and crazy sensitive.

Both over thirty and very clean-cut, the two men scan the place, then head straight for our table. The shorter one, a little stocky, black *Mod Squad* mustache and sideburns, removes his shades and takes out his ID—an impressive Federal-looking thing with a picture of the guy before he grew the facial hair. He shows it to me, then Sooz— agent somebody from somewhere. I'm too freaked to actually read it. People in the place start to stare, these guys are unusual clientele. Shoes, indeed.

Sooz puts her glasses back on, going into nerdy mode and, though she smiles at the two of them like they were customers at her place of employment, she uses her best studious student voice, "And how can we be of service to you gentlemen today?"

"Good afternoon, sir ... ma'am. I apologize for the intrusion." The agent smiles, thin-lipped. The second guy, the tall guy, stands behind him with hands politely clasped, chewing gum at a high rate of speed, dark sunglasses still on. I can tell he's looking at Sooz. "May I see a form of identification, both of you, please?"

I say, "Is there a problem, sir?"

"No problem. Just routine." His hand is extended, waiting.

I hand him my driver's license while Sooz calmly rummages through her purse. For a second I think maybe she's going to pull out a pistol and there'll be a gunfight amid the ferns and granola, and then we'd blast our way out and drive like screaming banshees southbound on the Pan American Highway, not stopping until we reach Patagonia where we'd live in a remote shotgun shack in the Andes subsisting on nuts and berries and penguins for the rest of our livelong days.

She hands him her license. I fervently hope it's clean, reasonably legit, though it occurs to me right then and there that I don't even know her address, where she actually lives in Chicago—maybe her license isn't even Illinois—maybe it's from somewhere else, but whatever address is on there I hope it isn't real, just like I hope this situation is just a passing figment. The agent studies both of them, hands them to his partner who takes out a little black notebook, bends over an empty table, scribbles in it.

The stereo blasts some stuff I've never heard before, clearly something new, obscure and progressive.

The first guy says, "Mr. Porter, Miss Kelliher, we're hoping that it would be convenient for you to see fit to help us with a bit of information that we are seeking."

I say, "Of course. What do you need, officer?" Perked up and helpful.

"No need to call me officer, sir. We are agents of SNARB, a special unit of the Executive Branch of the Federal Government—that's the Security Normalization and Review Board, Agent Schootz at your service." Motioning to his partner he says, "And this is Under Assistant Agent Brown." Under Assistant Agent Brown bows his head slightly.

I bow, too. "Pardon me."

Agent Schootz nods crisply. "I wonder if you could tell us about your visit to the home of one Dr. Ivor von Flarf this morning? We couldn't help but notice."

Sooz is alert, all ears. Like she's taking steno.

He tells us that von Flarf has heretofore had a very high government security clearance due to his advanced computer research and his discussions with various security-conscious government entities, it all being of such a sensitive nature relevant to national security and what not. Agent Schootz leans down a little closer to us, looks side to side as if the walls have ears, utters, "He is a *person of interest* to SNARB. So we are conducting a comprehensive review of his situation and his, shall we say, *reliability*." He eyes us skeptically, my hair in particular. "He does come into contact with certain unsavory types from time to time, him being in a university and all. And he is a *foreigner,* you know."

We nod in agreement.

He goes on, "Though apparently he *is* a citizen." Agent Schootz appears somewhat disappointed. "So I hope you will help us in our evaluation, come to the aid of your country, so to speak."

Sooz's face is expressionless as she sits there, a model of librarian blandness, blinking behind her glasses. There's no getting around this, so I ask them to pull up a couple of chairs, sit down. They sit. Under Assistant Agent Brown continues to examine our IDs, making cryptic notes and glyphs in the little black book in his lap. He looks up at Sooz. She smiles sweetly.

"May I ask the nature of your visit this morning?" This is Agent Schootz talking.

I tell them that Miss Kelliher and I were merely seeking Dr. von Flarf's advice on some technical matters. "You see, we are working on a computer project, a new invention actually, and since it is well known that he is an authority, well, naturally—"

"Of course. And you are, Mr. Porter, a student here at the university?"

I say, "No. I am a graduate of the University of Michigan. We were discussing ideas with Dr. von Flarf."

"And would those ideas have anything to do with advanced computer *networking* by any chance?"

Sooz can't hide her surprise. "Actually, yes they would. Why?"

"Nothing. Just figures." Agent Schootz produces his own little black notebook, scratches a few lines. He looks up, waits for us to say something, like he has all the time in the world.

Sooz unwisely fills the silence.

"Mr. Porter and I work together. You see, Agent Schootz, we—" she straightens up a bit, flexes her shoulders, "are *entrepreneurs*. Young people looking to start our own business."

Agent Schootz whistles softly. "Well isn't that something? What fine young people." Sooz lights up her charmingly shy smile.

Our lunch arrives, causing our visitors to reshuffle their chairs, again apologizing for the inconvenience.

Agent Schootz, eyeing Sooz's burger, says, "Please do not let us disturb you. Please." So we begin to eat. "So, technical computer ideas, is that right?"

"Yes, sir."

Under Assistant Agent Brown hands me my driver's license but keeps hers. Then he excuses himself, saying something about a routine check and hurries out of the restaurant. Sooz puts her burger down, sips her soda, touches the corner of her perfectly lipsticked mouth with her napkin, all the while giving me a stabbing look. Agent Schootz, noticing, says, "Just routine, Miss Kelliher, no cause for alarm." He studies her a bit. Behind those glasses, green eyes and ladies' tea party look, I know her fuse is lit. Then he asks both of us, "Notice anything unusual about Dr. von Flarf today?"

Sooz shakes her head primly. "No. I really don't know him at all."

I answer, "He *is* unusual, that's what's unusual about him don't you think? He's different. He thinks different." Agent Schootz looks a little confused. "Maybe if he was more normal, now that'd be unusual."

He considers that, slowly nodding, giving it some thought. Then he asks does von Flarf still have those fancy computers in his workshop over the garage and does he still like to listen to that strange long-hair music, you know, fancy classical stuff, and then out of the blue I remember that *that* was the music thundering on von Flarf's stereo when we had shown up—Mahler's Ninth, big, dramatic, mournful and dire.

I space out. I remember from an old music appreciation class—the Ninth is about death—mostly the death of a child and I remember that there is a weird chord motif thing in it—A, F sharp, and B—and then my mind jumps, trying to hear those notes in my head and then I think about Elliot and the dent in Felix. And then I think about how creepy it is that Agent Schootz seems to have intimate knowledge of von Flarf's workspace, like he'd been there before, like maybe he was there while we were on our walk and like maybe he might return there again soon. I begin to snap back in and I can see that Agent Schootz is talking to me but I'm not really listening. I'm looking at Sooz whose fire is burning underneath her expertly placid exterior, I'm sure of it, and I wonder if she's going to do something completely crazy like stand up and slap the guy then run out the back door, find the car and scram, careening out of town, leaving me with these two federal flatfoots. And then I marvel at how I, Pepper Porter, have come to be in such a situation, here in this joint in Champaign being quizzed by a couple of agents of the US government about matters of apparent national security, and how I am beginning to think I am such a tough guy and how I actually have the nerve to think of them as federal *flatfoots* like I am in some cheesy Sam Spade movie. But then I begin to see clearly that Sooz and I need to get the hell out of Champaign right then and there, because across the street in a phone booth I see Under Assistant Agent Brown talking with who knows who about Sooz's

ID, holding it up close then waving it around while he talks, then waits, then talks some more and I think that nothing good can come of such a thing, and that the sooner we are out of there the better, back to the big city, back where nobody knows her name and I'm just another longhair with a guitar.

I snap back in to see that Sooz is giving me a what-is-the-matter-with-you look and that Agent Schootz seems to be wrapping things up as Under Assistant Agent Brown is returning to the table, handing Sooz her license and then standing there silently as Agent Schootz says, "Well, I think that does it, for now. We thank you very kindly for your assistance." He smiles in a well-trained way and concludes, "If we need further information, we'll be in touch." As they leave and emerge out onto the sidewalk, I see Under Assistant Brown murmur something in Agent Schootz's ear. The SNARB guys disappear around the corner.

"Sooz, we gotta get out of here right now."

She shudders. "My thoughts exactly. And—what? *SNARB?* What the hell is *that*? Did you see that assistant guy screwing around with my license out there and writing whatever the hell he was writing about in that little black book of his? This is not good."

"No. It's serious. But let's wait a couple of minutes. You got the check? Okay, here's what we're going to do." I rattle off my plan and she sits back with a grin, impressed. "My word, you're getting the hang of this sort of thing aren't you?"

"I used to watch *Mission Impossible.*"

A couple of minutes later, Sooz takes the check, pays up at the cashier, walks out the door. She crosses the street, proceeds in the opposite direction from where the car is parked. Then I get up, put on my wrap-around sunglasses, walk out and perch myself next to one of the big empty wooden planters next to the Ten O'Clock Scholar's entrance. I hunch up my collar, watch Sooz head up the street, not too fast, not too slow. My job is to spot the tail, watch her back, see what I can see.

There are plenty of people on the street on that sunny Sunday afternoon—mostly college kids, some townies, some old folks out for a stroll, some cars looking for parking places. Nobody seems to care about Sooz.

She is to stop at the drugstore and buy the newspaper—the fat Sunday *Chicago Tribune*—then keep going. Stop and go, stop and go. I survey the street, looking for the big car I had seen near the von Flarf's or even Agents Fred and Barney themselves. Nothing.

I don't know what I'd *do* if I did spot a tail.

But per the plan, Sooz crosses the street at the light, walks back toward me on my side of the street. When she passes in front of me she mutters, "Anything?" I mumble "No goons." She proceeds to our car.

A few minutes later Sooz stops the Ford in front of me. I hop in, making sure that Felix is still safely sitting on the back seat.

I say, "Okay, now—train station, dump the car—it's better that way, more anonymous."

"I'm not so sure about this."

"You just call, who—Hertz?—tell them it broke down and they'll find it right there. Simple, plausible, nothing wrong with that. Did you pay with cash or credit card?"

"Cash. Simpler that way. Guess I'll lose my deposit but—"

"We'll figure that out later. This'll just let us disappear faster. It's worth it."

We wind our way through downtown Champaign, find the tracks—but a long slow freight train is rumbling through town causing a major traffic jam at the main crossing. The train station is on the other side, a couple blocks farther up.

We sit in the jam on the street next to the tracks, waiting.

"When's the next train to Chicago?"

"No idea. Probably soon."

She tells me that she gave Brown a driver's license with a non-existent address. She's pretty sure that it'll stand up to routine scrutiny. But you never know.

"Sooz, I have no idea where you live."

"Maybe you shouldn't. I think it's best that way." Her voice is tense and high-strung.

The train keeps on rolling.

"Jesus."

Finally, the long train's rusted caboose rattles past us and traffic starts to move. Things are kind of gridlocked with college kids crossing the street in front of cars, making things worse. We need to make a left, cross over the tracks.

"Look—up there on the right—on that street, at the intersection."

"What?"

"That looks like the car we saw at von Flarf's this morning."

An anonymous gray four-door is idling under the Standard Oil sign in a gas station at the corner about fifty yards ahead of us. Agent Schootz stands at a pay phone next to the car, phone under his chin making a call, facing the tracks—he hasn't seen us yet—Under Assistant Agent Brown must be at the wheel, waiting.

Our line of cars begins to move and, car length by car length, we move closer to the intersection and the crossing.

Sooz says, "Maybe it doesn't matter if he sees us, we're fine, maybe it's completely innocent." She drums her fingers on the steering wheel.

"But do you want to wait around and find out?"

"Okay, okay."

I sink in my seat. Then Agent Schootz, who's been watching the main street and train crossing, turns his attention to our frontage road and, still on the phone, sees us, looks straight at me. He says something to the phone, hangs up, begins dodging cars trying to run toward us. We get to the intersection but a truck passes in front of us heading toward Agent Schootz, between us and him, blocking him from view.

"C'mon, c'mon, c'mon let's go, let's go." Sooz sticks the nose of the Ford as far out as she can, waiting for the truck.

Then, as the intersection clears, Agent Schootz stands at the opposite corner waving at us. He begins to cross the street but, at that instant, a beat-up blue car coming from the opposite direction makes an abrupt left turn right in front of him, screeches to a halt, stopping him in his tracks. Agent Schootz bangs on the hood of the big car, yelling something at the driver. Sooz peels out, makes the turn, careens across the tracks just as the signal begins dinging—a train's coming, horn blasting. As we bounce over the hump of train tracks with the barriers coming down behind us, I look back and think that that blue car looks an awful lot like an old Electra 225—but I can't be sure.

Sooz makes a quick right on the other side of the tracks just as a northbound passenger train roars into the station. We whip into the long parking lot, amazingly find a spot right away, scramble like hell gathering up all our stuff—taking particular care about Felix—leave the keys on the floor mat, run up the station platform as fast as we can, jumping on the train at the last possible second. As the train moves out, whistle blowing, we stand on the shaky metal of the train car's steps wheezing, catching our breath. We look at each other, start to laugh.

The conductor's voice comes over the scratchy intercom and says, "Illinois Central, City of New Orleans, now operating express non-stop to Chicago's Union Station. Have a nice day."

 Track 7: Late Sunday afternoon

S OOZ, ASLEEP WITH her head on my shoulder, snoring softly, wakes up like she's been electrocuted as the City of New Orleans rattles and rolls through the quiet little city of Kankakee a couple hours later. She sits up, wiping the side of her mouth. "Did I drool on you? I did, didn't I."

"You did. Very endearing."

"Oy." She smooths her hair, pulls a little mirror out of her sensible purse, gasps, quickly excuses herself, heads for the ladies' room.

I've been dozing off and on myself, head bouncing against the window as the train races north. The snow grows deeper the farther north we go, and in the burnt orange light of the fading afternoon, the train zips through the day's hazy cold. Rivers are crossed—the Kankakee, the Illinois, unnamed creeks and culverts and then finally the gritty Cal-Sag Canal and its rusty barges that signal the beginnings of the outskirts of Chicago—gas stations, plumbing supply warehouses, gasket factories, plastic factories, used car lots, new car lots, big national distribution centers and regional headquarters, vast trucking freight depots with endless lines of loading docks, mostly empty of the big rigs on this average winter Sunday. Far ahead, the train's horn whistles at every crossing. We race between long lines of stopped cars waiting at the signals. The sun is almost down.

Sooz returns, plops down next to me with an exhausted sigh. The train car is nearly empty and we have commandeered two sets of facing seats. Our junk is spread out and Felix sits on the floor between the seats.

She says, "Listen to this. I just had a dream that I *knew* one of those SNARB guys. We were at that Dixie place and he was there in the booth across from us, actually participating in our training session—I think he was doing a little better than you, I'm afraid."

I'm insulted.

She goes on. "But he stares at me with these kind of dead eyes, you know now that I think of it, they were kind of kaleidoscope eyes, like the song. Very bizarre. Anyway, I looked back 'cause he looked somehow familiar, like I'd seen him before somewhere but I couldn't figure it out—second grade? High school? Then he takes out a clipboard and in a voice that sounds like my father, checks off our plan—Champaign. *Check*. Flarf. *Check*. Pitch plan. *Check*. Like he knew everything we were going to do. Then he reclined on our table—rather seductively, I might add—looked me in the eye and started babbling in some foreign language, like Chinese or Tibetan or something!"

"Jesus. What would Freud say about *that*?"

"Yeah. But you know, I think it wasn't you sitting there with me—it was that weird Hawgrim guy. That's when I woke up." An involuntary shiver shakes her body like a centipede has run up her arm. "What's that mean? I must be a real mess."

The train clatters through a crossing.

She looks at me and narrows her eyes. "That Under Assistant Brown guy, there's something about him."

"What? Really?"

"I don't know."

"Like maybe some guy from college, Ann Arbor? Or one of your past run-ins with other friendly agents of our federal government?"

"No. But SNARB? *SNARB*? I mean come *on!* I'm starting to think that it's completely bogus—those were no real FBI-type guys. J. Edgar would freak out if he saw the way those guys operate. I mean, please."

"You're the expert on governmental agencies." I try to remember the Under Assistant Brown guy, his bland emotionless face but he's already fading like a dream. "But if they're not real, who are those guys?"

"Right. Who *are* those guys?"

We consider the question silently while the train rocks.

Then out of the blue she says, "Ever since your brother appeared, I mean the one with your Felix guitar, everything changed for you, hasn't it? Things happening that really shouldn't—you get Felix back, your band gets a recording contract—no offense. Your record gets played, you guys sound *really* great, your tour, that third mic episode—suddenly everything is falling into place ..."

"And you reappear ..."

"And that guy from the UK wants you ..."

"... and you're here."

"Yeah. Wow."

The train's horn blows again way up ahead, long and mournful like a blues riff, and the train whips over a busy street—95th Street. Almost there.

I put my arm around her and she slips down in the seat, seeking warmth and comfort.

The train keeps on rolling.

But I'm worried about her. After witnessing that virtuosic performance in front of von Flarf, I'm beginning to see that she may be right. What she's doing really is hugely important and she's alone and ... and ... and we're closing in on Union Station, the end of the line, our final destination—we'll get off and she'll vanish.

My cheek on her head, I space out on the junk in the city's backyards. Abandoned cars, garbage cans, and weedy vacant lots filled with the unidentifiable debris of city life—busted wooden crates, disintegrating cardboard boxes, bald black tires, broken bottles and shards of shiny glass, newspapers blowing in the wind, and the occasional rusted major appliance. All that stuff used to be of value to somebody—made, bought and sold—what happened? Used up and thrown away—nothing's permanent, nothing lasts. What will an archaeologist digging and sifting the dirt by these ancient tracks a million years in the future think of us? What will *I* think of us—a lousy fifty years from now, if I live that long.

"Sooz, tell me where you live. I need to know, I mean what if ..."

"It's better you don't know."

The train slows and rocks through switching yards and crossings.

I protest. "I have no way of finding you. We get off the train, I go this way, you go that way and that could be ..."

"I'm serious. It's better this way. Just know that I'm not so far away."

"What's that mean?"

"That I'm not so far away, that's what it means." She touches my forehead and peering into my eyes, says that I must not let whatever's going on in *there* carry me away. That's her job.

Sooz tells me her plan for the next few days, the week ahead. She's going to go back to work, rest up and do a little research on this Fletcher Engel guy. She'll get in touch with me when she knows something.

"Besides, you've got a lot of rock 'n roll work to do. I suspect that you're going to be rather busy being a rock star soon as you get home."

Sooz says she works at seven—she makes it clear that a Bunny is never late.

The train stops.

It's about 6:30 as we hustle through the huge main hall of Union Station—almost churchy in its ornate, architectural grandness, with white marble and wide stone steps. The big schedule board clatters, listing all points and places to go in every direction down those long disappearing train tracks.

We're searching for the exit to the taxi stand. I don't want to find it.

I spot one of those cheap automated photo booths.

"Sooz, c'mon." She resists, at first saying she's late, but she relents and I drag her across the hall—we sit down inside and let it rip. I want her face on one or two of those little black and white strips of film, a permanent record immune to the shoes, SNARB, Hawgrim, or anybody or anything that might run her swirling down the drain. A salve for my sanity.

She sits on my lap as the flash starts to pop. I hold her tight, pulling her face close to mine and I strain to imprint the smell of her hair, skin, clothes, and breath on my brain so I won't forget what she's like in the flesh, in the real world. We laugh and pose—her smiling, then pouting, centerfold glam, and me doing rock 'n roll hair in the eyes, big star heroic. We try to look tough, mug-shot serious, haughty, then expressionless, and then the last one—the flash catches us looking into each other's eyes, her lips midstream in a word, and the word was *you.* A smile slips across my face and a high-speed sparking full-duplex connection happens between us—not exactly like the on-stage Dark Stranger mystery shots, euphoric and glorious—and it could've been sappy, cheesy, and over dramatic, too stagey like some soap opera shot, young and restless, but it isn't. I know it isn't. It's just good.

We look over the prints that pop out of the little machine slot. I take one look and point to the last one. "That's the one."

"How do you know?"

"I just know."

I hand her the first strip of three and she sticks it in her purse. I keep *the one.* We hurry off.

At the taxi stand she holds me longer than she should—she risks being late, she kisses me hard. She tells me it'll all be okay and I tell her it'll all be okay. I tell her that I won't lose her even if she wants to be lost and that I will find her if I have to. Then she opens her book bag, fishes around inside and pulls out a little slip of paper—the rainbow slash. She presses it into my hands saying *you might need this* and then, with her perfectly manicured finger she touches my forehead, her smile weary and diminished, and I let her go, watching as her cab takes off down Adams Street. She is gone.

Side 5: Everybody's in showbiz

WHEN I FINALLY WALK in the door of my Sooz-less apartment, tired and hungry, Dave hugs the hell out of me and then verbally beats me up for deserting everybody—"Where the fuck did you go?"—I elect to only roughly outline the events in Champaign, leaving out extraneous details like SNARB goons and ditched cars. Dave admits that if it wasn't for Creach's soothing influence they'd have put out an all-points missing persons alert, and that Hawgrim *is* a freak and I should've seen Creach deal with him at the truck stop ending a panicked phone call to the Feds or somebody with one deftly placed finger, and then calming him down like a firm but kindly uncle—which reminds me that I am going to have to figure out how to deal with the treachery of the reptilian Hawgrim. After I spend a long day's work back at the shop, sorting new records for Lazlo getting back into that groove, I stand in the little lobby of Checkers Records and notice that in the couple of weeks since I'd been there the place has been remarkably spruced up.

I have a private appointment with Harrison Creach.

The walls sport a series of new funky earth-tone stripes and the old, beat up furniture has been replaced with up-to-the-minute stuff that reminds me of the décor in the Playboy Club. It's got dark wood paneling and some sleek chrome chairs upholstered in thick suede the color of café au lait. Nicely framed photos of new Checkers Records artists, like Shine & the Funkolas, hang on the walls and right there in the center of the lineup—*us*, smiling and looking *good*—one of Flashy Ralph's outside train track shots. It's a sight to see.

Then, after being pleasantly greeted by the newly re-hired Mrs. Robinson—"Oh Mr. Porter, we've been expecting you"—the long-time Checkers Records receptionist who had been laid off during the label's dark years but has returned to replace the godawful shrieking door buzzer, revitalizing the place with the warmth of human contact, I am admitted inside.

The muffled sounds of musical mayhem—thumping bass, guitars, drums, and horns mashed up in a funky stew—filter down the halls, strangely distant like it's from some subterranean coalmine deep below Michigan Avenue. She leads me to the door of the control room. The big red recording light is lit. She smiles as we wait for the tune to end. We look at the floor, the ceiling, the walls. Then the music stops and the red light goes out. She opens the door and I enter.

Creach, seated comfortably at the board in a sensible beige sweater and brown slacks and speaking through the intercom, provides gentle encouragement to the musicians in the studio, who, through the big window, I recognize as Shine and the Funkolas—monstrous Afros a little ragged after the heat of the last tune. Seeing me, Creach springs the Funkolas loose and, with his reading glasses tipped up on his forehead and giving me a jiving high five, we adjourn to his office. He closes the door behind him.

Creach pours himself a cup of coffee from his coffee machine, asking me if I want some. I say sure and he hands me a new brown, orange, and white coffee mug with the Checkers logo all over it. The black coffee steams. I sip.

Creach looks like a man for whom things are happening. He's relaxed and satisfied with the recent rapid rise in fortunes at the label. His shoes shine and his slacks are as creased as an F sharp. He tells me that the Funkolas' "Jive Kangaroo" was announced as a new breakout hit on WVON that very morning, and that Bobby "Shine" Washington himself is scheduled to appear as a special guest on "Good Guy" E. Rodney Jones's morning drive-time show the very next day, and demands for a complete Funkolas album are coming in from record jobbers and sales channel flacks on an hourly basis since last week. Mrs. Robinson, whose telephone skills are impeccably professional, is amassing piles of pink *while you were out* messages for Creach about those boys. He says the sun is beginning to rise for Bobby Shine and his Funkolas.

I'm impressed.

He hesitates, asks me about my unscheduled side-trip on the way home. But the look on his face tells me that he probably knows everything anyway and is ready to move on.

I thank him for finding Felix.

"It's my job, young sir. He in good shape?"

I nod appreciatively. "Were you, I mean ... by any chance did you happen to be driving through Champaign—"

"I am always in the right place, son." He stirs a bit more sugar into his cup but doesn't take a sip. "But I will say this—I do believe that you are on a good path right now. All you've got to do is keep on walking, keep on easin' on down your highway."

Who *is* this man?

He stands up, walks to the window. They're barred, being a first-floor office and all. It's a standard city view of the between-building walkway, one of a million dimly lit brick and mortar canyons just like it all over the city.

"Pepper ..."

Mrs. Robinson's voice crackles across on the intercom saying she has another call for Mr. Creach, "It's Cathy Chartswell from WLS, Bob Sirott's production assistant."

"Mrs. Robinson, if you would be so kind as to take a message and assure Miss Chartswell that I will call her at my earliest convenience."

Smooth.

"Of course, Mr. Creach." She clicks off.

I whistle. "Man, those Funkolas are kicking ass, aren't they?"

"They are." He leans across the desk and looks me in the eye. "But Mr. Porter, I'll have you know that *that* call and most of this huge pile of pink that you see on my desk—" with both hands he lifts the pile of phone messages high above his desk letting the slips of paper fall through his fingers like great gobs of Monopoly money, then raising his voice in velvety disk jockey tone, announces "—are about *you* and your little old band!"

Holy smoke.

Mrs. Robinson buzzes on the intercom again with another call, this one from CKLW in Detroit. He asks her to take another message.

"See? It's *happening* my boy! Ho ho!" And then he jumps up— Cool Papa Spo-dee-o-dee appears from the distant past disguised as Harrison Creach and performs a neat twinkle-toes spin as deft and smooth as any full-fledged Pip—Gladys Knight would be proud. But in the middle of a twirl he stops short as if caught red-handed by the propriety police. Dignified Creach makes an abrupt return. He sits back down, smooths his sweater, straightens up the pile of messages on his desk.

"Pardon that rather ... unprofessional display. Now," he clears his throat, "let's get down to business." He winks.

Creach buzzes Mrs. Robinson and asks her to hold his calls as he is in a very important meeting with his *Top Artist*.

He proceeds to rattle off a seemingly endless supply of good news.

Creach tells me that our record—"Your Aunt is Cool"—is getting airplay not only down in St. Louis thanks to KXOK and Fat Phil, but we are being played right here in Chicago on big old WLS and its not-to-be-outdone archrival, WCFL. But wait, there's more—we're up in Milwaukee on WOKY and CKLW in Detroit, and he says it's kind of like a happy little virus spreading up and down Midwestern airwaves, viral and uncontrollable word of mouth from disk jockey's speaking on air. "But get this, my young friend—you're going to dig this—the B-side of that record, 'Burgers in Benton'?—has been picked up on that hipper-than-everybody FM station *WXRT*, right here in Chi-town!"

Whoa.

This bit of intelligence means that one of our songs, good old Burgers, is actually being taken *seriously*. Not that there is anything wrong with "Your Aunt is Cool" becoming a hit—that is unbelievable and amazing—but its sudden success smacked of *one-hit-wonderness*—a catchy and cute radio-friendly novelty tune but not *art*. Burgers is being played on the hipster airwaves of WXRT, choice of discerning listeners, musical connoisseurs, dare I say *musical snobs*, whose lives revolve around finding the next band, the next album, the next sound that just might lead to some new and undiscovered musical nirvana, a new high that is even higher than the last one, a high that is always *out there*, somewhere out on that horizon like a long-awaited letter from home.

It.

In other words, those serious listeners are just like me and *they* are the fans I want to have.

Creach lays it out for me—we need to get our band ass in gear. He has interviews and photo sessions and meetings with graphic artists lined up here in Chicago, and there are more contracts to be drawn up and signed and—oh yes, Rodger Slothwell called that very morning all the way from swinging London town letting it be known that his contract is in the *post* and due to arrive right there at Checkers Records any day now and would we be so kind as to sign *straightaway,* and when could he expect our first album to be available for British release and when might we expect a European tour to commence? *Jolly good.* He is talking big. But Creach says that first a regional tour must be planned and then national and then *international*—the UK, Europe, and then—a *world tour.* "No time to waste, my boy, not a moment to lose."

But Creach says that the most important thing to be done right now this week is this—write and record our first album. It needs to be out on the street within a month, maybe two at the latest.[67]

"Time to strike, Mr. Porter! While the iron is hot!"

So after making glorious plans, commitments, and setting deadlines, I walk out of Checkers Records flying high like one of those little waxwing birdies in Benld. I'm not a little prisoner bird, but one that has busted loose and escaped, flown out the door free and easy, a little bird on its way. It hits me that for this little while, I have forgotten about Sooz and everything in her bizarre and beautiful universe. And I have forgotten about Hawgrim. I put him out of my mind and think about her and about Creach as I pat my pockets searching for my keys in front of Otto, parked under the cold glow of a street light on South Michigan Avenue. I find the key and stick it in Otto's door, jiggling and then deftly turning it with just the right flick of the wrist to make it work, and as the door opens I feel the need to stop and look over my shoulder. Right there, on the east side of the deserted street, sitting on a closed-up storefront stoop in front of its rusted burglar bars is a long-legged guy in a dark coat and some kind of big hat.

---

[67] Creach also brings up the subject of management. It's becoming obvious that we need *professional guidance* above and beyond the production of our records—someone to look out for our best interests, provide advice and wise counsel in all areas of the business. In other words, he proposes to provide what, in actuality, he's been providing all along. So, we are now under contract with his newly revived management company, Starmaker Talent Services Inc.

"Hey! You goddamn sombitch! I been watching your goddamn car all this time, young white boy." He gets up and makes his shaky way across the pot-holed street with a nearly empty bottle of Thunderbird wine waving in his hand. Though he makes me nervous, I don't hop in Otto and tear out of there. The man sways in front of me—his black face grizzled with age, old man stubbled skin weathered and beaten up by life. His coat stinks of sweat and urine and his aromatic aura surrounds him like a big ten-foot bubble. Politely raising his hat and elaborately describing his vehicle protection services, he requests that a small contribution of a monetary nature be made. Saddened by his desperate ragged dignity, I hand him a dollar bill. He bows slightly, toasts me with a long swig of wine, expressing deep gratitude. Then he turns, retreats to his sidewalk perch, tossing the now empty bottle up against a wall, shards of glass skittering across the sidewalk, sounding like ice.

I haul Otto around in a creaky u-turn and we shake, rattle, and roll our way up South Michigan Avenue in the late night, past blank blinking stoplight after blank blinking stoplight, each one of them a silent question mark of societal guilt—like Sooz says—what's it gonna be, boy?

 Track 2: Later Monday night

DAVE: BEFORE YOU SAY A WORD, I'd like to comment on the contours of the beanbag chair.

I close the apartment door behind me.

Me: What?

Dave: The curves on that chair. Have you ever noticed how unbelievably *complex* they are? I mean, look at the deep creases right ... *there* (he reaches across the coffee table, touches a very specific point on the chair) do you see how it is so fabulously ... graceful ... do you *see* that?

Me: Mmm.

Dave: I never noticed it before. I never saw that. It's like that fabric, that stuff ... what is it?

Me: Vinyl.

Dave: Vinyl, yes, it's curved like ... a flame. Miraculous.

Except for the soft music on the stereo—Dave's album of Japanese koto music—the apartment is quiet, one light on, no incense or candles, nothing goofily weird or head shop strange. And as if he's discussing the status of his laundry, which is normally undone anyway, he tells me that he picked up a few buttons of peyote, mescaline, from somebody in the dressing room after the show at SIU, just a couple of grams. A glass of water stands half full on the floor next to him.

Me: You okay?

Dave: Yes. I'm fine. Couldn't be better. You see, I *am* and you *are*. And the legs of that table over there? Totally tubular.

I ask him if it is permissible to sit on the beanbag chair. He says it *is* what it *is*. He reclines on the sofa, observes the ceiling. I sit down quietly.

Dave: You know, I never noticed that this room, the ceiling isn't entirely square. (Laughs.) That's not the drug talking by the way, it's just a fact. Can you see that? (He points to the corner of the ceiling where the walls meet.) That? Damn. But you know, it doesn't matter, does it?

Me: What matters, Dave?

Dave: Its *is-ness*. It just *is*. And I ... am right here. Just where I need to be.

Dave goes on to discuss the intricate way the angles of the old bay window interact with the planks of the hardwood floor—their intersection horizontal, vertical, diagonal, and the amazing spatial relationships that have been there all the time and yet, he has never noticed. His peaceful manner spreads over me like an aura and I, too, try to *see*.

Dave: This room is like a painting, some amazing piece of art, like a Picasso or something, everything is art. You know he—Picasso—wrote about that somewhere and I can see it now and the *colors*—I'm so glad you painted it that color.

Me: It's white, off-white.

Dave: (sighs) But what a helluva white it is, a million different whites. I know you can't see that.

Me: It's so easy to be distracted by everything, the outer world, isn't it?

He looks like I have just said the most outlandish thing he's ever heard.

Dave: Yes! It's like a door that I never knew was there and yet ... there it is, right there in the wall. And I walked right through it. That cat was right.

Me: What cat?

Dave: This is the way we ought to *see*.

Me: (...)

Dave: Want some?

Me: Not now.

The koto record ends and the turntable's tonearm picks up, automatically shuts off. We sit in silence, broken only by the quiet whir of the fridge in the kitchen and the distant clank of pipes from the furnace in the building's basement.

Me: Perhaps now's not the best time to tell you this, but—

Dave: It's always the right time.

Me: It's starting to happen.

Dave: It is.

Me: (...)

Dave: What is?

Dave shifts on the sofa, puts his hands behind his head like he is reclined in a cozy hammock on a warm and windy day.

Me: It. *It!* The band, the music, all of it. Creach told me tonight. It's gonna get crazy, and it starts now.

Dave: Of course it is. I never doubted it. It is what it is. It just *is*.

And so begins a lunatic period of rock 'n rollness and musical wonders, broken only by my thinking of her nearly every seven seconds, almost as much as I think about sex.

 Track 3: Wednesday night

NOTHING. I HAVE HEARD NOTHING FROM HER. We're all back at Checkers Records holding our first post-tour band meeting and rehearsal. There are things to talk about, plans to be made, songs to go over—and Hawgrim.

I need to get my head together about him.

After what he did—his slimy proposal of consultations, his vague threats of menace should I not assent to his entreaties—not to mention his treacherous attempted phone call. How can I keep him in the band?

I resolve to fire his ass.

And the fact that it will be just as things are taking off will make it all the sweeter.

New keyboard player? No problem.

Here's how it will go:

We're all crammed in Creach's small office, gathered there to hear the *big news* that the fuse has been lit and our collective rock 'n roll cherry bomb is set to explode in the musical mental mailbox of kids everywhere, and that the band is poised on the edge of stardom, and then Creach'll say something like, "Boys, I want everyone to sign right here on the dotted line, a mere formality authorizing your full consent and participation in the exciting road ahead which will change your life and oh, by the way, change the world." Then, as Hawgrim takes the pen, poised to sign, I will rise up to halt the proceedings and, in a full-throated roar, which I know is uncharacteristic of me, I will say *not so fast, polka-breath—I'm afraid that due to your treachery and all-around weaselness involving the attempted intimidation of a certain young woman, a close friend of a member of this group— you have been uninvited to this party and you have been detained by the authorities at the border of this new and wondrous land, turned away—refused entry! Please hand over your set lists and regulation band bowtie.* And Hawgrim's head will droop in hangdog shame, offer not a word in his own defense because he has no defense and then, as I stand over him like a fearful Dickensian ghost in black robes of doom, I fervently point to the door, casting him out with a trembling bony finger. Hawgrim will rise like a prisoner in the dock, turning one last time to make a final pathetic appeal, but the steely heart of the Pepperian Ghost of Rock 'n Roll Future is hardened, and the door to Creach's office will slowly close in his face. And, being on the wrong side of my musical and cultural history, a thoroughly chastened Hawgrim will slink away into the cold, dark Chicago night.

That done, I will sit down and cheerfully say, "Now, where were we?"

But once again, before our meeting gets going, there is yet another scene in a men's room.

Speaking quietly, Creach says, "I know that you want to fire Hawgrim." He washes his hands, examines his teeth in the mirror for remnants of the fine dinner he has just hosted for us at Theresa's Barbecue just up the street. "I would advise against it, however. There's no good reason to do so and, if you do, I see nothing but trouble."

Creach lays out the worst-case scenario. Spurned by the band, Hawgrim, bitter and resentful—even more so than usual—wanders the streets of Chicago in a foul and dark mood, making insurance sales calls. He has both the motive and the opportunity for further skullduggery. He finds it a simple thing to do to contact the authorities, causing a catastrophic disaster for my young lady friend, me included, with no downside to himself, which is, let us make no mistake, always Hawgrim's prime motivator. Whereas, Creach goes on, if I was to refrain from this hasty, ill-considered action and keep him on board, albeit in some form of lukewarm keyboard purgatory, he will be more likely to *not* bring down the wrath of the authorities on my lady friend and myself, since that action would screw up and likely kill the band and any possibility of near-term financial, let alone musical success, for our young accordion-playing friend.

He looks me in the eye. "Do you understand my thinking, young Pepper Porter?"

"Yes."

He advises that I keep my friends close but my enemies closer.

Me? Enemies? This is nuts. I'm just a rock 'n roll kid with a cartoon guitar and a sorta-maybe hit record if you're tuned to the right radio stations at the right time, probably middle of the night, who knows? I have no enemies. But I decide to accept his counsel just the same. I see its wisdom.

So, amazingly, the rehearsal goes great. And why shouldn't it? Everybody is still juiced from the swing downstate and jazzed with Creach's long litany of good news. Hawgrim nods contentedly and is pleasant enough. And he doesn't say a word about Sooz. I know that he is just biding his time.

The next day, I hear nothing from her.

 *Track 4: Thursday night*

H AWGRIM AND I ARE standing in the narrow smoky hall in the back of the Quiet Knight, a hip Lincoln Park bar and music joint, having just finished setting up. We're about to play for a significant gathering of influential Midwestern rock 'n roll writers who are in town whooping it up for the week, seeing some regional talent— some on the way up, some on the way down. Creach has arranged this low-paying gig at the last minute, cajoling some old friend of his to let us have a slot opening for Archie Bell and the Drells, who technically aren't Midwestern and technically aren't rock 'n roll but are in town trying to restart after having some hits a few years earlier. Of course we're happy to have the gig, pay or no pay. It's good exposure. We'd play in a taco stand for free if we had to.

"Hello, Hawgrim."

"Hello, Boo Boo."

First time we talked since then.

"How're sales going? Aren't you in some big sales contest this month?"

Surprised that I asked, he says, "Closed a couple deals today." Getting into it, he sniffs with a self-assured satisfaction, scratches an itch on the side of his cheek. "So far I'm the leading producer in the district and if all goes according to plan, I'll be the proud owner of a fine *gold-plated putter*—with, I might add, my name engraved *right on the blade.*" He lights a cigarette, looks entirely pleased with himself. "Yep. My manager says my closing technique has gone from shit to gold in mere weeks."

"Outstanding. I don't know anybody with a golden putter."

He smiles thinly, puffing on his cigarette, narrowing his eyes like he isn't sure what I mean by that. He pokes me in the chest.

"Have you reconsidered your answer to my earlier question?"

"Which one?"

"That commie chick of yours ... she run into any ... trouble this weekend?"

"Brian, I've been thinking about my financial future and am thinking that a whole life insurance policy might be just the ticket."

His expression shifts gears like a V8, he automatically slips into sales mode.

"Pepper, that makes good *personal, financial, economic sense*. I'm so glad to see you thinking ahead." We talk about some numbers and he goes for a trial close. "I could have the papers drawn up tomorrow and—"

Creach sweeps around the corner, stands right between us, lets it be known that it is time to go on. He tells us that this is a very receptive crowd and they're all hoping that we'll be *fantastic* and *make their day*. Hawgrim, a little rattled with the interruption of the selling process, mumbles something, hurries off somewhere. Creach tells me, "Guy at the front table on the left with the glasses, the one of perhaps Asian ancestry? Stanley Wong-Garcia. *Rolling Stone*."

"I know that name. I've read his stuff."

"Indeed you have. Now pay attention to the man ... but don't pay attention to him. Know what I mean? Just play your music."

When I hop onto the little stage and as we're all plugging in, I tell Hawgrim that *whole life* seems to fit my *changing lifestyle's needs* and *investment objectives*. But on the other hand, I might be wrong— maybe more economical term life insurance would be smarter?

I just don't know.

There's a *you bastard* smirk on his face as he begins fiddling with the Baldoni. Dave thumps some bassy riffs, Ricky rolls his drums.

Then we rock the joint.

Creach works the room during our short set, handing out business cards and little promo kits with our new photo and a press release that he and I had whipped up that afternoon about how "Your Aunt is Cool" is sweeping the Midwest, and that Pepperland is a fresh new voice, an authentic American sound with deep musical roots in the heartland, reflecting the needs and desires of today's youth.

... the burning yearn of youth to find someplace far away, yet close to a cosmic home—someplace they've never been—lit by the lightning of music that crackles and pops like a sizzling roman candle, spewing sparks and stars straight out of the ground.

Or something like that.

We think it's a rather nice press release.

But Sooz would say it's all commercial marketing bullshit.

And she'd be right.

And then she'd resume coding.

After we finish up our set, which ends with a super tight rendition of "American Dirt" highlighted by Dave's newly fabulous lead vocal, and our just rolled-out three-part harmonies, featuring Ricky who is perched on his drum throne up under the low ceiling, hairy and imperial like King Farouk. It's more of that inexplicable magic that's been happening to us. Creach leads us around the room, beginning with Wong-Garcia, who is West-Coast cool. He hands me his card, telling me he likes our music and definitely wants to chat. We arrange to meet at his hotel the next day.

Afterward, Creach shoves the latest issue of *Rolling Stone* in my hand telling me to bone up, read Wong-Garcia's latest piece so I'll be knowledgeable, able to comment intelligently. He tells me to read the whole thing.

But as I sit at a table in the back of the room and wait for Archie Bell and the Drells to *tighten up* and *get down*, it isn't Wong-Garcia's article on Bob Dylan that catches my eye. It's this:

*   *   *

Excerpts from an Interview: *On the Lam in Nixon's America, Pt. 1. Rolling Stone, March 15, 1974*

Editor: There are political prisoners in this country. Some are behind bars, some are not—they live in a different kind of prison. They live in the underground, a shadowland where every move must be carefully considered, where fear of disclosure and its resulting paranoia is an everyday cold shot. Even while our government—the Executive Branch in particular—has shown its dark hand and may not last the year, the long arm and all-seeing eye of the FBI is forever probing and never resting in its goal of bringing these Americans to a twisted justice.

Recently, as it is the policy of this publication to freely report all the news that fits, your correspondent was able to meet with one of these political fugitives, who I will not identify, in a location that I will not disclose, in accordance with our First Amendment right to do so.

Our subject will be known here as *Grace*. We met in a busy working-man's café. All pauses, asides, and laughs have been left in so you can dig it as it went down.

                                       *   *   *

Rolling Stone: Why did you leave the Movement?

Grace: The Movement? It's gone. And because of death—far too much of it—there are things, inadvertent incidents that I must atone for. Of course, I can't be specific.

RS: Of course.

 G: But the egos, infighting, naiveté all contributed to it … money … certainly political differences, gender issues, sex … and the war's winding down and nobody cares anymore—the Paris Peace Accords—it's a new world. Armed insurrection? Forget it. And since I tend to have rather freakishly high standards of precision and execution, I decided to leave the group … and I wasn't really convinced that I was making a difference. I felt irrelevant.

RS: Patti Hearst?

G: And the SLA? Amateurs. Unrealistic goals. Nobody wins.

…

RS: Where do you see your generation—our generation in ten years time? Can we un-fuck what's been fucked?

G: I worry about us. I used to think that—like Joni Mitchell said—we were *golden*, stardust—but I think that at the end of the day, we're just like every other generation that's fallen off the turnip truck … albeit with a few unavoidable and … charming cultural twists that come with growing up in America in the middle of the twentieth century. [*laughs*] We're all going to have to make our own way one day—oy vey—it's happening now. Anyway, look out … this generation's going to be one huge bunch of all-American consumers. Politically? You could walk over there and say "hey man," and he'd say "hey man" back, but who knows where his head's at? He may look like he's a wild-eyed, anti-establishment, crazy freak, but he might just be worried about keeping his job, paying fifty cents a gallon, and for all you or I know, he voted for Nixon.

RS: You're pessimistic.

G: All could be lost. That old revolutionary, c'mon people, we're marching to the sea stuff, dreams of grandeur? Poof! Gone. Our role is to consume. [*pause*] A real revolution is like a million radio antennas picking up the same or similar signal creating a rhythm, a sympathetic vibration in a population, and *that* never happened. We failed to communicate. Despite that, I still have great hopes, and here's the ray of hope in these stormy times—there are areas of technology, computer technology that will be used for the common good, to empower those without a voice, to speed free communications among the people. Great things are happening in computer labs, even in garages and basements—right now. Unbelievably cool things. That's where the revolution will be.

RS: *Or maybe it'll be just another capitalist tool.*

G: It could make us smarter or it could make us dumber.

...

RS: *How do you survive?*

G: I've got a job in a place you wouldn't believe.

RS: *How does it feel?*

G: [*pause*] Sometimes I think ... I just might throw in the towel on this fugitive thing. It's a terrible life.

RS: [*silence*]

G: But then I snap out of it.

RS: *What will be your legacy?*

G: I don't want it said that I merely reflected my time, that I was a product of post-war prosperity, the Vietnam war, *Leave it to Beaver*, and TV dinners. I feel it is my role—or anybody's role for that matter, to transform my time. And I've only got so much time on the planet. But here's the thing, I firmly believe that there's a huge change coming, soon—something on the order of the Industrial Revolution, something as fundamental as that. It's big and it's going to happen. And I will be a part of it.

[*Our lunch arrives.*]

RS: *That's quite a big burger for ... well, I wouldn't have expected somebody such as yourself ...*

Grace: Gimme a break. I'm *hungry*. You have a problem with *women* ordering ...

RS: *Of course not. I apologize.*

G: Pass the ketchup, please.

[*nervous laughter*]
[*sound of ketchup bottle sliding across Formica table*]
G: Thank you.
RS: No. Thank you.

*   *   *

I am stunned. *Throwing in the towel.* There it is. She'd given me a few little hints about her frustration and fears, but here it is, laid out for everybody to see. I put the paper down, stare without seeing at the vanishing foam of my no longer cold beer. I don't even take a sip. Though after that brief, despairing comment, she recovered rapidly, talking of transforming her time rather than merely reflecting it and then put the interviewer in his place after his bonehead burger comment, she's more vulnerable than I have ever seen her.

But I am forced to put all of this into my mental back pages, because we spend the rest of the night chatting with the tough-minded rock 'n roll journalists that Creach keeps herding over to the little booth we have commandeered in the dark of the Quiet Knight. All four of us jammed in there talking big and acting cool, the sound system blasting old records of Chicago blues cats, and I bet that Creach knows every one of them. The writers hand me their business cards and it's like we're holding court—some look so young and babyfaced you'd think they write for college papers, and some are grizzled veterans of maybe thirty, and they're the ones drinking whiskey and tough-guy alcohol, but they all ask me about my influences, and what does that song about aunts—or is it ants—actually *mean,* and they want my opinion about the *direction of music,* and what about my politics and theories on religion, and what's the deal with that strange guitar and how about those bowties and who's ever heard of a band with an accordion player. Hawgrim steps right in and is salesy-smooth, asking what's wrong about shattering boundaries, breaking the rules, and everybody solemnly nods in agreement, and then they turn to Dave asking about the Kazoosh, which he enthusiastically describes as a marvel of musical stagecraft innovation. They laugh and somebody asks if we really are brothers and did we write tunes together, and he says yes, we are, and no, we don't, and then he gets into it, and I can see that he begins to think this is some sort of John and Paul press conference. He says that he always looks for the invisible door in the *cosmic wall of being*, which causes a perplexed silence, but then a couple of photographers, who have been snapping shots during our set, make their way through the smoky crowd and begin taking more pictures of us being cool. And then, after all that, Archie Bell and the Drells start up their set and it all comes to an end and she is on my mind again.

Hawgrim and Ricky head to the bar, chatting up the waitresses. I pick up the Sooz interview, start reading again. My eye keeps returning to the line about her throwing in the towel. Dave remains with me.

"Look at this. *Goddamn!* This is *her.*" I shake the paper, stab the page.

Dave scans it quickly. "Goddamn is right." He produces another beer for me. Therapeutically, he says, "Have another drink."

The music is loud, it's hard to hear. We have to shout at each other.

I take a long swig. "I want no fear in this girl's life. She's been on her own for so long, with nobody. Nobody!"

Dave reads some more of it. He hollers, "So what are you going to do?"

"I don't know."

"What?"

"I said I'm not sure." I avoid all the details.

The bass and drums thump away in a floor-buzzing funky storm.

"You are really freaked out on this chick, aren't you?"

"What?"

"I said you're really hung up on her!"

I yell back. "I am—it's like there's a million-watt neon sign flashing in my head, but I can't read what it says."

Dave thinks about that and swirls his beer. He drains his glass and shouts, "Happens to me all the time."

I'm not sure I hear him right but I go on anyway. "But then I read stuff like this—" I grab the paper back. "Jesus! In *Rolling* fucking *Stone*—and I just don't know. I've got to help her. She could disappear tomorrow."

The song ends and there's a brief period of low-noise while Archie Bell chats up the crowd.

Dave hunches over the table. In a conspiratorial tone he says,

"Strange times. And you know, this is *all related*. The Dark Stranger. The guy. I saw him again."

"Where?"

"At the Dixie." He looks at me hard.

"*What?*"

Dave tells me that he saw the Dark Stranger walking out of the Dixie with two packages of Twinkies and a soda in his hand—he walked out across the parking lot and vanished in the dark.

"What'd he look like?"

"The usual. You know, like Elliot." He takes a long swig and shrugs. "You were there, too, with her. Weren't you?"

I nod.

"I knew it, I knew it." He slaps the table. "Where?"

"The john. She ran out the back."

His eyes bug out. "Have you noticed that since the snowball fight and ever since you got Felix back, basically ever since we first saw him out there on the road outside the Dixie, things have changed and we have become fuckin' ... I'm sorry, *really* fuckin' amazing? Us, Checkers Records, the shows downstate, our actual sorta hit record, and now all this stuff with that chick of yours ... have you noticed?"

"Yes. It's all very weird. And *you*—your singing. I mean, we're all ..."

"... Unbe-fucking-lievable!"

The music starts up again. Archie Bell sings "Don't Let Love Get You Down."

Then I say, "What if we're crazy?"

"I don't know. If we're crazy, then everybody's crazy."

Which means nobody's crazy.

Later, we're loading everything into Otto in the grungy alley behind the Quiet Knight, Hawgrim tells me that he's going to work up a complete and comprehensive proposal for me outlining my insurance options. He'll have something drawn up for me in the next few days.

A couple of rats scuttle out of a big overturned garbage can, vanishing into the dark.

"Make no mistake though, Boo Boo—do not forget about our *other issue*." He takes off around the corner and is gone.

Side 6: Fragile

And so each venture
Is a new beginning, a raid on the inarticulate
With shabby equipment always deteriorating
In the general mess of imprecision of feeling,
Undisciplined squads of emotion.
T. S. Eliot, "East Coker," 1943

 Track 1: Friday morning

AMONG THE MAIL lying on the floor under the slot in the door
the next morning—including IBM's latest Annual Report, VP/
SPAS/OSS put me on their mailing list—I find a letter with a neatly
typed address to Mr. Martin Alan Porter. I tear it open.

It's a long letter from her. I'll spare you the chatty intro where she
complains about the sticky comma and apostrophe keys on her old
typewriter, and the fact that she has run out of whiteout so would I
please forgive the (very few) xxxx-outs. (She said she is also running
out of paper.) Then she gets down to it:

```
    I am spooked by those SNARB guys. You know how
I said that second guy, Under Assistant Brown
looked familiar? I figured it out. He was in the
MBA program at Michigan when I was there. I re-
member him because he was president of the Young
Americans for Freedom chapter on campus and had
the shortest hair in Ann Arbor. He was famous.
Did you ever see that guy? I'm pretty sure it was
him.
    I might've been a little famous too, for act-
ing up. Maybe he knew of me. Don't know. It's a
big place.
    Tomorrow I will spend some time @ my
undisclosed timesharing provider and do some
```

digging information-wise. There must be some data
on SNARB out there somewhere. I have my ways.

SNARB. And I was feeling so good after von
Flarf.

But the Plan must go forward.

I will also get back in touch with our professor friend tomorrow though his phones are probably tapped. There are other more efficient and new
channels. I want to know what he thinks. And then
I will contact Fletcher Engel. Are you ready?

I hate my hair this way. There, I said it.
It's vain and self-centered but I don't care.
This Bunny business can get a girl down.

By now you probably have seen that "Rolling Stone" interview that just came out. Did you?
You see, I have good days and I have bad days. I
was in a bad stretch when I did that. Very alone,
tired, depressed by the winter. It was about a
month ago and I really was thinking about throwing
in the towel. That was when I finally decided to
contact you. And here you are and I have new life.

Just as easy, it could all disappear and be
lost. As I write now it is the middle of the
night when everything is blackest and the mind
rummages around in its dark corners and sometimes finds things that should have been thrown
away but there they are, like forgotten junk in
a crazy man's basement. And then I tire of this
never-ending road and I'm a lunatic and I start
to think of just taking the bus down State Street
to Daley's police headquarters and TURNING MYSELF
IN. Just get the whole thing over with.

Then I'd spend the next ten or who knows how
many years behind bars while the entire technology revolution that I've been working for--my
revolution--just passes me by.

```
    Then I return to lucidity and rational
thinking.
    But I probably don't have much time left. This
is why I must come in from the cold.
    And you are my source of heat, Pepper my love.
Don't leave me alone.
```

There it is again. Fragility, uncertainty. Combined with such intelligence and courage.

What's a guy supposed to do when he gets a letter like that?

I go to the library to dig up what I can about SNARB.

I have a few hours before I'm due to meet Creach at the swank Palmer House Hotel for our little chat with Stanley Wong-Garcia, so I leave a note for sleeping beauty, knowing Dave won't wake up for hours. I grab my old canvas shoulder bag, hop a 151, head for the big library on State.

After failing to find anything that looks remotely like SNARB in any of the big, dusty US government reference books, and then feeling like a dumbshit for even thinking that there actually would be any public mention of such an oddball group, I decide to check the standard commercial registries. Nothing. Then I ask one of the nice lady librarians who, despite the obvious doubt showing behind her reading glasses, helps me get going with one of the fancy mechanical microfiche setups, and soon I am going through articles in papers like the *New York Times* and *Washington Post*—stuff about government security clearance policies in the past year. The librarian kindly supplies sub-referenced material through a University of Chicago database that has a terminal in one of the library backrooms that isn't available to the public.

So I sit alone in front of the microfiche projector in a dimly lit and quiet room filled with rows of identical machines scrolling through a stack of little rolls of the stuff, looking at what turns out to be dead-end articles about inexplicable things I don't care about and people I don't know.

I become engrossed in a strange article in the *San Francisco Chronicle* that's printed next to yet another thing about Watergate, Cuban exiles and presidential security techniques. The piece is about hand-made computers built in garages by freaks in California, wild and crazy stuff, the sort of thing she and von Flarf were talking about. Then a warm hand presses firmly on my neck and a dark voice in a library whisper says, "You'll never find what you're looking for that way, young man." Scaring the hell out of me, I jump. Then hot breath and a tongue enters my ear while a hand drops between my thighs. Sooz lets her shoulder bag fall to the floor, she kisses me hard, pulling my head up and back. She could've broken my neck if she'd felt the need—she is, after all, a well-trained operative.

Once again, she comes out of nowhere.

Making it sound like the sexiest thing in the world she coos, "I've had a productive day so far. How about you?"

In an unexpectedly smooth Hollywood move—I surprise my-self—swift and dripping with romance, I turn the tables on her, ex-ecute my own surprise maneuver, swinging her around in a dance hall dip, her back arched to the floor in surrender with our mouths pressed together in a grinning teeth-knocking and laughing liplock.

An older man in a wooden study carrel about thirty feet away wit-nesses this display with a hissing glare.

I whisper, "I got your letter."

She straightens herself out and shakes her hair out of her fuzzy white knit hat—the Mary Tyler Moore way she does it gets me every time—pulls up a chair. "Sorry. I was tired, needed to sleep."

"You sound better now."

"I am."

She tells me that she's already been in touch with von Flarf, send-ing an electronic message to him from a timesharing terminal in the library she has access to.

"I've made friends with one of the librarians. Older ladies tend to like me a lot you know. And they can be so sweet." She smiles de-murely.

"Electronic message, what do you mean, like a teletype?"

"It's a new world—*electronic mail*. Nobody ... I mean hardly any-body has access, but I do. Crazy, huh?"

"But how?"

"Don't ask. But von Flarf responded just like *that*." She snaps her fingers.

Apparently von Flarf has already run some preliminary mathematical models on Sooz's networking algorithms and likes what he sees—he says that *the numbers behave*. He got in touch with Engel and it was agreed that a meeting seems most appropriate.

"We need to call him. Now."

"Fantastic!" My gut begins to stew and it occurs to me that my life is flipping back and forth like a record—side one and side two. Sooz, music. Music, Sooz. Technology, band. What's the A side, what's the B side?

I don't know.

The man glares at us again.

She looks at my microfiche setup skeptically. I say, "Yeah, I didn't find anything out about SNARB."

"I did." She looks up and down the long hallway of the room—the man at the carrel appears busy. "From what I can piece together, it's a quasi-governmental, private entity that's involved with advanced technology and the military, specifically Fort Meade in Maryland." Narrowing her eyes, she whispers, "The NSA—the high tech spookiest of the spooks—the National Security Administration."

"Jesus. So who's Fletcher Engel?"

"A private investor with serious technology connections. That's all." She stands up—it's time to go. "Let's find a phone. Time to call him."

Track 2: Friday afternoon

I HAVE HALF AN HOUR before my interview with Stanley Wong-Garcia. As we're hurrying down the flights of echoey marble stairs of the big old library, Sooz tells me that SNARB appears to be connected to some vast pool of corporate money flowing out of the Mercantile Exchange right here in Chicago. She doesn't have a name, but her source told her that the retired chairman of some big conglomerate of Chicago financial services firms, a real John Bircher, is on a mission to hot wire the slow and inefficient process of organic high-tech development and nurture his own channel of the smartest high technology people he can find to fight the Cold War—talent-spotting and bird-dogging like-minded individuals, identifying useful ideas but keeping an eye on political and technology renegades, rooting out political undesireables and unreliables—and deliver the goods on a silver platter to the Fort.

"The Fort?"

"It's what they call the NSA. Hardly anybody knows what goes on in there, and that's just the way they like it." We arrive at the bottom of the stairs and stop. "They're one of the largest computer installations in the world."

"Where'd you get all this?"

"Out there. The network. You're gonna freak when you see all this stuff."

We find a bank of three pay phones in the main entrance, but they're the sort that just hang on the wall on dull metal shelves. I suggest that the constant whoosh of cold wind from the opening doors and street noise will detract from the business-like environment necessary for such an important call. Besides, one of the phones is in use by a guy who appears to be concluding some private and probably less than legal transaction. It feels like we're intruding on his personal space. Sooz picks up one of the phones anyway, but I pull her off and drag her out the door. She needs to sound good. Sooz says *c'mon it doesn't make any difference,* but I have already learned a thing or two from Harrison Creach and my earlier encounters with IBM and those others—impression and image is everything. I want her in an actual phone booth with a closing door.

"You don't want him thinking you're just some schmuck calling from a crappy pay phone."

So we hustle up State Street to the Palmer House Hotel, bastion of establishment propriety and society nightlife. Frank Sinatra and Debbie Reynolds had been there mere weeks before playing the glitzy Empire Room. Lots of pay phones and it's where I have to be in a few minutes anyway.

Sooz and I blow through the revolving doors and are immediately swept along with a surging tide of identical men in blue and brown suits. It feels like we've dropped into the middle of a surrealistic French film. It's mostly youngish guys about my age or maybe a little older, with sober three-piece suits straight off the rack at Brooks Brothers, recently shorn hair, thick mustaches, trimmed sideburns, all trying out earnest, boss-pleasing corporate expressions of no-nonsense, quota-making determination. It occurs to me that every one of them could be Hawgrim in disguise.[68]

Slowly rising up the narrow single-file escalator to the main lobby, Sooz first, then me, we emerge like wide-eyed subterranean explorers into a vast and secret cave festooned with Roman and Greek stalac-tite frescos circling high around the room. The hotel logo, an ornate blue "P" surrounded by a laurel wreath of gold, is everywhere, and as we stand gawking like hoosier ma and pa, stunned by the room, surrounded by a crush of very important conferees and chit-chatting dealmakers, an official-looking man with thick black glasses in a tux-edo approaches us. Tersely, he asks if he can be of some assistance. Clearly we, or at least I, don't fit in, and the watchful management must check me out before the hotel's paying guests are made uncom-fortable by my odd and hairy presence. Sooz, however, always looks good no matter what she wears. Would you have a problem with Jean Shrimpton in painter's pants? Of course you wouldn't.[69]

Cheerfully, trying to confirm my non-threatening civility, I greet him. "Thank you sir, but can you direct us to a telephone booth? I need to make a call ... prior to my *business* meeting with one of your *guests* that I believe is scheduled to occur right here in this lobby in about—" I check my watch, "—twenty minutes."

Surprised and vaguely disappointed, he directs us to one of the hallways that branches off the lobby's main cavern where, over the hall's entrance, a big banner is hung proclaiming a meeting of the *IBM Midwest Regional Commercial/Distribution & Wholesale Zone— Welcome New Hires!*

---

[68] Okay, Hawgrim does have that ponytail—a decidedly non-business feature. However, he, when necessary, can appear very conventional with his hair pulled back tight, nice suit and tie. A straight-on mug shot will reveal nothing freaky about him. He loves that ponytail. Soon, however, he is going to have to decide—the band or insurance sales or law school or something—things are about to explode one way or the other. But I suspect that a sure sign of his impending departure from the band will be the sudden disappearance of his ponytail.

[69] Jean Shrimpton—fabulously gorgeous English *bird*, supermodel of swinging '60s London town—made a seriously big impression on the young Pepper Porter.

IBM. My would-be employer, the empire of centralized computing power, symbol of informational oppression and ultimate target of
radical technology revolution. Or something like that. But for sure,
we are in the belly of the corporate beast.

I could've been one of these guys.

Sooz and I charge straight down the middle of the thick-carpeted
hall with rock star authority, and though the trainee tide seems to
magically part for us, it feels as if we're only a pair of hopeful spawn-
ing salmon pushing against a never-ending white water current,
jumping technical waterfalls, dodging businessman grizzlies. Sooz
and I are swimming upstream and I can't help but think that the unseen snags and undertows in this big wide river might easily wear
us down, bringing us in line with their entropic levels of lukewarm
equilibrium.

There I go again.

Despite her being surprisingly dressed down[70] in baggy white
painter's pants, beat-up sneakers, and an old down jacket, leggy Sooz
still presents a glorious sight—and sure enough, the hotel-imprisoned
junior executive entry-level horn dogs pick up her scent—she lets 'em
have it with a quick and oh-so tantalizing bunny hip-swivel that produces at least two audible gasps.

At the end of the hallway, all the phone booths are occupied. Men
are waiting impatiently, smoking cigarettes, reading newspapers and
magazines. We get in the long line.

I say, "So SNARB. They'd love to get their hands on … you."

"Sure. Why wouldn't they? And you *know* they've got some sort
of connection to J. Edgar. And if they got me—us—or anybody else
that's working on crazy stuff, and this is what I worry about—all this
amazing networking, all this technology, could go either way. It might
all disappear down a military black hole and go dark, or it could be

---

[70] Sooz: Dress code for an underground girl like me? Certainly not like some countercultural
envelope-pushing chick, which would be incredibly dumb and would naturally attract
unwanted attention. I'm trying to look good in a conventional sort of way. Not *too* good,
mind you—just blandly straight-world nice. Who'd expect somebody like me to appear like
I'm right out of the steno pool? Yes, I'm fully aware of the negative feminist socio-political
implications of this, but you do what you have to do.
Me: That'd be *some* steno pool.

free and easy for everybody. I mean, what if Gutenberg made some evil deal with the Holy Roman Emperor? Huh? What then?"

"Mmm. Bummer."

"We'd still be scrolling parchment."

"Like monks."

"Yeah. But SNARB, if they think von Flarf is no longer ideologically pure or something ... I don't know. And I'm probably gone already."

We stand silently, watch the river flow.

On the dark paneled wall behind us hangs a large oil portrait of a formidable woman, lit by its own polished brass lamp. It's the queenly Mrs. Potter Palmer, gracious and smiling in evening dress, presiding over her dead husband's State Street realm. Sooz says, "Potter Palmer—Pepper Porter. Ha! We're in the right place." She grabs my arm and hugs it close to her. "It's great about your interview and all your fabulous band stuff that's going on. I heard your song on the radio again this morning."

Sweet of her to say so. But I haven't thought of the band or the music in hours.

The line gets shorter. Traffic in the hall subsides. Two guys walk by carrying a big mounted poster—*System 370: Real Power for the Future.*

"Yeah, maybe it's starting to happen. But—have you decided what you're going to call this thing, your network? I mean, you really haven't named it, have you?"

"Who cares? Not sure that it's the sort of thing you name. It's just a carrier sensing bandwidth allocation algorithm. Earth-shaking, yes. Sexy? No."

I tell her that a name for the whole thing—the big picture—would be good. Something cool to attract the eye ... like a band name. I press her on it, tell her to think bigger, go further.

She shrugs.

I say, "Okay, Dave's on his trip of Eastern intrigue you know. So I picked up the *Tibetan Book of the Dead* yesterday ..."

"Doesn't sound like you ..."

"I remembered that Oppenheimer himself was this big student of the Bhagavad-Gita, so I thought ... anyway, the Fifth Element

of creation is the Ether—the green light path of the wisdom of perfected actions, I think it is—it's where Man will possess knowledge
that will replace mere faith or belief. Technology. QED."

"Wow." She's impressed with my esoteric knowledge.

The guy in front of us turns to check us out. He heard all this. Who
talks like that in the Palmer House Hotel? We both smile charmingly.

"The Ether ... something?"

"The communications Ether. Network of ether. Yeah, something
like that. And I'm probably not the only one to think of this. But what
do I know? There," I point at a booth. "That one's open."

She sits down in the booth, opens her black notebook—her
brains—repository of notes, numbers, addresses, logarithmic tables,
and who knows what, takes a deep breath, dials the number. I close
the wood and glass folding door for her, turn and retreat to the other
side of the hallway, stand next to Mrs. Potter Palmer. Somebody's left
a *Tribune* on a table—I grab it, begin flipping through it.

A familiar voice sounds in my ear.

"Boo Boo, my friend. What're *you* doing here?" I flip the paper
down and am confronted with Hawgrim in his Joe Businessman costume. His hair is pulled back tight and he's nicely attired in a blue
pinstriped three-piece suit with a snappy black leather briefcase. He's
standing in front of me with a suspicious look in his eye.

In the phone booth behind him, Sooz appears to have gotten
through to Fletcher Engel. She's talking, her free hand flipping her
pen like a baton, her back turned to the glass.

"You know the guy from *Rolling Stone* last night? Wong-Garcia?
Creach set up a little chat. Soon." I look at my watch. It is ten to two.

"Yeah, oh right. I'm sure you'll kick ass. Don't forget to mention
that I can play classical, too." I suspect he's offended he wasn't invited.

"So why're *you* here?"

"These big-time corporate shindigs are happy hunting grounds
for me and my kind. These junior executive types? They're insurance
prospect putty in my well-trained hands. That gold putter is as good
as mine." Sniff. "I've gotta make a call. You in line?"

I say no just as Sooz emerges from the booth. She instantly assesses my situation and, not wanting Hawgrim to make the connection between the two of us, gives me a quick lift of the eyebrows and without hesitating jumps into a new flow of people streaming toward the lobby. While Hawgrim reminds me that he'll have his proposal for me in the next day or so, Sooz disappears. Then he jumps into her vacant booth and slides the door shut.

I take off after her and soon find her standing by one of the huge Grecian urns in the lobby. She's upset, fishing around in her shoulder bag.

"What's the matter? Didn't it go well?"

"My notebook's gone—I must've left it in the phone booth." She roots around in her bag some more. "Is that awful Hawgrim person still hanging around there?" Her voice is tight, a little panicked.

"He's using the same booth—I'll go get it."

"Pepper, this is bad, this is very bad. That book is *so* important. My whole life is in there—what? No, no. You can't go up to him like that. I'll go."

She disappears up the hall. A minute later, she's back, panicked.

"He's already gone. And so's my notebook."

"You sure he's got it, I mean ..."

"I'm sure. I know I left it in there. I was so excited. Oh Pepper."

"Is your name in it, your real name?"

She hesitates. "No. I had the brains to rip that stuff out a long time ago—but he might be able to ..." She stops.

Harrison Creach appears at my side, his hand on my shoulder and says, "Mr. Porter." He bows slightly to Sooz and says, "Ms. Frommer, so nice to see you again. Can I be of some assistance?"

Sooz, freaking out that her little black book is gone but instinctively trying to turn on her natural charm for Creach's benefit, while at the same time realizing that he has just used her real name which only adds to her apparent state of panic, sputters and frets. She blurts out that her mobile Rolodex, her life, her network—the Plan—*everything* is in that book. And Creach, attired in his downtown businessman finery—blue blazer, fat tie in a subtly subversive Afro-paisley print, gray slacks with crisp creases, and apparently new cordovan Italian loafers—says with genuine concern, "I can certainly understand your concern, this is terrible. I believe that we should alert the hotel management."

He places a gentle hand on her elbow and says, "You come with me, Ms. Frommer. The concierge here is an old friend of mine. I've played the Empire Room many, many times. Don't you worry about a thing."

I take a look around and don't see Hawgrim. The coast is shaky but clear.

While escorting us to the concierge desk, Creach relates the highlights of a tale involving his friend Mr. Lionel McKinley, the hotel concierge, and the case of the absolutely lost, never to be seen again and highly valuable purse that contained the true-to-life and, one might suspect, spicy diary of Miss Peggy Lee—yes, *that* Peggy Lee—which incidentally also contained a substantial sum of money. But, amazingly, the purse was found intact through the good offices of Mr. McKinley, it being only just one of many similarly miraculous recoveries. He assures Sooz that Mr. McKinley is indeed *the man*.

As we stand in front of Mr. McKinley's ornate and P-emblazoned podium near the front reception desk waiting for him to get off the phone—he nods politely to us and slaps five with Creach—I whisper to Sooz that I need to scram because I'm worried about Hawgrim seeing us together. Who knows, maybe he has already. He'd just put two and two together then connect the dots and—bingo, that little book would become even more valuable and who knows what'd happen then.

"Yes, yes, get out of here. Go do your interview. I'll find you later and fill you in on Engel and everything."

Creach hears that and approves, appearing to know exactly what I am doing and why, indicating that he'd be with me shortly, just as soon as he's taken care of our Ms. Frommer.

Creach.

 Track 3: Friday afternoon

IT's STRAIGHT UP two o'clock as I hurry back into the lobby. The ancient clock over the palatial entrance of the Empire Room bongs out a couple of low notes. I scan the room thinking it shouldn't be too tough to spot a rock 'n roll journalist from *Rolling Stone* in a place like this. A whistle whoops through the foliage and I see Wong-Garcia waving at me from the lobby bar, drink in hand. His battered khaki vest, pockets stuffed with pens, pencils, and little notebooks, looks like it's been through the desert on a horse with no name, grimed with time and who knows how many rock star interviews. He looks younger than when I met him in the dark at the Quiet Knight, his baby-face camouflaged by a thick black mustache, with dark hair in a late-model Beatle cut.

"You're early." He shakes my hand, says that he can't remember the last time an interview with a musician has actually begun on time. I say something like shucks and he points inquiringly at his drink, probably a Scotch. I say no thanks and order a beer.

He tells me to call him Stanley.

So Stanley places a little mic on the bar, flips on his snazzy cassette recorder and jumps right into it. He asks me what I'm *trying to do* and, though I haven't rehearsed any answer to that one, I say that every time I pick up my guitar—my Felix the Cat guitar in particular—and every time that I play electrified with my brother and whoever else is in the band, I am trying to recreate *it*. I am yearning to experience *it*, that rare feeling that has enveloped me just a few times—a couple times in garage bands back home, a few times at high school and college gigs and then, most certainly and most recently it was the glorious mania that swept me and my brother off the stage that last Friday night in the wilds of downstate Illinois. I sang and pushed Felix so hard and my body was electric and sizzled with a current as rare and as exotic as … and I search for the word and can't find it, and there is nothing to express the simultaneous feeling of exhilaration, joy, internal harmony when everything lines up like polarized ions and electrical charges blasting through every bone and electron in my body, lifting me off the stage, sparks flying, words and notes flying up to the ceiling in the ancient old gym. It's about as rare and bizarre and weird and hard to find as—as—I can't think of anything else but Peggy Lee's purse.

Stanley looks at me like he's never heard such a thing. He tells me that I am one unusual cat, scribbles something in his notebook. He starts to ask me about the surreal, Dada and absurdist textual ramifications of an image like Peggy Lee's purse used in the context of rock 'n roll music, but then Creach walks up, puts his hand on my shoulder, cheerfully asks how things are going. He pulls up a barstool, shakes hands with Stanley, orders himself a ginger ale and winks at me like everything is gonna be all right just like Muddy Waters says.

Then the three of us chit-chat, talking big about Chicago's music scene, Creach describing how Checkers Records is well-positioned to break out new bands, both black and white such as ourselves and Shine and the Funkolas, when, over Stanley's shoulder, I notice that Hawgrim has reappeared and arranged himself on one of the comfy sofas on the other side of the lobby, half-hidden by a huge palm frond, sipping a drink in a large frosted glass. I can't really tell for sure, but it looks like he's leafing through some black book sort of thing.

Stanley returns to the question of the intertextual implications of my music and Peggy Lee's purse, particularly in the context of Watergate and the apparent decay of cultural life in America in the last half of the twentieth century. Which launches me into a discussion about how my strange and wonderful experience on and above the stage in Benld, Illinois, is emblematic of our times. He asks how so, and I say that just as the Romantic poets of the nineteenth century, going all the way back to Blake and his wild and crazy visions, were revolutionary responses to the entropy of their day—the perceived decay of early nineteenth-century culture. Stanley raises an eyebrow and I, gaining confidence, postulate that entropy is something to be feared, the spiraling down of creative life and the emerging gray blandness and musical mediocrity and the lukewarm cultural temperatures that inevitably occur unless the Artist, the Poet, the Adventurer swoops in to shake things up and be the antenna hoping to pick up on new wavelengths, finding faint traces of *it*.

I am rolling.

But while Stanley nods and makes scratchy glyphs in his notebook, and while I marvel about how someone is actually taking notes on the things that I say, Creach picks up the interview ball and runs with it describing a Renaissance of the city of Chicago and its culturally critical and historically significant music scene. He reminds Stanley of the electric blues and the wide muddy river that runs through town, and how it has been largely and undeservedly and criminally forgotten—I freeze as I see Sooz walk into the lobby, survey the scene and walk straight up to Hawgrim who looks up at her in dumbfounded slack-jawed awe.

Sweating it out and convinced she is taking a ridiculous risk, I see Creach notice the little scene. He puts his hand on my arm as he gets up and says, "I'll handle this." He excuses himself.

Creach hustles over through the ferns, dodging a tea-delivering waiter or two and then appears to excuse himself to Sooz, bowing slightly in her direction, then turning to Hawgrim and pointing back to me and Stanley at the bar. With a big grin on his face, Hawgrim jumps up, tossing the book inside his briefcase, snapping it shut and then striding over in my direction for his first big time rock 'n roll interview. He straightens his tie like Rodney Dangerfield.

Creach then speaks with Sooz who looks exasperated, pointing at Hawgrim and running a nervous hand through her hair.

Hawgrim slides his briefcase onto the floor between Stanley and me, hops on to Creach's barstool signaling the bartender for a vodka martini—"dry as dust, please." Stanley, who politely listens to Hawgrim's history of accordion lessons with the great Aldo Vanucci and his later deep admiration for the organ part of "In-A-Gadda-Da-Vida" that turns out to be a huge musical influence on the young Brian, steers the conversation back to the search for *it*.

Though a little rattled, I say that I think that *it* probably is swirling around in my head right there all the time like a chord that I know but have somehow forgotten and—strangely channeling my brother—I suggest that perhaps there is a lost chord, silent and eloquent, right there just beyond my guitar's strings on an invisible seventh string, tuned to a frequency that I haven't yet been trained to hear. But if I paid attention—paid attention effortlessly and with perfect calm—it would present itself. And I, like a Zen archer pulling back on that string and releasing the arrow—would find that beautiful and soundless chord.

Stanley puts his pen down and says that that is either the biggest bunch of dharma bullshit he's ever heard or it is profound and bizarrely wonderful. He ponders where he's heard it before.

Creach returns, asking if another round is in order. Hawgrim swizzles his martini and chomps his olive, drains it and says sure—his briefcase with Sooz's notebook is on the floor at my feet.

A bellboy frocked in a black and gold monkey suit and pill box hat, with a ringing paging sign that has the name "Brian Hawgrim" written on it, is in the middle of the lobby walking toward us. Naturally, Hawgrim notices immediately and calls him over.

"Phone call for Mr. Brian Hawgrim, are you ...?" Hawgrim nods. "Sir, please come with me, sir."

With a satisfied told-you-so sort of grin on his face, Hawgrim excuses himself muttering something about closing another big deal.

Creach, smiling, says, "Pepper, doesn't Mr. Hawgrim have a copy of that ... thing, that new press release ... maybe it's here in his briefcase. Pepper, see if you can find it." He picks up the case, hands it to me, then stands up on lookout.

Wide-eyed and frantic, but still jabbering about Zen archers and guitar strings for Stanley's benefit, I balance it on my knees and open it up. Inside is a rats nest of stuff—a bottle of aspirin, a small brown bottle of an unidentified substance, a toothbrush and container of dental floss, a small travel vial of Hai Karate men's cologne, a pack of Super 100 Camels, three Playboy Club matchbooks, manila file folders with prospect names scrawled on them including mine, his TI calculator, his Porsche 914 keys, some whole life brochures, term life brochures, cryptic actuarial tables, a dog-eared copy of the Interstate Metropolitan Citywide Insurance Company Employee Handbook, a pack of his business cards, a vinyl folder containing his clients' business cards, a slew of IBM business cards he must've acquired today, a black daily diary with names and addresses, a yellow legal pad in a black leather portfolio, a couple of Bic pens, today's *Tribune* and a worn copy of last month's *Penthouse*.

I look up at Creach. No notebook. What'd he do with it?

Creach closes the case for me, replaces it on the floor, apologizes to Wong-Garcia, launches into a discussion of the cultural roots of rock 'n roll.

A minute or two later, Hawgrim reappears, exasperated. "Some sort of fuck up. Not for me."

Creach pats Hawgrim on the shoulder and says, "Glad you're back."

The interview goes on for a while longer. Creach angles the conversation toward Hawgrim and further discussion of his keyboard influences, polka included.

Then Creach, seeing that Stanley is about to wrap things up, goes for the boffo finish.

"Stanley my friend, you'll be interested to know that our boys here," he hands him a sheet of paper with a *Billboard Magazine* letterhead, "and they don't know this—have just broken into the local Chicago Top 40—at number thirty-eight! With a star, I might add."[71]

Hawgrim and I whoop, but Creach shushes us and says, "But wait, there's more. Thanks to our just-signed exclusive UK distribution and recording contract with Terpsichorean Records—you've heard of that fine label, I'm sure, Stanley ..."

Stanley drains his whiskey. He's heard it all before.

"... our boys here are going to be the opening act for Mott the Hoople on the Midwestern leg of their soon-to-begin US tour!"

Another magical miracle.

So, after pulling myself up off the floor and amid general rejoicing and grooving around the barstools, Stanley, who seems genuinely impressed, congratulates us and alludes to fabulous new *Rolling Stone* publicity opportunities along with the possibility of him assigning a journalist to the tour to follow us around, getting the feel of life on the road for an up-and-coming middle-American band. He excuses himself and promises to be in touch.

Hawgrim, looking unnaturally pleased, checks his watch, informs us that he's got an important meeting. Then he reminds me that he'll get me those *numbers* the next day and tells Creach that he'll get him *his* numbers in a week or so. He takes off.

I look at Creach.

Creach shrugs. "Hey. The company is reviewing its financial situation."

"But with *him?*"

He ignores me. "Get that notebook." Creach finishes his ginger ale. "Tomorrow night. Recording session. More album tracks. See you then."

I run out of the bar looking for Sooz.

---

[71] *Billboard Magazine*—it's where you want to be—on the charts in *Billboard.* Number One with a Star. Yes, indeed, the music industry's weekly scoreboard.

The lobby, jammed again with a new throng of clean-cut IBM'ers and chatting tea-sippers, seethes. I thread my way through, a freak fish flopping on a businessman's beach. The same bellboy picks his way through the crowd with another call for somebody, and it makes me think about state-of-the-art communications, the transmission of information and unrooted trees. But I have no time to zone out. Cigarette smoke and the combined scents of matronly floral perfumes, locker room male deodorant, and powerful aftershave rises to the rafters painted with fat, grinning cherubs.

VP/SPAS/OSS, the very VP I interviewed with before, walks right up to me, crisply attired in a sober blue suit, white shirt, and sensible red tie. He eyes my hair, notes my attire.

"Well, well, well, it's Mr. Portmann, the young wizard of Ann Arbor, if I'm not mistaken."

"Porter. Martin Porter." I shake his hand.

"What brings you here? I mean," he assesses my non-company-man appearance, "you've certainly changed a bit. Reconsidering that ill-advised decision of yours last year?" VP/SPAS/OSS chuckles to himself.

"Good to see you again, sir. No, but I'm still keeping a hand in the computer world and—"

A younger clone of himself comes to his side and whispers in his ear. VP/SPAS/OSS apologizes, tells me we should do lunch sometime, excuses himself, saying something about how important it is to stay abreast of the times.

Alone in the crowd again, I do a 360—periscoping above everyone—looking for her. A blonde head, her white knit hat maybe camouflaged by a gigantic fern or palm frond or hidden behind a mammoth Grecian urn. Turning to the Empire Room staircase, turning to the escalators, to the mezzanine, turning to the long front desk mobbed with newly arriving guests—men in tan trench coats and wintery gray houndstooth Chesterfield overcoats, older men in felt fedoras, thick-framed glasses, some with leather briefcases in hand and newspapers under their arms, running late, looking for deals and making calls, making dinner reservations tonight, and *where can a guy find a little companionship in a town like this*, with clinking glasses, muzak, and talk rippling around the room.

No Sooz.

Mr. McKinley. Almost spotlit underneath the heavy overhang of the mezzanine level where the warmer lights of the registration desk and black-suited clerks handle the new wave of incoming guests— Mr. McKinley's gaze zeros in on mine, sharp-eyed and insistent. He beckons me over.

"Young man, your lady friend asked that I make sure you received this message." He presses a white Palmer House envelope into my hand saying, "I'm afraid that we have not yet located the young lady's notebook, but please be assured that all our powers of search and item retrieval are at work." His voice is professional, relaxed and confident, with no trace of doubt. "Fear not, Mr. Porter. It is not lost—it will be found." His eyes meet mine and won't let go.

On any other day and if he were speaking about anything else, I probably would've just thanked Mr. McKinley for his time and forgotten about it, moved on. But this little black book is clearly a big deal—no simple collection of names and numbers—it is a directory that leads in all directions of her life and in all directions of technology and, in the wrong hands, unpredictable results could occur. A bright red line is drawn under its cosmic importance, and Mr. McKinley's fervent and steady gaze stops me in my tracks. There, for a moment, mist clears and I glimpse the road ahead and I know where to go and what to do but only for a moment, because it disappears and the headlights of my mind go back into the fog and reflect blindingly right back in my eyes, like I am driving in a cloud and I can't see ahead at all. But there, for a second, I *saw*.

Mr. McKinley blinks twice, snapping me out of it, and smiles. I thank him, head for a big potted fern out of the flow of traffic. I tear at the envelope, blowing it open just like Johnny Carson.

I pull a rainbow slash out of the envelope, exactly like the one from the week before at the library—artsy, handmade, and psychedelic. On the back, in her very precise hand:

Marshall Field's, 8F. Now.

I look up, my body tense, my hand starting to shake. Out in the midst of the lobby, I see Hawgrim making his pitch to a couple of well-suited young computer execs.

He's got the notebook. I just know it.

The execs are wowed with his powers of persuasion—they stand in front of him, rapt. In mid-sentence, he glances my way, sees me through the foliage, grins, winks.

I give him a thumbs up—*yeah Mott the Hoople, man*—and then I carefully replace the rainbow slash in the envelope, stick it in my shoulder bag, elbow my way to the down escalator, head to the street.

 Track 4: Late Friday afternoon

T HE EIGHTH FLOOR of the Marshal Field's on State Street, the flag-ship store, the one covering a full city block with ten floors of ev-erything any serious shopper could possibly want, contains the fancy lunching spots, coffee shops, gourmet food and candy stores and the venerable Walnut Room, which serves frumpy food favored by grand-mas and great aunts from all over the city.

After holding the elevator door open for a group of little old ladies armed with big purses and tasteful green and gold Field's shopping bags stuffed with treasures, I emerge from the elevator, try to imagine where I might find her in such an un-Sooz place like this. I study the floor directory, trying to get my bearings in the maze, feeling like a long-haired cheese-hunting rat.

"I just love Frango Mints. Don't you?"

Sooz materializes at my side with a little green box of the choco-late mint concoctions that have been the dietary downfall of my own, otherwise vice-less, dear mother. Popping one in her mouth, savoring it, she says, "But I'm really worried about the Plan."

She leads me to a big old wooden bench in one of the quieter halls interconnecting many of the food emporiums. We sit down. "You know, these things are … are almost sexual, they're so good. Sure you won't have one? Hmm?" She waves the box under my nose, munches her mint.

Sooz had fled the fancy hotel straight for the eighth floor of Field's, frantic for a Frango fix.

"You're freaking out, aren't you."

"I am. But Frango Mints can make it all better. Did you know that?"

"Really?

"Maybe not quite."

"You're a Bunny, watching your weight ..."

"A girl's got to have what a girl's got to have and these ..." She selects another one, sits back, smiles. "Besides, I'm a regular at the counter here."

"Aren't Frango Mints just upper-middle-class bourgeois opiates for the masses? Wouldn't ... granola be more your speed?"

"Bleah."

"What's with women and Frango Mints? I just don't see it." She pushes the box under my nose again.

I reluctantly take one, consider it, nibble and think—women and music, women and chocolate.

Then she brings me up to speed on everything. She tells me that her call with Engel had gone beautifully—he asked some smart questions, testing her knowledge, and then she just flat out forgot her notebook.

"I'm an idiot. I don't do things like that. I just ... I don't know."

She bit into another Frango Mint.

I say, "We'll get it back."

"He's *your* friend."

"Right. Hawgrim's got it."

She lets that sit there for a few beats. "*Must* get it back." Then, "But Engel said he'd like to meet us—get this—at the *Playboy Club!*"

"What? What kind of intellectually rigorous plugged-in wizard of technological connections would want to meet *there*?"

"Captain of industry. Men. I don't know. My place of employment."

"What's the matter with him?"

"And von Flarf will be there. They've been talking."

"When's the meeting?"

"Next Tuesday. Eight. And I'm working then. And no, I didn't or couldn't tell him that that's where I work and I will in fact be on duty at that time."

She says Engel is heading out of town on Wednesday and it's meet then and there or nothing until he gets back in a couple weeks. Engel had been thoroughly briefed by von Flarf about Sooz and the Plan. He expressed a certain amount of enthusiasm for it, told her that he thought he might be able to be of some assistance to her moving things ahead—he looks forward to meeting her—and her assistant. Me.

"I might be able to trade nights with one of my Bunny buddies but I don't know ... I have to make it work."

Sooz sighs forlornly, looks up and down the hall. The hall has become strangely quiet, deserted. The afternoon rush has evaporated. She murmurs, "SNARB was at the Palmer House. I think I saw those guys. Agent whatshisname and that Brown guy."

"No! C'mon. It's that paranoia again. Don't ..."

She drums her fingers on the Frango Mint box. "I can't tell you how important that notebook is ... my past, names and numbers, calculations and ... wait." Peering over my shoulder down the hall, she whispers, "Don't turn around."

We hunch down like we're deep in conversation. I hear the slow click of heavy heels on the parquet floor far down the hall. Then nothing.

"He's gone."

"Who?"

"Probably nobody. Ghosts. Like your Dark Stranger. I don't know." Her face is washed out, her amazing cheekbones stark and tightly drawn, color draining.

That's it. I say, "Okay. Let's go."

"Where're we going?"

"My place."

We hop on the next down elevator, go to the third floor—women's foundations and lingerie—hurry through the vast store, crossing through the ancient middle section of the building that arches over the street-level loading docks to the Wabash Street side—men's furnishings—transferring to the east escalators, me watching our backside, hoping I don't see those SNARB guys or anyone else who looks creepy.

"How's your Mr. Creach know my real name?"

The ancient escalator with wooden slats in the treads creaks and rolls as we ride down to the main floor. From on high I see nothing but perfume counters and miles of aisles of ladies' scarves, stationery—diaries, schedulers, little black books—and glittery chandeliers.

"Who knows? Nothing about Creach surprises me now." The escalator ends. "Let's go." We head for the street.

Figuring that we'd have better luck snagging a cab on the slightly less-crowded northbound side of Wabash under the El, and that if we're being followed it might be a little less expected than the both of us just taking another 151 northbound—our typical route. I consider myself cagey. Out on Wabash, we scamper across the street dodging traffic. I stick up my arm and a big old green and white Checker pulls over.

I tell the driver, "Water Tower Place." The guy flips the flag down and we take off.

"Water Tower Place?"

If we're being tailed, going straight to my place would be exceedingly dumb, so I tell her that our getting lost in a crowd in that fancy urban mall would give us much better odds.

"And you think that these guys aren't pros? C'mon. They've probably got this cab bugged for all we know. Why don't they just take me?"

I look at our driver in the rearview mirror. His eyes meet mine. He shrugs, asks if us kids are okay and are we sure about Water Tower Place. I say we are. Sooz slumps down in the big seat. I turn around—a line of cabs identical to ours is behind us as we race up Wabash under the dark and rusting El—every taxi with who knows who going who knows where.

I pick up her hand, hold it between mine.

"Look, there's no reason to be so completely freaked out."

"Oh? Tell me more."

I try to talk her up.

"C'mon, Sooz. We're moving ahead—you've got a date with this Engel guy. Von Flarf too—and they love your stuff—they're wowed! It's gonna be great." She turns away, looks out the window. We take a right onto Wacker Drive and the dark monolith of the IBM building appears across the river, then the tall apartments of Marina City—round and puckered like a pair of big city corncobs. "So you've lost that book—a minor, temporary inconvenience. I'll get it back—I don't think Hawgrim'd really want to mess with you, us. And who knows, maybe that Palmer House guy will find it."

A thin smile crosses her face and in the slanting shadows of the cab amidst the canyon of the city, I think I might be getting a glimpse of an older Sooz, a hint of a future Sooz—maybe it's the slight crease in her lips or the way she's holding her head—older.

"And SNARB? What were you telling me about paranoia?" I ask. Sooz is silent. Then I say, "I know what you need."

She looks at me. "But do you know what I want?"

The cab makes a fast left turn just beating the light, swerving onto northbound Michigan Avenue. Sooz slides across the slick vinyl seat straight into my arms and then the cab accelerates across the metal grating of the drawbridge over the river, taxi tires whining higher and higher like we're about to take off, screaming off the deck of a heaving concrete aircraft carrier. We lift off the north side of the bridge, airborne and silent with only the whoosh of air and the howl of the engine, but then the squeal of the brakes ends the takeoff, as the cab halts at the signal in front of the gargoyled Tribune Tower.

Sooz remains in my arms. She snuggles deeper.

Her voice is muffled in my coat. "This life is getting old."

And it occurs to me that even if it all goes great, I have no idea what might happen to her if Engel steps up and points her in the right direction, to new contacts, new opportunities, a new life—she might be gone. Just like that.

In the midst of the gray and white marble, glass and weird jungle greenery hanging from fat planters in the artificial light at Water Tower Place, she and I lean on the fat round brass railing overlooking the cavernous atrium.

"I never come here." Sooz marvels at the glitter of this vertical city mall—elevators in crystal tubes, the boutiques, the fat shopping bags, the fur coats. "This isn't my kind of place—all this ... stuff—sure isn't the revolution I had in mind."

We watch the scene. It's time to get out of here.

Sooz says, "I thought I was so sure about things—I knew what to do, the lines were drawn. The mission was so clear—finish my work, get the technology out there. Now, I'm ..."

A little girl, not more than three or four years old, bundled up in a fuzzy pink parka, appears in the middle of the mall, alone, no parent in sight. It's hard to miss her—a little teddy bear loose on her own in Water Tower Place. We watch as she toddles along, looking a little worried.

Sooz says, "That's not right. She's lost. Some parent isn't paying attention."

We watch a bit longer—still no one shows up to whisk her away in a gust of parental relief. People notice her, look about, hoping to see the panicked mother or father hurry over, a mother and child reunion. But no one does.

Sooz hurries over to the little girl and I follow behind. She instinctively switches into camp counselor mode, kneels down in front of the child, talks with her quietly and calmly, takes her hand and the two of them—Sooz and this little lost girl—walk hand in hand into the nearest store, Rizzoli's, to call mall security. A minute or two later a uniformed security guard hustles into the store. On a bench by the main cashier, Sooz sits chatting with the toddler who seems to have a lot to say and is now content having made a new big sister friend. Sooz listens intently.

I stand away from the scene, not wanting to complicate things as Sooz speaks with the security guard, while still keeping the very important conversation going with her little admirer. Sooz looks up, gives me a smiling wink.

And that ... is *it*.

That's the moment—right there—too late to stop now. Headlights, spotlights, and shining searchlights all swing around and my path lights up—the fog is gone.

The parents show up—a young couple not too much older than us, pushing an empty stroller, he in a three-piece suit, she straight out of Bonwit Teller's—sweeping the little girl up in their arms in a waking-up-from-a-nightmare relief. They thank Sooz profusely, clearly embarrassed, though it's evident that the father is the negligent party.

We leave the store and I take Sooz's arm, drag her to the elevators.

At the little flower shop on the ground floor, I buy Sooz a single long-stem white rose. The florist wraps it carefully in thick green paper reminding us to be careful of the hidden thorns. Sooz lifts the flower to her nose and breathes deeply. "Now you're getting a little sappy, don't you think?"

I am. But I don't care.

Emerging from the back entrance of Water Tower Place into the busy tunnel of limos and taxis shared with the Ritz Carlton Hotel, we're shivering—my arm around her keeping her close, she's relaxed a bit and is letting me take over. We cross the street, stand on Chestnut like a couple of tourists staring up the black-girdered flanks of the John Hancock building, a city block wide at its base, tapering elegantly to the top, ninety-five floors above, where the thick band of white light that crowns the building has just been flipped on, shining like a giant lighthouse on the lake. The cold wind whips through the man-made steel and stone ravine as I pull her across the street. After spinning through the doors of the Hancock lobby, I buy a couple of tickets to the observation deck on top. We jump into the express elevator and rocket to the top.

Pushing through the heavy glass doors of the Sky Deck—a big room covering the entire ninety-fourth floor—we stop in our tracks. The sun is dipping below a growing bank of dark clouds far out on the suburban horizon, shining a light-show orange above the jeweled amber lights of the city that are imprinting themselves on our brains like an electric map—vast and stretching away from the dark of Lake Michigan behind us, streaming to the north, west, and south never ending, arrowing sure and big-shouldered confident.

With her white rose in hand and the two of us arm in arm, slowly making the circuit around the hushed and mostly deserted space, its floor to ceiling windows dark, framing the immense display of the city, Sooz perks up, the lost little kid incident calming her down, giving her a chance to refocus.

One time around and we stop at the center of the long west window. After a while, she says, "Pepper. I've come up here before." I give her a look. "Yeah, I have. Actually many times and always at night. I love this place."

"Me too."

Theatrically, she steps to the window, touching the glass with both hands. "And I've stood right here, and this scene—this scene!—the lights, the grid of Chicago laid out so precisely and perfectly—looking like the printed circuit board of a monstrous computer—always stuns me into silence. But beneath all this," she waves her hand, the one with the rose, "there's a perfect chaos with good and bad flowing like electrons in these streams of light. And we live in this—we are the electrons."

I stand behind her. We watch the city breathe.

Then she says, "Okay. Let's go."

"Where are we going?"

"My place."

 Track 5: Friday evening

THE CAB RIDE IS LONG—stuck on northbound Lake Shore Drive at rush hour. She keeps her thighs pressed against mine, her head on my chest as traffic inches along with change-in-the-weather rain beginning to speckle and sparkle the taxi windows as her hand finds its way through my coat to my jeans, lightly fingering.

Her place. And I'm stunned. Only three blocks from my apartment, east on Wrightwood across Clark almost to Lincoln Park—the Martha Washington Apartments for Women, an old brick edifice built back in the '20s when the residences were grand and ornate. Since then, the building has come into a state of genteel decay, broken down into much smaller *efficiency* apartments—rents are pretty reasonable—Sooz says she only pays about $170 a month. She's been there since the summer of '73, nine or ten months. Yes, it's mostly middle-aged and older women and she had to go through a small vetting process, but Sooz can be so charming and can be whatever you want her to be—in this case, a bookish, single career girl, intense and focused on her work. And Miss Margaret Ruth Jones, the building's administrator, beginning the interview somewhat skeptically, warmed quickly to the natural niceness of Miss Grace Kelliher and soon Miss Jones introduced her to many of the building's long-term residents. Sooz, posing as a technical writer working on projects for an engineering firm in the Loop. The ladies said they liked her *moxie*.

So close. She says she knew that I was right up the street but she didn't get in touch. She says she thought about it, thought about it so much—she moved to the neighborhood for that very reason. But she hadn't been ready to make the move to get back together, she needed time and didn't want to drag me into things just yet and she was busy working on the Plan, buried in the library and waiting tables at the Club. So she watched.

We wait for the elevator in the building's quiet lobby, meticulous plastic flowers in grandmotherly vases perched on mahogany tables, flaking gilt trim on the ceiling, walls hung with elegant old still lifes, mostly apples and shadows in deep browns and ivy greens, sailing ships and colonial eagles, scenes of English fox hunts, prim little chipped chairs cushioned in fraying floral patterns arranged neatly but hardly used. Sooz pleasantly greets a well-dressed, silver-haired woman emerging from the elevator, whispers that male guests are accepted but not desired.

She concedes that I am accepted *and* desired.

Sooz had done her surveillance tradecraft on me and had come to know where I'd go and when, which is kind of spooky, her telling me this as we go up the old elevator to her apartment. She says she'd been right *there* buried in a book sitting in the diner at the corner next to the plate glass window as I headed home, or standing in the phone booth at the gas station or buying a paper at the newsstand on Diversey. She says sometimes I walked right by her and she'd watch me head up the street. There I was, just going along singing my little songs to myself trying to get something, anything, going and she'd been there, right there watching and waiting. I was so blind, didn't see, making no eye contact on the tough streets of Chicago.

We pad down the hushed hall of the seventh floor.

"What made it the right time?"

"Shhhh." She puts her finger on my lips.

Turning the key in her lock, she has me go in first. I feel like I'm dropping further into her own systems-level code. She is revealing a bit more of herself.

She lives in a studio in the back of the building with a decent, but low-rent, view to the south over alleys, water towers, and air conditioning. The big masts and antennas on top of the distant Sears Tower on the southwest corner of the Loop peek through lesser concrete and steel crags. Her low platform bed, neatly made with a thick down comforter covered in unadorned muslin and bunches of embroidered pillows arranged on it all in white—warm whites, off whites, cream whites, ruffled whites, Marilyn-Monroe-blonde-reclined-and-ruffled-in-the-sheets whites—is centered underneath the two double hung windows. An ornate but threadbare Oriental rug lies on the hardwood floor. A portable typewriter, a sheet of paper wound in the platen and ready to go, sits on her small, white desk. Bookshelves made of unpainted planks supported by cinder blocks line one wall, filled with engineering texts and fat plastic binders with what looks like green and white computer printouts—probably listings of programs she's compiled at some computer service bureau somewhere in town. On a little nightstand by her bed is a beat-up paperback copy of *Wuthering Heights* along with the writings of Rousseau, Shelley, some radical French cats and some other SDS pamphlets, papers and stuff I don't recognize.[72] A few unidentifiable hunks of computer hardware sit on the floor by her desk amid a collection of flat gray ribbon cables, raw circuit boards, a small oscilloscope, her basic black telephone, and a small radio. The room feels like an adjunct professor's homebrewed computer laboratory—von Flarf would be right at home.

There are no curtains in the windows. We're on one of a million small stages in tiny glass prosceniums on every street and in every building in the nighttime city. She motions for me to turn the lamplight off and suddenly the room darkens, but fills with the dimly splashed light of the city. There is never darkness, only the never-ending urban glow that's cold and damp and harsh on the streets, but turns gold and warm here on the seventh floor in a small efficiency, high above sidewalks, storefronts, and back alleys.

We're hidden and invisible to the world. I'm standing in the middle of the room in the midst of her private world, amazed that it seems as far away as Venus yet as close as the 151 bus stop, and I try to comprehend as much as I can, seeing and understanding and hoping that I can really begin to know this wondrous heart. She stands behind me breaking into my thoughts, pulls at my coat. I drop it from my shoulders, she places it next to hers in the closet, returns wrapping her arms around me from behind, her head on my back, and I hear her sigh as she squeezes me, clinging and hanging on—her message of stay with

---

[72] And I thought she read only tech stuff. Sooz asks if I can see that the moors of Yorkshire are just like Chicago—cold, windy, and lonely—and she says that reading *Wuthering Heights* has given her a place to escape. Even if it is on cold misty moors, they're far away from hard streets full of storms and wind and rain and snow, and even if Heathcliff is crazy—and maybe she is, too—it's still escape. But she says that sometimes she feels like Cathy, and that someday she imagines that she might fade away, lost in a rainy windowpane doomed to haunt the moors and Sir Laurence Olivier.

me, stay with me, and then her hand drops below my belt and clothes are shed and her perfect curves slide with mine in a yin and yang of fevered coupling.

Sooz and I fall to the bed, early spring raindrops spatter on the window, misting with silvered wires of rain lit by city lights. Inside, we are warm and dry under mounds of her comforting down and white linens, safe and protected. Her hair pours and brushes my face and her tongue is on mine. My hands trace the French curve of her neck, dropping to the elegant soft C of her back. She is silhouetted in the rain-sparkled window. Her eyes flutter and the arrows of rain rise, and the warming wet wind gusts and thunder rolls over the city. She opens her eyes, smiles, and pulls me closer while the rumbles of the city sound below us, horns and trucks and people vanishing seen and unseen between buildings and parked cars. The lights of the distant towers blink, the rains come down and our perfect motion rises and falls and rises and falls until it can be held no more. And the storm ends and I hold her and she is the rain and I am the clouds and we are the light.

Her room is silent. Drops of rain run down her windowpanes in stuttering streaks. She breathes. I listen, remembering. I pull the Shelley from her nightstand, open the book, find this and read to her— *Make me thy lyre, even as the forest is, what if my leaves are falling like its own, the tumult of thy mighty harmonies ... scatter, as from an unextinguished hearth, ashes and sparks, my words among mankind, the trumpet of a prophecy, oh Wind, if winter comes can spring be far behind?*

I say, "You weren't an English major," and she says, "I certainly wasn't," and I say, "I never knew you were into this sort of thing," and she says, "there's lots you don't know," and I say, "how true that is," and she says, "you read it so very well," and I say again, "*make me thy lyre,*" and she says she already has.

And then a cat jumps up on the bed and scares the hell out of me— it's Snowball, the Revolutionary Cat—he snuggles with Sooz, ignoring me, but Sooz tells me not to worry, she loves me, too.

Sooz dreamily says that Snowball requires considerable attention and if he doesn't get it, then things can get pretty unbearable in that little one-room apartment, let me tell you—other than that, he's a great cat. She says it will be to my advantage to make friends with him.

Snowball eyes me suspiciously and growls when I very tentatively scratch the top of his head.

"See? He loves you."

So she plops that cat onto my chest, rolls over for a look at the clock. Snowball yowls and scrams.

It's a little after seven.

Sooz shrieks, scrambles over me—which, once again, is a pleasurably fleshy experience—muttering that she's got to be at work by eight for the late shift at the Club and a Bunny is never late. I refuse to let her go, cuffing her wrist until she kneels by the bed so I can successfully plant one last big one on her. Then she runs into the bathroom.

The rainy night love spell is broken.

Sooz emerges from the bathroom, does her basic makeup as fast as she can, sitting at her little dressing table that she's set up in the oversized closet, distracted, running late. I lean against the closet door. Construction of her official Bunny face has begun—however, I learn that the final and actual Bunny face is always applied at the Club.

Looking into the mirror at me over her shoulder, she stops and asks, "Where's it all leading to? I mean you, me ... my project, your music ... and—" motioning darkly to the street, "them."

Uh oh.

"I mean, really. Are we both ... like, like two trains on different tracks going different ways?" She resumes lipsticking.

My downstate railroad dream and the disappearing V of the tracks replays in my head.

"Absolutely not. We're on the same track, just different rails— we're going to the same place. I think."

She pauses again in the middle of lipstick application and cracks a little smile and says, "You're hopeless." Then, "But where will the tracks end ... I'm sorry." She smacks her lips at the mirror—the radical technology Bunny revolutionary. "You know, I've been thinking about your concert the other night—those kids in the crowd, you know, those kids with the bowties. They were so cute. And it was all for *you*. Amazing." She considers that like it's an elegant solution to a complex equation. "And your brother—both of them. Truly impressive." Flicks her eyebrows.

"Dave says it's unbefuckinglievable."

"He's right."

Finished with the face process, she throws on a simple not-too-sexy-for-the-bus wrap dress, steps into a pair of flat walking shoes and says, "Let's go."

She almost kisses the cat.

Snowball senses my departure, immediately sits up in an annoying display of triumph—a miserable cat grin on his face—pleased that she snuggles with him and not me. And while Sooz strides out the door ahead of me, buttoning her coat, I glare at him and flip the lights off. Snowball hisses.

Out on the street, she tells me that I have to be at the Engel meeting in my best suit and tie and that I should bone up on communications-I/O subsystems and operating system-level connection theory. She thinks Engel might go in that direction. I'm her expert there. She tells me to go to the library and find the IBM Systems Journal from last quarter. There's some pretty good research in there—unexpectedly radical stuff for a big company. And also a recent *Popular Electronics*.

"*Popular Electronics*? You're kidding me."

"No, really. Check it out—it'll give you a good feel for all this. It's a new world—I know a few guys out in California, old Michigan types, around San Francisco, Palo Alto, you know, Stanford, places like that. Unbelievable work. They've got this home computer club thing going—can you believe it? Very *out there*, cutting edge—well, it's amazing."

"Incredible."

She had details on all that in her notebook but, well—it's gone.

"I've got to get it back."

Then I remember—I tell her how I ransacked Hawgrim's briefcase but didn't find it. She gives me an admiring look, says that there's no doubt about it—he's got it. I say that whatever it takes, we'll get it. She snuggles on my arm, things warm up again.

I will get that notebook back.

Wrightwood is dark and quiet—parked cars and apartment buildings. It's an established residential neighborhood with a mix of stately

Victorian mansions long subdivided into smaller units, old high-rises built before the war and glassy new ones with big-time city views. The original residents, aging, not too prosperous, are being slowly replaced with younger people—folks like us—former kids newly enrolled in the rat race of make-a-living life.

Rain, nearly freezing, begins to fall again. She flips up her umbrella. Lights are reflected in the wet black streets—cars cruise by slowly, hunting for parking places. Back on the street, we both automatically restart the scanning process—quick glances between buildings, then a look at a big Buick, a big Ford slowly following behind us hoping we'll get in a car and vacate a spot—us just wishing them away. A wave of gloom washes over me and I think why don't they just take her—or us? If they—whoever they are—know it's her, why don't they just swoop in, nab us and be done with it, end of story?

Maybe they don't exist.

Reading my mind, she says, "It's not the FBI I'm worried about—at least I don't think I am—they're big and clumsy and methodical. It's those SNARB creeps—or whoever they are. I just don't know what their game is—von Flarf, me—I don't know."

We wait for the light at the corner on Clark. Out of the blue, sounding a little unsure of herself, she asks, "Do you love me or the idea of me?"

"What?"

A Loop-bound 151 appears a block or so up Clark, rumbling toward us, so we make a dash across the street against the light, dodging a couple cars, getting in the bus stop queue.

"Sorry I'm being so weird right now. Look for a note in your mailbox. Or somewhere." The bus pulls up. I try to smile for her.

Sooz pushes a key into my hand. "If something happens to me—Snowball, please look after him." She kisses me hard, pulls back to look into my eyes and says, "Thank you for everything. It's won-won-wonderful." I hold her hand until the bus door nearly closes on it and she's gone.

Sleet. So I duck underneath the awning at the corner diner fingering the key, turning it over in my hand, try to decipher the messages I've just been sent.

I run the couple of blocks back to the apartment, arrive cold, wet, and hungry. Dave is gone. I find some cold pizza and come up with a plan.

As I'm wolfing the last piece, Dave walks in with a particularly vibrant shit-eating grin on his face but before he can explain I fill him in on the notebook—what we're about to do.

 Track 6: Later that night, very early Saturday morning

"I S THAT THE HOUSE?"
"Haven't you ever been to Hawgrim's place?"
"Hell no. Why would I?"

It's the middle of the night. Dave and I are on a *caper*.

We are both in burglar black including gloves and itchy knit watch caps pulled down low over our foreheads, crouching behind a long evergreen hedge that lines the alley behind Hawgrim's huge house on the elegant east side of Hinsdale. He still lives with his mother, the queenly Beatrice Gladys Jones Hawgrim. His father, Mr. Brian A. Hawgrim Sr., left the planet years ago.

A suburban possum scurries from behind a garbage can and scares the hell out of us.

"Jesus Christ." Dave shivers. "Do we have to do this?"

I look him in the eye. "Dave, we've been through this. Her notebook is of cosmic importance."

"Right. Sorry." He pulls himself together.

Fortunately for us, Hawgrim lives in the coach house above the ancient garage, not unlike von Flarf's nifty lab set-up in Champaign. Mrs. Hawgrim, resting peacefully high in the master suite of the main house, will not be disturbed as Dave and I seek to visit her son's residence.

"You sure he's not here?"

Intelligence sources—Ricky—indicate that Hawgrim is on a date—off in pursuit of some poor unsuspecting young thing, oiling his seductive way across the floor of another female heart. I have determined, therefore, that the coast is clear and that not even Hawgrim would bring his briefcase on a date. It is very likely that the notebook is here.

"Do you see his car?"

Hawgrim drives a red Porsche 914. His Baldoni barely fits.

We peer through the dirty garage window, see only his mother's monstrous Cadillac Fleetwood Brougham d'Elegance resting like a snoozing whale on the cracked concrete of the ocean floor.

"Okay, he's gone. Let's go."

I have been to this place, many years before—a high school party complete with catered weed, beer, and hard liquor, while Mrs. Hawgrim was traveling in Europe, her faithful son holding down the fort entertaining half the senior class. I remember the secret hiding place of the key, provided by young Brian for the benefit of partygoers—high and inside one of the old wrought iron light fixtures by the garage door. The light is unfortunately lit. I'm betting that Hawgrim still keeps an emergency key in this very excellent location. I reach up, feel around and sure enough it's there. I am ecstatic. There will be no breaking. Only entering.

The neighborhood is silent—the only sound is the faint buzz of the streetlight at the end of the alley. Otto is parked blocks away on a route that Hawgrim, if he inconveniently returns, will be unlikely to take. Hinsdale's Finest, however, are likely to regard Otto's presence as suspicious, so we need to move fast.

"C'mon, c'mon." Dave is winding up.

I turn the key in the door lock and we are admitted to the garage. Dave closes the door behind us. We scamper up the old wooden stairs, stop at Hawgrim's door. This is it—it's now or never. My heart is pounding. I push the door open.

We flip on our flashlights.

Hawgrim's second floor setup is well ordered. The big double bed is nicely made, pillows artfully strewn, rugs aligned, a pair of sleekly modern chairs perched in front of a huge 25-inch Sony Trinitron and wet bar, complete with bar stools and wine rack along one of the walls. His big-speakered stereo is lined up underneath a window—a Tony Orlando album rests on his turntable.

We point and laugh.

Hawgrim's color scheme is black and white—a definite sleek bachelor pad vibe. We are in the belly of the beast.

Dave goes to the window, assuming his lookout post. He opens it so we can hear what's going on outside, cold air rushes in. We are above a pair of old garbage cans along the side of the coach house, hidden from the street light. Quiet.

Hawgrim's desk is neatly organized—a nice leather blotter, a twin pen set with his name engraved on the marble base and two framed pictures—one of his mother captured in a rare smiling moment and the other an autographed photo of an older gentleman with a heavy mustache and accordion. I look closely—it's Aldo Vanucci, his beloved accordion teacher and musical guru.

I don't see his briefcase. I open all the drawers. While the temptation to throw the contents all over the floor, just like a cheap detective show, is strong, I resist. I carefully close them.

There is no notebook.

"C'mon, c'mon, c'mon." Dave hisses, but maintains his vigilant sentry position.

I check under the bed, I check the closet, his dresser, under his pillows, everywhere. Nothing.

The bathroom. The shower, under the sink. Nothing.

Then the linen closet.

What kind of guy has a linen closet?

There, on the top shelf underneath a set of fluffy black towels, is the briefcase. I put it on the shaggy rug on the floor, stick my flashlight in my mouth and open it up.

"Car! In the alley, right now." Dave's voice gets higher when he's freaking out. He's a soprano at this moment. "Porsche. It's him. 914. Holy shit!"

I hear the approaching roar of Hawgrim's snazzy mid-engine machine.

A fat black notebook is right on top of the pile of stuff in the case—it wasn't there in the Palmer House, but it's here now. I grab it, shove the briefcase back in its hiding place.

The Porsche screeches to a halt below us, idling noisily in the alley, radio blasting—Hawgrim climbs out and is opening the garage door. The entire house shakes.

Dave, after dropping to the pavement, banging his knee on one of the garbage cans sending its top rolling around like a plugged nickel, tries to silence the spinning lid while Hawgrim careens the car into the garage. In a yogic contortion, I try to pull the window shut behind me before I bail. I let go and fall on Dave and the lid, crunching his hand causing him to yelp and me to twist my ankle as we fall in a heap on the concrete. And while Hawgrim sits in his car listening to the end of, yes, it's our song—"Your Aunt is Cool"—his rumbling engine still on, we, the valiant wounded, flee, hopping and cursing down the alley. We are gone.

Two blocks later we jump into Otto, fire him up and we wheeze out of town, notebook in hand.

We're stopped at the train tracks in downtown Hinsdale. A long freight train is rumbling through the dead quiet town.

I open the notebook and fan through the pages.

"Well?"

"This isn't it! It's Hawgrim's schedule planner, name and address thing." The train drowns my howl of despair.

 Track 7: Saturday

A FTER SLEEPING IT OFF, bummed, discouraged, and racked out till noon, then soaking my ankle in a hot tub, I'm tempted to stand outside her building and just watch but decide against it, figuring that would be pathetic and a bad security risk and anyway, she said she'd get in touch. Instead, I limp back to the State Street library and wade through IBM Systems Journals, finding the *Popular Electronics* she mentioned and making correlations with her Plan and better understanding what she's getting at, boning up for the big meeting with Engel. I do it again on Sunday.

Dave examines his hand and says he'll never play bass again.

He lies.

I don't hear from her.

Side 7: Close to the edge

Track 1: Monday night

WE'RE AT CHECKERS RECORDS, setting up for the night's recording session. I'm still limping. Hawgrim appears. He has his swaggering businessman's briefcase with him—probably containing the paperwork for my new peace-of-mind-generating and economically sound insurance policy—it occurs to me that if I could buy Sooz some of that peaceful mind stuff, I would.

There is no inkling from Hawgrim of anything being amiss, no hint of any alleged burglary in Hinsdale.

Hawgrim says, "Hey, Mr. Martin Alan Porter, prospective long-term customer sir—I've got that *thing*, what we talked about, right here for you." He holds up his briefcase for me to see.

The big studio door opens and in walks Creach.

He once again congratulates us on our triumphant couple of downstate *concerts*—not gigs—makes a point of highlighting that distinction, saying that we have crossed a serious threshold, and with the addition of our new relationship with Rodger Slothwell and the very successful rock writer's night session at the Quiet Knight and growing radio airplay, things are starting to roll. He reviews the latest station playlists he's picked up from his station contacts—they're all encouraging—he reports on the very successful interview Hawgrim and I had with Stanley Wong-Garcia of *Rolling Stone.* Then he casually mentions that he is particularly proud of our very own *glamour puss* Dave and his *photo-modeling session* that took place the night before with a photographer from *Tiger Beat* magazine, who had been in touch with Creach since seeing St. Louis Ralph's shots over the weekend on KSHE's just-out newsletter. *Tiger Beat*—the last time I read that magazine was during the first season of the *Monkees* TV show back in '66, the only source of reliable news coverage for young Monkees fans. And now here they are—shooting dreamy pix of my brother. *Tiger Beat*, the teeny-bop rag that made David Cassidy and

Bobby Sherman famous, always on the hunt for pretty pop stars with the potential to make the young girls scream.

I had no idea.

Everybody stares aghast at Dave, who immediately claims that it's good for the band and besides it's just a teenybopper thing and who's gonna ever see it anyway? Much abuse is then hurled at my brother, including my questions about what exactly is his favorite color and what are his turn-ons and turn-offs when dating girls.

Creach tells us to cool it. "Like I said before—it is time that we get down to business. And as such, I'd like to make an announcement." He clears his throat dramatically, maybe a little uncertainly. "Boys, I'd like you to meet Mr. Flash Freehly." He turns and with an upraised arm like Monty Hall at door number one, the big studio door swings open and some long-haired guy enters the studio carrying two battered guitar cases.

Creach says, "I've asked Flash to sit in with us tonight. I think he'll fill in a number of blank spots in our sound, add some needed texture, color—a bit of professional *oomph*."

Flash Freehly, baby-faced, tall and rock 'n roll skinny, with curly blonde hair parted in the middle hanging to his shoulders and smiling freely, nods humbly at all of us.

Creach adds, "Flash is a fine session guitarist here in town—a first call rock 'n roller, been in a bunch of bands around here, even had some hits—he and I have worked a number of sessions in the past and, well, I think he'll be good for the band. Perhaps even as a permanent member. Maybe. If necessary." Creach, like a parent at a seventh-grade birthday party, gestures for everybody to make nice. "Of course, only if everyone is amenable." Creach bows in my direction, a faint smile on his face. "Naturally, as your newly appointed band manager and with the *fiduciary* responsibility that comes with that territory, I believe it is within my purview to make such recommendations, and/or decisions."

Dave, Hawgrim, Ricky, and I stand there with mouths hanging open, shocked at Creach's audacity. They all look at me like I had something to do with it.

Creach says, "You'll find that Mr. Freehly is already very familiar with much of your material—he's done his homework."

Flash seems to be the very model of long-haired charm and hippie enthusiasm. Despite that, he shakes our hands with manly gusto—looking each of us in the eye like we were always taught, saying he is looking forward to helping out, being a *team player*. Then he says, in an unexpected gravelly voice, "It's an honor and a privilege to work with you dudes."

Creach says, "Play your guitar, son."

Flash proceeds to set up his gear, whip out one of his electric guitars. It's a beaut, an old sunburst Gibson. He plugs it into a Marshall amp in the corner that I had always avoided because of its seriously intimidating look—big, loud, and dark—he lets it warm up, then rattles off a series of roaring tuneful riffs which somehow turns into a medley of our greatest hits.

Now, another man might be outraged that his little songs have been stained with such a blatant display of technical virtuosity many light years away from their humble origins—me and Felix strumming away on my bed staring at the ceiling on dark rainy nights—and another man might be offended that the simple soul of his little tunes appears ripped off, hijacked, and dipped in a soufflé of slick show biz flair, and I might be convinced that I—the artist—by letting this happen might compromise all of my principles of musical authenticity and cosmic integrity. I might have a problem with all this, but I don't. A warm breeze of calm wafts through the musty studio of my mind—Flash is good, Flash is earnest, Flash is strangely familiar.

Creach pats me on the back, sings that old line, *everythang gonna be all right,* disappears into the control room.

We rip through most of our concert material and lay down good solid tracks. Dave, continuing his newly cosmic trend, sings like he's never sung before, Hawgrim and Ricky are right on and the tunes come together amazingly well—the smiling Mr. Flash adds licks here and there that are not overbearing or intrusive, but are produced from his listening to the music with an obviously professional ear that knows how to serve the song—how to be there when needed and to back off when not.

Creach is right. Everythang gonna be all right.

I introduce a new song—I sit on a stool with an unplugged Felix and sing "Shelley's Lyre"—a softly pale ballad of *rainy streets and soft white sheets and my lover's touch that meant so much and I feel her music kindling fires in my heart that burned so much higher and would that it were possible that I would not tire before she could indeed make me her lyre.*

Yes. I know. The words still need work.

We take a break. I go up to the control room to talk to Creach.

"How's the beautiful lady of 'Shelley's Lyre'? A lovely tune, a nice piece for the middle of the album. Maybe we can get a synthesizer in here and Hawgrim can—"

"Hawgrim? On *that* tune? I don't think so."

"Of course. Very foolish of me."

"But you think it's good? I don't know."

Creach gestures for me to sit down.

"You haven't found her black book yet, have you."

I shake my head. I tell him of our dumbshit burglary.

"Well, I'll be *goddamned*. I was wondering why you were limping." Laughs. "We've got burglars in this band! Hoo-we!" Looks at me admiringly. "Ah, but don't worry. You'll get that thing back." He uses a pencil like a drumstick, bouncing the eraser head on the console. "You okay with Mr. Flash? He's got your best interests in those fingers of his."

"Yes."

"That's a very professional attitude."

"Thank you."

He drums some more. An awkward silence.

"One more thing, Pepper. I've been debating about whether or not to tell you this." He sips his coffee, hesitating. "I want you to know that things are very likely going to change around here. Actually, not just around old Checkers Records—the entire industry is changing—the days of little labels like us are pretty much gone."

Creach is uncomfortable. He crosses his legs, then uncrosses them. He never crosses his legs.

"Conglomerates—they're taking over. Big money's buying up the industry, touring, venues, distribution—hell, the Czecholiewski family has been approached by a couple of the majors. They apparently want to buy little old Checkers Records, no small part thanks to the promise and potential of you and the boys—and our back catalog, of course. I'm trying to do right by you, but I want you to know this."

"Why?"

"You need to know it. It's a new day."

"Is this good or bad?"

"I don't know. Could go either way." He shows a little flash of impatience, probably just due to the fact that he finds himself in the unfamiliar position of not knowing. We silently share that feeling for a few beats.

Then, almost whispering, "Which prompts me to ask—what's going on in that hairy head of yours, Pepper Porter?"

High wire current flips on in my body.

"Just where you headed, my young friend?" He looks me straight in the eye, points at my head. "Methinks you approach a fork in the road."

I shake my head. I don't know.

"You got a map in there?"

Yeah, right.

"You've got a helluva future—one way or another. It could be extremely ..."

Yes.

"Don't fuck it up."

I nod. I won't. I hope.

Then with a forced smile, he rattles off another pencil drum roll. "You better go deal with Hawgrim."

With all that swirling around in my brain, I find Hawgrim waiting for me in the hall outside of the control room, cigarette hanging from his lips and a slim red binder with the fancy black and gold Interstate Metropolitan Citywide Insurance Company logo emblazoned on it in his hand.

"Whole life insurance is a wonderful thing, Pepper my friend. And you know what the real benefit of whole life really is?"

"What." I slump against the wall.

"Peace of mind—your ability to sleep at night and not worry about ... things."

Sigh.

He puffs, blows a smoke ring at the ceiling. A long ash falls on the beige linoleum floor.

"I've got your commie chick's fat notebook—quite provocative reading. And she, I might add, is quite the little number herself. Gorgeous. We met at the Palmer House. But you probably knew that."

My heart goes into its usual Hawgrim sputter. "I'm so glad you found it. She'll be very grateful to have it back."

"I'm sure. However, there's just one thing, a small *finder's fee*, if you will."

He launches into a description of the contents of her notebook. "Upon perusal, I see that we're talking apparent Weather Underground addresses—people, places—I tell ya, your little brainy babe's got quite the network of unsavory fiends—I mean friends."

"What do you want, Hawgrim?"

"Mostly, she's got whole sections of bizarre-looking notes—equations, graphs, weird formulae and technical cryptic scribbly things—indecipherable to most, I'm sure. But to those in the know, well ... there's no telling."

He motions for me to follow him down the hall away from the control room.

"Boo Boo, do you know how to compartmentalize? I'm quite good at keeping various aspects of my life completely separate—no cross-talk or fuzzy interference between, say, my business life and my musical life."

"You're not doing a very good job of that right now."

"Oh, but I am. I'm thinking that our little old band here just might be some sort of success—things are starting to happen. Who knows?—maybe twenty, thirty years from now, your little songs—I mean *our* little songs—could be a little gold mine as many of our generation enter their golden years nostalgic for the good old days—I'm trained to look at the long term, you see. Which brings me to the point. The policy I have drawn up for you will generate real cash value for you down the road. We're talking big bucks when you retire in, shall we say 2015? Nice chunk of change."

"So I sign up for your insurance, start paying you an arm and a leg, you win your gold putter and I get the notebook back, right?"

"I win my gold putter, quarterly bonus—hell, this and the Creach thing'll put me over the top for the year—but I also get half of the publishing rights to all *our* songs, in perpetuity. It'll be Lennon/ McCartney, Jagger/Richards, and Porter/Hawgrim. I can see it now ..."

"You fucker."

Creach sticks his head into the hall, sees us down at the other end. "Do you boys mind? Back to work." He shoots me an inquiring look, ducks back in.

Hawgrim resumes. "It's very simple. And you get the nasty incriminating little book back, no questions asked. And we go on our merry little band way. Everybody's happy."

He claps me on the back, we go back into the studio.

The rest of the session is awful. At least for me. I can't concentrate, I forget the words, I mess up chords, intros and endings and the whole thing feels to me like the music actually deserves to be in Dave's cheesy *Tiger Beat*. Or maybe not even. Oblivious, Hawgrim plays as well as ever, offering me annoying encouragement. Looking to get something going, Creach has Dave step up, sing some leads— he's fantastic and Flash dishes out solid guitar work and harmonies that even sound kind of like me. Ricky, twirling his sticks as he sits on his throne, shakes his head, sensing the weirdness.

Creach finally pulls the plug around four in the morning, tells us he'll see us the next night. He takes me aside and before he says anything I mumble, "Fuckin' Hawgrim."

Everybody else clears out of the studio.

I sit down on a piano bench bent over with Felix between my knees, hair in my eyes, wiped out. Creach straightens his trousers, sits down next to me, crosses his legs. His shoes are shined so bright I can see my face in the black leather.

"What happened?"

"He's got Sooz's notebook and he'll return it for a small fee—me buying a whole life policy ..."

Creach starts to laugh. "Helluva closing technique!" He stops laughing. "I'm sorry."

"... and half the publishing rights to all my songs."

Wide-eyed, Creach marvels. "Well I'll be god*damned*. Our own little accordion-playing extortionist—Brian Hawgrim—pleased to meet you!"

He uncrosses his legs and joins me hunched over.

"You know you shouldn't fool with those publishing rights. Some serious coin to be made there, if and when we—you—really get going."

"Maybe I should think of it as an insurance policy, you know, for her."

"You'd do that?" He whistles softly. "It *is* a problem. But nothing that can't be handled. In some way."

I notice how amazingly quiet the studio can be—with no amps, no guitars, no hiss, no hum, no rattling snare. A ceiling light glints off of one of Creach's shoes and a way out of this mess begins to spin on the turntable of my mind.

"I'll be late tomorrow night—I have an important thing going on downtown."

"Then you'd best be at that thing. When can you make it here?"

"Eleven work?"

"I think we'll be fine—you do what you need to do. We can get things done. Your brother, he sounds pretty good—despite that *Tiger Beat* shit."

After a silently exhausted ride home in Otto, *Tiger Beat* Dave, still looking as good as Bobby Sherman at the corner of Hollywood and Vine, stoops to scoop up the mail inside the front door of the apartment. He hands the little pile to me and says, "You got no problem with me singing leads like that?"

I flip through the mail.

"You were great."

"How about this *Tiger Beat* stuff?"

"If it's good for you, it's good for the band."

I find what I'm looking for.

Dave yawns loudly, says *namaste, man* and goes into the kitchen to forage for food.

I tear open the plain white envelope and a rainbow slash falls out. In her perfectly neat hand, it reads *Tuesday's the night. Meet you at the Acropolis 7:30. Hope you've got my book. Love and Revolution—*

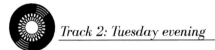

A FTER ANOTHER LOUSY night's sleep—wading through strange and bizarre dreams, like being stretched out on a couch being questioned by a faceless shrink wearing a tall pointy wizard hat with half moons on it, then suddenly being forced to climb the endless stairs of the Hancock all the way to the top because the elevator is broken only to be met in the Sky Lounge by Felix the Cat himself who, also reclining on a couch smoking a joint, is playing *a guitar with my face on it* asking if I love Felix or just the idea of Felix—I wake up exhausted.

I go to work and spend a long but sunny afternoon working for Lazlo shelving new records, listening to XRT, hoping to hear one of our tunes. I don't.

So I show up at the Acropolis Diner a little early and sit in a window booth, swilling a cup of heavily sugared coffee, fully suited and tied, waiting for Sooz. The place is busy. Looks like a regular crowd.

As scheduled, at 7:30 and just as the light at Rush and Bellevue changes and the WALK sign comes on, she appears, and like the model for *Charlie* perfume she comes cruising across the street full of confidence and gorgeousness—crisp tan raincoat over a darkly elegant pantsuit, perfectly tailored, slightly flared and draped beautifully at just the right length over shiny black high heels, serious black leather valise in hand, her big round glasses framing her face, her blonde hair freshly curled. She looks like she means business—this is not Bunny Sooz. This is professional kick-ass-and-take-names, you-gotta-problem-with-my-femininity Sooz, ready to wow the hell out of Fletcher Engel.

Sooz, after sweeping into the diner, scans the place, sees me, approaches with that same perfumed stride. Without saying a word, she bends down and lays a tongue-heavy kiss on me that leaves me breathless. Then, with her red Revlon'd lips at my ear she breathes, "*That …* was for our fabulous night."

Carefully, she hangs up her coat, sits down, begins drumming the fingers of both hands on the table.

She says, "I'm nervous as hell. A bit scared actually—I mean this is it! Right now. Everything I've been working for." She eyes my attire. "You look very nice. Thank you for being here, for being ... with me."

I lean across the table, take both her hands and assure her, "You've got nothing to worry about. You know your stuff and I bet that Engel is just dying for you to be amazing—he *wants* to hear your story. And von Flarf will be there—you know he digs you—it's gonna be great."

Her hands are cold.

"And I found that Systems Journal and the magazine—I'm all boned up."

She smirks.

"No really. I got the background and that stuff *down*. I'm ready." We talk a little bits and bytes. She's impressed. We're good.

Sooz glances at the door. "Have you seen—you know—those SNARB guys?"

"No. And I bet you haven't either, right? Forget about 'em— whatever or whoever they are—they're just a distraction from your— our—purpose. Just do it."

She pulls from the black valise a freshly minted copy of the Plan bound in one of those clear covered plastic report binders, riffles through it, showing me some of the new charts she'll use to pitch Engel, all very meticulously done on graph paper—bell curves depicting network traffic under various loads—some stuff I haven't seen before. She says it's based on new calculations and right *there*—that segment of the parabola right where the bell peaks and begins its descent, shows that her mechanism for sorting and smoothing out data traffic works—*controlled statistical arbitration of a shared media*—at speeds nobody has ever thought possible and is unlike anything out there that she—and apparently von Flarf—had heard of.

"This network'll be *hyper fast*—remember, we're changing paradigms here."

"What about that name thing we were talking about?"

Sooz says, "Remember that all this is just part of the puzzle here but yeah, I have—let's call it the *Hyper Ethereal Transmission System*—"

"Catchy."

She rolls her eyes. "It's about *connectivity*—and we all need connectivity."

"I'm into it, yeah—connectivity—but only with *you*. Not somebody else or even—" I recall her parting shot the other night, "the *idea* of you—I am into you."

She nervously brushes an invisible hair off her face. "Right—the idea of me. That wasn't fair. Sorry."

Nevertheless, I quickly review her query in my mind. What, exactly, is not to love about the *idea of Sooz?*

Benefits:

    A. Gorgeous.

    B. Brilliant. A *self-starter*. A *go-getter*.

    C. Currently employed as a Playboy Bunny.

    D. Little kids love her, she loves them. Charming, gracious.

    E. Paradigm shifter. And responsible.

    F. Those legs. That face. Those eyes. (Perhaps redundant—implied by items A and C.)

And G. She *will* change the world. I just know it.

On the down side:

    1.Wanted by Federal Authorities. It's a problem.

    2. Not all that impressed with my music.

    3. Eats like a horse.

    4. Sometimes snorts when she laughs.

    5. Uncertain future.

    6. Annoying cat.

Making rapid calculations, I discount the negatives as merely adding desirable "color"—an essential value-added spice to any relationship. I come up with an answer.

Yes.

I am in love with the idea of her. No doubt about it. But I deem that a shallow, unacceptable response, even for a twenty-three-year-old confused rock 'n roller. However, isn't she the embodiment of the idea? Existentially speaking—existence precedes essence, or is it essence precedes existence?

Sooz rattles my cage and I check back into reality.

"Hello—are you there?" She snaps her fingers in front of my face. "What about my notebook?"

"Hawgrim confessed, holding it for ransom. But Dave and I tried to get it. We burgled his place."

"You *what*?"

"Middle of the night. He was gone. But he came back and we had to scram." I tell her the whole story.

She's disappointed but impressed. "You just might have a future in this line of work."

"But I think his appointment book, names and phone numbers will be very useful."

"Interesting."

I tell her about Hawgrim's "finder's fee."

"No!"

"Don't worry. I've got a plan."

"Tell me."

The radio behind the counter sings about teaching the world to sing in perfect harmony and I have the sudden radio-induced urge for a Coke.® But then my song crackles over the airwaves behind it and everybody in the place immediately stands up, fruging in the aisles, boogalooing with the waitresses, the off-duty cop, the two old guys at the counter, the rumpled brown-suited salesman with his order pad, call reports, expense forms, and receipts spread out on the table in front of him, the taxi driver with his sports page, and the three older women who look like they work at Marshall Field's in the Frango Mint department. Everybody rocks out. And then they all sing along with the chorus in an impossible world of perfect harmony—aunts are indeed cool.

All that didn't really happen.

But my song does come over the radio. People ignore it and go on eating.

So, with Sooz shaking her head, I groove and get *down* a little bit in the booth on my own, tapping the high-hat cymbal of the chrome sugar dispenser, the tom-tom of my empty plate and the bass drum of the booth bench.

Sooz relaxes a bit, says, "It's growing on me—I mean, it's really pretty good."

"It's damn good."

"I take it all back. Maybe you *can* change the world with your little songs."

"You don't really mean that. And there ain't no paradigm shift in 'Your Aunt is Cool.'"

"Maybe a little."

"Maybe a little."

I drum roll the table.

She smiles. "Pepper, you were saying … a plan?"

I tell her what I've got in mind.

"That sounds crazy." She hunches over the table, her shining green eyes narrowed, whispers, "But it just might work."

I look at my watch.

"We gotta go."

Immediately shifting gears and going into meeting mode, Sooz hands me a complementary Playboy Club Key good for one night only and we hurry over to the entrance on Walton, she motor-mouthing the whole time, rehearsing and telling me yet again that my purpose is—yeah yeah yeah, I remember. Before we walk into the Club, she straightens my tie.

 Track 3: Tuesday night

DINA, THE BUNNY I'd made friends with when I sat slumped at the bar that first night just before Sooz appeared, greets us, welcoming me back with a wink. She makes kibitzing Bunny talk with Sooz while I mentally rehearse my own humble little introductory spiel. Dina escorts us back through the Club and its confusing warren of rooms and passages to a secluded booth occupied by the professorial Dr. Ivor von Flarf in an oddly cut Germanic sort of suit coat with very thin lapels and a plain black stripe of a tie, smoking a gaudy Meerschaum pipe. On the other side of the curved booth sits a smiling gentleman, angular and balding with short spiky gray hair, casually but elegantly attired in a crisp blue blazer, black turtleneck, and gray slacks—Fletcher Engel. He and von Flarf extricate themselves from the booth, rise to shake Sooz's outstretched hand—both he and von Flarf innately courteous, well-bred, welcoming and small talking as we sit down ordering drinks, getting settled around our big half moon table. Sooz is in the middle next to Engel, under large, artfully illuminated photos of the '64 Miss June and the '68 Miss September. Von Flarf and I are at the opposing horns of the plush curved sofa.

Engel's business card shows only his name, telephone number, and the simple title—*Investor*.

He drives the evening's agenda. My intro spiel goes out the window.

Truly charming and with great consideration for our comfort and well-being, Engel, after talking about the weather and the traffic coming into the city that evening, turns the conversation to me. I say that I'm there as a good friend and advisor of Miss Grace Kelliher and that I have a small measure of mainframe systems level programming, communications subsystems architecture and design experience. I am also a professional musician and, again, am there in support of the young lady.

Engel nodding at Sooz, smiles. "A young woman ought to have an escort in this day and age, don't you think?"

Engel probes my background a bit and I discuss my experience at Michigan, describing the systems I worked on. I also mention that I had been offered a job at IBM, but turned it down. He seems to already know that. I mention a few names. He's impressed but mentions bigger IBM names—CEO, Chairman of the Board, a Senator. Then he asks about my current career, gets me talking about my recent musical successes which prompts him to promise to put me in touch with one or two West Coast people he knows that might be in a position to be of some musical assistance. He asks if I've heard of Tony Orlando.

He turns to Sooz, asks about Miss Grace Kelliher's technology background and current employment, says he's a bit puzzled at how she seems to have flown under the radar, almost completely.

Demurely, Grace speaks of her time in Ann Arbor and her work in electrical engineering and computer science. She indicates that she currently works as a tech writer for a small publisher here in town that Engel hasn't heard of but it is of no matter. He summons our Bunny, satiny-green Marilyn, and dinner orders are placed. Almost immediately, four mammoth shrimp cocktails, each surrounded by a vat-sized mound of shaved ice, appear on our table, delivered by two particularly statuesque Bunnies who very discretely flash comradely and conspiratorial nods at Sooz and then vanish in the dark.

Watching the disappearing Bunnies, Engel says, "Miss Kelliher, your past is indeed impressive. Though I'm curious why you did not complete your degree." He selects a particularly large curving shrimp, swirls it in cocktail sauce and chews thoughtfully.

Formally and succinctly, she states, "I hope to complete my studies in the future. But I was very driven to explore this and other areas of interest outside of academia."

"Passion. I like that—one doesn't always need that piece of paper in order to make a difference."

Von Flarf, apparently reaching his fill of shrimp, pushes his icy vase toward me, kindly asking if I'd care to finish it.

I gratefully accept.

Engel says, "Ivor isn't much for seafood."

Von Flarf relights his pipe.

Dabbing his lips daintily with a napkin, Engel then tells a bit of his own story. He too has an engineering background, did his undergrad work at Iowa State, well known for its pioneering work in large computing after the war. Sooz, gaining confidence, asks if that isn't where the roots of Control Data, CDC, were put down—in the fertile black technical dirt of central Iowa. Engel smiles, says it certainly was and, warming up to this obviously knowledgeable young woman, describes his early work in innovative core memory storage technologies that ended up becoming a central part of the huge technical computing mainframes that CDC—where he was an early employee—went on to build in the '50s and '60s, machines that ultimately became critical to government and military installations around the country, many very sensitive, dark and black. Enthusiastically, he begins to talk about a site at the Air Force Weapons Laboratory at Kirtland Air Force Base in Albuquerque but catches himself, saying that that was really neither here nor there, but *my gosh there are some very interesting applications out there, aren't there?*

Sooz is listening intently. I am taking notes.

Wistfully, he says, "Oh, we were *coining money* as fast as an Iowa cyclone could blow your house down in those days."

Engel goes on, saying that he retired early and these days lives up on the leafy, well-to-do North Shore of suburban Chicago. He provides monetary, technical, and business development consultations to highly specialized and extraordinary engineering talent, "such as yourself, Miss Kelliher," as well as offering talent-spotting services to other clients—private investors, private industry, government and, of course, the military.

Sooz does not flinch. Dinner arrives. Engel makes a show of thanking our Bunny—"Thank you so much, Marilyn my dear."

Far away in the main part of the Club, music begins playing—jazzy piano, bass, and drums.

A New York strip medium rare, large baked potato, and steamed vegetables along with a house Caesar salad for Engel and Sooz—identical orders for similar tastes. Pleased, Engel orders another bottle of '67 St. Julien for the table. Though clearly amused at Sooz's chow-houndness, he makes no unseemly mention of it.

More war stories of CDC and its battles with IBM and, as the wine flows, Engel talks of his work during the war. He was a low-level functionary—a young man on the make—in the Office of Strategic Services, the OSS, precursor to the CIA.

"But the life of a spook wasn't for me. It was rather dreary, actually." He smiles. "This is much more exciting. Don't you think?"

He leans across the table as if the walls had ears and says, "I have had the honor to have played small roles in the invention and implementation of world-changing technologies—transistors, semiconductors, rotational disk storage, and more recently, microprocessors. And I am always on guard, always on the lookout for new and amazing marvels." With his eyes on Sooz, "Perhaps you may have that opportunity, too."

Bunny Marilyn clears away the remains of dinner and takes my order for coffee and Bananas Foster—I can't resist—and small glasses of Port for Engel and von Flarf. Nothing for Sooz. Marilyn gives her a quick wink.

Engel, cheerfully lighting a cigar, says, "But enough about me. It's time to hear from you, Miss Kelliher." He sucks on the stogie till it lights, politely puffs a little cloud away from Sooz. "You come highly recommended by my good friend Dr. von Flarf—he is one of our best and most ... *reliable*—" he pauses, faintly underlining that last word, before concluding with, "talent spotters."

Von Flarf, who has remained mostly silent and very obviously deferential in every way to Engel, nods in a heel-clicking Teutonic manner. However, I get the feeling that he is somehow uncomfortable with all this.

Sooz hands her fresh new copies of the Plan to everyone at the table, me included, and launches into what I think is an eye-poppingly spectacular, well ordered, crisply clinical, and devastatingly convincing description of her means of statistically arbitrating data traffic on a high-speed, shared network media. Engel, following along and now using reading glasses that perch on the end of his nose—enabling him to peer over them at Sooz and occasionally me with a disconcertingly penetrating raised eyebrow—encourages her, genuinely fascinated, interrupting only a few times to clarify various details, obviously testing the depth of her knowledge, probing for weaknesses and gauging her poise, but always with an engaging and reassuring smile.

"Please go on, Miss Kelliher."

She arrives at the end of her pitch, then goes for the big finish.

"So what I have described enables a completely new way of building a data network—it helps move the world from its centuries-old, restrictive, dead and dying analog basis to a digital foundation. It is revolutionary, an epoch-making paradigm shift that, with various other critical computing components I know are under development as we speak, will change the world because—and I have learned this from my friend Mr. Porter here—to the end user, the way it works and the applications yet to be invented that will take advantage of it, will be completely indistinguishable from magic. Thank you very much for listening."

There is a moment of silence. Engel removes his glasses and sits back in the booth. He begins to clap, slowly, in a Wrigley Field big-handed way, von Flarf joining with more of a drawing room reserved courtesy. Other diners in the room stare.

"Extraordinary, simply extraordinary." His cigar has gone out, unused during her pitch—he tries to take a puff but quickly abandons it in the ashtray, totally distracted. "Miss Kelliher, allow me to cut to the chase. While I am aware of the existence of at least one other somewhat similar private initiative elsewhere in the country—Palo Alto to be specific, I have certain friends highly placed in government technology laboratories—are you familiar with DARPA? I'm sure you are—and I most certainly would like to recommend that you enter one of the facilities. Probably Lawrence Livermore National Labs, don't you think, Ivor?"

DARPA. Livermore. Hydrogen bombs and Cold War weapons research. A cold shot runs up my spine. This is a deal killer.

Von Flarf vaguely nods.

Engel goes on. "These are facilities where, with ample funding, you could pursue your research with the goal of bringing it to fruition as soon as possible. Of course, you would have to undergo certain security background checks—rather in-depth I'm afraid, but purely a matter of course, you understand. I'm sure there would be no problem there—I know some highly placed people." He smirks in von Flarf's direction. "Actually, I believe that in order to save time, a few preliminary inquiries may already be underway." Von Flarf sits expressionless.

Engel, in a stagy whisper, says, "You will be famous."

Sooz closes her copy of the Plan.

Smiling graciously, she says, "Thank you so much, Mr. Engel. Your kind words and encouragement are very flattering. I am truly overwhelmed." And she looks it. "However, I wonder if I might excuse myself for a moment while I consider all this, and powder my nose." She glances at me. "Mr. Porter, would you join me, please?"

Engel and von Flarf chivalrously rise as Sooz extracts herself from the booth stuffing her small purse into her leather valise, grinning with some good-natured exasperation, "Oy, this darn makeup! Be right back." She smiles winningly.

We hustle through the Club. The vibes are getting weird.

Passing the main bar and little stage, standing among a crowd of aging jazz lovers swirling Manhattans and swilling Double Gibsons, I notice that Oscar Peterson is at the piano—"Green Dolphin Street" whirls around my head once again.

Bumping through the crowd, heads turning in her wake, Sooz tells me that this is clearly a disastrous dead end, that she could never in a million years go to work for DARPA.

I know that to be true.

She stops in her tracks and turns to me. "What am I supposed to do?"

As she says that, with "Green Dolphin Street" surging in volume—

I see two men standing about thirty yards away at the other end of the darkened room beneath a palm tree and yet another portrait of a naked busty blonde—their backs up against the wall, shades on, nearly matching blue suits—Agent Schootz and Under Assistant Agent Brown.

The moment I see them, they see me—my head above the crowd like a balloon—Sooz probably still unobserved. They begin to elbow their way toward me.

"Sooz, SNARB, those two guys, right over there. Here they come."

She doesn't turn, wastes no time. Sooz reaches up, pulls my head down, kisses me hard, looks me in the eye and says, "I'm gone. Don't look for me."

And she disappears into the crowded, martini-clinking piano bar dark.

Brown and Schootz split up—Brown heading for the main entrance of the Club, Schootz coming right at me. I turn and spot a familiar landmark—the hall with the men's room. I dash over, duck in.

Being the middle of Oscar Peterson's set, the men's room is deserted except for Mr. Roosevelt, who makes no fuss—he is simply perched on his stool elaborately folding the fluffy white hand towels. As if no time had passed, he asks, "So how has that oh so fine recording deal worked out for you, young sir?"

"Just great, Mr. Roosevelt."

I begin to think that diving into the men's room was a really dumb idea, a dead end with no way out, when in walks Agent Schootz, calm and cold, crisply polite, his shades still on. He says, "Leaving so soon? We'd like a word with you and your friend."

"You must have the wrong guy, sir ..." The door opens and Under Assistant Agent Brown bursts in.

Brown, seeing Schootz, says, "I lost her, just like that." He snaps his fingers.

"Twerp!" Schootz turns to me, "Well?"

Then Hugh Hefner walks in.

Mr. Roosevelt winks at me.

The two SNARB guys, awestruck, stand with their mouths open while Hef, in one of his maroon smoking jackets, holding his pipe, chats easily with them, asking if they're having a nice time, telling them that Oscar Peterson is a *real gone cat*. I edge toward the door. Hef goes about his business, asks if they'd seen the new issue, just out today. They say no, which, after he finishes up, prompts Hef to pull out a few Polaroids of the new Miss April, and that was all she wrote.

I slip out the door unobserved, with Mr. Roosevelt right behind.

He touches my arm, asks that I follow him.

We make our way through one of the hidden doors where we spot Bunny Dina, who has a shaken look on her face, standing in the bright lights of the kitchen, a bit of mascara streaked on her cheek. Mr. Roosevelt confers briefly with her, turns and says, "Come with me."

Down a back staircase smelling both of disinfectant and grilled red meat, Mr. Roosevelt says he is leading me to the back door of the Club—the secret entrance designed to allow employees—Bunnies in particular—to come and go with discretion and in complete safety. We enter a long, narrow but well-lit, perfectly clean and clinically white passageway furnished with occasional grandmotherly vases of flowers on small antique tables and closed circuit TV security cameras mounted on the wall every twenty-five feet or so.

We walk and walk and walk, wordlessly.

Oscar Peterson's music sounds over speakers mounted alongside the cameras. "Green Dolphin Street" finally ends.

We turn corners, go up and down a few staircases—I have no idea where we are or where we're going.

Finally, we hustle up a narrow set of stairs, open a door and enter what appears to be a small apartment building lobby—a nicely appointed wood-paneled room, carpeted, with comfortable chairs, more flowers, and a small chandelier. There is a heavy, round-topped oak door. It appears to be the only way out.

Mr. Roosevelt says, "I can go no farther. She went this way." He points to the door. "You're on your own now, son." He shakes my hand, bids me goodbye, vanishes back down the passageway.

I open the door, find myself standing under a small striped canopy on a street in front of what appears to be an older upscale apartment building doorway. There is a doorman, elegantly uniformed in black with a red bowtie. With a tip of his tophat, he greets me. "Good evening, sir."

The doorman looks a bit like Hugh Hefner.

He says, "She told me to give you this. She said it would remind you of—well, you know what."

A snowball.

"Taxi, sir?"

Befuddled, I mumble, no thank you.

"Have a pleasant evening, sir. And good luck." He returns to his duties by the door, rocking slowly on his heels, whistling a jazzy tune.

Chestnut Street. The Hancock Building towers to my right, the marbled back of Water Tower Place to my left. I am a full three city blocks from the Playboy Club.

Snowing. Raining. The black streets glisten. The street is empty.

The snowball is melting in my hand. I wind up and fling it, perfectly starring the stop sign at the corner with an exploding splatter of snow.

I slump against a lamppost. She's gone. Again.

At my feet, a small white piece of paper blinks at me, soaked by the rain but familiar. I pick it up—its colors blurred and streaked—a rainbow slash.

The following is an unreleased rock opera, the double album of my mind—*A Night in Pepperland.* This is what happened next:

Side One

LOUD MUSIC DRUMS THRUMS AND HUMS deafening my brain on the dark end of Chestnut Street and I'm still slumped on the streetlight dazed and confused and the music explodes out of my ears like strobing flashes of her rainbow lightning thundering and echoing down the empty street and everything speeds up—My heart metronomes in high gear my ears are hypersensitive my eyes grow beach ball big and I hear it all every last little bit of this psychic white noise twentieth century harsh discordant and screaming five key signatures at once half of them from detuned guitars and prepared pianos and the rest from unknown power sources stacked with violent volts and angry watts and I windmill a screaming guitar around my head and fling it through a street-level window where fifty fifteen-inch speakers blare ten or twenty channels of static and the glass splinters and shatters and then I wrap the guitar around the iron lamp post and the guitar vanishes because she's gone she's gone she's gone and then all is quiet and a beer can rolls down the middle of the street blown by the wind like a dented runaway bowling ball clanging on the pavement about to veer into the gutter and then the world turntables down going from 78 to 45 to 33-1/3 rpm—The one true speed in revolutions per minute and I realize that I must have a revolution in my head this minute the next and the next and I catch my breath—a horned moon appears above between the white of the twin antenna ziggurats and I touch the Hancock's smooth black steel and zoom to the top sky deck where she says she likes to be and the darkened rain-streaked glass frames the orange bright grid of the city channeling live current through every street and every junction but clouds smear the view and half of it is gone in a second shrouding the circuit board avenues that glow and beat with a rhythmic submerged light and a few couples walk arm in arm slowly doing romantic laps around the hushed sky lounge as flashbulbs pop amid the quiet and emptiness—oh—Sooz—no—and

Side Two

THE STREETS BREATHE through great steam vents from deep tunnel pipes—I can feel the city's lungs and I am part of its breath exhaling outside the State Street-that-Great-Street Central Library and it is closed tight dark and locked but I mindlessly pull on the doors and rattle chains—behind me a grizzled panhandler sez spare change brother can you spare a dime for a cup of coffee—I fish a linty quarter out of my pocket but it's probably only a nickel and he is grateful and begins to tell his seaman's tale of the Great Lakes waterfront wharf working plying passage through the locks gone to ports east and points west and all points in between heaving ore ships from up on the Iron Range sailing to the dark satanic mills forging sheets of steel and twin I-beams and alchemizing Thunderbirds and though I try to concentrate he fades and loses interest and swigs his own Thunderbird and wanders away and my turntable spins down some more and I circle the library all the way around one city block testing entrances looking for the unseen doors in the wall where she might have gone seeking shelter from the storm—Checker-topped cop sez where you going flower punk and I blather something and move on and a trio of rats cross my path eyes shining on their way someplace I have never been

LIKE A SPINNING SPOOKHOUSE WINDOWSHADE a fat scroll shrieks in a Marshall Field's high fashion window and it's her Plan that projects itself in the eyelid movie theatre of my mind—It rolls a million frames a minute and some psychedelic lady who sez call her Queen Fab she smiles sweetly and laughs through her nose and sez I was wondering when you'd get here so let me take you on a little trip—She's in some electric Glinda the Good Witch outfit threaded with a million little fibers of light each slowly waving in her unseen karma current tentacles of tiny jellyfish hypnotizering and electrificationing and she holds a dime store costume wand sparkly and slightly crooked and topped with a cardboard star that's bent and creased from overuse—And we are comfortably seated in Sooz's electronic carrier silvery and sleek and open like a V8 go kart from the future and Queen Fab and I are flying straight into the words of Sooz veering between lines and letters and riding the curves of the graphs and then orbiting high over the throbbing grid of the city amidst vast shining clouds of streaming charged electrons and crazed datagram packets bits and bytes all jabbering at once chaotic but miraculously ordered and there are no collisions and it all magically works and it is hyper ethereal just like she said it'd be and Queen Fab turns and shakes my shoulders and sez you too must shine a light in this entropic night and she tosses me a flashlight but the batteries are dead she only shrugs and a little fog clears in my brain as the question comes back to me and lights up across a blazing block-long State Street marquee and Sooz sez you gonna play your little songs your whole life or change the world then Queen Fab sez dig this junior and she pulls the plug and the globe goes dark lights out and the oceanic mesh of light is replaced with closed cybernetic sinister structures with no doors no windows inert and featureless and all roads leading there and none leading out and it is all command and control and central intelligence and terminal and it's up to you—Queen Fab sez listen to what the music tells you listen to what the technology tells you listen to what you tell you and I can show you no more and she waves her wand and the funny car sputters to a halt and disappears while a 151 roars up and I get on and go furthur.

Side Three

FAR AWAY IN THE LYSERGIC NIGHT of Chicago's Old Town maybe she's here hipsters and hookers hassle me and it's raining again and my hair is soaked as the city begins to run down growing colder away from the electric glitter and glam of the Loop—Distant sirens waver in the west but here broken glass and needles lay washed up in the gutter and surgical cords tourniquet around arms and the haunted eyes of slaves stare out of darkened doorways hunting for veins as I avert my eyes and then I'm mugged by two jittery kids who take all they can find and somebody slugs me in the face and I stagger backwards and they find everything and I end up in a doorway that reeks of piss and sweat sticky with sweet alcohol and I have found nothing and have nothing

I KNOCK ON HER DOOR softly softly knowing she won't be there—Just a scratching inside and a pathetic muffled yowl as I use her key and jiggle the lock and the door opens—Snowball the cat fed and cared for by the nice building ladies takes one look at me and disappears under the bed in the darkened room lit only by sulfurous city lights—The unused bed made up neatly—She's gone—I sit on the bed and listen to the sounds of the building breathing and radiators gurgling and the middle part of something playing just beyond my ears that I can't hear then but there's a quick staticky segue on the radio station of my mind and I am hung up but then Snowball warms up to me nuzzling my leg and then jumps in my lap—Maybe her scent is all over me maybe Snowball decides that I'm the only way out and he'd better make nice and the radiator sputters and ticks and the apartment is cold gimme shelter—I bury my face in her pillow fall asleep in a trickle of blood and dream and there she is and then

ANGRY FEARFUL MUSIC FUZZTONED GUITARS stab me awake but there is no shelter and Snowball is stuffed in my shirt and we are out on the street chased by the mad bull of the twentieth century lost on the streets of Chicago red-eyed hard charging up Clark Street and across Fullerton and I have no choice but to run bloody-shirted and frantic in my own weird Pamplona in the Lincoln Park 1968 of my mind and there's no place to run no place to hide while scrawled rainbow slashes begin to appear and they're on L-stations alley walls overpasses underpasses burned-out cars and wavering on crumbling

brick walls and torn billboards forming your own personal runway and I am drawn to the next place because the Dark Stranger stands
Side Four

ON A BEND IN THE RIVER slow city sewer stinking stagnant just north of the city on ruined Goose Island under an ancient bridge behind weedy warehouses and derelict factories with busted signs and broken windows and rusting water tanks—Chicago Conglomoration Corporation and International Consolidated General Enterprises mossy with overgrown dead end forgotten rail spurs and crumbling loading docks—Beneath a blasted tree and between the tracks are rumpled shadows around a weeping fire and sparks fly up freeing fleeing fireflies blown by hot gusts of the city's breath—Like Huck and Jim traipsing across a snag ragged dark island in the center of the great river Snowball and I follow muddy paths toward the flames Snowball huddles in my coat clinging to me his claws reaching through my shirt and his little heart fluttering—Behind us is the great city's pile of steel and glass lit up and stainless—The ghosts around the fire are wrapped in blankets and cast-off coats others in tin sheds and camped in big derelict packing crates among the cattails and what look like burial mounds then a boxcar bull of a man with a topless porkpie hat and wild gray hair streaming from under the brim like Bozo the Clown wrapped in a torn greatcoat stands and calls out—Who the hell are you brother—a baseball bat flicking in his hands and I stop but he relaxes as Snowball cries and I smile peaceably and he offers me coffee and a cracked saucer of milk for Snowball while he eyes me up and down then the shadows reveal faces and they're all lost and shuffled out of place misfit native sons left behind bona fide losers former winners and players to be named later and then a kindly woman touches my face it's bleeding again and she dabs a clean cloth damp and warm and tells me she can fix me up real fine—the head man asks why you here son and I pull out my crumpled rainbow slash and show him and he smiles and nods and passes it around the fire while somebody hands me a tin cup of gritty cowboy coffee—I seen that sign years ago—them weather cats those crazy ass revolutionary kids—he shakes his head and narrows his eyes—But they don't come around here no more—those kids are all gone—probably grown up and got real jobs working over there—He nods toward the emerald city—May as well be a million miles away—you know those lights never go off—They always on—But ain't no connection 'tween here and there my brother and see that telephone pole over there it don't stop here it just passes through and that's the way we like it—I ask again have you seen this recently—and a girl—a beautiful girl you'd remember her—she been here?—And he takes his hat off and ruffles his crazy Einstein hair taking a closer look and sez I think I know who you talking about son and whistles quietly—He sez come with me and we climb over a little hill with a half-dead battlefield black tree and there on a shed and there on a plank behind matted dead leaves is a little painted rainbow slash weather beaten and badly faded—She was here once but now she's gone they all gone and ain't never coming back

FAR OUT OVER THE LAKE THE FIRST CONTRAIL OF THE GRAY MORNING sparks and trails fuzzy spiraling wisps lit by the rays of the rising sun—Inbound DC-10 to O'Hare on final—Snowball and I shiver and shake awake in Otto parked by a chain link fence topped by barbed wire in a gravel grassy parking lot at the end of a runway at Lawrence and Mannheim awakened by the roar—The windshield fogged up and frosted—Standing outside as the aluminum bird screams overhead and I am hanging on the wing as the wheels touch down and there are puffs of smoke as the big tires skid and roll on the cold concrete of the runway centerline—The ticketing hall is crowded with hurrying people in gray browns and blues and fine United and American uniforms and Snowball and I make it through security and stand at the crowded departure gate for flight 9 to San Francisco—I think again about what Engel said he said something about Palo Alto and I fear that she might really be gone.

Side 8: I am he as you are me

 Track 1: Early Wednesday morning

SNOWBALL AND I LEAVE O'Hare, dejected and exhausted. A lunatic night. She's gone, but my life is not.

We drive out of the parking garage against the flow of early morning daddies leaving on a jet plane. I'm heading back to my apartment, but at the airport exit where I have a choice—head into the city on the Kennedy and back to Wrightwood *or* turn south and follow the mighty Tri-State Tollway south, the road back to a very old place— I turn. I must do this. After the unreal reality of the night, I must confront the truth—the historical truth of what really happened, not what I think happened, somehow draw the scrim of virtual childhood memory aside. It's time.

Twenty minutes later, as the sun is rising higher, burning off low-lying ground fog, and the early morning school buses are rumbling around town, I park the van on the street beside a park in the village of Hinsdale. It's a dead spot in the road. I have not been here since then. The accident.

Deadman's Hill rises in the park like my own hometown Everest, dark, scary steep. It rears up over the commuter train tracks like a man-eating monster surrounded by quiet homes of the executive class. I grew up in this town. I know this place.

The park, a remnant of the great forests of the last century, is for kids and dogs and where the hill flattens out, there is a playground with swing sets, slides, and monkey bars on old gravel. A concrete fountain, now frozen and dry, waits for summer. Green wooden benches need paint and are empty.

Early morning sunlight flecks the bare branches of the trees. I hear one bird sing, high in the canopy. The bird has probably just returned from a long winter somewhere far away.

Snowball perches on my shoulder like a pirate parrot. He isn't purring. His eyes stare and his claws dig through my coat. His fur ruffles my ear.

I'm drawn to this place for the first time in many years. Since Dave and I passed up the hitchhiker on the road in the black night, since she reappeared projecting the end of one world and the beginning of another, since I have seen my crazy visions of Elliot on streets and stages casting about blindly in the search for *it*—I come here, where I will find *it*, him.

Why not? It's the only place I haven't looked.

I've avoided the hill. After Elliot was killed I didn't come here. Not even years later. This side of town became walled off, forbidden and alien. Dead. I asked no questions, got no answers. I thought I knew. Though I didn't want to know.

Standing at the bottom of the hill, it isn't so big. Not like I remember it. In fact, it's surprisingly small. From the bottom, with my back to the train tracks, I am right there, right *there* at the place where it all went so wrong—the sidewalk goes up the hill, splits in two, comes together again near the summit—one path rising steeply to the right, curving over a knoll then ascending rapidly to the top. The other veers to the left and is more gentle, a roundabout path from peak to the junction, the V where the path divides, where on the descent, the two become one again, creating a chute ending at a small bit of grass and the street.

A commuter train roars behind me, city-bound, filled with fathers and sons and brothers and sisters and mothers and daughters, aunts and uncles, everybody that's still alive, still here. Waves of long dead leaves, winter's debris, blow at my feet. The train heads east, horn sounding, then fading. Silence returns.

It was me. Not Dave. I was there. I am the one.

*   *   *

A kid banged on our screen door.

"C'mon, get your rod! We're going to Deadman's Hill, let's go."

Our bikes were freedom, hot rods for cool kids.

"Your brother coming?"

They wanted Dave. But I found Elliot. He was fooling with my guitar.

"Elliot, put that thing down and get your rod, kid. We're going to the hill."

He jumped up, ran to the garage, hootin' and hollerin'.

Mom said be careful. We rode off and last I saw, she was on the front porch watching us leave. She waved.

Guys at the hill, bikes loaded with baseball cards snapping in the spokes, doing the run, riding between slalom gates of rocks and stones set at easy, intermediate, then impossible intervals, skidding at the bottom. An incredibly complicated system of team scoring was in place. Some kid with a watch with a second hand kept time.

Elliot and I were a team. But we fell way behind, marooned in last place. He was only six.

I made him do the easy course. He had no problem with that. Tentatively, he eased down the right side. No need for a skid at the bottom. He was happy. A big whoop to prove it.

I thought he did great. Guys laughed. I told them to shove it.

My runs were good, screaming down the left side, heroically laying rubber at the bottom.

"Porter brothers stink."

I remember now.

"Pepper, I can do the hard one. If I do it will we win? Will we? I'll do it."

"Porter brothers are losers."

"Elliot, you can't do it. It's not worth it."

He was mad, about to cry.

I looked down the hill, checked the V again—the hard course, the easy course. On the tough side, the slalom gates of stone were fiendishly tight—I had set them that way. I did it. For the last round.

I remember now.

Guys on their bikes, leaning on their big handlebars, racing slick tires, and banana seats, waiting. "What's it gonna be, dickbrain losers?"

I went to the V in my head, I chose.

"Okay. Go Elliot. You go. You show 'em."

I sent him down.

Big smile. He wiped away the almost tears.

"Okay, Pepper. I'm gone."

He pushed off, got to the V, I panicked, "Turn the other way, the other way, take the easy route." He didn't. He went left, took the hard run and that was *it*.

*   *   *

I told him to go. I told him.

I break down, my knees buckle in the wet grass and it all comes out. Chest heaving, I weep.

It was me.

That bird, high in the tree, is singing. There's only one. Only one song. Snowball looks up, begins to purr. It's a little cedar waxwing, like the one I became at the sound check in Benld, flying amid the rafters high above the stage. Only this time, I am me and I am he and he is me.

The little bird spirals down through the bare trees, flies around my head, perches on the furled edge of the empty fountain. His call is fast, ecstatic, he trills and swoops and hoots and whoops. Like a guitar solo I've heard all my life, always always and never-ending.

The cedar waxwing, sleek and smooth, black beak, a black racing mask on his eyes running to a blonde feathery crest, tips of red on his gray and dusky brown wings, yellow-tipped tail, is a rock 'n roll bird in feathered finery, the most elegant I've ever seen. He's talking to me, he's got lots to say. I listen closely, I close my eyes, I zone out. I listen with my inward eye.

::::   ::::   ::::   ::::   ::::   ::::   ::::   ::::

It.

The cedar waxwing chirps once more, flies up and disappears over the hill.

I sit for a while. Peaceful. Resting. Snowball is curled in my lap, asleep. I pick him up and we drive home.

I am free.

I'm back in the apartment. *I Love Lucy* is on. With the sound off. Dave, in his threadbare mystical bathrobe, is seated on the beanbag, meditating. His mantra—*om, om, om*—hums softly like the refrigerator in the kitchen.

I sit quietly and wait.

Soon, Dave opens his eyes. He smiles, refreshed.

I say, "Dave, I went back there. To the hill, I hadn't been there since *then* and all these years. Maybe I'm nuts, but Elliot was there. And Dave, back then, that day—it was me. Me. It was me."

Silence.

Dave sips his tea. "Mmm. I always suspected you thought that … I didn't really know. But we never talked about it, so …"

"I was nuts."

"Mom, Dad … did they know you thought—"

"I don't know. Never talked about it."

"Naturally."

I Love Lucy ends. Snowball crawls into my lap, purring, reminding me—she's gone. My body, electrified and exhausted, is running on empty.

We sit. The radiator gurgles and burps.

Dave says, "You and that chick. You and the band. You and Creach. You and technology. You and me. Know that I am he as you are me and we are all together. Aren't we?"

We hug like brothers rarely do.

The rest of the day, I sleep like I'm dead, grateful, peaceful.

The sun crawls across the floor. I wake up. Sooz. Her notebook. My life. My past, my future. Lost in a mazed map of off ramps and on ramps and endings and beginnings, real and imagined, historical and fantasy, twined choices—the V's of life. A strange new energy stirs inside of me.

The hill. Cedar waxwings. Elliot. Peace.

 Track 2: Late Wednesday afternoon

I WALK INTO HER apartment building, checking on her place again, hoping. The ladies at the desk downstairs have come to know me. And they seem to like me. When they worry that it's been so long since they've seen her, I tell them that Sooz is on a business trip. They smile proudly. I tell them that I'm taking care of Snowball. The ladies ask if they can make dinner for me. I politely decline. They are so nice.

I let myself in again. The place has been ransacked, turned upside down, and shaken hard. Her desk is ripped apart and all of her files have been taken. Her phone is gone and her small collection of electronic hardware is missing.

Fuckin' bastards.

Track 3: Wednesday night

CREACH TELLS US THAT our song has gone to number 11 on the local charts. We're starting to make some real money and we're recording our first album, which is almost done, and we're rehearsing for that big tour with Mott the Hoople—there's only a month to go before we leave.

We have gigs scheduled at places previously unattainable. And constant rehearsals and recording and interviews and rehearsals and recording and interviews.

All fabulous.

But Hawgrim asks me—"What's it gonna be? What about our deal?" The end of his fiscal year approaches. He's under sales quota pressure.

Thursday
Nothing from her.
I make a phone call.

Track 4: Saturday afternoon

I HAVE AN APPOINTMENT with Mrs. Beatrice Gladys Jones Hawgrim. I am to meet with her in the comfort of her own home—today, a nice Saturday afternoon. The purpose of my visit, as I very respectfully tell her on the phone, is to discuss a matter of great importance— I have some concern about her son's future and I need her help. She quickly, graciously consents to my visit.

Dave and I arrive in front of the stately Hawgrim home—winter-dead vines of ivy climb the fine brick walls, a few hopeful spring crocuses stick their heads up in the empty garden beds that line the long walkway to the heavy black oak front door.

We are there for afternoon tea.

We are on time.

Further, we are attired in our best, our only suits—my Flarf and Engel suit, it's been cleaned since *that night*—pressed shirts, shined shoes, and sober ties, clean-shaven and well groomed. Our hair is slicked down, pulled back. We look like missionaries. We do not want to scare Mrs. Hawgrim. On the other hand, she is Hawgrim's mother.

In my hand I have a small green and gold bag—a Marshall Field's shopping bag. Frango Mints. A simple, tasteful, and civilized gift. I have learned that you can't go wrong with Frango Mints.

In my other hand is the same Joe Businessman briefcase I used in those IBM interviews. In it are Hawgrim's brains—his own *notebook*, filled with names, addresses, telephone numbers, miscellaneous doodles, scratchings, and his daily schedule.

Hawgrim's notebook contains a name of mutual interest. Fletcher Engel.

I ring the doorbell. Dave, slightly apprehensive, stands safely behind me.

Mrs. Hawgrim, a husky, formidable woman in a sensibly sober floral suit and beautiful camel-colored cashmere sweater draped over her shoulders, opens the big door.

"Mr. Porter, I've been expecting you." I introduce myself. She gives my hand a firm shake, smiles. Her hair is seemingly perma-sealed in a bell-shaped helmet of chestnut brown that matches her sculpted eyebrows, arched in what appears to be a look of perpetual disdain.

I introduce Dave. He bows slightly and she says, "So nice to meet the both of you, although I'm sure we've met, Pepper, back in your high school days, yes?"

"Yes, ma'am."

She sighs. She has been down this road before.

Mrs. Hawgrim appears to have been at an *event* this afternoon. A nametag is still pinned to her sweater. "Please, come in."

Mrs. Hawgrim is chairwoman of the Hinsdale Women's Club.

As she leads us through the imposing entry hall, she chats pleasantly about today's luncheon fund-raiser in support of the Equal Rights Amendment in Illinois. "It's so important, don't you agree?"

We sit in lovely comfy chairs arranged in a large, light-filled room that is lined with carved mahogany, paintings, large Chinese vases, fine porcelain figures, and bookshelves that actually look used. A baby-grand piano sits in the corner.

Noticing my interest in the piano, she says, "Yes, Brian, like his father, is the musician. It's a beautiful instrument. Mm." She pauses. "May I pour you some tea, Pepper, Dave?"

From a delicate china tea service, she pours small cups for us, offers cookies.

"I'm afraid that I'm very tired of that annoying accordion of Brian's. I have no earthly idea what he sees in it. Honestly, I'm not sure I understand anything about my son these days. Sometimes I wonder—where did he come from?" Long-suffering smile. "He seems to have rather strong views on things. Just like his father, if I do say so."

We sip our tea. Dave compliments Mrs. Hawgrim on her exquisite choice of brew, a nice dark Prince of Wales. She is pleased.

I present the Frango Mints. Mrs. Hawgrim is very appreciative and perhaps impressed with my obvious good breeding. "Oh, I just love Frango Mints. Don't you?"

"Yes, ma'am."

She eagerly opens the box. "Would you like one?"

We say yes, please.

Mrs. Hawgrim savors her mint, regards me in weary expectation. "So. What has Brian done *now*?"

One minute later, while I am describing the situation in which a particularly brilliant female friend of mine from the University of Michigan who has done years of research in computer science and has developed an amazingly important new technology, she says, "Stop right there, please. She is your girlfriend, is she not?"

"She is."

"And she has performed this research and has come up with all this remarkable work in today's world, this man's world—"

"Yes ma'am."

"I must meet her. By any chance, does she accept speaking

engagements? Oh, the girls at the Women's Club would find this young woman so inspiring!"

I tell Mrs. Hawgrim that, sadly, this fine example of the best in American womanhood is not able to accept speaking engagements at this time, however, down the road, I am very hopeful that something could be arranged.

"We can wait." She zeros in on me with narrowed eyes. "So. Brian?"

"Mrs. Hawgrim, my friend misplaced her critically important research notebook while at an event at the Palmer House. Oddly enough, Brian found it, but will not give it up … unless I buy a rather expensive Whole Life insurance policy, which at this point in my life is rather expensive and—"

"Say no more." Mrs. Hawgrim, huffing and puffing, bolts from her chair and strides into the entrance hall. She hollers up the stairs, "Brian! Come down here this instant!"

She returns to the room, steaming.

"He's here? I had no idea …"

"Pepper, it occurred to me that your visit might be … awkward." Mrs. Hawgrim smiles grimly and taps her foot. "I made sure that he was available."

Brian Hawgrim, in a beat-up Hinsdale High School Red Devils sweatshirt and torn sweat pants, slinks into the drawing room in stocking feet. His mother stands in the middle of the room—judge, jury, and executioner. She reviews my story for his benefit.

"Young man, is it true that you have *pinched* this poor girl's *notebook*, a document clearly very *important* to her and perhaps of importance to our nation's *technological future*, to say nothing of the future of *women in industry*? And you're holding it for *ransom*? Is this *true*?"

Brian, his eyes on the carpet, mumbles, "Yes, Mother."

Mrs. Hawgrim then launches into a lecture about doing the right thing and respect for women and what's the matter with you anyway and no son of mine participates in such loathsome skullduggery, does she make herself clear?

"Yes, ma'am."

"Well, do you have this notebook?"

"Yes, ma'am."

"I'm waiting."

He leaves the room and after a few uncomfortable minutes, he returns, notebook in hand. Hawgrim gives it to me.

I open my briefcase, hand him his.

Hawgrim's eyes bug out.

I thank Mrs. Hawgrim profusely. She escorts us to the door, making apologies for her son, asking that I keep in touch. "I will look forward to hearing more about this remarkable young woman."

From the front step, I remind Hawgrim—gig tonight. See you there!

 Track 5: Saturday night

FIRST GIG SINCE she's been gone. I'm distracted, a little distant. *It* doesn't happen. But Flash Freehly sits in for the first time. He's good. We are competent and professional. Even Hawgrim. No words are exchanged.

There are Felix the Cat t-shirts scattered in the crowd.

I should be reading her notebook.

Side 9: We can be together

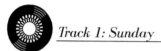

A FTER GETTING OVER the awkwardness of actually opening her notebook, which very definitely feels like some kind of violation, like watching brainwaves flick and run on somebody's encephalograph, I turn to page one:

Information Wants to be Free

—is carefully inscribed on the inside of the cover in blue ink in her meticulous, precise handwriting. Like a title. Like a motto, like a call to arms. Vintage Sooz.

A few of the earlier first pages in the notebook have been removed, carefully razored out, leaving scant evidence of their previous existence. She told me that she had had the brains to delete the more obviously dangerous or perhaps out of date contact information. The current first page is revelation enough for me.

Account Access

Computer access. This is what she's been doing at the State Street library. Here, in clear and well-documented detail, are what appear to be the keys to the kingdom, like the old password from Michigan—here is her timesharing account information at the University of Illinois, granting some level of access to the ARPANET—the web of big computer centers spread across the country.

It's all laid out.

I look at my watch. Noon. Library's open.

Notebook in hand, I jump on the 151, head downtown.

After flashing my old Michigan student ID to the nice lady attendant on the fourth floor of the library who waves me through with a shake of her head, I'm admitted to the terminal room. It's small and cluttered with metal filing cabinets, shelves of thick, bound printouts of who-knows-what, a few noisy teletypes, two large microfiche readers and one small computer terminal—a sleek, plastic-encased display device—a CRT with a keyboard.[73] Nobody's here but me.

I sit down at the terminal. I open the notebook.

Account access: *illinois.edu*

System Login: datarevolutionary

Password: porthuron

There's a phone number. Then a heading—

Mail Box Protocol

Electronic mail. Address: gkelliher@arpanode.illinois.edu

(What a cleverly efficient way to address a message. Finally, someone has figured out a use for "@." I'm impressed.)

Password: snowball

(Naturally.)

She's gone, but here is a path that may lead to her. Maybe I can find her.

There is an *acoustic coupler* device connected to the terminal interface. It's a *modem*. It's a strange looking, recently introduced contraption. A telephone handset is inserted into its two black audio receptacles that look like stereo headphones, and a telephone keypad is then used to dial the communications access phone number of the target computer center. I've seen some of this stuff in the computer magazines I've been reading. I've been away from the game for a year. But I'm impressed. Technology marches on—the terminal will communicate with the remote system at 1,200 bits per second.

Lightning fast.

I flip on the terminal. On the black screen, a small green cursor preceded by a > begins to flash at the top left corner of the screen.

I've been here before. I know how to deal with text editors.

I set up the acoustic coupler, dial the number, sit back and wait. Muffled gibberish leaks from the modem. The cursor continues to flash. I'm not sure it's actually working.

After a tense minute or so, the green cursor races across the top of the screen and then a simple request is made:

---

[73] It's a Lear-Siegler ADM-3A dumb terminal, which means its got no brains, it relies on the remote computer system for everything. With an RS-232 interface, it's new and it's pretty good-looking.

Login

Password

I type.

Thirty or forty seconds goes by, the cursor flashes blankly, I begin to think I'm dead but then ... I'm in. The following green text appears top left:

>****Welcome to U of I CompSci/ PDP-11 ARPANET Gateway****

So cool. Talking to myself, I say, "This is great!"

The cursor flashes, waiting.

I know my way around PDP's. I begin to play the keyboard. This could get very interesting, but I've got to focus.

Soon, I find something called

>*Mail Box Protocol.*

I see a list of messages. To her. An *electronic mailbox*.

Fantastic. We only had hints of this stuff at Michigan. There was a mainframe-based TSO messaging system but it was really clunky.[74] *This* is slick.

I'm in her mailbox. But I'm creeped out. I don't want to read this stuff. I'm not supposed to be here.

I look anyway.

There are only four messages, they appear to be administrative stuff, the sort of thing that used to be posted on bulletin boards in the computer lab at Michigan—batch processing schedules, BASIC compiler upgrades. Things like that. Nothing to see.

So I move on, I need to send a message.

The library attendant pokes her head in the room, asks if I'm doing all right, need any help. Hasn't seen me here before. I smile, say something about Ann Arbor and that I'm doing fine. She's seems satisfied and closes the door.

The cursor flashes. Waiting.

It occurs to me that Sooz may be logged in *right now*. It's possible that this system doesn't care if there are two *datarevolutionarys* logged in simultaneously. We used to trade logins all the time.

Who knows?

---

[74] TSO. IBM's Time Sharing Option. Nobody likes it.

But what if she *is* logged in? Right now?

What then?

That'd be fabulous.

I wonder if her timesharing account time is limited. And the phone line. Who's paying for this? I'm hoping that the library has a WATS line.[75] I need to keep moving, otherwise this exercise is going to be very expensive.

After a few failed attempts, I figure the thing out and am typing her electronic mail address amid fields of low-level systems gibberish. Since I have no account of my own and am logged in as Sooz, I am going to send a message to myself, to her, to gkelliher@arpanode.illinois.edu.

I compose my message carefully because, what if she's been hauled in? After all, they ransacked her place, but I don't want to think about that.

Still, what if her timesharing account has been blown? What if SNARB or somebody else is on the other end? How will I know if I am communicating with *her*?

And how will she know that *I am me*?

I have to be careful. I type.

>*Your notebook is in good hands. Are you?*

Send.

That's it. The message is sent. I sit back, notice that my heart is pounding and my mouth is dry. There's a water cooler down the hall. The attendant nods as I walk by.

I drain a few paper cups of cold water. The fourth floor is deserted.

I return to the terminal. I'm still logged into the system. The cursor blinks at me.

I go back to her mailbox. My message to her is there. Of course. It was self-addressed to me/her.

But there's a new message. A reply. From her.

She's *here*. Like *magic*. I'm ecstatic.

It says:

>*Very good news. Please verify identity.*

---

[75] *Wide Area Telephone Service.* AT&T (Ma Bell) offers flat-fee, unlimited long-distance lines. Big companies and governments use them. If you can find one, they're great for calling home or faraway girlfriends.

I'm crushed. So clinical. But of course it must be like this.

I can't use my name and I can't use her name. I could be SNARB. She could be SNARB, looking for her contacts, probing her network. Fear, uncertainty, and doubt well up inside me.

This is a very bizarre form of communication, but it's all I've got.

I think about it. I'm tapping my foot, drumming my fingers. Then—

>*I know your favorite song. Rgds, Felix.*

Send.

A few minutes go by. Nothing.

I stare at the screen.

Then the cursor races across the screen and the terminal display reads:

>*Hello datarevolutionary. You have been logged off. Timeshare account exceeded. Have a nice day.*

WHAT THE FUCK?

I pound the desk and curse evil robotic systems administrators.

 Track 2: Sunday night

I GO HOME, DIVE INTO HER NOTEBOOK. It's actually a big book, a standard 8½ by 11 size, not one of those little black book things. Maybe half an inch thick, filled with long stretches of text, formulas, diagrams, clippings from news articles, and mimeographed sheets. It's a counter-cultural, technology-based, whole earth catalog.

I fall asleep but I wake up again.

I'm *awake*.

I try to work on a new tune or two but I can't concentrate.

I return to the notebook. There's the front page of an underground newsletter from Palo Alto, California. *Computer Lib*. The cover is a black and white drawing of a power-to-the-people fist. Revolutionary. Stark. Urgent.

Across the top of the sheet are the words—*You can and must understand computers NOW.*

Like a bloody banner nailed to a generational mast. *This* is the future, this is the next big thing, this is radical, this is where the revolution will be. And she is plugged in. She has been wired.

And so am I.

She's got an ad clipping from *Popular Science*—a miracle *home* computer, something for a *person*, not a department—an entire computer right *there*. A box on a desk looking bizarre and powerful— a machine not built by IBM but made with microprocessors, silicon chips from companies with science fiction names—Intel, Zylog, and Altair. Barely more than a set of circuit boards, I see that this is the window on her world—this is what she's been talking about and I remember seeing something like it on one of von Flarf's workbenches down in Champaign—power to the people.

But I read that this crazy little computer doesn't *do anything*— it sits in the photograph empty and inert awaiting instructions. Instructions.

Software.

I feel the presence of a crossroads, a place on the map in my head—*Pepperland Pepperland Pepperland*—where music and magic and euphoria and this strange new technology intersect and make a difference. It's bubbling with the same mystery as a string of gloriously loud power chords in that downstate barn where there is onstage enchantment, and the tracks begin to converge and I can see way down the line.

And inside my head, in the little datacenter of my mind, I feel new synaptic connections being made and old ones being restored, retuned, and fired up. Heavy maintenance and upgrades are taking place.

There's a folded mimeographed flyer inserted in between pages:

"Are you building our own computer? Terminal? Or some other digital black box? Meet like-minded subversives—the Homebrew Computer Club."

A meeting is scheduled. In somebody's garage in Menlo Park. Next month. *Next month!*

The rest of the night, I watch moon shadows drift across the floor. Her tidal pull is immense.

I'm going to do it.

 *Track 3: Monday morning*

I'M BACK IN THE terminal room at the library. Nobody around, the terminal is available. I go through the login ritual. Where yesterday the process was miraculous, today it seems to take forever.

Finally, I get in.

There's an email in her mailbox. One message, nothing else.

>*Sing it for me.*

Jesus. Is she toying with me? But again, this might not be *her*. And *where* is she? I can't be too careful and neither can she.

I look at the timestamp—the email was sent last night.

I type.

>*If I sing that song, unpredictable sexual results may occur.*

Send.

That ought to get her. Only I would know that and only she would know that I know.

I pace around the room. Five minutes go by. Ten. Maybe she's not there. Maybe during the night, there was a knock on her door and jackbooted agents of SNARB or who-knows who pushed their way in, guns drawn with bayonets affixed and she's really gone this time.

Then finally—

>*Won-won-wonderful. Now. Know that this mailbox is likely monitored.*

>*Encrypt ALL future messages. Please refer to page nine in my notebook. Cease*

>*using your current terminal. You are likely being watched. Leave now. Alt*

>*location in notebook. Oh. Cipher keyword is REVOLUTION.*

This is her. But in four short lines of text, she takes me from wild and crazy flying high to crashed, burned, paranoid, bumping along the bottom.

The door opens. A standard-issue man-in-gray enters the room, suit and tie, close-cropped black hair, brown briefcase in hand. Like another SNARB guy or a variation on Engel. He nods pleasantly, sits down at one of the microfiche readers on the other side of the room, opens his case, removes a roll of film, loads the machine, begins viewing it.

I type.

>*Msg received. Understood.*

I don't hit send. I think about it.

I delete it.

I sign off, pack up, leave.

The man in gray does not follow me. I think I'm in the clear, no tail.

On the bus, I refer to page nine—two pages of an alphabetic table, twenty-six rows, twenty-six columns—a *Vigenere Cipher*. Rows of alphabets stacked on top of each other, the first row beginning with "A B C," the second beginning with "B C D," and so on. Using her keyword—REVOLUTION—I'm going to have to figure out how to communicate with her.[76]

I flip farther through the notebook, searching for her alternative computer access location. By the time the 151 is up on Clark Street nearing my stop, I find it, buried in the back—an underground radical bookstore in a basement near the University of Chicago in Hyde Park. How'd she find that place?

I am energized, I am a technology rock star.

 Track 4: Three weeks before we leave on tour

DAVE IS MORE COSMIC THAN EVER. Continuing the downstate trend, he's screamingly good in the studio and on stage—out of his head on the bass, singing like he's never sung before—and he's taking more leads and writing songs. They're good. He sings. He sounds great. I sing harmonies.

---

[76] Blaise de Vigenere, a sixteenth-century Frenchman came up with this scheme—a polyalphabetic cipher, meaning that the same letter of a message can be represented by different letters when encoded. Cool. Avoiding the State Street library, I conduct further research at the branch on Fullerton to figure out how the Vigenere system works. Using her keyword, I can construct messages that she can decrypt. While this system is certainly not strong enough to fool professionals for long, it's good enough to slow them down. I go for it.

Creach says, "Yeah, sing those songs, Cosmic Dave!" I know Creach has been schooling my brother—now professionally known as Cosmic Dave, thanks to wildly successful on-air interviews with friendly jocks and a few pithy comments by E. Rodney Jones on his morning drive-time show.

One of Dave's songs, *The Subconscious Sleep of Unconsciousness (Part 1)*, has an amazingly tuneful hook of a chorus that, upon first hearing, inserts itself into one's brain, winding itself around the cerebellum like a rock 'n roll tapeworm. Creach hums it while he's at his desk. Mrs. Robinson sings it.

Incredible.

Creach decides to release it as a single. E. Rodney Jones plays it. Miraculously, WLS picks it up. It's an instant hit.

Dave talks about doing a solo album.

Creach whistles, says, "It could work."

Flash is now part of the band. He's fabulous. He can play guitar like me, sing like me, sing like Dave, or sound like himself. Flash is perpetually cheerful. Hawgrim, amazingly, is happy. It's like nothing ever happened. He says he got a big commission check. I don't ask about the golden putter. Besides, Sunshine and Luna are in town. Ricky smiles.

We will kick Mott the Hoople's ass.

But despite all this, something's wrong. Dave may be cosmic, but he ain't dumb.

 Track 5: Two weeks before we leave on tour

I 'M SITTING AT OUR beat-up kitchen table. Her notebook is open to page nine, the keyword carefully printed across the top of a big yellow legal pad. My overall purpose: Dispel all fear, uncertainty, and doubt—FUD. No FUD. In her. In me. In all of society.

Insanely nuts.

I have composed what will be my next email to Sooz. And now, I am about to encrypt that message. Letter by letter, character by character. Terrible way to communicate. As result, the message will necessarily be terse, with no emotion, no romance, not like me at all.

Dave walks in, sits down, drums his fingers. Stares at me. No cosmicity on display.

I stop encoding, put my pencil down.

"What're you doing? That's her weird notebook, right?"

"Right."

"Soooo glad we got it back."

I show him the cipher tables. "I'm *communicating* with her. It's kind of strange and elaborate, but it has to be this way."

A siren wavers in the distance, fades like a song. We stare at the table.

He says, "All this computer shit you been doing. Where the hell's your head at, man?"

"Well, I'm— "

"I see what's happening—are you ... you're not really going to throw it all afuckingway and run off with ..."

"I don't know."

Wide-eyed. "Who would know? Susie Creamcheese?"

"You've been fabulous. You're the star. Everybody loves Cosmic Dave."

"Jesus Christ! You're really gonna do it, aren't you ... it's all being set up, Creach, Flash, Mott the Hoople—"

"Dave, your interviews, *Tiger Beat,* it's all happening and you—"

Dave hisses, "Bullshit. Fuck you and your goddamn cat guitar and fuck you for ever getting this fucking thing going and fuck Creach, fuck Hawgrim, fuck Sooz, and fuck Mott the Hoople."

"Dave."

Pounds the table. "Fuckin' computer shit, goddamnit."

He sputters, runs his hands through his hair. Tries to compose himself.

Silence. The phone rings, loud and shrill, we both look at it. Rings and rings. We don't answer. It stops. Minutes pass. Temperature drops.

Quietly, Dave says, "I haven't seen him in weeks. You?"

"I think so, I mean, maybe."

"Wish I could."

Another siren, this one more distant.

He stomps off. I hear him rooting around in the kitchen, then the back door slams and he's gone.

I walk to the front window. Dave appears on the front sidewalk, stops, sees me watching. He gives me the finger, disappears.

For hours, I stare at the wall, I can't strum Felix, I can't listen to tunes, I can't read, I can't write, I can't eat, I can't do anything.

I sit.

It's getting dark.

Something slams against the big front window, scares the hell out of me. I look—a little brown and yellow bird, cradled on the scraggly bush with a trace of blood on its beak. It twitches amid the green buds. Dies.

Snowball rubs my leg.

Her notebook remains open on the table. Page nine. Sooz. My yellow pad ready, key word REVOLUTION across the top.

I encode the first word: ORD
The resulting text is: FVY

I go on. It takes me over two hours to finish it. When it's done, the message is a nonsensical string of letters, chaotic. High entropy.

In the low-ceilinged, overheated basement of an actual Gothic seminary in Hyde Park on the Southside, hidden among the flying-buttressed, Rockefeller-funded dreaming spires of the University of Chicago, is a bookstore. Down a flight of smoothly worn stone steps beneath tranquil cloistered gardens, Left Bank Books is an endless warren of small rooms, each filled to capacity with highbrow political and academic books, a vast repository of knowledge, information, and revolutionary thought.

I ask for the timesharing system and am unquestioningly led to a dented door next to the hard-working furnace. A key is produced and I am left in a tiny room with a single terminal, modem, and printer. Soon, I am back on the ARPANET system in Champaign.

In her mailbox, there's a message to her, me. It's been over a week since I logged in. I've been going nuts, making this plan, figuring out the Vigenere Cipher. And Hyde Park isn't exactly next door. Her message is a few days old. She's alive, still free.

It's unencrypted. I'm surprised.

>*Felix. Am working on a short-term project of seriously grave consequence. Getting so close to the end but I don't know when we'll finish. But then what? Where are you? Please know, truly, notebook is of secondary importance. It is you that I want, you that I need. Sending in clear text. Dumb but I don't care. Where are you?*

Whoa. For Sooz, that's completely out there, heart flying like a flag. My fingers tremble.

I type wildly.

>*I'm here. Critical message to follow.*

Send.

The big boiler behind the rickety wall of my small cell roars into life again, steam pipes clang, hot water flows.

I begin the tedious process of typing my encoded message. After twenty minutes, checking and rechecking, I send it.

That's it. It's gone. I have no idea what she'll do.

I wait. Ten minutes. Twenty. The furnace goes through a few heating cycles. But there's no reply. I log out.

On my way out, the clerk asks for sixteen dollars and change for the long distance call. Fortunately, I've got the dough. I pay up happily and head home. Nobody appears to be following me.

 Track 6: A Monday night, 2 a.m.

NOW I AM FINALLY GOING TO RECORD that song—her song— "Dreaming's Done." I have convinced Creach to allow me to do it alone—I play piano, sing, am a one-man band allowing no one else in the studio other than Creach, who sits up in the glowing control room listening, twiddling dials. I overdub a few other instruments and harmonies. The song is too tightly wound around my heart to open it up to anyone else. Maybe I'm a little embarrassed.

It goes well. After a few hours I'm happy with it. Creach says that it is finished and he can add no more.

It's the last song on our album.

The studio is silent, only the faint ticking of a cooling amp. I sit, unwilling to leave.

Creach, over the intercom, says, "And you, young Pepper Porter, now what?"

Yes. Now what.

Despite everything, I'm clinging to a flipped-over sailboat in a raging sea of FUD.

 Track 7: One week before we leave on tour

I HAVEN'T HEARD FROM HER. I've managed to get back to the bookstore in the seminary dungeon almost every day. Nothing. Where is she?

And Dave? He and I haven't talked much. He's meditating a lot again. We are both quietly professional.

 Track 8: Tuesday

FOUR DAYS BEFORE we leave on tour, I am seated comfortably in the library's periodicals room. I see the following item in the *Washington Post*, today, April 30, 1974:

"In an unexpected twist in a convoluted case, Senator Sam Irvin (D-TN), speaking before reporters in the Senate Judicial Committee Room, announced that the mysterious erasure of the 18½ minutes of President Nixon's conversations possibly regarding Watergate with H. R. 'Bob' Haldeman on June 20, 1972, has been explained with at least some of the missing audio partially restored. The Senate Advisory Panel on the White House Tapes, headed by Richard H. Bolt, Chairman of Bolt, Beranek, and Newman and Founder of the MIT Acoustics Laboratory, working in secret and in conjunction with Dr. Ivor von Flarf, a University of Illinois Professor of Electrical Engineering and Computer Science, and Miss Grace Kelliher, a research assistant, said that the recovered portion of the missing conversation, while shedding no new light on the alleged Watergate cover-up itself, does reveal the existence of a heretofore unknown organization within the Executive Branch. Senator Irvin said that the Security Normalization and Review Board (SNARB) is a super secret and clearly illegal entity, and very likely involved in the subversion and misdirection of Congressional funding of high technology, attacking certain people named on the White House Enemies List and directed by the Committee to Reelect the President (CREEP). A third gentleman, a Mr. Fletcher Engel, apparent Managing Director of SNARB, was a very active participant in the June 20th Oval Office conversation in which, reportedly, illegal White House manipulation of the FBI, the existence of a high-technology enemies list and Federal witness intimidation plans were discussed. Senator Irvin said that this could have serious negative implications in the preservation of American technological leadership. Though little is publicly known about Mr. Engel, Senator Irvin indicated that a subpoena has been issued and a Grand Jury investigation is pending while ..."

Yes. I say yes, I say yes.

I am back in the bookstore timesharing dungeon. There is a single message from her:

PIN

I decode it.

YES

Yes.

I am back in the apartment at the kitchen table, reading a mimeographed California home computing newsletter. Dave bursts in the back door, slams the latest *Tiger Beat* on the table.

"*He's* here. I've seen him." Stabs the magazine. "Here."

"Hell're you talking about?"

He tells me that while I've been off toiling in bookstore dungeons hunched over timesharing terminals, during our time of uncomfortable silences, he's been getting his head together, going further into serious meditation.

Dave, peacefully seated underneath a budding apple tree on the north side of that pond in Lincoln Park, felt the gentle presence of the Dark Stranger. There, his antenna tuned and calibrated, Dave gained enlightenment, knowledge of the ultimate reality. He says it wasn't exactly Elliot or the guy in the black coat and hat and all that and the magazine didn't exactly *speak* to him, but if a little cedar waxwing can somehow communicate with me, then this copy of *Tiger Beat*, the one with David Cassidy on the cover and the little photo spread about Cosmic Dave right *here on page 9*, can communicate with him. Dave *knows* it to be true.

"What'd the magazine say?"

"It is what it is and let it be so. I am an instrument of the cosmos and you need to do what you need to do and so do I, oh my brother."

I feel better and so does Dave's inward eye.

 Track 9: May 4, 1974

Today is the day. We are leaving. The band is flying to St. Louis, first stop on Mott the Hoople's *Roll Away the Stone American Tour.*

Dressed in our best traveling rock star costumes, we're holding court in the fancy round restaurant on the upper level of O'Hare. Cosmic Dave, appearing as Brian Jones circa 1967, is stunning in striped bell-bottoms, brocaded long coat and what must be a ten-foot long white scarf twirled around his neck. Hawgrim, Ricky, Flash-the-New-Guy, and Creach are outstanding, too. I have my new snakeskin boots on, but other than that, I am drab compared to my brother and everyone else.

We're loud, we're fabulous.

Creach is on a phone at the other end of the restaurant. He waves at me, motions for me to join him. He hangs up the phone.

"That was the president of Columbia Records. Wants to meet you."

I stare him down. "Bullshit."

"I told him, Clive …" A thin, mirthless smile twists his lips. "Hell, Pepper, thing about you is …" he's speaking carefully "… you are not going to be one of those coulda, shoulda-type cats. Fork in the road comes … and you take it."

We laugh.

"And don't you worry about that Brian Hawgrim, Pepper Porter."

"I won't."

"Well, yeah, I know, but he's under control. You know he won that goddamned golden putter—it was the end of his fiscal year and he made Checkers Records one helluva deal on insurance—liability, fire, health, life—you name it."

I grin and shake my head.

Hawgrim.

The boys are whooping it up across the room, flirting with the waitresses like rock stars should. Cosmic Dave looks good, confident, leading the charge.

"And your brother? Isn't he something?" We marvel at the scene.

Then Creach's arm is around my shoulder, he speaks quietly. "But you listen to me, Pepper Porter. Things happen everyday that we just can't explain—and I sure as hell can't explain all this. But I'm good with that. I think you know what I'm talking about."

I nod.

He says, "Don't you worry about a thing. It's all going to be all right. Women and music."

And I say, "Music and women."

Creach shakes my hand and says, "I'm heading to the gate. See you on the other side."

Huh. The other side.

He gathers the boys together and shepherds them out of the restaurant. Dave stays with me.

He says, "So."

"So."

"Yeah."

"I'll call you."

"You will?"

"Yeah."

"Jerk."

"Creep."

We hug.

I look at my watch. It's time.

Cosmic Dave, rock 'n roll splendiferous and leaning against an illuminated United Airlines billboard—*Fly the Friendly Skies*—at the head of the E concourse across from gate E-1, removes his aviator sunglasses, peers into the terminal and asks, "She coming?"

I'm standing next to him, Felix at my feet along with a small, blue plastic cat carrier containing a surprisingly quiet Snowball.

"She'll be here."

The E concourse is a non-stop river of people, mostly business-men in three-piece suits, sober ties, and brown shoes—men on mis-sions, leaving town and making deals or flying in for the big meeting in convention city, walking fast, avoiding eye contact, places to go, people to see. Flight announcements drone.

There are two airplane tickets in my shoulder bag, heavy with lyric sheets, books, magazines, newspaper, my copy of *The Transmis-sion of Information*, a copy of Sooz's Plan, a map of California, and securely tucked in an inside flap, her notebook.

Across the busy concourse on the upstream terminal side are two men standing on opposite ends of a row of newspaper vending machines. They're both reading a paper. Like a B-movie, they flip their newspapers down simultaneously and peer at us through dark glasses. Suspiciously, doubtfully, with malice in their hearts. It's Agent Schootz and Under Assistant Agent Brown.

"Dave—"

And then everybody in the concourse is a SNARB agent, flocks of them, hordes of them, cheesy sunglasses everywhere and I'm thinking we gotta get outta this place, and I'm breathing heavily, panicky.

They leave. It's not them. It's sister paranoia hissing in my ear. I calm down.

Dave says, "Jesus. Keep cool, man." He turns me around and kneads my shoulders. "C'mon. She'll be here. She said she would and she will." Turns me around and looks me in the eye. "You got your antenna tuned right?"

"Sorry. Yes. I'm in tune. You?"

"Perfectly."

I look at my watch again. It's time.

Snowball stirs, scratches the side of the cat box. A little yowl. The pick in my pocket's going nuts.

I almost don't recognize her. The real Sooz, fake blonde Bunny curls gone, her piano black hair growing back straight, a little spiky— she's running through the crowd with that old peace-signed bag on her shoulder, open peacoat flying like a sail. The human river parts and she jumps into my arms. I swoop her off her feet, spinning, hooting, hollering.

Sooz hangs on, she doesn't let go.

I hand her a plane ticket.

Flight 909, ORD-SFO, San Francisco. Palo Alto, Menlo Park— Pepperland of computer dreams. I say, "You and I've got civilizational paradigms to shift. Computers to build—in garages! You coming?"

"I am."

"There're crazy computer subversives out there—"

"Better be."

I pull her close and whisper in her ear—I sing that song—yes, dreaming's done.

And she says, "Silly boy—no, it isn't."

Cosmic Dave.

Dave is gone. I look around. Nowhere.

Up ahead, the wide tile-floored concourse divides—E continuing left, F going right, a traffic-efficient V. Dave, standing at the V, is smiling, making sure to catch my eye. He turns, disappears down the F concourse to St. Louis. Time is getting tight.

I think I see a tall guy in a long coat and black hat hurry after him. Our flight's boarding.

Pepperland Discography

SIDE 1

The Beach Boys. *Pet Sounds.* "Wouldn't It Be Nice." Capitol Records. 1966. (Pepper's Theme)

Crosby, Stills, Nash & Young. "Ohio." Originally released as a single in May 1970, the studio version was not released on an album until *So Far*, 1974.

Iron Butterfly. *In-a-Gadda-da-Vida.* Atco. 1968.

Tony Orlando and Dawn. "Candida." Bell Records. 1970.

Oscar Peterson. *The Sound of the Trio.* "On Green Dolphin Street." Recorded at the London House, Chicago. Verve. 1961.

SIDE 2

Jefferson Airplane. *Volunteers.* "We Can Be Together." RCA. 1969. (Sooz's Theme)

Jefferson Airplane. *Crown of Creation.* "Lather." RCA. 1968.

SIDE 3

Bob Dylan. *Highway 61 Revisited.* Columbia. 1965.

SIDE 4

The Rolling Stones. *Their Satanic Majesties Request.* "She's a Rainbow." London. 1967.

SIDE 5

The Kinks. *Everybody's in Showbiz.* RCA. 1972.

SIDE 6

Yes. *Fragile.* Atlantic. 1971.

SIDE 7

Yes. *Close to the Edge.* Atlantic. 1972.

SIDE 8

I am he as you are me. The Beatles, *Magical Mystery Tour*, "I am
   The Walrus." Capitol. 1967. And The Beach Boys, *Carl and the
   Passions/So Tough*. "All This is That." Capitol. 1972.

SIDE 9

Jefferson Airplane. *Volunteers*. "We Can Be Together." RCA. 1969.
Mott the Hoople, *All the Young Dudes*, RCA. 1972.
The Beatles. *Yellow Submarine—Nothing is Real* (original soundtrack).
   "Pepperland." Original film score composed & orchestrated by
   George Martin. 1969.

Checkers Records Artists (partial)

Scratchy Fenwick and His Itchy Zoot Suiters. *The Many Moods of
   Scratchy Fenwick*. Including "Do You Like Tractors" and "North
   Dakota Love Call." Written/produced by Harrison Creach. 1953.
The Cat Daddies. "Who's Yowling at My Window?" and "If I Was
   a Three-legged Cat (Would You Still Love Me?)," 1962 (written/
   produced by Harrison Creach)
Shine & The Funkolas. "Funk-o-Sicle," "Chocolate Bloop," "Jive
   Kangaroo," 1974 (written/produced by Harrison Creach and
   Bobby Washington)
Pepperland. *Pepperland*. "Burgers in Benton," "Freakout in Coal
   City," "Your Aunt is Cool," "Windblown American Dirt," "151,"
   "The V," "If I Were a Rich Man," "The Transmission of Informa-
   tion, (Part 1)" "Peggy Lee's Purse," "Shelley's Lyre," "Lysergic
   Night," "She Kissed the Cat," "Charlene," "This Whole Life,"
   "Queen Fab," "The Subconscious Sleep of Unconsciousness (Part
   1)," "Dreaming's Done." May 1974.

Terpsichorean Records Artists

The Thamesmen. "Don't Cross the River (Without My Heart in Your
   Pocket)," The What, Nigel and the Pub Crawlers.

Acknowledgments

Pepperland would not be resting comfortably in your hands without the inspiration of these amazing people:

Jill, love of my life, unfailingly *there*. Mark Stevens, old friend, a writer's writer, close reader, editor, rockin' bassman, and tireless cheerleader. Clint McCown, who asked, "So what?" at a critical moment. Larry Sutin, a gentle teacher who showed me how to go from here to there. The fabulous faculty and staff of the Vermont College of Fine Arts. Mira Perrizo, editor extraordinaire of Big Earth Publishing. Q Lindsey Graham. Shana Kelly. Robin Oliveira. Sheila Stuewe. Jeanne Gassman. Miciah Gault and everyone at Hunger Mountain. Jim and Pat Williams, founders of the feast. Jack Kerouac. Thomas Pynchon. Albert Murray. Raymond Douglas Davies. Robert Metcalfe, co-inventor of Ethernet. John Patrick Erlman. And Mary Lu Fennell, Professor Emerita of English and World Literature, Principia College, who, a million years ago, told me I could write.